Every Step You Take

"A sharp, well-plotted novel that I thoroughly enjoyed from beginning to end. Judith Kelman's quirky investigators and surprising plot twists create a very fine story. Sure to delight old fans and new readers alike. As unusual as it is entertaining."
—Nelson DeMille

"Fans can relax and rejoice, because this new one's a corker. It has all the suspense, wit, romance, and surprises that we love."
—Nancy Pickard

"Kelman's a pro and *Every Step You Take* . . . is very hard to put down. The twin strands of the story interweave with surprising fluidity and skill."
—*San Francisco Chronicle*

"Slick, savvy . . . sharp, clean prose and a pace that moves forward on flashes of heat lightning. No one does it better than Judith Kelman."
—Thomas H. Cook

"A dizzying dance of plot twists."
—*Times Union* (Albany, NY)

"A powerhouse of a thriller that hooks you from the first page. Kelman will hold you spellbound with her mix of compelling characters and stunning psychological suspense."
—Harlan Coben

"[A] beautifully choreographed climax. This . . . Kelman thriller is a true nail-biter."
—*Booklist*

"[A] fascinating, exciting, and enthralling thriller . . . Kelman keeps the surprises happening. The climax is a total shocker."
—*Midwest Book Review*

W9-COD-476

continued . . .

Summer of Storms

"Taut and assured . . . swift pacing . . . [a] smooth page-turner that's sure to have fans reading into the wee hours of the night." —*Publishers Weekly*

"Past and present converge with dizzying speed . . . Tough-minded, exceptionally well-written suspense. The break-neck pace never flags, and the grittiness of New York settings and people is just right." —*Kirkus Reviews*

"Sends shivers up and down the spine . . . [An] absorbing novel." —*Midwest Book Review*

After the Fall

"Riveting . . . loaded with suspense, smart characters, and wonderfully acute observations." —Susan Isaacs

"A page-turner . . . disturbing and suspenseful." —Phillip Margolin

"In stylish, energetic prose, Kelman reveals surprising new twists." —*Publishers Weekly*

"Strongly effective . . . reveals the hypocrisies and malevolence sometimes lurking behind leafy suburban comforts." —*Kirkus Reviews*

"Judith Kelman provides her readers with her usual thought-provoking, superb tale . . . chilling." —*Midwest Book Review*

THE
SESSION

JUDITH KELMAN

JOVE BOOKS, NEW YORK

THE BERKLEY PUBLISHING GROUP
Published by the Penguin Group
Penguin Group (USA) Inc.
375 Hudson Street, New York, New York 10014, USA
Penguin Group (Canada), 90 Eglinton Avenue East, Suite 700, Toronto, Ontario M4P 2Y3, Canada
(a division of Pearson Penguin Canada Inc.)
Penguin Books Ltd., 80 Strand, London WC2R 0RL, England
Penguin Group Ireland, 25 St. Stephen's Green, Dublin 2, Ireland (a division of Penguin Books Ltd.)
Penguin Group (Australia), 250 Camberwell Road, Camberwell, Victoria 3124, Australia
(a division of Pearson Australia Group Pty. Ltd.)
Penguin Books India Pvt. Ltd., 11 Community Centre, Panchsheel Park, New Delhi—110 017, India
Penguin Group (NZ), Cnr. Airborne and Rosedale Roads, Albany, Auckland 1310, New Zealand
(a division of Pearson New Zealand Ltd.)
Penguin Books (South Africa) (Pty.) Ltd., 24 Sturdee Avenue, Rosebank, Johannesburg 2196,
South Africa

Penguin Books Ltd., Registered Offices: 80 Strand, London WC2R 0RL, England

This is a work of fiction. Names, characters, places, and incidents either are the product of the author's imagination or are used fictitiously, and any resemblance to actual persons, living or dead, business establishments, events, or locales is entirely coincidental. The publisher does not have any control over and does not assume any responsibility for author or third-party websites or their content.

THE SESSION

A Jove Book / published by arrangement with the author

PRINTING HISTORY
Berkley hardcover edition / January 2006
Jove mass-market edition / October 2006

ISBN: 0-515-14189-5

JOVE®
Jove Books are published by The Berkley Publishing Group,
a division of Penguin Group (USA) Inc.,
375 Hudson Street, New York, New York 10014.
JOVE is a registered trademark of Penguin Group (USA) Inc.
The "J" design is a trademark belonging to Penguin Group (USA) Inc.

PRINTED IN THE UNITED STATES OF AMERICA

10   9   8   7   6   5   4   3   2   1

DEDICATION

For Peter S., a man as fine, thoughtful, dear, and caring as they come. And for glorious little Caroline. My heart runneth over.

ACKNOWLEDGMENTS

I am most grateful to Rikers Island chaplains Rabbis Herbert Richtman and Moshe Kwalbrun for their time and input. Thanks also to the inmates I met at Rikers who shared their experiences on the inside and out openly and courageously.

Anne Ziff, dear friend and therapist extraordinaire, and Dr. Nora Brockner, near sister and top-notch psychiatrist, are always generous with their professional insights and sage advice.

Thanks also to Jennifer McCarthy, who breathed real life into P.J. For a novelist, there may be no greater gift than finding the clone of her imagined protagonist and having the opportunity to pick her nimble mind.

It's always a pleasure to work with my friend and editor Natalee Rosenstein, and with her wonderful team at Berkley, especially Leslie Gelbman.

Peter Lampack, my literary agent, is a truly extraordinary representative and consigliere. I would only wish him on my best of friends, and I'm delighted to count him as mine.

CHAPTER

1

■ **I should have said** *no* **or** *absolutely not* **or simply** shaken my head in the unstinting negative. *No* was the correct answer, the one that could have averted the train wreck my life was about to become. But at that moment, it seemed out of the question to turn Jeannie Bagshaw down.

It was the first time she had asked me for anything. In fact, she had barely spoken a word to me until that fateful Monday nearly a year ago, when she showed up for her scheduled counseling session in my office at the Rose M. Singer Detention Center for Women on Rikers Island, known to insiders as "Rosie." Jeannie appeared in the doorway, a scrawny wraith capped by a riot of rust-colored, broken Slinky curls, as I was heading out to see her in her cell. Until then, that was the sum and substance of every one of our biweekly sessions: I *saw* Jeannie, though not at all clearly, as she cowered beneath the bottom bunk in her cell, hugging her pale skinny legs, scared eyes skittering in the shadows like spooked mice. Time after time I stood for the allotted hour and talked to her, coaxing and encouraging, hoping the sheer weight of my stubborn persistence might somehow get through.

But it had not, not once in the eight months since she arrived on the *Rock*, as Rikers was often called, after her arrest for acting crazy in the wrong part of town. You simply did not pull off your clothes and stand naked in the beam of a blazing streetlamp in front of the elegant Sutton Place brownstone of Mr. And Mrs. Allston Grainger IV, especially not in the middle of Alls and Taffy's annual black tie fund-raiser to benefit orphans from some appallingly poor (though thankfully very faraway!) country. You certainly didn't screech like a hoot owl while exposing your pale, scarred, bony form, stealing attention from the brilliant Natalya Sakharova's rousing performance in the Graingers' parlor of Brahms's "Double Concerto for Cello and Violin." According to the report of the incident that had crossed my desk, Sakharova was nobody's definition of a good sport.

As the psychologist assigned to Jeannie on the so-called Women's Mental Observation Unit, my job was to determine why she had pulled such a stunt and determine what nifty pill or magical insight might guarantee that she would stay clothed and invisible to people like the Graingers once she was released. But until that fateful morning, about all I'd managed to elicit from her was the occasional sneeze.

So imagine my astonished delight to find her standing at my office threshold in a pea-green T-shirt and khaki cargo pants. She held out her child-sized left hand to show off the white twist tie bound to her ring finger and announced that she and Lolly Rasweiller were engaged.

"To be married," she said in an eerie, dead-ball monotone. "Week from tomorrow."

"Married?"

"Lolly and me. Down in the day room. Twelve noon."

That's when I should have said no. Though I'd never run across such an edict, what Jeannie proposed was almost certainly against one, or perhaps several, of the encyclopedic prison rules, not to mention asking for all manner of trouble. This was a psych ward, after all, the very definition of all that was dangerous, unpredictable, and unknown.

"Why don't you have a seat and tell me more about it."

"Lolly and me."

"Yes, Jeannie. Tell me about you and Lolly. I'd love to hear."

She stood rooted in the doorway, staring past me at the featureless gray wall.

"Come in and sit, Jeannie. Please."

"Tuesday."

Her eyes were sinkholes, sucking light from the harsh fluorescents overhead. Not yet twenty-three years old, and life had long since tripped the breaker in her soul.

"Honestly, I think it should wait until we've had a chance to talk it through."

"In the day room. Tuesday. Noontime. After *The View*."

"I hear that you want to do this, Jeannie. But first we ought to talk about why, try to figure out what it means for you."

Her gaze fell. "Dearly beloved," she explained to the desk. "We are gathered here."

"You know it wouldn't be real or hold any legal weight. Plus, legally, you're already married."

She tensed so hard her stick limbs quaked. "No!"

"All right," I soothed. "Let's put that aside for now. The wedding is only part of the issue. What happens next if you do this? We have to consider the consequences. Think about how things might change."

"Dearly beloved. Tuesday. Twelve noon."

"I have to give this some thought, Jeannie. Why don't I do that and let you know in a couple of days?"

Now her lusterless eyes locked on mine and her face spawned a pained, crooked grin. "Something for Jeannie."

That hit me hard. Precious little in her life had been for Jeannie. Her intake report chronicled a history of unimaginable abuse. Born to rabid fundamentalists who had seen her flame-red hair as the Devil's mark, she'd been variously threatened, whipped, neglected, and reviled. Her parents had invented unthinkably brutal means to exorcise Jeannie's demons. They'd held her head under the bathwater until she turned blue; made her sleep outside in the dead of winter; and forced her to fast for days on end.

Jeannie's first attempted escape was a tragically misguided marriage before she turned sixteen to a local boy named Charlie Booth. Booth turned out to be another sadistic nutcase, whose brutality made her parents' seem benign. My strong suspicion is that Jeannie finally took leave of her senses to get away from Booth. Or at least, she tried.

"For Jeannie," she echoed. A rare trace of resolve infused her expression; and I caught a hint of what she might have been in a world devoid of horrific cruelty: a puckish, pretty, headstrong little girl.

And so I mutely went along. I failed to say no to her. And that started it all.

■ **Except for the murder, the wedding went remarkably** well. Ragged rows of cement-toned plastic chairs flanked the makeshift aisle in the day room. The two dozen or so female inmates currently in residence on Rosie's Mental Observation ward shuffled in, doing the heavy tranquilizer waltz, and claimed seats without argument or incident. Big Millie Williamson, whose clerical robe had been fashioned from a king-size bedsheet, stood poised to preside behind the stainless-steel medication cart that would serve as a podium. Having murdered her husband, a fire- and gin-breathing Baptist minister, Big Millie considered herself more than qualified for the job. Twisting his head like a jar lid until his neck snapped had earned her fifteen years in an upstate lockup for the criminally insane. Millie had passed the time honing her persecution fantasies and collecting bogus mail-order degrees. She now qualified, in a manner of speaking, as a preacher, lawyer, osteopath, off-shore oil-drilling specialist, manicurist, pastry chef, demolitions expert, meteorologist, and golf pro, to name a few. Millie was no shrinking violet, and she had what it took to assert her preferences, nearly three hundred pounds of galloping, in-your-face, paranoid schizophrenia that landed her back on Rikers every spring, as predictably as dandelions and flies.

The day room, painted the green of overcooked peas, stood ready for the celebration that would follow the trading of vows. Two cases of classic Cokes perched beside a wedding cake assemblage of Dunkin' Donuts on the card table. A few primitive drawings taped to the walls made a stab at festive decoration, as did the mound of paper napkin confetti the designated flower girl had dumped prematurely near the door. The TV sat dark and silent for a welcome change, a clear indication that something major was afoot. Outside, where such things mattered, the weather was ideal.

As the second hand on the ancient wall clock twitched past noon, Big Millie bashed the medication cart with a clubbed fist, signaling D'Shawn and Tyree to start the processional. The pair had been practicing Mendelssohn's Wedding March with maddening compulsion for days, D'Shawn trumpeting the melody in brassy bass notes through her puckered lips, while Tyree's taffy-pulled fingers tapped triumphal flourishes on the huge pregnant swell of her abdomen.

Bah bop bwee bah!

Jeannie started down the aisle on the arm of Bobbye Sunday, her cellmate, who'd agreed to give her away for a fee of three Marlboro Lights and a package of Kit Kats. They walked in sync with the music, step by measured step. My breath caught and my eyes filled with the diabolical reflex that can drive even the sanest among us to cast away all reason and take the plunge.

Dah dee doo wah!

The bride wore bright white tennis shoes minus the forbidden laces and a long, white, form-fitting gown crafted from a case of inmate-quality toilet paper. The papier-mâché headpiece roosting in her paprika curls was fashioned from a clever blend of denture adhesive and strips torn from last month's edition of the prison newsletter: the *Rikers Review*. Behind her trailed a cathedral-length train made entirely of pages from failed parole applications. They swooped and fluttered as she walked, like wind-whipped sails.

Dwee bop bee dwee op, do dwee dah do bwee.

As Jeannie approached the end of the aisle, Lolly

Rasweiller lumbered in from the hall. Duct-tape tuxedo stripes rode the outer seams of her prison-green cargo pants, and her Department of Corrections T-shirt featured black Magic Marker lapels and an ink-drawn bow tie. Her mud-brown hair was cropped even closer than usual, a stingy line of scrub framing hardscrabble features. Lolly was a human glacier, not normally given to shows of sentiment, but I could tell she was as gut-punched as I had been by the sight of Jeannie done up—however strangely—as a bride.

Big Millie drew a menacing finger across her broad, squat throat, and D'Shawn and Tyree went still. "Marriage is an institution. And so's this penile colony. So I say, why the doodad day?"

Several heads in the audience bobbed in firm agreement. This was a place for psychos, after all.

"When Reverend Herbert and me got hitched, that was some kind of Colonial Williamsburg, believe you me. That rotten sumbitch was a whole nother rawhide all by his own self." Millie popped off a fat, wet laugh that sent her beefy midsection heaving. The hysteria threatened to spread in nervous tics and titters, but Millie got a grip and went serious before it took dangerous hold.

She laid one hand on a battered Gideon Bible and snaked the other back to scratch her double-wide rump. "Anybody got problems with this: You got to pop fly or roll mop right now."

The silence held, and Big Millie peered down her squash-blossom nose at the bride. "You here because you here, girl? Nobody done laid a twelve on your sister Pearl or nothing like that?"

Jeannie grinned shyly. "I do."

Lolly did as well, and Big Millie offered her version of the standard, albeit bogus, pronouncements about how they were now married in the eyes of the Lord and the governor by her nonexistent authority. "Now, you two go on and have yourselves a big old smoochy hootchie pie."

As they were leaning in to do so, the alarm sounded. A series of deafening whoop sounds was trailed by a long mournful howl. Then bells clanged in riotous cacophony, and the whoops began anew.

I raised my hands. "Stay calm, everybody!" Of course,

they couldn't hear me above the incredible din much less the flares of panic firing in their minds. Mental patients are like dry tinder. The least little spark can set them off.

I looped my hand through Big Millie's cocked elbow and endeavored to nudge her toward the door. Given her size and sheer mulishness, this was about as useful as trying to redirect the tides. I was relieved when she changed course on her own and aimed for the corridor that led to the yard. The others followed in a frightening stampede.

"Whassup? They a fire?" Big Millie roared. "They a nuke killer accident?"

"Let's not get ahead of ourselves, Millie. Could be just a drill."

"Drill my butt. Bet you another one of them whoosh-zoomers went down. Damned things just fall out the sky anytime they feel like it, and *kerboom!* One of those big-ass seventy leventies falls on you, you are so *splatchoo.*"

"We'll find out, Millie. No point worrying about it in advance."

"This ain't in advance, girl. The shit is happening *now.*" She wrenched free of my grasp and charged like a crazed bull elephant. "Incoming. We got incoming! Splatchoos is falling out the sky. The beagles has landed! Hurry up and get your crazy asses out this place fore it blows!"

Suddenly rough hands shoved me from behind. I staggered off balance and bashed into the cold tile wall. Heart stammering, I braced there, shrinking from the racing hysteria behind me.

In moments the manic throng had passed, the alarm stilled, and I heard the reassuring sound of rabid guards barking orders in the yard, countering the chaos, restoring the shaky calm that passed in here for normalcy. Clearly, this had been a drill.

My lower back ached where I had wrenched it. Hobbling toward the yard, I tested the sore spot with a knuckle. Not too bad, I concluded. Nothing that a hot bath, a couple of extra-strength something or others, and liberal doses of whining wouldn't cure.

"You okay, P.J.?" The question came from a waddling Tyree, who sported a dazzling grin and a greased-sugar mus-

THE SESSION ■ 9

tache. She had hung back despite the alarm, lured by the far more urgent call of the waiting doughnuts. She was eating junk for two, after all.

"I'm fine, Tyree. Thanks for asking."

"That wedding was so gooood! D'Shawn and me blew us some real good tunes, didn't we?" She offered an energetic reprise on the belly drum.

I caught her fingers and held them still. She was giving me a headache, so imagine the poor fetus.

"You did, Tyree. You worked hard."

"And Jeannie looked real fine, didn't she, all out from under the bed like that and everything?"

"She did. She seemed happy."

"I helped make the dress, you know. Wrapped her up just so."

"That was nice, Tyree. Very creative."

"Took some real doing." She leveled a finger down the hall, past the door to the yard. "Damn. Now it's ruined. Look at that."

I tracked her gaze to a fluffed white heap on the floor. At first I took it for a pile of laundry, abandoned at the sound of the alarm. Then, squinting, I made out the arc of a spine and one small, stark white tennis shoe, dangling at an impossible angle. My knees went soft, and I forced back a bitter swell of bile.

Tyree waddled ahead of me and leaned over Jeannie's inert form, yelling as if the girl could hear. "Look what you did. You gone and ruined that dress. You get up right this minute, you dumb, lazy thing! Get up and brush that fool dress off!"

I caught her by the shoulders, turned her away, and steered her swollen body toward the yard. "Let Jeannie be, Tyree. She needs her rest."

"She's hopeless, that one. Tell you that much. Fool girl's hopeless as they come."

As she drifted out into the bracing sunshine, I walked numbly back to the spot where Jeannie lay. Only then did I notice the spreading crimson stain on the rear of the toilet-paper gown and the spray of bloody droplets on the wall. Her face was a stone-gray pedestal for the eternal flame of curls. And I knew without getting any closer that Tyree had called it correctly. Jeannie Bagshaw was as hopeless as they come.

CHAPTER

3

I was completely prepared, though as too often hap-
pens, not for the thing that occurred. When I arrived at the
office of my boss, Will Creighton, Chief Calvin Daley was
seated at the desk. Creighton, the decent, dedicated psychiatrist who oversaw the prison's rambling complex of psychological services, stood off to the side, next to a bookshelf
neatly packed with journals and texts. Normally Creighton
projected the reassuring air of a favorite uncle with his affa-
ble face, dove-gray eyes, and cappuccino froth of stark
white hair. Normally I could rely on him for a ready smile,
good advice, and a quick infusion of optimism, no matter
how bleak the situation. But today my boss stood glum and
impassive.

Chief Daley was a big man in every intimidating sense of
the word, known for his merciless tongue and incredible swift
sword. Since he'd taken the helm, violent incidents on Rikers
had been slashed by an astonishing ninety percent. When
something went wrong, Daley saw to it that the responsible
parties paid quickly and dearly. During his quarter-century
tenure in the NYPD, the man had been a legend, credited with
quite the collection of prize collars, and he was bent on rising

to the same mythic proportions in the corrections phase of his career. Less than two years on the job, and he had already inspired a Lord's Prayer of his own: *Give us this day, our Daley dread . . .*

"You're late, Lafferty."

"I came the minute my session was over, sir."

"Late," he hammered home the accusation. "And screwed."

My cheeks went hot. "I understand that the wedding was unorthodox, sir. But there was a valid therapeutic rationale."

"Therapeutic you say?" He leaned back and planted his size-twelve, spit-shined wing tips on Creighton's scarred wooden desk. "Do tell."

"Jeannie Bagshaw was pathologically withdrawn. Terrified of everyone and everything. She barely ever said a word. Until the matter of the wedding came up, she spent most days huddled under the bed, hugging her knees."

He clapped twice, two sharp, lethal reports. "Well, bully for you. Look what you've accomplished. You fixed it so she's not terrified anymore."

"Coming to me, asking for the wedding, was a major breakthrough for her."

"Is that so? You often bury your breakthroughs, Lafferty? Is that your *therapeutic* goal?"

"All due respect, sir. The wedding didn't cause Jeannie's death."

"No? You sound like the kid who offs his parents and then throws himself on the mercy of the court because he's an orphan. Spare me the lame excuses."

"I hear you, sir. Of course, I'm terribly sorry for what happened, and I take full responsibility for allowing the wedding to go on."

Daley snickered. "You just don't get it. She's not very swift, Creighton, is she?"

Creighton coughed into his fist.

"Dr. Creighton had nothing to do with any of this, sir," I said. "He didn't even know about it."

Daley seemed to be considering that as he worked his right earlobe, kneading the bumpy road of piercing scars from the days when he'd worked undercover in narcotics, his hip-hop street gear set off by cornrows, a thicket of earrings, and the nasty scorpion tattoo on his neck. "Is that true, Creighton? You were completely in the dark about this wedding business?"

My boss shrugged, leaving it to me to come to his defense. "He was, honestly, Chief. It was all me; every bit of it. I acted entirely on my own."

Daley dropped his feet and leaned in, strafing me with a shot of bitter, coffee-tinged breath. "Not that you deserve it, Lafferty, but I'm going to teach you a couple of things nonetheless. You remember the song about the old lady who swallowed a fly?"

"I do, sir. That was a favorite of mine as a child."

"Good. So I'd bet an experienced, highly educated, maybe brighter than she acts forensic psychologist like you can tell me what killed the old lady."

"I can. It was the horse she finally swallowed to catch the cow."

He wagged a chiding finger at me. "You're forgetting a cardinal principle of cause, effect, and culpability. You're forgetting that what starts a chain of events is responsible for what happens in the end. The old lady swallowed the fly, for whatever reason, on her own, setting her *suicide* in motion."

"I suppose you could look at it that way."

"That's the only way to look at it. Drop a lit match in the woods; you're responsible for the forest fire. Create a dangerous breach of prison discipline by consenting to an idiotic mock marriage between two criminal crazies; and any blood that flows from that is on your hands. You caused Jeannie Bagshaw's murder as surely as if you'd carved the shiv and shoved it in her descending aorta all by yourself. That was your handiwork. Your homicide. You read me, Lafferty?"

Difficult though it was, I kept still. When you're in deep shit and sinking fast, the only sane response is to keep your big mouth shut.

Daley's face was florid now, and the scorpion tattoo twitched with the rabid thudding of his pulse. "And here's lesson number two. You thought you were doing Creighton a favor telling me that he was oblivious to what you were doing? That he didn't know?"

I tried to catch my boss's eye as the chief ranted on, but Creighton refused to engage. Or maybe he understood, as I did not, what was coming next.

"Well, here's breaking news for you, Lafferty. It's his *job* to know what's going on. It's his *job* to keep tabs on the fools who work for him. It's his *job* to keep those fools from stepping on their own dicks or whatever else they've got to step on. It's his department, which means that the buck—and the bodies—stop right there!" He took vicious aim at Creighton's heart. Had that finger been loaded, my poor boss would have keeled over cold.

"Please, Chief. This is my fault. Dr. Creighton is not to blame."

"Oh, really? It's all on you, Lafferty? You're sure of that?"

"I am, sir. You're right about my screwing up. I made a big mistake in allowing the wedding, and I'm sorrier than you can imagine. But please know that this job means the world to me. I'm prepared to do whatever it takes to make things right. Anything, sir. You name it."

Daley stared at me for a long time. And then his head bobbed slowly up and down. "You know? It's the strangest thing, but for some reason, I'm feeling generous right now. I'd say you can count this as your lucky day."

"Oh, thank you, sir. From the bottom of my heart, you won't be sorry. I can promise there won't be any such misjudgments from me ever again."

He was smiling now in earnest, a rare, and frankly terrifying, sight. "Of course there won't. You're not going to get the chance to screw up again. You're finished here, Lafferty. Done. *Kaput.*"

"Sorry? I don't understand. I thought you said—"

"Explain it to her while you take her to her office to get her things, will you, Creighton? Tell her she should consider herself damned lucky I'm not hauling her incompetent butt before the DA on charges of manslaughter, reckless endangerment, and worse. Make sure she understands that if I hear so much as a peep out of her or ever even have a reason to think about her again, I will see to it that she's brought up on every charge I can come up with. Tell her the only way she's ever coming back to Rikers is in a DOC van with a warrant up her butt and government-issue bracelets on her wrists."

Creighton's eyes squeezed shut, and the breath he'd been hoarding escaped in a rush.

"And while you're at it, give her boss fair warning, too. Tell Willard Creighton that if he can't stay on top of his people and keep them in line, he can just pack up all his handy dandy degrees and certificates and precious little awards. He can go hang out a shingle in some musty little room and spend the rest of his life listening to angst-ridden, impotent stockbrokers and their fat, annoying, narcissistic wives. Tell him I think he's got too many outside distractions. I think his plate's too damned full, and that's why some things are bound to slop over. Tell him he'd better get himself in gear and straighten the hell out so he can concentrate on what he's paid to do around here. Is that clear, Creighton? You get the picture?"

My boss's lips pressed in a grim hard line.

"I'll take that as a yes. Now, you're going to march your former employee out of here, give her ten minutes, max, to collect her things, and then see to it that she's on the next bus off the island. Make sure you let security know she no longer exists. I'll see the word gets out to everyone else."

At that, I found my voice. "You can't simply fire me like that, Chief Daley."

"Oh, and why is that?"

"It's not reasonable, that's why. I was only doing what seemed to be in my patient's best interest."

"Right. And now I'm doing what seems to be in the best interest of the institution. Call me a neat nut, but I just hate having blood on my floors."

"My record up to now has been impeccable, Chief Daley. I've had excellent reviews, commendations."

"Pack them up and take them with you. Bet they'll make nice souvenirs."

"Please, Chief. All I'm asking for is another chance. Dock my pay if you want, put me on probation."

"I'm putting you on the next bus out."

"That's arbitrary, Chief. Arbitrary and unfair. I'll bet anything it wouldn't hold up."

"Hold up to what? Are you threatening me, Lafferty?"

■ **Creighton's concept of my salvation was precisely** what I needed least. He strode into my office with Mrs. Perfect, of all people, in tow as I was sorting through my desk drawers, separating pocket change from paper clips, lint-encrusted cough drops, some sticky brown substance of unknown origin, and snippets of paper scrawled with some of the countless things I had sincerely intended but failed to do. *Send Aunt Nora a get-well card for the hip replacement* (preferably before she dies). *Gift for Martin's baby* (now in kindergarten). *See Picasso exhibit* (which closed two years ago). *Don't miss the once-in-a-lifetime look at the* (spectacular and long gone) *Hale-Bopp comet.*

Mrs. Perfect was queen of the prison's volunteers, always ready to tackle a bold, new, well-intentioned project. She had the energy, determination, and hordes of stylish friends to pitch in and pull it off. Still, I suspected that her primary function in life was to make the dismal likes of me look even more pathetic by comparison. Her hair was a silky obsidian drape; eyes the blue green of sun-stippled pool water; skin smooth and bright as a freshly laundered sheet. She had one of those unforgivably perfect bodies that smack of impeccable input,

Herculean output, and unparalleled genes. Perfect had fabulous posture as well, the proud-boned, chest-up, shoulders-back sort of stance that made you want to stow your sorry, slumping self in a trunk in the attic and lose the key. Her clothes were gorgeous designer things, tailored to showcase her perfect form. And she could stride about in nosebleed high heels without a trace of agony or clumsiness. She was devoted to family, community, and the doing of good deeds. Perhaps most intolerable, she was unfailingly pleasant, thoughtful, charming, gracious, and polite. And I thought to myself as she floated toward me on a cushion of unassailable self-possession, haven't I suffered enough?

The answer: apparently not.

"P.J., you've met Nina Present, haven't you? She runs the volunteer services at Rikers. Has for years. Can't imagine what we'd do without her."

"We've met. Sure. Many times."

"Always a pleasure, P.J." Perfect proffered a smooth graceful hand. "I'm a great admirer."

"Of my? I mean of me?" In addition to everything else, people like her made me sound as if my tongue had slipped a cog.

"Absolutely. You have the most amazing way with the inmates. I watched you calm Big Millie down last week when the phones were out of service and she got so upset."

"She was convinced she had a conference call scheduled with Meryl Streep and Michelangelo to talk about collaborating on a musical comedy."

"You were wonderful with her."

"Kind of you to say, Mrs. Present, but apparently, being good with the inmates doesn't count for much. Chief Daley has let me go."

"Dr. Creighton told me. And I think it's dreadful. You will be sorely missed around here. No doubt about that."

I shrugged, battling outrage and tears.

"Maybe I can help," Perfect went on. "I understand you'd like to continue working in the forensic field."

"Doesn't much matter what I want. Rikers is precious close to the only game in town."

"A large percentage of New York City's prison population is housed here, true. But there are other programs and facilities. I've gotten to know them through the work. If you like, I can make some calls, see who might have openings."

"You'd do that?"

"It would be my pleasure."

"That would mean more to me than you can imagine, Mrs. Present. I'd be forever in your debt."

"Not at all. I can't guarantee anything, but I'm glad to try."

"Thank you."

"And please, call me Nina."

"Thank you—Nina."

She caught Creighton's eye and something inscrutable passed between them. "I'm a little concerned about the interim," she said. "Even if we do find an opening, the interview and hiring process would take time."

My stomach seized. "I'd better hurry up and find a job flipping burgers, then. Or serving them up. My landlord is not the understanding sort."

She smiled, and I noticed, to my perverse delight, that she had a tiny chip in her right front tooth. "I hope you won't consider me intrusive, P.J. But I believe I can help there as well. If you're willing to take on some private patients to tide you over, I'd be glad to pass the word. There's no shortage of people in need of a good counselor."

"Private practice?" I'd gone into this field to work with the criminally insane: murderers, sex offenders, interesting folk like that. Counseling normal people with standard, off-the-rack neuroses struck me as the equivalent of leaving the Yankees to play whiffle ball.

Creighton raised a traffic-stopping hand. "It doesn't have to be permanent. Besides, it's important to get back into to the real world every so often. It'll help you keep things in perspective."

"I'm not saying no, Dr. Creighton. I'm hardly in a position to say no to anything. I'll confess I've developed quite the fondness for eating regularly and sleeping indoors."

"Good, then." Nina Present dipped into her butterscotch ostrich Kelly bag and handed me an embossed card. "If you'll give me your contact information, I'll put out some feelers right away."

"Thanks. You're a treasure." She was, in fact, but I found I loathed her much less for that than I had.

Creighton walked her out. I tuned to his soothing voice and the crisp strike of Nina Present's footfalls as they faded down the hall. I placed my meager belongings into one of the nest of cartons that had materialized in my office while I was out getting canned. Daley was a detail man, not the sort to lop someone's head off without first setting out a pan to catch the blood.

I used a section of the morning paper to wrap a framed picture of my parents. There they were, aglow with twined affection, just months before that black day seventeen years ago when their car hurtled out of control on a slick, back country road. Next I packed another photo that held an ancient image of my twin sister Caitlyn, my big bad brother Jack, and me, all caught in that gangly twilight between sugarcoated innocence and the ugly truth. That was back before Jack's illness bubbled up like sewage and soiled everything, back when the future loomed as a bright, boundless possibility.

As I was about to seal the box, I spied a book of mine on the windowsill, propped up by a dead cactus I had meant to water regularly, but as the evidence showed, cacti do not thrive on fine intentions alone. The slim volume had been given to me by my sister, one of those thinly veiled insults Caity tries to pass off as a gift. This one was called *Personal Best* and the message in a nutshell was: *If you work really, really hard, maybe someday you won't suck quite as much as you do now!*

When I picked it up, out flew a long-forgotten snapshot of Rafe and me, from our wedding. I found it difficult to relate to the young woman smiling back at the lens, neon with happiness and a miraculous makeup job, or the young man beside her, whose irresistible fervent idealism turned out to be such a monumental deceit. There we were, holding on to each other as if we would never let go, about to take those weighty vows as if we had the slightest clue of what they meant or how to go about upholding them.

Creighton was back to carry out the chief's final edict and escort me out. "She's quite something, don't you think?"

"That she is."

"Having Nina on your side can make all the difference, P.J. Never underestimate the value of influential friends."

"I don't, Dr. Creighton. I'm more grateful to her than you can imagine. And to you."

He leaned in for an awkward hug. I took in the mingled scent of fresh sweat, lime aftershave, and mentholated shaving cream. Something in the mix reminded me, most painfully, of my dad.

"Ready?" he asked.

"Not even close."

He winked. "You'll be fine, P.J. My money's on you."

"I'd watch that, Dr. Creighton. You're betting on a known loser."

"Nothing of the sort. Mark my words. In a little while, this will all seem like a distant bad dream." He tipped his head toward the single carton I had filled. "Is that everything?"

"Yes."

"I'll get it."

I stole a glance at the wedding picture of Rafe and me. The sensible thing would be to toss it, and I feinted toward the wastebasket to do just that. Then, reconsidering, I set it face-down in the box and sealed the lid. I've never been the least bit good at letting go.

CHAPTER

5

■ **The two-lane bridge linking Rikers Island to the bor-**ough of Queens spans little more than a mile, but that day, the ride felt like that slow, grim, final sail across the Styx. The bus slogged along in the tangle of emptied supply trucks and vehicles hauling workers and visitors who had completed their business on the island. Others carried prisoners who were making trips to court or medical appointments, and would be back.

Still bristling with shock, I stared through the grime-streaked window at the glinting face of the East River and the conga line of planes lifting off with a crushing roar from neighboring La Guardia Airport. It always struck me as curious that most of the tens of thousands of people who fly over Rikers each day, not to mention the millions who live nearby, are vaguely aware at most that the prison exists. This remains true despite the fact that Rikers, with fifteen thousand inmates, happens to be the largest penal colony in the world. The island, once the private estate of the seventeenth century Dutch settler for whom it was named, was purchased by New York City in the 1930s and swollen by putrid landfill to its current sprawl, which spans half the size of New York's massive Central Park. Today the complex includes ten jails, one for women and nine for men, in addition to the huge floating prison ship docked on its shore that was built to ease the perennial overcrowding. Most of the people housed here are detainees, awaiting trial but unable to make even the most nominal bail. For want of a few dollars, plenty spend weeks or even months in a dismal cage. Some are in for civil offenses, like failure to pay child support or proper respect to a judge. Tax-paying citizens spend hundreds of dollars a day to warehouse these nonviolent and legally innocent people in jail. We could park them at the Waldorf instead, and pocket the change.

Thousands of employees arrive on the island daily to work in the jails, schools, kitchens, barbershops, bakery, commissaries, chapels, auto repair shop, car washes, clinics, and the staggering array of other facilities required to meet the astonishing complex of inmate needs. Thousands more come to visit in a grim ritual that is far too often handed down from generation to generation. In all likelihood, I was the only one, save Jeannie Bagshaw, leaving today against her will.

As I was thinking things couldn't possibly get worse, they predictably obliged. The bus was packed. My seatmate, a plump, blowsy, gum-cracking Hispanic woman with inch-long, rainbow-painted nails, commandeered my attention with a sharp elbow jab to the ribs. "You got a husband inside?"

"No."

"Boyfriend?"

I shook my head tightly.

"Must be your brother, then. Am I right?"

"Sister," I said. Caity's level head and firm shoulders could accommodate the lie. For my brother Jack, it cut far too close to the truth.

"What she in for? Drugs?"

"I'd rather not say."

"Drugs. I knew it. Same here. My man dropped a dime on a cop in Bryant Park, would you believe? Not the first time, either. They don't come any dumber. Tell you that."

I forced a hollow smile. "Please excuse me. There's something I have to read."

She stared as I rummaged through my purse. Nothing in-

side but a couple of pens, a capless Chap Stick, a half eaten
Reese's peanut butter cup, a crumpled twenty-dollar bill, a
sprinkling of change, my maxed-out Visa and equally over-
taxed MasterCard, a pair of hopelessly scratched drugstore
sunglasses, and Nina Present's card. I ran my fingers over the
reassuringly sturdy card stock, trying to believe she would do
as she said. Get me a job. Find me clients to pay the bills in the
meantime. Didn't it all sound too good to be true?

As that thought crossed my mind, the bus lurched to a halt.

"Must be one of those security checks," my seatmate
huffed. "Pain in my *culo*."

Up ahead, police cars formed a barricade, slowing the traffic stream to a drip. It could well be a security check, a fairly
common occurrence. If something or someone significant
turned up missing at Rikers, this span was the only logical escape route. Swimming away in the river's cruel currents was a
superhuman feat under the best of circumstances, and at this
time of year, when the water still ran with the harsh winter
chill, impossible to do for long enough to make it to the opposite shore alive. Rikers was designed to thwart surreptitious
boat launchings, so the bridge served as the main line of
scrutiny and defense.

"Ramon's my man's name," my seatmate said. "Brains or
no, the guy is some kind of something. Know what I mean?"

"Listen. I've had a really bad day. So if you'll excuse
me . . ."

She tossed her henna-streaked hair. "You think it's a picnic
for me? Ramon's not easy, you know. Man acts like I sent him
up with my own two hands. Like it was my brilliant idea he
should go drop a dime on Mr. Plainclothes. Everything's always my fault. Try that, and see what bad is." Tears spilled
from her round dark eyes. Keening shrills matched the heaving of her chest. All eyes around us turned to stare.

"Shh. Take it easy. Please."

She plucked a crumpled tissue from her flowered tote and
trumpeted through her nose. "You got no freaking idea."

"That's true."

We inched forward as a car ahead was cleared. I watched
as a brawny cop in dark glasses leaned through the window of

the dark blue Cherokee that was next in line. Another officer crouched to examine the car's broad undercarriage, while a third rummaged through the mass of motley possessions stuffed in the trunk: baby stroller, mesh bag crammed with laundry, sack of Kitty Litter, split logs, giant bag of unbleached flour, hockey skates, beach blankets, drum set, toy golf clubs, lawn chair, mulch.

Methodically he replaced it all, rechecking each item as if he'd never seen it before. Finally he slammed the hatch and moved on to a DOC van that was ferrying six prisoners downtown.

"Think they could move any slower?" My seatmate peeled the foil from a stick of gum and shoved it in her mouth. "I look like I got all day or what?"

"Security." I shrugged, not wishing to appear for or against it.

"Must be that murder," said a breathy voice from the seat behind me.

My seatmate wheeled around. "What murder?"

"Someone on women's M.O. went down during a fire drill. Got stabbed in the heart or something and bled out."

"Sweet Jesus. You hear that? Is that the worst?" My seatmate jabbed my ribs again.

"It is."

The guards had reached us now; a pair of them boarded the bus. They went down the rows, checking each passenger, until a uniformed sneer in aviator sunglasses came to us.

"Your purpose on the island today?"

"Visitor," my seatmate said.

"Employee," I muttered.

"Liar," my seatmate trumpeted. "Lying sneak of a freaking rotten spy."

"See your ID?" the cop said.

I slumped deeper in my seat. "Former employee," I amended. "They took it when I left."

His jaw twitched. "Come with me, please. Step off the bus."

"It was on Chief Daley's instructions. You can check with him."

"Outside, lady. On your own steam or the hard way."

Chatty Cathy refused to move to let me pass. She just sat there, a big heap of smug indignation, as I struggled to get by.

On the roadbed he edged uncomfortably close. "You P. J. Lafferty?"

"Yes. How'd you know?"

"I know everything," he said. "Like I know P.J. stands for *Poor Julia*. I know you're called that because you're such a hard-luck story. Parents killed in a car wreck. You're left with a deaf twin and a crazy brother. Poor, poor thing."

"Stop. You have no right to treat me like this. I haven't done anything."

"No?" he said. "I heard you set up one of your patients on the nut ward and got her offed. I call that doing something."

"I've already answered to Chief Daley. I don't have to put up with you!"

"Temper, temper. Better watch it, Lafferty. That mouth of yours might get you in even bigger trouble if you don't keep it zipped."

I pulled a breath. "All right. You've had your fun. Let's call it a day, shall we?"

He planted his hands on his hips. "Can't let you go until I make sure you're clean. What's in the box?"

"My personal things."

He had hauled my carton out of the bus along with me. With a Swiss Army knife, he slashed the tape, upended the box, and dumped my meager belongings on the pavement. I heard sharp crackling as the glass shattered on the picture of me, Jack, and Caity.

He stuck out a hand. "The purse."

I passed it to him, eager to have this done.

He emptied my handbag, piece by piece: topless Chap Stick, MetroCard, peanut butter cup complete with my dental imprint. Crumpled twenty. Handful of quarters, nickels, and dimes. He eyed my credit cards with disdain, as if he some-how knew I'd strained the limits of the lenders' patience yet again. Nina Present's card came next. His thumb left a murky blotch beside her name.

Peering into my purse, he frowned. "My, my. What have we here?" He plucked out a small plastic bag filled with white powder.

My scalp erupted with prickles of fear. "That's not mine. I never saw it before."

"Not smart. Judges don't take kindly to employees dealing."

"That's ridiculous. I'm no dealer. Ask anyone."

"Come now. Surely someone who digs around in scrambled brains for a living can come up with something more original than that."

"I'm not coming up with anything. It's the fact. Someone put that there to try and get me in trouble. Maybe you did it yourself."

"Are you accusing me of planting evidence, Ms. Lafferty? Because if you are, you'd better be prepared to prove it."

"I'm not accusing. Simply saying it could be so. I had nothing to do with it. That's all I know."

"That's what they all say: the guilty ones."

"It's the God's honest truth. You have to believe me."

"I do? Let's see what we've got here." He shook his head grimly as he unsealed the bag, moistened his pinky, and dipped in. His finger glistened with the damning evidence. "I'll give you one more chance to change your story. Things will go much easier if you come clean and cooperate."

"There is no other story." My voice had climbed to a desperate shrill. "I wouldn't go near that wretched stuff. That blasted poison stole my brother. Nearly put him in the ground. Listen to me. Please!"

He sniffed his contempt. "You're not very convincing."

"Drugs get planted. You know that."

"Sure I do. What I find hard to believe is that your brother took a near fatal overdose of table sugar. I mean, the stuff may not be very good for you. Rots your teeth and all. But calling it lethal poison is a little much."

With that, he twitched out laughing. Nothing funnier than my terror, it would seem.

"Hilarious. Why don't you take it on the road?" In a fury I threw my things back in the box and wrestled my purse from his grasp. "You should be proud, Officer. Takes real talent to do such a dead-on imitation of a horse's ass."

When I turned to board the bus, he caught my arm and squeezed it full of pain. "Not so fast, Poor Julia. I've got a message for you from Chief Daley."

"Daley sent you?"

He edged closer, so his breath raised a shiver. "The chief is very angry with you, Lafferty."

"I figured that out when he fired me."

"That would have been the end of it, but you had the gall to threaten a lawsuit. Not smart. Not at all. The chief doesn't want you to forget that he's in charge. He wants to take you down, that's what he'll do. Any time, any place, you keep that in mind. This was only a sample of how he can thank you if you play things wrong."

CHAPTER

6

■ **My mother liked to say her girls were split-hair, spit-**close identical, except that I couldn't listen and Caitlyn couldn't hear. Naturally, given that our veins ran with the broadest Celtic irony, I went into the listening game and became a psychotherapist, while Caity has always traded with astonishing success on her ears.

If ever there was a dime to be made in deafness, Caity did. She taught and tutored hearing-impaired kids. Ran focus groups; trained sign language interpreters and served as one in the courthouse and onstage. She developed a broadly adopted program to promote deaf tolerance by putting sound-swallowing earphones on what she called the ear bigots, forcing them to go about soundless, clueless, and scared. Most notably, my sister has become quite the celebrity, having penned a wildly successful series of children's books about a deaf girl named Eva Everheart who shares Caity's talent for lip-reading and discerning nonverbal cues. Using those skills, Eva, now age ten after seven installments and countless millions in print worldwide, solves crimes, spies for the government, repairs broken relationships, tutors adults in the art of parenting and other things, conquers bullies, averts disasters, heals international rifts, you name it. This scrawny child, reminiscent of me and Caity as kids in all her willful, dark-haired, mulish glory, has emerged as an iconic superhero for children and adults alike. She can do anything she sets her mind to, obstacles need not apply. In that way Eva is virtually identical to her creator, except that she's not real.

Caity bumped my front door open with her hip and entered jostling a quartet of overstuffed grocery bags, a large designer tote, a gift bag from the nearest liquor store, and a paper cone brimming with the kind of bright, cheery flowers I detest. A large ring of keys, including the one that allowed Caity to invade my apartment at will, dangled canine fashion from her mouth.

As usual, she was dressed in the finest, best, and most fashionable, in other words, nowhere near my style. Like Nina Present, my sister knew how to pull it together, while my talents ran more toward tearing things apart. On the positive side, I had found a sensible, mature, satisfying response to this. I seethed.

The sight of her, like most everything else today, threw me. I hadn't expected to see Caity. But of course that's how it would be. My sister always turned up when I needed her most or least.

She set the bags on the counter, freeing her hands to sign. "I feel like cooking," she informed me, fingers wavering like flames beneath a pot.

"What a coincidence," I gestured back. "You feel like cooking, and I feel like a truckload of donkey dung."

"What's wrong?" she gestured broadly, as you might to a child. "You look horrible."

"Bless you. Just the encouragement I need."

"Well, you do."

"That's because I am."

"Horrible why?"

"I was fired."

"No."

"Yes."

"For what?"

"Nothing."

"What kind of nothing?"

I told her about Jeannie Bagshaw coming to my office, the ill-fated wedding, and the bloody craziness that followed the alarm.

"How could Daley blame me for her murder, Caity? Isn't that insane?"

"No," she gestured sharply. "Predictable."

"Predictable how?"

"You did something you knew was wrong; and it went wrong." She snapped her fingers crisply. "Simple."

"That's not true. I made a professional judgment."

"U-n-p-r-o-f-e-s-s-i-o-n-a-l." She finger-spelled one sharp, accusatory letter at a time. Caity's signing reminded me of birds. Depending on her mood, her hands could be lazy gulls, jittery hummingbirds, nasty vultures, or, at their most emphatic, startled geese exploding from a blind.

"Sometimes you do unorthodox things for the good of a patient. I deal with human beings, Caity, not made-up characters who behave any way you please. In case you've forgotten, real life happens to be much messier than sitting at your computer, playing God."

"It doesn't have to be. Not like this. You asked to get fired." Her fingers flew in angry staccato, cutting her irritation into a fine, even dice. "Begged."

"I did no such thing."

Her hands wavered harshly in front of her chest. "Did."

"Thanks." I scowled as hard I could without making it impossible for her to read my angry lips. "I can't tell you how it warms my heart to know you're here for me—all sympathetic and understanding—when I need you most."

"You're the one who's not there for you, sister dear. You're your own worst enemy."

"If you'd seen Jeannie Bagshaw fighting for what she wanted, acting like an actual person for a change, you would have done the same damned thing."

"I would have asked someone higher up. Covered my butt, at least."

"Pity we all can't be as wise as you."

"True." Her index finger arced up from her lips. "But you can try."

She turned her back on me and focused on the stove. Caity

was a mediocre cook at best; make that mediocre minus, but never one to let a lack of ability stand in her way. Despite the fact that her sprawling apartment featured a glorious gourmet kitchen and daily cleaning help, she insisted on coming to my very humble abode when she felt right trying her hand at overly ambitious dishes, leaving me to cope with both the indigestion and the mess. Today, from the look of things, the menu was quail, wild mushrooms, and one of her odd salad combinations that were always far better in theory than in the mouth.

"The truth is I'm scared," I confessed to her back. I always found it much easier to open up to my sister when she was oblivious.

She hacked a shallot into harsh, uneven spikes and brushed the pieces from the cutting board into a pan sizzling too hot with oil. Caity jumped back comically as scalding bits leaped out at her. "Shit!" she howled in the weird, swallowed nose sound that passed for her voice.

"There are precious few jobs in my field. Remember when I got out of school? I couldn't find real work for almost a year. I had all I could do to keep life and limb together selling athletic shoes and tending bar."

She began dredging a flock of tiny, pin-boned quail in a slimy mix of cornmeal, flour, and insufficiently beaten egg.

"What if Nina Present doesn't come through? It could be just talk, you know, empty encouragement. I could lose this place, Caity. I could be homeless. Or worse, have to move in with you."

She hefted a large plastic jug of vegetable oil, poured an absurd excess into my remaining fry pan and cranked the heat up far too high. Half measures were never my sister's way. In short order, the oil thrummed ominously and threw off seething wisps. As she was about to immolate the first of the quail, I bolted from my chair, wrenched her arm away, and flipped the burner to low.

"Mo-der-ate," I said with patronizing exaggeration. "I'll thank you not to burn yourself to a blistered crisp in my apartment. I've got more than plenty to worry about without having a screaming French-fried know-it-all on my hands."

"What would I do without your expert advice?" She turned

away again, flipped the heat back to maximum, and dumped in the breaded birds. Wretched twits settled in without so much as a sputter. I didn't need to see the smirk on Caity's mug to know it was there.

I settled down again at the scarred oak table in the meager area that served as my combination kitchen, living room, dining room, library, media center, parlor, solarium, office, and den. My small square bedroom and tiny bath were at the rear. What Manhattan apartments lack in space, they more than make up for in the laughable cost per square foot. Rents are as outrageously high as is my unshakeable opinion of the city. I simply adore the place in all its loud, crowded, untenable splendor. The quality of life here may not be top-notch, but the quantity of most everything except space and solitude suits me perfectly. So does my tiny morsel of the island, this rented apartment on the first floor of a private house on a quirky little anomaly of a dead-end street sandwiched amid all the normal, orderly blocks in the East Eighties. I love it here, despite Caity's outspoken view that my place would benefit hugely from a liberal sprinkling of kerosene and a match.

"Why not find a new apartment while you're changing things? You know this place gives me the creeps." Caity signed this backhand, overhead, with the uncanny timing of someone able to read my thoughts. Word has it that this can be true of twins, but in our case, the street only ran one way. I couldn't begin to understand my sister, much less read her diabolical mind. In my opinion, her doing it to me constituted felonious mental trespass. If there was justice, I could shoot her in the head for this and walk off whistling a happy tune.

"Then feel free not to come here anymore," I suggested to her back. "Feel free to stay in your sanitized, homogenized, three-bedroom, three-and-a-half-bath, white-glove brat apartment with the in-house gym, stunning river views, and the hot and cold running blow jobs. I'm more a cramped, cozy, no-frills, tatty hovel, self-service sort of a girl."

She peered over her shoulder with tight, suspicious eyes. "What did you say?"

"I said, just because you happen to be chilly doesn't mean I have to put on a coat."

"That would be true," her hands flew sharply, "if you had the sense you were born with."

"Okay. I give up. Congratulations. You've managed to kill the one teensy-weensy crumb of self-confidence Daley missed. Excuse me while I go off in the corner and shrivel up."

Caity wiped her hands on a dishtowel and wrapped me in a hug. "I'm sorry."

I wriggled free. "Forget it. I'm fine."

"That's mostly true."

"It's a dumb job. That's all. Not the end of the world."

She crossed her fingers and waved them toward her ear. "Right."

"I'll get over it. In fact, I'm practically over it already."

"What did Daley say? Will he give you a recommendation?"

"Sure, Caity. In fact, he already did. He strongly recommended that I disappear."

"Seriously."

"Seriously, he threatened me and then sent one of his uniformed goons to follow up. Make sure I got the message. If he feels like ruining my life, that's exactly what he'll do."

"That's nonsense, P.J. What could he possibly do to ruin your life?"

"I got a sample, and it wasn't pretty. The cop he sent planted what looked like a glassine envelope filled with heroin in my purse. If it had been real, I could be looking at twenty-five to life."

She flipped the quail, now fried to tobacco-colored leather. "He's just trying to scare you."

"And succeeding."

"Don't take it seriously. Daley's not an idiot. He's not about to lay his career on the line over you."

"Of course not. The nerve of me to think I might be worthy of hatred or revenge."

"You are, sweetie. You definitely are. I didn't mean that."

"Do me a favor and let's not talk about it any more. OK? Why don't you concentrate on wrecking the food so we can get this blasted dinner over with?"

Caity frowned at the charred quail as if they were to blame for their own sorry plight. "You have macaroni and cheese?"

"Cabinet above the stove."

She doffed her million-dollar shoes, clambered onto the counter, and retrieved the mix. "A little comfort food is what you need, along with the nice Barolo I brought to wash it down. Later we can brainstorm; figure out your next moves."

"I already know. I'm going into private practice until I can find a new job."

"You're joking."

"Dead serious."

"But you swore you'd never do that. I thought only serious psycho criminals were good enough for you."

"*Never* happened to come along a lot sooner than I expected."

She rolled her eyes. "How are you going to find patients?"

"This is New York. The big hassle. Plenty of stressed-out head cases to go around."

Her moves grew more frantic: sniper birds bent on attack. "What are you planning to do? Stand on the corner and shoot them with tranquilizer darts? Put out a net?"

"So happens a highly influential and very well-connected woman has offered to send me referrals."

"A Park Avenue fairy godmother." She waggled two taunting fingers before her chin, the sign for *cute*.

I countered with a sign suggesting that she was welcome to have carnal relations with herself. "Her name is Nina Present, and she happens to think I'm wonderful. Anyway, I don't give a damn whether you believe me or not."

"May I ask where you're planning to see all these patients you don't have?"

I hadn't gotten that far. "Right here, naturally."

"You think it's natural to invite nutty strangers into the totally unprotected place where you happen to live alone?"

"I'm not going to be treating rapists and serial killers. They'll be regular people with standard problems, nice folks in need of a bit of advice, a little clarity, and a sympathetic ear."

"And how, pray tell, can you be so sure of that?"

"I can't, Caity. You're absolutely right. Truth be told, you can't be sure of anyone. There are plenty out there who'd just as soon run you through a wood chipper as give you the time of day. And to look at them, you'd never even guess they owned a wood chipper."

"That happens to be true, P.J., and you—of all people—should know it."

I threw up my hands. Dealing with my sister, I'd developed quite the sign system of my own. "Sure, Caity. If I were sensible, I'd barricade myself in the closet and booby-trap the door."

"Why don't you think it through for once? You have no doorman, no security, and your landlord is never home. As usual, all the other lights were out when I showed up."

"I told you, the woman who owns the place is a photographer. She's either taking pictures or holed up in her darkroom developing them."

This was the ever-so-slightly misleading truth. What I had not told Caity was that my landlord did these things in Tuscany, where she lived. She'd inherited this house several years ago and decided to hold on to it as an investment. Except for my apartment, the rest of the place was basically a large, very expensive storage bin. In exchange for keeping an eye on things, admitting necessary repair people, clearing the junk mail from her mailbox, and promising to inform her should anything go wrong, I had use of the ground floor for an unconscionable, though still below-market, rent.

"Except for us, this place is empty as a tomb," Caity went on.

"Tombs aren't empty."

"Right. They're full of reckless idiots like you who put themselves in harm's way and then get exactly what they asked for. Go on and make an even bigger mess of things, P.J. See if I care."

"You do. You love me dearly."

"Not so dearly when you insist on acting like a jerk."

I gripped her wrists to shut her up. "I'm not you, Caity. Damn it! I'm doing the best I can."

She wrenched free and gave me the look of someone who hates you as only you can really hate yourself. "No, you're not."

"I'm doing the best I can," I said again, pounding home one word at a time. "And for your information, your cooking sucks, and your stupid books are way overrated, and those pants make you look like the old lady after she swallowed the cow."

Of course by then, she had long since turned her back again, so I was railing at the insensate air. If you want to make me scorching mad, try rubbing my nose in the truth.

CHAPTER

7

■ **I cracked the spine on my new, burgundy mock-**leather appointment book and inscribed the names and vital statistics in a scrupulous hand. *Ted and Clarissa Demetrios (couples counseling). Molly Adler (mother Stephanie. With-drawal, poor achievement. Rule out anxiety/depression).*

Nina Present had passed along these two referrals in as many days and assured that more would be forthcoming soon. In addition to patients, she'd offered all manner of helpful advice. I'd had to work up the courage to ask what she thought I should charge. When she answered, without a trace of irony, that the going rate for private therapy in New York City these days was two hundred dollars or more per session, I almost lost my jaw. I had to whittle her down to one seventy-five to still the galloping palpitations, but even at that heady level, I'd spent hours since multiplying deliriously. A mere eight sessions a month would cover my rent. That left ample time to pay the rest of my bills and then some. I could actually envision working off my student loans at last, kissing chronic debt and deficits good-bye. I even dared to imagine raising my rates to the market standard if ever experience and confidence allowed. Private practice might turn out to be more tolerable than I'd thought.

With only five minutes remaining until my first scheduled appointment, I cast a critical eye around. My furniture was a mongrel mix of hand-me-downs, thrift-shop buys, and castoffs I had rescued from the curb. Still, the deep red convertible sofa was comfy enough, as were the Mutt and Jeff of green armchairs. A fresh box of Kleenex perched on the chrome-and-glass coffee table beside the empty cookie tin I planned to offer up as a place to deposit dysfunctional ideas and other emotional debris. The stuffed rabbit and teddy bear I'd picked up on sale at the nearest Duane Reade drugstore sat ready to offer their comforting services, as did the artless crocheted afghan I'd churned out during one of my rare, and mercifully short-lived, flings with domesticity.

The sound of the bell set my heart stammering. Ted Demetrios, a squat, timid-looking soul with a crash helmet of chestnut hair and licorice-framed glasses, stood on the small landing outside my door beside his wife, Clarissa, a willowy, patrician blonde. She claimed the larger of the armchairs, while her husband stood stiffly, awaiting instructions.

"Why don't you sit right there, Mr. Demetrios?" I said. "And I'll trade with you for my chair, Mrs. Demetrios." I let that and them settle in. Therapy is a dance that requires careful choreography.

"May I call you Clarissa and Ted?"

Her nose wrinkled in distaste, but she grudgingly agreed. His nod was barely perceptible.

"So what brings you here today?"

Her eyes flashed. "I came home early from a bridge game last week and found this—this pervert strutting around in my things."

The accused flushed a hot, dusky pink.

"Lucky me," she sniffed, "married to a hairy, repulsive Victoria's Secret model."

At that, he drew a ragged breath.

"I hear that you found that upsetting, Clarissa. But personal attacks really aren't useful. I'd like you to try to express things in terms of how they felt for you."

"Repulsive. That's how it felt. Disgusting, humiliating, and repulsive. He made me sick."

The rest of the story emerged in bitter bites. The marriage had started under water and rapidly sunk from there to worse. It was obvious that Clarissa had chosen Ted to spite her parents. He'd been so blinded by the attentions of someone so attractive and desirable that he'd never dared to consider whether there was anything of value beneath the glossy exterior. Finding little else to enjoy in the relationship, Clarissa delighted in making Ted suffer. Her torments ranged from humiliating comments to disappearances that lasted for weeks at a time.

"Why do you leave like that, Clarissa? I'm sure you understand how frightening and difficult it must be for Ted."

"Because every so often I need to breathe," she said, "without having to catch a whiff of him."

We had not yet reached the first of their eleven miserable anniversaries when the session clock ran out.

"If you want to try to resolve your issues, I recommend that you both come in twice a week for individual work in addition to our sessions together," I said.

"Fine. Whatever," Clarissa said.

Ted sat in mute misery.

"This is going to take a great deal of difficult work, Clarissa. Are you sure you're prepared to commit to that?"

"My husband will have to commit to it and make the necessary changes. Divorce is simply out of the question. Unacceptable to my family and to me."

Though I strongly suspected their marriage was a teardown, they were the only ones who could issue the condemnation order and summon the wrecking ball. This was one of those good news/dreadful news situations. On the upside, they'd be filling six of my hours each week at one seventy-five per, enough to sustain me quite nicely even if nothing else panned out. On the down, I would have to be there with them to earn my keep.

A two-hour gap loomed between those delightful lovebirds and my next appointment. Armed with a spoon and a pint of ice cream, I went online and cast around for innovative approaches to healing disordered relationships. Thinking in the field evolves constantly, and while I'd always kept abreast of developments in forensic psychology, I hadn't followed the broader psychological literature religiously. The electronic editions of the major professional journals gave me some useful ideas. Beyond that, quack advice abounded. One self-avowed "expert" chalked up vicious behavior like Clarissa's to Ted to "normal marital sadism."

Rafe, in his typical perversity, chose that particular moment to call. "You busy?"

"Yes, as it happens, I am."

"I heard about what happened at work, P.J. Are you OK?"

"You heard? It was on the news, was it?"

"Caity told me. So how are you?"

"Dandy, Rafe. And busy, like I said."

"Caity tells me you're taking private clients."

"Quite the nifty news source, my sister."

"How's it going?"

"Very well, actually. Which is why I'm so busy. You can tell Caity that when you two have your daily chat about how to run my life. Tell her I'm busy, and not amused."

"Ease up, P.J. She just mentioned it, that's all. No one's trying to run your life."

"Someone is, but no one's succeeding. Thanks for calling, Rafe. You take care."

"Wait. I have tickets to *Players* Thursday night. Got great reviews. Want to go?"

"I'm busy Thursday. Thanks anyway."

"How about getting together Friday, then? We could see a movie. Maybe grab a bite."

"Busy Friday, too, Rafe. Busy, busy."

"I don't suppose the answer is going to be different if I pick, say, next Michaelmas?"

"As I understand it, that's the whole point of divorce. Each of us gets to spend Michaelmas alone."

"It's been more than a year, P.J. There's no law that says we can't be friends."

"I wouldn't be so sure of that. As you know better than most anyone, Mr. Prosecutor, there are laws for most everything."

"OK. I get the message. I won't push."

He had. He was. He would. And Caity, bless her meddling

heart, kept encouraging him. Until Rafe and I split, the pair of them hadn't given each other the time of day, but as soon as the marriage dissolved, they'd formed a cozy, maddening alliance. "Bye now. Enjoy your Michaelmas."

"Call if you change your mind, P.J. Anytime."

"Sure, Rafe." I was tempted to suggest he hold his breath until that happened, but I resisted.

With only a few minutes remaining before my next session, I reviewed my notes. On the phone Mrs. Adler had described her daughter Molly as willful, rebellious, and poorly motivated. With increasing frequency, the child opted out of social engagements. Molly was talented in dance and swimming, but had stopped putting adequate effort forth in both and sometimes refused to attend class altogether. In addition, she was moody and acting out in school. Stephanie Adler was convinced that her child needed therapy and medication to arrest and reverse this ominous trend. Then she dropped the punch line: Molly was four and a half years old.

The little girl most certainly had a problem, and when the bell rang it was standing at my door, swaddled shoes to glasses in Chanel. Stephanie Adler wore a pink tweed suit, chunky gold jewelry, and a hard-etched scowl. With her bony form, stingy features, and sun-scorched skin, she bore an uncanny resemblance to one of Caity's immolated quail.

Molly had emerged from a much hardier end of the gene pool. The little girl was three feet of robust, flame-cheeked exuberance with springy blond pigtails and a wide, toothy grin. She sported bubblegum-pink knit pants, pink-and-white saddle shoes with candy-striped laces, and a rhinestone-studded Hello Kitty T-shirt. Hands on hips, she peered at me. "Are you the sigh-college-us?"

I knelt to greet her. "I am. I'm P.J. And you must be Molly."

"Nuh-unh. I'm Mr. Magoogle."

Her mother wrenched the child sharply, warping her giggles into a howling rain of tears. "What did I tell you? No silliness!"

"Come in, please."

Stephanie Adler perched on the couch, placing the maximum possible distance between herself and her child, and recited her litany of complaints. Molly had failed to gain admission to a decent preschool. Given the little girl's continued refusal to apply herself, failure to secure a place in a prestigious private elementary school seemed inevitable. Surely, her life would slip in a tragic downward spiral from there, and how on Earth was a parent to deal with the disgrace?

I gathered paper, markers, and a sticker book and invited Molly to play at the table. Once she was happily diverted, I sat with her mother. "I think you and I should meet again when Molly is not here and talk this through."

"She's the one who needs the work, not me."

"You and her father are responsible for Molly's well-being, Mrs. Adler. If any issues involving her are to be solved, you're the key."

"Her score on the ERBs was simply atrocious. An utter embarrassment, if you must know. Way below her capabilities. And after I engaged the best tutor in the city."

"You had her tutored for the preschool aptitude test?"

"Certainly I did. I want Molly to have every advantage. But she's lazy and stubborn. And I fail to see how my talking to you is going to change that."

"I'm sure Molly wants nothing more than your approval and acceptance."

"Nonsense! She's doing this out of sheer defiance. That's her way. Anything to get my goat."

"Children develop at their own individual pace, Mrs. Adler. They're not all ready for structured academics at the same time."

"Then she had better get ready. The world is not going to wait around while she acts like a silly infant."

A novel treatment came to mind: therapeutic strangling. If only the food weren't so rotten in jail. "Why don't you wait here while I talk to Molly for a while?"

"As well you should. She's the one who needs a talking-to."

At the table, I drew a crude face. "So tell me, Molly. Who is Mr. Magoogle?"

"He's the funny man in my most favoritest storybook."

"Can you tell me the story?"

"Uh-huh. Mr. Magoogle loved to bake pies. He made pies out of cherries and berries and clocks. He made pies out of shoes. He made pies out of socks. He made car pies and tar pies and green pies and pink. He made near pies and far pies and pies that could think."

"That's enough!" her mother demanded. "That book is pure silliness, and as soon as we get home, I'm throwing it in the garbage."

"No, Mommy, please. It's my very bestest book in the whole world!"

"Don't whine!"

"I think Mommy's trying to say she's feeling frustrated, Molly. Do you know what frustrated is?"

"Nuh-uh."

"It's when you want something and you just can't make it happen, no matter how hard you try."

"Like when you want to play with the big kids at the playground and they say 'No! You're too little! Go away!'"

"That's exactly right."

She nodded gravely. "Mr. Magoogle can make pies out of anything, even soap."

"That's because it's a made-up story."

"Soap pies would taste yucky."

"Right again. Some things are just perfect for making pies, and other things are better for washing hands with," I said with a pointed gaze at her mother. "People, too, Molly. Some are good at singing and others can't even sing a note, but they're extra good at riding a bike."

"I can sing. Want to hear?"

"I'd love to."

"Three little speckled frogs, sat on a hollow log, eating the most delicious bugs—yum yum . . ." Her voice was light, bright, and tuneful. "One fell into a pool, where it was nice and cool. Now there are two speckled frogs, dum dah dum dum dum dum."

I applauded her performance and noted that Stephanie Adler clapped a grudging time or two as well. I felt a tiny twinge of hope that she might turn out to be what famed child psychiatrist Bruno Bettelheim had termed a "good enough parent," one capable of learning to accept the delightful child she'd been given, rather than trying to mold her into some preconceived, unrealistic ideal. But before I could complete the thought, the witch reverted to wretched form.

"Enough foolishness. Show the psychologist what a smart girl you are. Show her how you can write your whole name."

"But I don't want to, Mommy."

"I don't care what you want. Do as I say!"

The child's expression melted from defiance to defeat. Listlessly she took up a thick blue marker and formed a stiff-peaked *M*.

"Concentrate!" her mother said. "You can do much better than that."

"I can't. That's my very bestest."

"No backtalk, Molly! Do it right!"

She scrawled another *M* and another, forging a row of craggy, deteriorating bumps.

"Stop that this instant!"

The child scribbled in a mounting rage, hard slashing lines that shredded the page. She refused to stop, even when her mother shook her shoulders roughly, even when she yanked Molly's pigtail so hard, I felt the pain.

"Stop! You're hurting her!"

The woman gasped. "Don't you dare tell me what I can do with my child! The nerve!"

"There are better ways to communicate with her," I said as evenly as I could. "I'd be glad to show you."

"You'll do nothing of the kind. What could Nina Present be thinking, recommending someone like you? I can't wait to tell her how inept you are."

"I'm sorry you feel that way."

"Come along, Molly. Mommy made a mistake. We are leaving this horrible place and this dreadful person this instant."

The child circled me widely, thumb in mouth, and clutched her mother's hand.

"That's a good girl," Stephanie Adler crooned. "I'm going to take my good, big girl out for a yummy strawberry milk-shake and then buy her a brand-new dolly with beautiful blond hair."

The door slammed with an icy ring of finality. Peering through the blinds, I watched them walk down my tiny block and disappear around the corner. My stomach drew in a knot of fear. This could well mark the end of my record short career in private practice, not to mention my fleeting flirtation with solvency.

Then perhaps the effort had been doomed from the start. Stephanie Adler had certainly reinforced my long-standing preference for criminal psychotics. Compared to her, the worst of them made sense.

■ **I thought it best for Nina Present to hear about the** Stephanie Adler debacle first from me, straight from the horse's ass, so to speak. But when I picked up the phone to call her, I found the line alive.

"I have a collect call from a Matilda Williamson. Will you accept the charges?"

"Matilda?"

"Big Millie, tell her," came a frantic squeal in the background. "Tell her I got something to tell her. Tell her this shit's big!"

"It's OK, Operator," I said. "I'll accept the charges. Put her through." Inmates at Rikers were entitled to three free calls a week, but Millie always exhausted her quota right away calling administration again and again to beg for more.

"One moment, please."

"Don't you be giving me none a that *one moment please* crapola. P.J. got to hear this shit NOW!"

"Go ahead, please," the operator said.

"You hear what happened, P.J.? You believe that shit or what?"

"Slow down, Millie. I don't know what you're talking about."

"Talking 'bout that Jeannie girl, that's what. Talking 'bout how she got herself dead."

"What did you hear?"

She snorted. "Not what I heard, shrinky dink. Ask me what I seen."

"Fine, Millie. What did you see?"

"Seen that girl's sumbitch husband, that's what. Big as day, he was. Sneaking 'round out back behind the yard."

"How do you know it was Jeannie's husband?"

"How many times I seen that sumbitch's picture hanging right there on the wall in Jeannie's cell? How many times I seen him show up all wanting to visit Jeannie, trying to get her coaxed out the cell so he could get his nasty-assed paws on the girl, all playing nicey nice, like he wasn't the baddest sumbitch ever lived. That sumbitch made my Reverend Herbert look like a big ole sweetie pox."

For Millie, this was sensible, rational talk, the kind she was able to pull off when she was taking her medication. "You're absolutely sure?"

"Absotootly, posilootly. No one knows bad sumbitches better than me. I got me a regular P h sumbitch D."

"I mean are you absolutely sure it was Jeannie's husband."

"Was his face right up there front of his head. No doubty bouty. Man I saw was Jeannie's husband Charlie Sumbitch Booth. Clear as day. Woulda called sooner, only you know how it is. Those illio-missionaries been spying on me again, so I had to wait till they finally ate themselves one too many cannonballs and fell asleep."

Then perhaps she wasn't taking every single dose. "OK, Millie. I hear you. I'll look into it."

"You do that. And while you're looking, look into what in the name of covering up his guilty ass that sumbitch Booth was doing with the lawn hose. Washing the blood off his guilty ole face and hands is what. Washing the blood off his fancy-assed Air Nike shoes."

"You're sure this isn't one of your hallucinations? Like the cannibals and the missionaries?"

"I'm sure as they come, lady. Surer even. You ever hear of

a lucy nation blowing over on you in the breeze? Ever hear of a lucy nation spraying your big ole ass and getting you rockem socking wet?"

"It's possible, Millie. We've talked about this, remember? Hallucinations can seem incredibly real."

"That man was real, all right, and so was the blood on him. You go on and check it out. You go get his DNA and his CIA and his Howdy Dunnit. You make that nasty sumbitch pay for what he done to that poor Jeannie girl. You make him pay full retail plus shipping, tipping, whoop-de-doo, and tax."

"I'll do the best I can."

"Don't you go be giving me none of that can-can shit, girl. Just do-do it, you hear?"

Calling the police seemed sensible, so that's exactly the useless thing I did. I explained that I had information about a recent killing at Rikers. True, there was a chance this would come to Chief Daley's attention, but surely he'd view it as a positive to have Jeannie's murder solved. The desk sergeant I spoke to at my neighborhood's 19th Precinct said he'd send someone over right away.

A squad car appeared with the prescient speed of my local Chinese take-out place. Two officers emerged and strode to my door. In charge was a plump attractive caramel-skinned woman whose name badge identified her as Martinez. Her slim, balding partner's badge read Sheriff, one of those destiny names that made it far more likely that he'd turn out to be a cop than—say—a serial killer. Martinez fired questions at me while Officer Sheriff took notes.

"I understand you have information about a murder, Ms. Lafferty?"

"I do. A few days ago one of the inmates on the Women's Mental Observation Unit at Rikers Island was stabbed to death during a fire drill. Her name was Jeannie Bagshaw. A witness called to tell me she saw Jeannie's husband, a man named Charlie Booth, behind the yard after the killing. He was using a hose to wash off Jeannie's blood."

Martinez nodded gravely. "The witness. What's her name?"

"Matilda Williamson."

"And she called you why?"

"I knew her while I was working at Rikers, as a psychologist."

"You're no longer there?"

"No."

"Because?" Martinez asked.

I swallowed hard. "I was dismissed."

"Because?"

"Because someone had to take the blame for Jeannie Bagshaw's murder. And I happened to be the handiest choice."

She tapped her index finger against her lips. "Matilda Williamson is a psychologist, too?"

"No."

"What then?"

"An inmate."

"On M.O.?"

"Yes."

Martinez's face signaled the rapid approach of a cold front. "Are you telling me your witness is a mental patient?"

"She is, but in this case, I believe she's credible."

The cop rolled her eyes. "May I ask what kind of a mental patient?"

"I'm afraid that's privileged information; but in my opinion, what she told me was true."

"In your opinion."

"My professional opinion, yes. Can't you at least question Charlie Booth and see what he has to say?"

"Sure. And the next time someone claims to be Jesus Christ, I'm going to hit him up for a nice miracle. Loaves and fishes for the whole neighborhood maybe. Or better yet, the winning ticket in a hundred-million-dollar lottery. Imagine the mess of loaves and fishes I could buy with that."

"Booth is a sadistic abuser, Officer. He injured Jeannie many times and everyone knew it. Are you going to sit back and let him get away with her murder?"

"Of course not. What I'm going to do is find the guy and string him up on the strength of what some certified nut job claims she saw. Or stone him maybe, depending on my mood. And then you and I are going to get all gussied up and have our hair done so we'll be ready to collect our medals and ride the float of honor in the parade."

I went sheepish. "You can't question him?"

"Look, Ms. Lafferty. Here's how it is. I'm a single mom with three kids. I've put in eighteen years on the force, and I'm looking forward to collecting my pension and being able to take in a nice little second income on the side. That way I can put those kids through college, maybe grad school if that's what they want, try to give them a leg up."

"I can't see how questioning a suspect would get in the way of that."

Her tone went sharp. "No, you can't see. Fact is you may be a student of human behavior, but you don't know your butt from a hole in the ground when it comes to how things work on the force. Fortunately, I do. And that's how I've gotten this far. I follow chapter and verse. I take my vitamins, say my prayers, keep my nose clean, and do my best to never shoot myself in the foot."

"But what if he did kill her? Doesn't chapter and verse say he's supposed to pay?"

She spewed air. "You worked at Rikers, so I'm willing to bet you do know a little something about criminal justice in this country. There are very clear, very specific rules, and the law says we have to obey them, like it or not. And yes, sometimes people get away with serious crimes, even murder as a result, even though that's not how things are supposed to go."

"No. It isn't. That girl was minding her own business, not hurting anybody."

"We can't be sure of that, can we?" Martinez said. "We weren't there when she bought it. Maybe she got exactly what she signed up for. People get killed in jail. By definition, it's a bad, brutal place."

"Jeannie Bagshaw was a timid, gentle person. She didn't have a violent bone in her body. She was abused by sadistic creeps her whole life. First her parents, then Booth. It's not right."

Officer Sheriff was still scrawling elaborate notes. Martinez set a hand on the page to stop him. "I'd advise you *strongly* to drop this and mind your own business as well, Ms. Lafferty."

That notion refused to go down. "I can't see why you wouldn't investigate, at the very least. You could find out if Booth was at Rikers that day. See if he has an alibi."

"I can't. I won't. And neither will anyone else in the department. We don't take marching orders from mental patients. Not from mental patients or the people who believe them, no matter how sincere and well-intentioned they might be."

"So Jeannie's death simply gets written off like a few stray pennies on an accounting statement? Take the loss and forget about it. Is that honestly how you think it should go?"

She turned to Sheriff. "Do me a favor, Mike. Go outside and check the tires."

"Tires are fine. The car was checked last week."

"They were looking a little low to me. Can't be too careful about vehicle safety, I always say."

"All right. Sure. I'll check them when we leave."

"No, Officer. You'll check them now." When he hesitated, she added, "The tires and the procedure manual, Officer. The part about who reports to whom and what happens when someone refuses to follow a direct order. You be sure to check that, too."

He made his way out the door, mule walking and muttering under his breath.

Martinez skewered me with dark, angry eyes. "Let me give you a bit of advice, Ms. Lafferty. Sometimes it happens that you feel like you're walking on firm ground when in fact all you've got under your feet is a shaky little termite-infested plank. All it takes is one wrong step, and you're in for a big, nasty fall. You read me?"

"I don't read you as someone who wants to see an innocent victim's death go unpunished."

She puffed her lips. "No one would accuse you of being easy."

"You really think it's OK to forget about it, to pretend Jeannie Bagshaw's murder doesn't count?"

"No, I don't. Turn up some good, solid evidence or a witness who has something better than chili con carne for brains, and I'll do everything in my power to help you see her killer put away."

■ **Getting the information I needed would take** management-level access at least. I tried to reach my former boss Will Creighton, but got no answer in his office at the prison, on his cell phone, or at his home. I left a trio of messages, but from past experience, I knew it could be days before I heard back. With four little kids, the Rikers job, and a staggering number of outside involvements, Creighton was way overextended. Calling Chief Daley to report Big Millie's allegations crossed my mind, as did several other devilishly clever forms of suicide.

Rikers was closed to visitors on Mondays and Tuesdays. No exceptions. If Charlie Booth had been at the prison on the Tuesday of Jeannie's murder, as Big Millie claimed, it could only have been as an employee, an outside contractor, a dignitary invited for a VIP tour, or an inmate. The latter was easy enough for me to find out, if you consider something on a par with chewing off your own foot easy.

I picked up the phone and let my fingers do the balking. First, though I knew it like my own, I couldn't summon the number to mind. After I looked it up, I misdialed again and again. Forgot to press the 1. Neglected to input the area code.

Hit the asterisk instead of the 7. Pressed End when I meant to hit Send.

Eventually I ran out of delaying tactics and let the call ring through. "ADA. Lafferty."

"Hello, Rafe." I hated that we had the same last name, even though it was technically his. Changing mine back to Goldstein, my maiden name, had seemed too monumental a task. Plus, try looking and sounding like the typical milk-pale, jet-haired, blue-eyed "black Irish" girl with an indelible brogue and a name like Julia Goldstein. The unlikely surname had come courtesy of a grandfather who had passed through Ireland selling piece goods, swept my grandmother off her staunch Catholic feet, eloped with her, spawned my father, and died before my birth. Caity had no trouble pulling off the laughable incongruity of our last name, but identical though we were, I could run rings around her when it came to being awkward and inept.

"P.J., hi," Rafe said with a galling excess of enthusiasm. "What a nice surprise! Change your mind about getting together?"

"No, Rafe." I was tempted to point out that hell hadn't yet frozen over, but I was angling for a favor after all. "I need to know if there's been a recent arrest or contempt citation against a man named Charlie or maybe Charles Booth. In his twenties, early thirties maybe."

"Checking out the new boyfriend, are we?"

"Right. Quite the clever detective you are. So happens I've been trying for months to hook up with a nice, eligible felon, preferably an ax murderer, but no luck so far."

"Someone you're planning to work for, then? Because if you feel the need to do a background check, I'd advise you to trust your instincts and stay away."

"No. I'm not planning to work for him."

"Same thing if he's a potential patient, P.J. Actually, you're probably best off not taking on any men at all. Better safe than sorry."

I chuckled. "Come now. After all those billions you've locked up, I can't imagine there'd be any bad ones left roaming free to do a girl harm."

"Still a few, but I'm working on it."

"How comforting." The line hung with thick, weighty frost. This was the largest of the hopeless abysses that gaped between us. My ex believed that society's best answer for most ills was to put away as many people as the cages could stretch to hold. In my strong, unshakable, and perhaps rabid opinion, jail was too often nothing more than a means to place bars and barbed wire between us and *them*: the different ones, the ones who made us uneasy in whatever unpardonable way. Granted, plenty deserved, even demanded, locking up for their own good or the general safety, but many others would be far better served by treatment, school, and the resources it would take to set them on a better path, or better yet, all three. Jail was prep school for advanced criminality and graduate-level craziness, a place where the basic rules of humanity took a backseat to Commissary credits, prime chairs near the television, and precious extra minutes on the phone.

"So why do you want to know, then? Exactly what is your interest in this Booth guy?"

"Let's say it's personal."

"What kind of personal?"

"The personal kind."

Rafe sighed. "Must you be so difficult?"

"You're the one being difficult, Rafe. Either tell me you'll help or say you won't."

"What else do you have on the guy?"

"He was married to a girl named Jeannie Bagshaw. They met as kids somewhere in the South."

"Not much to go on. Charles Booth is not exactly an exotic name."

"Maybe not, but how many could have been arrested recently in New York?"

"You'd be surprised."

I strained to dredge up details from what I'd read months ago in Jeannie's file. "He does something in the building trades I think. Lives in Queens. Astoria comes to mind, though I can't swear that's right."

"You have a description?"

Like Big Millie, I'd seen Booth's picture countless times, glaring at me from the wall in Jeannie's cell. "Dark hair; dark eyes. I suppose some might say he was decent-looking, but not in a way that would draw a person in."

"Distinguishing marks?"

"Those eyes of his were definitely distinguishing. Had this look about them like burn holes in cloth."

"I mean tattoos, P.J. Scars and such. Editorial observations don't make it into police reports, no matter how charming they might be."

I bristled mightily at that. *Charming*, indeed. "He wears a gold earring shaped like a lightning bolt. At least, he did in the picture I saw. Bit of a crooked mouth, too. Peaked higher on the left, so he always has the sneer."

"Grew up in the South, you said. Any idea where?"

"Can't say I do."

"That's a big help, P.J. The guy once lived in the South. Narrows it right down to only eighty, ninety million people."

"That's what I have. Will you help, Rafe? Or not?"

He played me through a long, irritating silence. "I can try," he said finally.

"How long do you think it'll take?"

"Busy, busy here, too. I'll get to it as soon as I can."

"Sure thing, Rafe. I read you loud and clear. Thanks anyway."

"I'll do it, P.J. That's the truth. Have a little patience for a change. And please, whatever you do, don't get it in your head to take after this character on your own."

"Is that an order, Mr. Prosecutor, sir?"

"No. Definitely not. I am absolutely, positively *not* telling you what to do."

"That would be refreshing."

"I'll get right on it. Shouldn't take long at all."

"Sure. I'll bank on it."

"You can. Now promise you'll sit tight until you hear from me."

"I won't move a muscle, Rafe. Not even if it cramps."

"I mean it, P.J. Don't screw around. The guy could be dangerous."

"Give it a rest. It never entered my head to go after him." And in truth, until Rafe brought it up and forced it into my innocently bystanding brain cells, I hadn't given the reckless possibility a thought.

CHAPTER

10

■ **It was dead simple, which should have warned me off** then and there. All I had to do was call Rikers Island and ask to be put through to the chaplaincy office. A cadre of imams, rabbis, ministers of various denominations, and priests served the prison complex. In addition to conducting services and overseeing the distribution of modified ceremonial items like electric candles and sacramental grape juice, they were routinely informed of the inmates' critical life events: births, dire illnesses, graduations, marriages, impending releases, and, when the need arose, deaths. I described myself, with defensible accuracy, as a friend of Jeannie Bagshaw's and asked what, if any, funeral arrangements had been made on her behalf. Had she been destined for a crematorium or one of the thousands of anonymous graves in New York's massive Potter's Field on Hart Island, I would have reached a fortuitous dead end. But no, the clerk informed me that her body had been released by the medical examiner's office late yesterday, and she was to be buried this very afternoon at St. John's Cemetery in Middle Village, Queens. So I was in luck, though of course I had no way to tell what kind or how deeply and hopelessly I was destined to get mired in it.

A quick check on the Internet turned up the cemetery's address, subway directions, and the fact that Jeannie's remains would be keeping eternal company with some of New York's most infamous wise guys, including "Lucky" Luciano, Vito Genovese, and John Gotti. In life, Gotti had been known as the "Teflon Don," but apparently the Grim Reaper had managed to make the last bit stick.

I donned a black turtleneck and blazer and black running shoes, the closest thing I had to proper funeral attire. In a lame attempt at anonymity, I pulled my hair back, clipped it near the crown and slipped on a baseball cap. I grabbed my scratched drugstore sunglasses for good measure and headed out.

It was lucky that I'd allotted plenty of time given the trudge I had from the subway station to the cemetery and the even longer one that followed, tracking the convoluted directions I was given at St. John's administration building to the rectangular pit, draped in hopsack and bounded by hillocks of fresh-turned earth, where Jeannie Bagshaw was to be interred. Her solitary plot was wedged between the highly extended Nunzio and Ingles families. Jeannie would be laid to rest behind a thick stone bench engraved with the legend: *Enzo Nunzio—beloved grandfather, devoted husband, father, and brother, loyal friend*.

My plan was to observe the people who attended Jeannie's burial without having the favor returned. I settled on a gravesite marked *Mary Margaret Connolly—Angel on Earth and in Heaven, RIP*. Mary Margaret lay at a reasonable distance from Jeannie's patch of ground, and her plot offered favorable sight lines.

I knelt on the cool, hard ground and set to routing out the stubborn weeds and errant grasses. Perpetual care, which according to the small bronze plaque on the headstone Mary Margaret's family had sprung for, certainly didn't begin to approach my mother's scrupulous gardening standards. Not close. Mary Margaret's berth, a meager space that seemed too small by half to lay down in, much less stretch out in comfortably, was pocked with scraggly dried clumps, unsightly wild things, and a large, discouraging scatter of dirt-encrusted rocks.

At first I kept an eye on Jeannie's gravesite as I worked.

But more than half an hour still remained before the scheduled start of the service, and I soon yielded to the lulling warmth of the sun on my back, the hypnotic rhythms of the plucking and tamping, and the velvety richness of the earth as I worked it through my fingers and inhaled its dark, primal scent. My mother had taught me how to coax meltingly sweet squash, beans, and tomatoes from our meager, hilly, shade-burdened yard in County Kerry when I was a child, and the love of the soil has never left me, diehard city girl though I may be.

The conditions here were a far cry from the small, ancient graveyard swaddled in the shade of Ste. Catherine's Church near the town of Tralee, where my parents had been lowered into the ground. Though they'd been obscenely young, still years shy of forty when their car went off that slick serpentine road, they'd left precise, detailed instructions for what they wanted done with their bodies when the time came. Home to them had always been Ireland, and that's where they wished to return. At Ste. Cat's, volunteer congregants, most longtime friends and neighbors of my folks, saw to it that everything was lovingly, perfectly maintained. That was the local way. Perpetual care was for the giving, not for sale. If you were sick, the townsfolk brought hot hearty meals in covered baskets. If you were dead, they brought seedlings and gardening gloves, stooped on the ground, and set to work. When Caity and I went back for a visit some years back, we were comforted to note that our mother would have viewed their patch of ground with smiling approval. The soil bore a downy coat of new grass and lush heather framed their stones. Paper white narcissus filled the squat stone planters that had been set to mark the boundaries of their plot. *Now there's a proper job,* my mother would have said.

And didn't Mary Margaret, celestial, terrestrial angel that she was, deserve a proper job as well? In life, I pictured her as a strapping, modest woman, fingers worn blunt from a life of endless chores. From what it failed to say on her gravestone, she'd been single and childless, so I imagined her as the doting favorite auntie. I conjured her with smiling eyes, gifted at storytelling and the stove. I could almost taste her roast chicken, cooked so tender it all but fainted off the bone when the boisterous clan piled in after church for Sunday supper.

Absorbed as I was in the gardening and the fantasy, I failed at first to notice the small group assembling at Jeannie's grave. When I glanced that way again, a stooped, white-haired couple stood in the shade cast by the minister, a giant, stocky wisp-haired man with bulldog jowls and the spongy nose of a heavy tippler. A chunky girl came up next, snarling on her cell phone. "That bitch ain't coming to the party, you hear me. I don't care who she's doing. She shows up, I'm gonna throw her sorry ass out the door!" She was dressed in a flounced floral blouse over bandage-tight white Capri pants, wobbling on high-heeled turquoise mules. Following her, a thick pewter-haired woman appeared with a small, ginger-haired boy in tow. Next, an attractive, coffee-skinned woman arrived, toting a briefcase. She clasped the small boy by the shoulders and gave him a reassuring squeeze before backing away to stand off to the side.

Charlie Booth was last to show up. He bumped up the slim, winding cemetery road in a dark green pickup with a gnarly carburetor and country music blasting from the radio. He made a conspicuous exit from the cab, slammed the door, and then loped around to the passenger side, where a hay-toned blonde in a lavender miniskirt, neon pink blouse, and thigh-high bruise-colored boots emerged. Swaggering toward Jeannie's grave, he draped his arm around the woman, hand grazing the formidable bulge of her breast. Booth sported a studded leather motorcycle jacket over a grimy T-shirt and acid-washed jeans. His coal-nugget eyes blazed in the glare, and shards of fractured light spat from the lightning bolt in his ear.

Barely a word of greeting passed between Jeannie's mourners. They traded glances ranging from wary to grim. The minister waited until their attentions turned to him. He cleared his throat and eyed the heavens, where a steady line of low-flying planes roared toward the nearby airports. Except for Booth, everyone peered up with him, squinting against the sun's fearsome glare.

"Jeannie Bagshaw was a flower in want of its bloom. Cut down and too soon faded, far too soon." He tracked the group through a long, weighty silence, punctured by the howl of passing jets. "To those of you who loved Jeannie, this must seem a particular tragedy. She had her difficulties, to be sure, but she had many special abilities as well. Jeannie was a kind, loving girl with a good heart. Surely, with the good Lord's grace, she could have fulfilled the possibility that her untimely end so brutally erased. The person who took that life, the one who stole Jeannie's future and her promise, bears a harsh, indelible stain on his soul."

As the reverend went on, his preaching timed to the silent respites between the planes' din, Charlie Booth tapped a cigarette from his soft pack, lit up, and blew a lazy plume of smoke. He aimed for the clergyman's face, but the insult was deflected by the breeze.

The minister tipped his head down toward the wizened white-haired couple. "To Jeannie's great-grandparents, Hiram and Isabel Bagshaw, I wish peace, comfort, and healing from this dreadful loss." His gaze settled on the middle-aged woman next, and the boy beside her. "To Dennis John and Lottie, and to the other relatives and friends gathered here, I wish that the memories of this gentle, loving soul stay with you and sustain you. I urge you to cling to those moments when Jeannie was well and strong, when her spirit shone bright and true." Finally he turned to Booth. "And to Jeannie's husband, Charles, I wish the light of the good and merciful Lord to shine upon you, lead you out of the darkness, and show you the way."

Booth whispered in his girlfriend's ear. She burst out giggling and then muzzled herself with a hand.

"Jeannie placed her love and loyalty in your hands, Charles. Honor that, and you honor yourself. Deny it, and be denied. That is how it must be for every one of us, for each of God's children, here and in the hereafter."

Booth twirled a finger in the air, signaling his impatience to have this done.

The minister stared stone-faced at his prayer book. "The Lord is my shepherd, I shall not want . . ."

Before the final *Amen* faded, Booth steered the blonde back toward the pickup. As the others filed past, he pulled her close and drilled for her tonsils with his tongue.

Everyone's fear of the man was palpable. They circled him with downcast eyes, except for the girl who had been talking on the cell phone. She chanced a smile and a flirtatious little wave, both of which Booth ignored. The woman with the briefcase stopped for a moment to talk to the woman with the little boy, and then strode off. Booth watched as the blonde opened the truck's passenger door and then slapped her fulsome rear as she slithered into the high-riding cab.

I cursed myself for failing to bring a notepad and pen. For what it might be worth, I scratched the make, model, and license number of the pickup in the soil so I might better remember it. Toyota Tacoma; CZV 832.

When I gazed up again, I found myself trapped in the crosshairs of Charlie Booth's menacing sights. With a pointed scowl, he stubbed out his smoke on the nearest gravestone. Scorched by the threat, I looked away and fiddled with the grass. I knelt there, insides churning, until he drove off and the livid blast of his engine faded in the distance.

Now I cursed myself for coming here. Rafe was right. It had been a stupid, dangerous thing to do. But then, evil eye aside, Booth had no way to know who I was. So no harm done.

Rising, I swiped at the filth on my hands. The hard-packed dirt framing my fingernails begged for soapy water and a brush. My knees bore dark, damp oval earth stains, my sneakers were mud-caked, and I dreaded the long trip home. All I'd managed to confirm by coming here was the appalling inadequacy of their perpetual care. Then what on earth had I expected? Charlie Booth might not be a paragon of strategy and control, but he wasn't about to show up at Jeannie's funeral wearing something that proclaimed: *I murdered my wife and all I got was this lousy T-shirt.*

I retraced my steps through the cemetery that suddenly seemed devoid of other living souls. The wind whipped up, shaking the trees like angry hands, deepening my eerie disquiet. A plane dipped low with a monstrous growl, trapping me in a cloud of menacing gloom. I had the unshakable sense that I was being watched. I kept glancing back, expecting to find Charlie Booth trailing me instead of my own timorous shadow. What if he circled his truck around again? What if he'd kept a distant eye on me and found some way to follow me home?

And what if the sun forgot to rise tomorrow? And what if my nose grew thorns?

Seeking distraction, I read the names and legends carved on the stern granite markers I passed. *Clara Gartner October 21, 1928–May 10, 1986, Beloved mother; devoted wife; RIP. Leonard P. Hauptman, March 2, 1912–May 14, 1996: Gone but not forgotten. Sally Jane Sternbeck, May 3, 1983–May 2, 1994. Light of our lives.* I could well imagine what Caity would have them chisel on the stone above my head when I lay decomposing in a box. *Here lies Poor Julia. If only she'd had more time to get it right.*

Finally I spied the administration building in the distance and the wrought-iron gates beyond. Eager to be done with this place, I sprinted toward the road. Soon I was damp with sweat, breathing in shallow bursts. Still, I kept running full out until I came within a few paces of the exit. As I slowed, a pleading cry sent me nearly out of my skin. "Stop! Wait!"

"What the hell!"

"Sorry. I didn't mean to startle you."

The voice belonged to the pewter-haired woman from Jeannie's burial. The small boy she'd come with hovered at her side. Freckles peppered his heart-shaped face under hair reminiscent of carrot curls. He was dressed in an outsized plaid shirt and khaki shorts cinched tightly at the waist. Scrawny arms and slim knob-kneed legs gave him the look of a baby scarecrow. The woman clutched his hand. Her prim black dress had faded to a purplish iridescence, and her ankles swelled like ripe fruit over squat, sternly-laced black shoes. The black purse clutched beneath her arm had the dry, crazed look of old plastic. "I didn't want to intrude while you were visiting your loved one's grave. Figured you had to come this way sooner or later. You're from the jail, right?"

"Have we met?"

"Saw you at the women's prison not long after they put Jeannie in that awful place. Administrator on the observation unit asked me to come help fill out some forms. Jeannie pointed you out. You were her doctor?"

"Psychologist. I worked with her, yes."

She extended a gnarled, pale hand. "I'm Jeannie's aunt: Lottie Dray."

"P. J. Lafferty."

"I know. Jeannie talked about you a lot."

"It's hard to imagine Jeannie talking a lot about anything."

"Not in that place. Not when she was scared near to death all the time."

"Did you speak to her often?"

"She called first thing every Sunday to talk to Dennis John. Didn't she, sweetie? Your mommy never forgot. Not once."

"Mommy? I didn't know Jeannie had a son."

"Sure did. Dennis John was Jeannie's pride and joy. Best thing ever happened to her, Jeannie always said. Remember how Mommy used to say that, sweetie, how you were her very best thing?"

The little boy kicked the ground, stirring a gritty fog.

"There was nothing in her chart about a child," I said.

"No? Can't imagine why not." Lottie drew the boy close, and he melted against the spongy comfort of her legs. "Hardest thing for Jeannie was having to leave Dennis John when they took her off. Poor girl missed her little love something fierce."

"I want my mommy, Aunt Lottie! I want Mommy now!" His voice was a quaking filament of grief.

"Shh. It's OK, sweetheart. Mommy's all fine and happy and beautiful where she is. Remember like I said?"

"But why can't I see her?"

"Because Heaven is way far off. Farther than Alaska even. Farther than China or Japan or Neverland; that's why."

"So why can't I go see her there?"

"Because no one can get into Heaven until God decides it's their time and sends his beautiful golden chariot to pick them up. But your mommy can see you, clear as day. In fact, she's watching right this very minute, so hurry and dry those tears and stand up straight and tall."

She produced a crumpled Kleenex, and the child rolled his little shoulders back while she blotted his eyes.

"There, that's better. Bet Mommy's smiling now to beat the band."

Dennis John gazed upward and chanced a tight, little wave.

"That's the way, cutie pie," Lottie crooned. "That's my big boy. Dennis John turned five last month," she declared with a lilt of pride. "Hard to imagine, but next year he'll be starting school. Time sure does fly."

I crouched to face him. "Nice to meet you, Dennis John. I'm P.J."

"Like pajamas?"

"You're right. It is. How are you doing?"

His eyes pooled with tears. "Mommy got real sick so she had to go far, far away to Heaven."

"I know. I'm sorry that happened."

"Like my fishes."

"Your fish are in Heaven?"

"Daddy broke the bowl, so they got dead." His eyes stretched to accommodate the monstrous memory.

"There now, sweetheart. It's okay." Lottie hiked up his shirt as she hugged him, exposing a livid, arc-shaped scar. She caught my eye, making sure I took note. "I have to talk to the nice lady alone for a minute. You wait right here—OK?"

She walked me several yards away and whispered. "Charlie smashed the fishbowl in a fury. Then he sliced Dennis John with the broken glass."

"My God!"

"Afterward, he wrapped the boy up in a towel so the blood wouldn't mess his precious truck. Dropped him at my place and took off. Didn't even wait to make sure I was home. But lucky I was. Cut was deep and bleeding something awful. Took twenty-two stitches to close it up. Doc said a little deeper, and the glass might have punctured a lung. Or his heart even. Could have killed him."

I shuddered. "How much time did Booth do for that?"

"Time? Charlie? Never happen. He wasn't even arrested."

"Didn't you report it?"

"You bet I did. Hospital did, too. I've called the cops about that monster a thousand times, but nothing ever comes of it. Complaints just up and vanish."

"I don't understand."

"Who could? Plenty about Charlie Booth doesn't add up." She fixed me with her tense, troubled gaze. "Look, Ms. Lafferty, running into you here today is the first thing that's given me any hope at all."

"I have no special powers, Ms. Dray. Believe me. In fact, if there's the opposite of special powers, that's what I have."

"Jeannie trusted you. Of everyone in that dreadful jail, she said you were on her side."

"Turns out that didn't count for much."

"Did so. Meant the world to that girl to have someone she felt she could turn to."

I shifted uneasily.

"I live nearby. Be a big favor if you'd come with us. I'd like to show you something. Maybe bring things a little clearer."

Dennis John edged toward the gate. "You stay put, lovey," Lottie called. "Just be a quick minute more. Then we'll go have lemonade and cookies, like I said."

I eyed my wrist, where the watch would have been if I'd been wearing one. "I should probably be getting home."

"Please, Ms. Lafferty. It'd mean more than I can say."

I understood exactly what it would mean: getting in deeper, stepping further into Charlie Booth's world.

"Only take a few minutes. After that, you want to walk away, forget all about it, fine."

"Come on, Aunt Lottie," the little boy whined. "Time for lemonade and cookies."

My eye strayed to him. At that moment—as the sun struck his pale, freckled face and dense red curls—he bore a heart-breaking resemblance to his mother. I pictured Jeannie as she had looked less than a week ago at my office door. I could still see the glint of hope in her eyes as she made her case about the wedding, the thing she'd so wanted that had turned out to be her bloody end: *something for Jeannie.*

The child edged close, took my hand, and tugged. "Come on, P.J. It's time now. Let's go!"

I understood that we had reached a critical pass in the negotiation. "What kind of cookies?"

"Chocolate chip."

"With nuts or without?"

He frowned as if the question was too lame too merit a response.

"Yellow lemonade or pink?"

"Aunt Lottie?"

"Lemon color, of course. Make it myself. Cookies, too. Toll House are fresh today, plus there's still a couple of oatmeal raisin and some of my extra-special peanut butter chips in the freezer. Only take a minute to thaw them out."

"Homemade peanut butter chips?"

"Like you never tasted, if I do say so myself."

"Then what are we waiting for?"

Dennis John grinned smugly as I trailed him and Lottie out the gate.

CHAPTER

11

■ **Lottie Dray's building perched half a block from the** Myrtle Avenue subway station and resembled a wedding cake whose day had long since passed. Graffiti and ragged cracks marred the stained, tiered ivory facade. A window near the roofline and another on the penultimate floor were cracked and held together by strips of silver duct tape. Tall garbage bag pyramids flanked the entry door. I recognized this as precisely the kind of rundown, seedy, mildly dangerous place that would drive my sister mad, so naturally I found myself musing about whether they had vacancies and how much rent I might be able to save by moving to Queens, if all else failed.

The lobby was ripe with musky animal scents, cooking grease, spoiled milk, and stale tobacco. Two stern wooden chairs and a swayback sofa were chained to the yellowed linoleum floor. The elevator was nailed shut, caked with grime, and out of order. We crossed to a cement-walled stairwell and trudged up five long, narrow flights. Bare bulbs dangled overhead, spilling bilious light on metal stairs strewn with cigarette butts, crumpled gum wrappers, crushed beer cans, and a solitary, serpentine blue sock.

In stark contrast, Lottie's apartment was pin neat and

homey. Cascading spider plants in white hanging pots graced the tiny foyer along with cross-stitched platitudes in slim metal frames. *Sit awhile and have a smile. Home is wherever you find love.* Beyond was a small living room with facing brown velveteen love seats, tables fashioned from TV trays, and a flimsy armoire that showcased flowered dishes and a large, clunky television that was a dead ringer for the one my parents had donated to Goodwill decades ago. That led in turn to a kitchen so narrow that the vintage sixties harvest gold appliances had to line up in stern single file.

Lottie plumped the already plump pale blue throw pillows, straightened the small threadbare rugs, and tidied the crocheted doilies on the love seats. She aligned the window shades and cracked all the windows to allow a meager influx of what passed in the city for fresh air.

While she fussed, I asked Dennis John where I might wash my hands. He led me to the kitchen, and I scrubbed with dish soap in the sink. After I was passably clean again, the boy offered to show me around. First, he pointed with pride at a brightly scrawled page dangling from a refrigerator magnet that advertised AAA Atlas Exterminators (*Is something bugging you? Call us!*).

"That's my work," he said with solemn pride.

"I like your work. Such bright colors."

"This is my chair," he went on, settling a proprietary hand on the pale pine ladder-back nearest the door.

"I see."

Next he opened the pantry closet. "That's my peanut butter; and that's my jelly."

"Lovely."

Lottie ambled in with a green-and-navy striped T-shirt draped across her arm.

"Here, sweetheart. Let's change before your snack."

He raised his arms, and she tugged off his plaid shirt, exposing the arc-shaped scar that framed his ribs. "There now, you run along and play in the bedroom. I'll bring your drink and cookies there."

Lottie got Dennis John settled. Then she retrieved an album from its hidden perch atop the ancient television. With a pained sigh, she sank onto the love seat nearest the door. Her face went chalk pale except for the bruise-colored troughs beneath her eyes.

"Are you all right? Can I get you something?"

"Never mind about me. That boy's the one needs worrying about. Let me show you, Ms. Lafferty. Please."

The album cradled in her lap was soft blue beneath a protective plastic cover gone syrupy with age. On the front, smiling diaper-clad cartoon infants crawled beneath the buoyant title: "It's a boy!"

This was far from the standard baby book meant to chronicle a child's milestones. Lottie had photographed, dated, and described in detail horrific examples of Charlie Booth's brutality. As she paged through, even more gruesome captions came to mind: *baby's first beating and black eye,* the lid split like a bruised plum and swollen nearly shut. *His first step and first trip to the emergency room,* where X rays confirmed that his tiny right arm had been cracked like a wishbone. *First time the child was thrown down stairs,* leaving him a mass of welts and bruises with three unimaginably painful broken ribs. *First internal bleeding. First concussion. First Communion of the damned.*

The next photo was an extreme close-up of Dennis John's neck. A disembodied hand held back his springy red curls so the camera could record a half moon of rough-edged dots. On this page, there was no written description.

"What's that?" I asked, unable to accept what my instincts were stridently suggesting.

"What it looks like," Lottie breathed. "Cigarette burns in the shape of a *C.* Charlie likes to brand what's his. One time, he burned his initials on Dennis John's back." She turned the page again and there it was, *CB* rendered in raw angry welts.

"Jesus!"

"The slashing with the glass from the fishbowl was way worse. You saw the scar around the boy's ribs. Charlie made a giant *C* that time. There it is right after it happened. She turned the page to a picture of the wound while it was still raw-edged and scored with black sutures.

"It's unbelievable. How can he get away with a thing like that?"

"Don't know. But that's how it is. Always has been. Charlie

does whatever he pleases and no one says boo. That's how Jeannie wound up on the mental ward. Booth took up with that other woman he brought to Jeannie's grave. Wasn't the first time he went off catting, but this one was different; serious. He wanted Jeannie out of the way, so he got it in his head to have her branded crazy. Guess he figured that way he'd still have her close by and handy if he ever changed his mind. So he made up that ridiculous story about her standing in the altogether in front of some fancy people's house on Sutton Place, screaming wild. Wasn't true, not a word of it. But it didn't matter. Cops carted Jeannie off and locked her up just the same."

"You're sure it wasn't true?"

"Dead sure. I was with Jeannie when it was supposed to have happened. Charlie was acting even meaner than usual that day. Scared Jeannie so she asked me to come by and keep her company. After I got there, Charlie left, but Jeannie was afraid he'd come back, so she asked would I stay. We were together all day and through the evening. I told them that, the cops, people at the jail, everyone. Didn't make a bit of difference. They took Charlie's word over Jeannie's and mine."

"But the Graingers filed a complaint against her. I saw the report."

"Whole thing was a phony. Go ask those fancy people if you like. They'll tell you they never filed any report. Charlie saw something about that charity thing with the concert and all in the paper, and that gave him the idea. Paper was open to that article right on their kitchen table, like he didn't even care who knew it was a flat-out lie."

She was still turning pages. Pictures of injuries Booth had inflicted on Jeannie followed the ones of their battered little boy. I couldn't say which was harder to look at: the raw, angry wounds on Jeannie's face and body or the dead, empty look in her eyes.

Lottie came to the last entry, a shot of a painfully young Jeannie shortly before Dennis John was born. Her lip was bloodied, and the white man's shirt she wore to accommodate the pregnancy was open to expose a large, nasty contusion on her distended abdomen.

"Thank heavens Dennis John is with you."

She shook her head. "Problem is he's not. Not officially. He stays with me most of the time, but Booth has legal custody. He gets to take the boy when he feels like it. Brings him back to me when he's had his fill. For days afterward, Dennis John has these terrible screaming nightmares. Boy begs not to have to go with his daddy, begs and cries so it breaks my heart. But the courts say that's how it has to be."

"There has to be some way to keep a little child like that away from an abusive parent."

She sighed. "Used to believe that, but no more. One time, a year or so back, I plain refused to let Charlie take the boy. He started in on Dennis John soon as he came to pick him up. Child was so upset, I couldn't stand it. So I put my foot down and told Charlie no. I said he had no right to see his son if he was going to treat him so mean. Wasn't an hour later, three cops came banging on my door. Accused me of kidnapping. They put me in handcuffs like I was a dangerous criminal. Walked me out like that in front of all the neighbors and drove off with the sirens on, lights flashing. Never felt more ashamed in my life.

"I got taken in for what they call an arraignment. Had a lawyer from the legal aid I'd never even met. Man barely knew my name. Couldn't make the bail, so I spent three days in the jail down at the courthouse, the one they call the tombs. They locked me up with drugged whores, and worse. Hell on Earth, that place was. People fighting all night, ranting crazy. People begging for a fix, screaming, messing themselves. Don't know why they finally let me out, but thank God they did. One more day and I think I would have clean lost my mind."

"It's terrible, and I'm sorry you had to go through it, but you were right to try to protect Dennis John."

"That's all I've ever wanted to do, believe me. But I'm running out of time, Ms. Lafferty. Got a cancer in my blood. Been going on for years and getting worse. Docs keep trying this and that, but it's hopeless. No one wants to say so, but I know."

"But they can cure things now, even the worst things."

"Here's the thing about your own death coming. They may try to fool you, to boost you up, but deep down, you see the truth. You go along with the treatments, you try. But you know right where you're headed nonetheless."

"I'm so sorry."

She shrugged. "I've lived my life. But that little boy deserves a chance at his. Charlie Booth murdered Jeannie, Ms. Lafferty. I know it like I know my name. Bet you anything she was cut in the shape of a *C* or *CB* the way Charlie likes to do. Someone doesn't stop that man, I'm terrified Dennis John will be next. Once I'm gone, Booth will have no place to leave the boy when he gets tired of him. Jeannie's grandparents are too old and sick to care for a child. Both of them are mostly gone in the head by now, got no memory to speak of and need caring for themselves. And that cousin of his, Lacy Pierce, got her mind on other things, if you know what I mean. Plus crazy as it sounds, she's sweet on Charlie Booth. Always has been. Girl doesn't have the sense to come in out of the rain, much less look after a boy."

"But if the cops won't listen, how can Booth be stopped?"

"I'm thinking you're young, strong, and smart, Ms. Lafferty. Plus you're a psychologist, which means you understand how people tick. I'm just a plain, simple woman nearing the end of the road. But I know Charlie Booth. Watched him plenty over the years. I kept an eye on him like you'd watch a snake slithering out back behind your house. Maybe you can't get rid of it, but you know it bears watching, and you do. So it occurs to me that maybe if we pull together, you and me, we could figure a way to fix it so that man gets what he's got coming and Dennis John can finally get the chance to feel safe."

"Who will take care of him after—?"

She sighed. "If his daddy is out of the picture, have to be foster care. That nice black lady who came to Jeannie's funeral, Emma Wolcott, is a social worker for the state. She's a friend of Dennis John's teacher, so that's how we met. Emma knows the whole story. She hasn't been able to do anything about Charlie, either, but she's ready to step in and do what she can to find Dennis John a real good placement when and if the time comes that Charlie ever gets what's coming to him. If that comes to pass, maybe Dennis John gets lucky and he's put with good folk who see what a fine little boy he is and take him in permanent. Emma's keeping her eye out, hoping."

"That's good."

"Would be. Child deserves a break, that's sure. Amazing

thing about Dennis John is how regular he stays, how kind and dear, even with all he's been through. Boy has a good soul like his mother. But he's strong inside, which Jeannie was not. That's what's gotten him this far."

"My favorite definition of *lucky* is being able to deal with what you're dealt. Being resilient is a big part of the battle."

"True. But it won't count for anything unless someone gets him out from under that father of his." She eyed me expectantly. "We could do it, Ms. Lafferty. I know we could find some way to fix Booth's hide: you and me."

How I ached for Dennis John. I knew only too well what it was to have the ones you loved and trusted wrenched away, to lose the very ground you'd learned to stand on. "We could try."

Lottie pressed her hands to her chest. "Thank you, Lord. You can't imagine what this means. I've been so worried for that boy, thinking of him left with that—that thing that's his father—after I'm gone."

"I want to help, but honestly, Miss Dray, I'm sure there must be someone who could do a better job."

"You're the right one, Ms. Lafferty. I know it."

"Please. Call me P.J."

"You call me Lottie, then. Aunt Lottie, if you like."

"OK, Aunt Lottie. I'm flattered by your confidence, but I think it's misplaced. I'm no expert in criminal investigation. Far from it."

She smiled weakly. "Here's the thing. Jeannie knew she could count on you. It's like those chickens can sense when an earthquake's coming and get to fussing long before things start to shake. Jeannie was like them. Girl could tell up front who was good and not."

"Then how on earth did she wind up with Charlie Booth?"

"That was her father's doing. Her old man lost a bet to Booth. Gave him Jeannie to pay it off. Jeannie's mother, that's my sister, went along. Think she was glad to get rid of the girl. Jeannie was all of fifteen."

"Gave her to him? What's wrong with those people?"

"What wasn't? Jeannie's folks were a lot like Charlie. The pair of them had something missing inside. Sister or no, they weren't altogether human, if you ask me."

"Certainly sounds that way."

She slumped in her seat. "Forgive me, P.J., but I'm a bit worn out. Dennis John will be fine playing on his own awhile, so you're welcome to stay if you like, or go. There's paper and a pen in the kitchen. Be good if you'd leave your number. Mine's seven-one-eight—two—three . . ."

Her chin lolled to her chest and her hands dropped to her sides. I slipped the album off her lap and replaced it out of sight above the television. Then I copied her number from the phone and wrote mine on the pad beside the sink.

Dennis John was sprawled on the floor in Lottie's small blue bedroom, happily engaged with a pair of Matchbox cars, staging collisions, making *vroom* sounds, acting in the timeless, classic manner of smart, imaginative little boys.

"Do you need anything, sweetie?" I asked.

"Nuh-unh." He squealed in imitation of slammed brakes, and then crashed two tiny sports cars, head-on.

"I'm going to go, then. Aunt Lottie's resting—okay?"

"Mm-hmm."

"Nice meeting you, Dennis John."

"Want to have a playdate some time?"

"Sure. That'd be nice."

"Tomorrow?"

"Tell you what. I'll talk to Aunt Lottie, and we'll work something out soon as we can."

"Promise?"

"Definitely."

"Okay. Bye." He backed the cars apart and sent them zooming on another collision course.

It warmed me to see him like this, enjoying an oasis of normalcy. I trapped the heartening image in my mind's eye and let myself out.

CHAPTER

12

■ **The next morning, when I took my habitual stroll** around the corner to buy the paper, Rafe burst out of the neighboring Starbucks and blocked my path. His thick hair, the color of wheat toast, showed telltale signs of his habitual nervous finger-raking, and his starched white shirt bore a sizable brown splotch from the molto yuppie-o grande ridiculoso expensivo cup of something or other he held that still dripped on the pavement.

"P.J., hey. What a coincidence!"

"Coincidence, Rafe? You live twenty blocks and at least half a dozen other Starbucks away. I think it would be more accurate to call this stalking with caffeine."

"Actually, it would be more accurate to call it doing you a big fat favor." He set the drippy container on the rim of a mock terra-cotta planter and plucked an official-looking page from the overstuffed briefcase that drooped from his other fist. "I ran down that guy you wanted to know about: Charles Booth."

"That's great, Rafe! Wonderful. I really appreciate it. Thanks so much."

When I reached for the document, he whipped it away and

slid it back inside his case. "Let me buy you a cup of coffee and explain."

"Explain what? Either Booth has a recent arrest or he doesn't."

"It's not that simple. Legal stuff, you know."

I stood my ground. Somehow, accompanying my ex into a Starbucks, especially my very own neighborhood Starbucks, felt far too intimate. "Try me."

"Forget it, then. If you can't stand to spend five minutes with me, don't call asking for my help."

"Fine, I won't."

"Fine, don't."

Much as I was enjoying the infantile spite-fest, my thoughts swerved to Lottie and Dennis John. "Okay. You're right, Rafe. I'm sorry."

"Could it be?" He twirled a knuckle in his ear. "Did I actually hear you admit to being wrong?"

"I appreciate your getting the information for me. It was a big fat favor, as you said, and I shouldn't be snotty about it."

"I'm impressed, P.J. Very mature."

"My not being snotty does not mean you have to be extra snotty to balance things out."

"I said that in all sincerity." His face went mock innocent beneath the slick of righteous hurt. Rafe had that brand of wide-eyed, dimpled, boyishness that made you want to pinch his cheek. And right then, I ached to pinch it black and blue.

Mahood, the towering Sikh Indian man who manned the neighboring news kiosk, had followed our testy exchange. "Beautiful day," he said, turbaned head bobbing like an oil crane. "Perfect for have a coffee together."

As if things weren't bad enough, here was my very own newspaper vendor pleading Rafe's cause. Whatever happened to the good old days, when setting a toe on someone else's turf would buy you an armed escort out-of-town, or better yet, a bullet in the back? With a pointed frown at Mahood, I allowed Rafe to steer me inside.

"Coffee?" he asked with an excess of cheer.

"Tea."

"Cookie? Scone? Danish? Lowfat cranberry muffin?"

"Just tea, Rafe. Tea and what you found out about Charlie Booth. That's all I want."

While he waited on line, I claimed the sole vacant table, a black laminate lozenge on a rickety chrome stand located hard by the napkins, stirrers, sweeteners, cup holders, and trash. All the more desirable spots had been commandeered by the standard Starbucks denizens: pairs of new moms with napping infants; writers hunched over laptops; and cops with time on their hands and a suspiciously high-end taste in hot beverages.

Rafe ferried my tea on a tray along with a fresh mega-whatever for himself and a paper plate heaped with unsolicited pastries. Leave it to him to taunt me with calorie-packed temptations just when I was getting ready to prepare myself to seriously consider thinking about planning to try to lose weight.

I reached back over my shoulder for two sugars, but scored a pair of artificial sweeteners instead. Even as I cringed at the thought of the cloying chemical aftertaste, I ripped the packets open and dumped them in my tea. What could be better than a bit of self-spiting idiocy to counter Rafe's grotesque allegation that I was acting *very mature*?

He broke a scone and passed me the far larger piece. "So how's it going?"

"Fine."

"Really? You're enjoying the private practice thing?"

"It's fine."

"Really?"

"Really." I broke a fragment from the edge of the scone, the part where virtually all the calories have been leeched out by the baking process. "So about Charlie Booth."

"First tell me why you want to know."

"A personal thing. I told you. Anyway, it's a long story."

He leaned back and crossed his legs. "I'm all ears."

I blinked first. "Booth was married to one of my patients. So I'm curious."

"*Was* married?"

I stirred so hard, a tornado swirled in my tea. Rafe had a way of burrowing under a person's skin and sticking like a burr. Next thing you knew, you were picking out china patterns and mooning over dresses that made you look like a demented sugarplum fairy. "He was, yes. This patient died."

"May I ask how?"

"Sure you can ask, Rafe. The Constitution gives you that right."

"I thought you were through being snotty."

This time I bit the scone as if I was mad at it, not him. "I asked you for a simple piece of information. Is it really necessary to make me jump through all these blasted hoops?"

He cocked his head like a hopeful poppy. "I just want to help. I care about you, P.J. Is that so terrible?"

Now, why in the name of all that's blessedly mule-headed and irrational did that make my treacherous eyes pool with tears? I coughed into my hand to cover the grotesque show of emotion and then tossed back a repulsive swig of tea.

Rafe held the coy, slant-jawed pose. "So how did this patient die?"

"What's the difference? If you want to help, tell me what you found out about Charlie Booth."

"Sickness, accident, suicide, or homicide?"

"Yes."

"Which?"

"OK, Rafe. You win. She was murdered. Stabbed to death. Happy now?"

"This guy Booth did it?"

"They don't know who. She was found dead in the corridor after the fire alarm sounded and cleared the place. There was chaos. Probably deliberate. Apparently, nobody saw."

"But you think Booth did it."

"I don't think. Not unless it's absolutely necessary. Now would you please tell me what you found out?"

Holding the scowl, he slipped on his rimless reading glasses and scanned the printout he'd brought. "There's no record of any civil or criminal charge against a Charles or Charlie Booth in New York in the past year. No outstanding warrants or convictions for anybody matching the details you gave me in the national crime database going back twenty years. But I did turn up a juvey record for someone named

Charles Proffett Booth from 1985 in South Carolina. Could be your guy."

"Sounds right. The place and the timing at least. What was the charge?"

"No way to tell. Since he was a juvenile, the record was sealed."

"Can't you get one of your fellow enforcers down there to open the seal and have a little look? Just let you know what the charge was?"

"Sealed doesn't mean literally sealed like Academy Award envelopes. It means the record is unavailable, protected from scrutiny so the kid gets a fresh new chance. Anyway, I work on the right side of the law, P.J. Bending the rules happens not to be my way."

"You don't need to tell me, Rafe. That much I know." I glared at him while the unspoken accusation hung like a stench in the air. Two years ago he had refused to intervene when my brother was arrested for possession in New York. I'd begged Rafe to step in and try to steer Jack into a program where he might get some help, rather than jail, where he never got anything but wilder and sicker. But no, my then husband did nothing and let Jack be flattened by a system that didn't begin to understand or meet his needs. Now Rafe sat blankfaced, as if he had no idea what I was talking about, cloaked in that shiny, stain-resistant, self-righteousness that made me yearn to bathe him with my tea.

"So that's the story," he said, slipping the paper back in his briefcase.

"You're sure there's been nothing on Charlie Booth since? Nothing recent?"

He studied the pastry plate and had the nerve to nab the selfsame lemon square that had been beckoning seductively at me. "Nothing I could find. Not under that name anyway."

In retaliation for the lemon square, I claimed what I took for a cheese Danish, Rafe's runaway favorite, which he would save for last to show off his maddening restraint. "But he could have been there under another name?"

"Unlikely. They check ID, run background checks. This isn't the Keystone Kops."

"But it's possible."

"Sure. So are flying elephants. So are polka-dotted swans."

I tucked eagerly into the Danish, only to discover to my dismay that it was pineapple, which I hate. Somehow, I managed to swallow the gluey mass. Then I slid the remains beneath a paper napkin.

"How about running his fingerprints to see if they match any recent arrests?"

"I could do that, only I don't happen to have his fingerprints."

"What if you got them?"

"No, P.J. Absolutely not."

"No what, Rafe? I asked a question is all. That's no call to leap off the rails."

"No? You're thinking of getting fingerprints from someone who bumped off his wife and I'm supposed to take it calmly?" His finger popped up. "I have a better idea. Why not jump off the Empire State Building? See how well you can fly."

"I never said Charlie Booth bumped off anyone. I said they don't know who killed Jeannie."

"But he's the prime suspect in the case."

"There isn't a case, Rafe. And there isn't a prime anything. Everyone's pretending the whole thing never happened. Hoping it'll go away."

"But not you. You'd rather jump in with both feet. Dance your jig on those hot, flaming coals."

"There's more to this than you can begin to guess. Contrary to how you see the world, some things aren't all black or white."

"And some things are. Poking around in a murder case is dumb and dangerous. This is not some interesting little hobby a person takes up because she happens to be underemployed. And hear me, P.J. I'm not running the guy's prints, no way, no how. Not even if you bring me his hands on a plate."

"I'm not a reckless fool. So happens I'm doing what needs doing, not vanishing up my own behind, looking for trouble like you think."

"You don't have to look for it, P.J. Put yourself out there and trouble will find you soon enough."

CHAPTER
13

■ **The Chief Medical Examiner's office is on First Avenue** at Thirtieth Street, hard by Bellevue and New York University hospitals. Much of the 1960s building is faced in blue and white porcelain tile on an aluminum backing, giving it the look of a massive bathroom wall. Inside, in addition to offices for the M.E. and staff, are laboratories, lecture halls, a library and museum, several autopsy rooms, and, of course, a morgue. Since the tragedies of September 11th, the facility has served as the repository for victims' remains and the DNA samples on toothbrushes, hairbrushes, and other personal effects that relatives donated in hopes that those remains, some of them unimaginably tiny fragments, might be identified. Though the process has slowed to a trickle, the identifications continue to this day. Rikers Island could be depressing at times, but the prison complex was Disney World compared to this.

A whippet-thin, pretty young Chinese woman sat at the desk. Her nameplate read Laura Chu. A man in a suit had come in ahead of me to request a death certificate. While I waited for that transaction to be completed, I stared at the inscription on the wall above Ms. Chu's head: *Raceant colloquia effugiat risus. Hic locus est ubi mors gaudet sucurrere vitae.*

I hadn't used my Latin since high school. But sure enough I found it still stuck deep in my brain where Sister Calvin Mary of the Sacred Heart Academy had hammered it all those years ago. I translated haltingly: "Let conversation cease; let laughter flee. This is a place where death delights."

How uplifting!

She was ready for me now, and I tucked my sour mood behind a smile. "I'm hoping you might be able to help me, Ms. Chu. I need the report on a recent autopsy."

"You the prosecuting attorney on the case?"

"No."

"Spouse of the deceased then? Next of kin?"

"Well, no. Not exactly."

"What exactly?"

My smile was growing stiff. "I'm an interested party."

Her head bobbed with approval. "You're the deceased's attorney? Sure. I'll just need to see credentials and proof of representation."

"Not that kind of interested party. I was a friend."

"Sorry. Friends don't qualify."

"Who does?"

She enumerated on long graceful fingers. "If there's been a crime, the defense or prosecuting attorneys. In a civil situation, the decedent's personal legal representative, a spouse, or other next of kin and various state officials that may qualify, depending on their interest in the matter."

"For example?"

"Well, if the deceased was a mentally retarded person in the care of the Department of Mental Retardation at the time of death, the DMR commissioner would have the right to request an autopsy report."

"Let's say, just for the sake of argument, that she was a prison inmate."

"In that situation, someone in administration at the Corrections Department would have to make the request. If you're none of the above, you'd need an order from a Supreme Court judge, which you're not going to get if your only interest is as a friend." She cracked her gum. "Sorry."

"Why so restrictive?"

"Privacy issues. Like that."

"I thought death records were public."

"Nope. You thought wrong."

My mother always said you could catch more flies with honey than vinegar. But that assumed you wanted to catch flies. "Don't you think all that hush-hush cloak-and-dagger stuff is just the least bit ridiculous? I mean it's not as if the dead girl really cares."

"I don't make the rules." The look on her face let me know that were ever she granted the privilege, there'd be a big fat rule against me.

I smiled harder. "You know? I don't actually need the report. I don't even have to see it. All I want is one tiny piece of information. If you can just take a quick look and get me that, I'll be out of your hair for good."

"What makes you imagine for one minute that a sane person would do something that could get her fired, just because you ask?"

"I'm not suggesting anything like that."

"Oh, but you are. That's exactly what you're asking. And I'd really like to understand your thinking here."

"And I'd like you to. Is it okay if I sit?"

She pointed to the scatter of chairs behind me. "Knock yourself out."

I nearly did, dragging a wood-framed armchair swaddled in bloodred upholstery that turned out to be far heavier than it looked. "My name's P. J. Lafferty, Ms. Chu. The murdered woman was a patient of mine in the Mental Observation Unit on Rikers Island. She was stabbed during a fire drill that I'm sure was triggered to cover the crime. No one's been charged, but her husband is the likely suspect."

She took up a pencil and tapped an ode to nervous impatience on the broad oval cocoon that served as her desk. "You're a psychologist, you said; not a cop?"

"Right. For some reason, the cops haven't been interested in this case."

"Maybe they figure she's better off."

"She's dead. That's not better off than much. Anyway, this isn't about Jeannie Bagshaw. Not anymore. There's nothing anyone can do to help her. But there's a child involved, a little boy."

"And exactly how is seeing an autopsy report going to help some kid?"

"Dennis John is Jeannie's son. He's been left in the custody of his father, a man named Charlie Booth. I've seen hard evidence of the abuse Booth has inflicted on that child, practically from birth. Doesn't take much imagination to see where that could lead."

"That's too bad about the kid, having his mother murdered and all. But I still don't see how you get from any of that to the autopsy report."

"Booth likes to mark what's his. In the past he's burned his initials on Dennis John's neck and back with a cigarette, and he cut the boy around the ribs in the shape of the letter *C*."

She cringed. "Nice guy."

"He marked Jeannie also, several times."

"Thought you said her name was Bagshaw. If this guy Booth was so big on marking what's his, why did he let his wife keep her maiden name?"

I'd asked Lottie the same question. "He didn't let her, he insisted she do it. Crazy as it sounds, he decided she wasn't good enough to take his name. Wasn't worthy. But he saw marking people as a whole different thing, a claim of power and ownership, I suppose. If the autopsy indicates that Jeannie was slashed in the shape of a *C* or *CB*, it would be hard for the cops to ignore. I'm sure I could use that to get them on the case. Otherwise, chances are sooner or later Charlie Booth will send his son here, too. That little boy is looking forward to starting kindergarten. It'd be a shame if he had to miss that and all the other exciting possibilities in his life because of a silly rule about who's allowed to get the official read on how his mother died."

"All you need to know is the shape of the lethal wound?"

"It's not a stretch to call this a matter of life or death."

Her eyes went vague, and I could read the battle raging behind the frown. She could do what conscience dictated or follow the seductive trail of her own self-interest.

"Please, Ms. Chu. You can make all the difference for that little boy," I urged.

Her hands twirled up in that lovely gesture of surrender. "OK. You win."

"Thank you so much. You can imagine what this means."

"Unfortunately, I can."

"You're doing the right thing."

"And I'm going to try to do it without getting my head handed to me. I'm on my lunch break in twenty minutes. Wait for me at the northwest corner of Thirty-first and Second in half an hour."

"Absolutely. I'll be there. Bless you, Ms. Chu."

"Please. Let's just get it over with and then forget it ever happened."

"Sure. Absolutely. Whatever you say."

I fairly floated out of the building. A bracing breeze ruffled spindly, smog-nourished trees that were spawning their first spring buds. Sunlight glinted off the soaring amber, bottle-green, and smoked-glass buildings. New York's stately skyline preened against a pool-blue sky.

I imagined Officer Martinez's expression when I told her about Booth carving his initials in Jeannie's lethal wound. I wouldn't gloat. No need for that. All that mattered was securing Dennis John's safety. All right, maybe I'd gloat just a wee bit. The answer had been right there in plain sight, if only the cops had bothered to open their eyes.

At our designated meeting place, I leaned against a plate-glass storefront and settled in to wait. Time, in its typical perversity, slowed to a maddening sink drip, and nothing I tried helped to hurry it along. I couldn't think of a tune to hum or a puzzle to ponder. The pickings for people watching were grim. Everyone who passed struck me as medium, average, or beige, and quite a few qualified as all three. The street was full of dull cars and unremarkable commercial vehicles. Not a crisis or calamity as far as my seeking eye could see. Even the pet parade was boring. Nothing but standard breeds on normal leashes trailing their ordinary owners. What I wouldn't have given for one measly eighty-five-year-old woman sporting a miniskirt and a feather boa or a two-year-old in a stroller wearing designer sunglasses and chatting on a cell phone. I would have settled for a simple near collision or a diverting bit of apoplectic road rage. But no, from the look of things, all of New York's legions of weirdos and whack jobs had taken the day off. Or maybe there was a major, all-inclusive nutcase parade in progress in some other part of the city. I couldn't think of any other way to explain the stifling drought.

Finally the longest thirty minutes in recorded history elapsed. I peered up, down, and across the street, as I'd done about ten thousand times, but there was still no sign of Laura Chu. Five more minutes slogged by, and another two. What if I was standing in the wrong place? Might she have said First Avenue instead of Second? Or maybe she'd said Second but meant First and planted that as the destination in her head. My heart hammered wildly as I bolted to check. I was painfully aware that even as I raced back toward the M.E.'s office, she might be headed westward on a different block. My mind ran in frantic circles. I could all but hear her thinking that because she was a few minutes late, I'd had the gall to leave. So the hell with me and my out-of-bounds requests. If this was so damned important, I would have waited.

Sure, I could go back and explain. Throw myself on the mercy of her court. But it wouldn't take much for her to read my convenient absence as a sign that she shouldn't have agreed to cooperate in the first place. This was risky for her, and who the hell was I? Probably some crackpot out to stir a vat of trouble. Worse, I could be an investigator for the city or state, testing to see whether she was willing to break the rules.

I ran full out. On the fly, I confirmed that she was not standing within three blocks of the medical examiner's office in any direction. I charged back to the place I'd been sure she told me to meet her. Flares of panic fired my mind. This was too important. I could not, must not, would not screw it up.

Still no sign of her. My cell phone had only one battery bar and not much better reception. Through the crackling static, I strained to catch the number for the Medical Examiner's Office that the information robot reeled off. I repeated it to myself again and again as I dialed. Thankfully, the call went through on the first try. But the phone rang six times in desolate refrain after which I was switched to voicemail.

Where was she? What the hell could she be doing? There hadn't been time for her to change her mind and chicken out. Discounting the life of a five-year-old boy couldn't happen that fast.

"There you are."

Laura Chu had snuck up behind me as I my head swerved incessantly in search of her.

"I thought you weren't coming."

"I looked every place; the report's not there."

"Someone has it out, then?"

"There's no such thing as having an autopsy report out. The original stays in the files. If someone is authorized to have a copy, we make one. Same with death certificates. Our office is responsible for keeping the permanent records permanently."

"Then maybe it's not ready yet."

"That can't be. If it wasn't, Jeannie Bagshaw's body wouldn't have been released for burial, especially in the case of a homicide. Sometimes it takes awhile to get back certain tests or tox screens, but the basic postmortem should definitely be on file."

"Maybe it was misfiled. Did you check everywhere?"

"I did. Believe me. It's seriously strange."

"What if someone misread her name? Or misspelled it? What if—"

She tamped the air. "Would you stop? I'm trying to think."

I couldn't keep the words from bubbling up. "But couldn't someone have simply made a mistake? Isn't there a way to search through all the recent files for Jeannie Bagshaw?"

"Great idea! Which is why I already did that!"

"Oh."

"Look. I know you're anxious about this. Believe it or not, it shows. And I want to help. I feel for that kid; I do. I've seen what's left after the worst abusers do their worst, and if I can help stop such a thing, I'm all over it. But I can't get you something that doesn't exist."

I waited patiently for a good ten seconds, and then meekly raised my hand. "Is it OK if I say something?"

Try though she did, she was far too pretty to pull off the stern schoolmarm face. "You may speak."

"You said yourself that they wouldn't have released Jeannie's body for burial unless the report was finished. So it must exist. It just doesn't exist where it's supposed to."

That brought a grudging nod. "I can't argue with that."

"Good. We agree."

"So the question is where?" she said.

"That's one of the questions. The others are why is it missing and who took it?"

"*If* someone did," she corrected.

"Fine. If someone took it, why?"

"I can tell you it's pretty weird."

"What if you let the M.E. know it's not in the file?"

"And how, pray tell, would I know that unless I'd been snooping around trying to find a file I had no business snooping around about?"

"Couldn't you say you were doing a routine check to make sure the reports are in place?"

"Sure I could," she said. "I could also say I got the information from a little green one-eyed man on a UFO."

"Bad idea," I conceded.

"Extremely."

"You have a better one?"

"Sure," she said. "It's simple. All we need is for someone authorized to make an official request for that particular file. The M.E. is not about to admit an autopsy report has gone missing. He'd pull out all the stops and get to the bottom of it ASAP."

"And he'd get the report back?"

"He'd certainly try, but it wouldn't matter as far as you're concerned. He keeps copious notes, plus digital photos and a tape recording. Everything he found on Jeannie Bagshaw and every other corpse he ever examined is filed away in his office as a backup."

"That means we don't even have to get someone to request the report."

"Hold the phone! Don't even think of asking me to sneak into the boss's office and look through his personal records. No way, no how."

I put on my pure innocent face, the one I'd practiced again and again as a child in the vain hope that my mother would blame Caity once in a while, instead of always pointing the accusatory, and generally accurate, finger at me. "Of course I'm not. That would be much too risky for you, I understand

that. I have another idea, and if it works, we can put this thing
to bed."

"And if it doesn't?"

"I'll jump off that bridge when I come to it."

CHAPTER

14

■ **The line snaked down the block and around the corner** from the sprawling Barnes & Noble flagship store at Rockefeller Center. A dozen grainy overblown posters featuring Caity and her deaf super-heroine Eva Everheart smiled at me from the display windows: *Meet the author, Caitlyn Goldstein, live today!*

My appearance stirred a ripple of excitement, but before I became the bogus target of a fan feeding frenzy, the genuine article pulled up in a white stretch Lincoln Navigator. Caity emerged along with her personal assistant, her sign-to-speech interpreter, her editor, her publicist, and two of her publicist's assistants. All of them looked remarkably perky given that their day had commenced with a five a.m. pickup for hair and makeup before Caity's interview on *Good Morning America*. That had been followed by two other signings after which my sister had delivered the keynote address to over two thousand attendees at an Irish Historical Society luncheon fund-raiser at the Waldorf-Astoria.

A cadre of guards and fawning employees from the bookstore hurried out to greet them. My twin spawned a plastic smile and waved in regal fashion as the doting entourage spirited her inside.

Her signing was scheduled to last for an hour and a half, and would end, as they always did, precisely on the minute. During the allotted time, Caity would captivate as many fans as happened to show up for the event and sell as many books as the store's buyer had had the foresight to stock. Not one of the hordes who had stood waiting on line for hours would feel in the least shortchanged or even recognize that the author had not spent more than ten seconds, maximum, either signing, speaking through her interpreter, or smiling beatifically while she basked in an avid reader's adoration, to seal the deal. I have seen fans of all ages at these events drift off in dazed contentment after a brief audience with Caity only to queue up all over again, having suddenly remembered that they'd neglected to pick up a signed copy of the latest Eva Everheart for some random soul, perhaps one as yet unborn.

Was I jealous? Certainly not. True, Caity was successful. *Wildly successful* would not overstate the case, but so was I. My role on such occasions was to support my sister, i.e., fade into the woodwork until it was time to tell her how brilliant and charming she had been. And at the risk of seeming immodest, I was very adept at this. Of course, I could have lived without the dubious privilege of attending these frequent events, but Caity and I had negotiated an agreement on the subject years ago, and a deal was a deal. After debate worthy of an international tribunal, I had agreed to show up at her New York–area book signings, launch parties, and award ceremonies in exchange for a blanket exemption from all readings and rubber-chicken events out of town and those in town at which she was not slated to receive a major prize, a medal, or an honorary degree. Getting out of those dreary book-and-author luncheons, where Caity always told the same damned jokes and recounted the identical bogus story about how she'd come up with the idea of Eva Everheart, had felt like a major coup in itself. In the myth Eva had appeared to Caity in a dream. In reality she'd outright stolen the idea from a deaf kid she'd worked with years ago who'd kept demanding to know why there weren't any deaf superheroes. She had based the character on yet another deaf child she'd worked with whose lip-reading skills were the most amazing she'd ever encountered. And the rest, as the saying goes, is revisionist history.

As part of the complex treaty, Caity had ceded all rights in perpetuity to make me feel guilty by saying I was "all she had" and that I was, therefore, somehow duty-bound to put up with no end of bad food, stale speeches, and mind-numbing boredom for the benefit of her insatiable ego. In truth I was far from all she had. In addition to the legions of fans, the entourage, and any number of devoted friends, my sister had two long-standing suitors. There was Mr. Absolutely Right and Mr. Unbelievably Ideal. Bachelor Number One was adorable, funny, accomplished, and nuts about Caity. Bachelor Number Two was handsome, brilliant, fascinating, accomplished, and nuts about Caity. They were fully aware of each other, which had only served to intensify the competition. So they were forever vying to outdazzle my sister with their extravagant attentions. For Caity, choosing between them boiled down to having to give up beluga caviar for vintage champagne or vice versa, so she'd concluded that the only sensible answer was holding on to both.

While Caity held court at the signing table, I wandered about, marveling as I always did in these megastores at the astonishing diversity of books. I challenged myself to think up a topic that hadn't merited a single volume, much less an entire section, and this proved to be devilishly difficult. Just when I thought there wasn't one book devoted to yaks, for example, I would stumble on an entire Zach the Yawning Yak series in the children's area or find a spiffy new tome on classic yak cuisine (incredibly low in cholesterol!) among the cookbooks. Flatulence, I noted, had spawned an entire genre.

But even that fascinating pursuit paled after a time. Seeking fresh diversion, I drifted into nonfiction and found myself, as I always do eventually, in the section devoted to true crime. Selecting a title at random, I leafed through the fascinating tale of a nineteenth-century serial killer who had sought to blunt the hurt and humiliation of being jilted by trying to kill off every woman in all of England who happened to bear his former girlfriend's name, which was Claire. This had triggered a highly targeted panic. Claires throughout the United

Kingdom began changing or lying about their names, not to mention tossing their personalized jewelry, stationery, clothing, and monogrammed towels. Clairs, Claras, and even the occasional Carol followed suit, on the chance that spelling happened not to be the killer's forte.

The next book I plucked from the shelf was about two teenage boys from Kansas who had gotten it into their warped little minds to recreate the adorable shenanigans of the James Brothers. The kids took turns playing Frank and Jesse, robbing convenience stores instead of banks and holding up Greyhound busloads of touring senior citizens in preparation for the train robberies they intended to graduate to later in their criminal careers. That lofty dream was dashed when a silver-haired retiree on one of their bus heists turned out to be a retired cop packing a .45 and a carry permit.

Finished with that, I drifted to the front of the store and stood around until I caught Caity's publicist's assistant's eye. Despite the fact that my sister was oblivious to my existence on such occasions, she often sought proof of my attendance after the fact. Observing her now, I tried to imagine what it must be like to have the avid adulation of so many. Caity looked radiant in her fabulous red suit and twinkling jewelry, fresh as a parched plant after a nice, long, healing soak. With my luck, if my desiccated ego was ever treated to a soak like that, I'd get root rot.

Back in the crime aisle, a book entitled *Dark Reckoning* caught my attention. The jacket bore the dark haze of a brooding night sky. The cover art was a stylized demon's face with feral yellow eyes rendered in gleaming holograms that tracked my gaze. I flipped to the introduction by the author, Albert Dunston.

"The events chronicled on these pages are as true as they are unbelievable and as unbelievable as they are true. Until I learned about Blake Madigan, I questioned the existence of pure evil. Weren't those two words inherently contradictory? Pure evil struck me as an oxymoronic absurdity on the order of 'guest host' or 'jumbo shrimp.' But there was nothing contradictory or equivocal about Madigan. He was pure evil incarnate. No other words could begin to describe what he did."

I read on, viewing the horror that was Blake Madigan

through the eyes of the writer and far more chillingly, his victims, who happened to be his young wife and two little girls. Madigan had set up his home, an isolated cottage in the woods of northern Maine, as an experiment in terror. He had selected his wife carefully, an unsophisticated, poorly educated runaway. She had come to him free of outside ties: no relatives, no close friends, no one to worry about her, question her whereabouts, or even notice that she had seemed to drop off the end of the Earth. Madigan kept her prisoner in the house. He even forced her to give birth to all her babies at home, despite the fact that their first child, a son, had been ill-positioned and died during Madigan's botched attempt to yank him free. Madigan had stuffed the dead infant in a trash bag and discarded him at the local dump.

As I read, my emotions ran from revulsion to admiration for the strength and spirit that had somehow enabled his youngest daughter to survive. Had Gail Madigan not escaped and lived to tell the story, what had happened in that house might have remained a gruesome secret. That had been Madigan's evil intent. He chose to torture, and when he tired of that, to destroy his family and move on to the next victims. And he fervently believed that he had the right to do so. At his murder trial, where he'd insisted on serving as his own attorney, he had put forth that warped reasoning as his defense. His wife and children belonged to him, to do with as he pleased. In an irate rant, he'd claimed it had been illegal for the police to violate the sanctity of his home and seize evidence, even though they'd had a valid search warrant and despite the fact that the evidence they'd discovered in his cabin included the remains of his dead wife and older daughter. In Madigan's view the entire case against him hinged on an unconstitutional law through which the government sought to limit his inalienable right to pursue his sick definition of happiness.

As I read, my thoughts kept flashing to the striking similarities between Blake Madigan and Charlie Booth. Both men possessed their victims and then brutally destroyed them. Both saw complete vicious control as their right. Neither showed the slightest hint of mitigating remorse or humanity. From the pictures I'd seen in Lottie's album, Booth was about as pure an embodiment of evil as Madigan.

And here was someone who had studied such creatures far longer, harder, and at much closer range than I ever could. The brief author bio on the jacket flap stated that Albert Dunston had devoted the bulk of his four decade career to the analysis and pursuit of brutal sadists like Blake Madigan. The book's publisher was Aureus Press, a small imprint of one of the major New York conglomerates. Their offices were only a few blocks away from this very bookstore. There, with any luck, I could find the people who had acquired the rights to the manuscript and worked with Albert Dunston to bring the book to press. They would surely know how to reach him. With their help, I could seek the man's wise input right away. So here I'd happened upon the right book by precisely the right expert whose contacts were nearby. And wasn't that the winking eye of fate?

When I gazed at the clock again, I was startled to find that the time for Caity's signing had expired. By now my sister's fawning retainers would have spirited her out to the waiting limo. I pictured her in the rear of the giant stretch, stewing over my unthinkable tardiness and building quite the head of indignant steam. With reluctance I set the horrific account of Blake Madigan on a shelf and hurried out.

The moment I opened the door to the stretch Navigator, Caity shot me with a poison-eye dart. Her hands flew in sharp, angled swipes. "How kind of you to honor us with your presence, P.J. Thanks for being so considerate, *really*."

"You're most welcome," I said.

Caity's signing birds burst wild. "I've been going since four o'clock this morning, for Christ's sake. The last thing I need is to have to stand around on one foot waiting while you disappear."

She wasn't standing at all, but I decided to let that go. I also declined to state the obvious. She hadn't been waiting for me at all. I'd passed Caity's publicist pacing outside the store, jabbering on her cell phone, deep in some heated negotiation my sister had elected not to interrupt.

Unable to resist the chance to annoy her further, I fed my response through the interpreter, a dowdy, forty-something woman named Trudy. "Would you kindly tell my sister that I did not disappear? I happened to be absorbed in something interesting and lost track of the time."

I held the Cheshire cat smile while Trudy relayed my words. When she finished, I hastily continued before Caity had the chance to respond. "And please explain to Ms. Goldstein that watching her peddling her little books happens not to be nearly as fascinating as she might think."

Trudy looked startled, as if I'd slapped her. But her face quickly shifted into neutral as she signed what I had said. Caity's hands started flapping beside me. I refused to look her way, but I caught the angry breeze.

Trudy, who seemed a churchgoing, God-fearing sort in her long navy skirt and prim white blouse, squirmed as she prepared to deliver the diatribe my sister launched in return. "Ms. Goldstein says that if it acts like an ass and sounds like an ass, it's an ass."

I held the smile, which now framed hard-clenched teeth. "Kindly tell Caity she's got a bit of something green stuck between her teeth. Salad maybe. Must be from lunch."

From the corner of my eye, I caught the lovely horror blooming on my sister's made-up face. On the small screen, that thick, bilious foundation gave her a glow of eager, outdoorsy health. In person, and especially in close up, she looked as if someone had slathered her with an unfortunate shade of mortar and was waiting until the time was right to add the coat of bricks. She pulled a compact from her purse and retracted her lips. Then, as I continued to stare at the interpreter, she launched an airborne attack, hands poised to deploy a payload of deadly ire.

Trudy's eyes bugged. "Ms. Goldstein is a little upset."

That gave my sister a spanking-new target for her rage. Caity told the interpreter off in no uncertain terms. I caught the sign for *boss* and the swift swipe of her right fingers over the heel of her left palm, which meant *fired*.

Trudy slid toward the limo door and grasped the handle. Caity caught her by the elbow and drew her back to her seat. She circled her hand above her heart, the sign for *sorry*. Then she flared and bowed her fingers in front of her face, invoking grouchiness as her excuse. Trudy was an excellent, reliable interpreter with the kind of nondescript appearance and rice-pudding personality that posed no threat at all to Caity's monopoly on the limelight. Unlike me, my sister was generally able to resist the urge to torch her own house.

A few minutes of gentle coaxing ensued. Caity's signing smoothed like gentle gliding birds. The warmth of her practiced charm quickly melted Trudy's pique.

Dripping petulance, Caity turned to me again. "At the least, you could admit that my signing the new Eva Everheart is more important than your mooning over some dopey book."

I faced her squarely and let my own hands fly. "It wasn't about you, so I don't expect you to understand."

"Try me," she signed with the finesse of a woodpecker.

"Why bother? I'm sure you couldn't be less interested."

"And I'm sure you're full of bull!"

"You want to go into this now? Here?"

Caity smirked. "Unless you need more time to make something up."

"Now it is, then."

Trudy averted her gaze, allowing us the privacy to spill a bit of sisterly blood. The others didn't know how to sign, so they couldn't follow our conversation, though I, for one, had no qualms whatsoever about letting my sister show off what a self-centered jerk she could be.

"I happened to be reading something about a serious crime."

"That patient of yours who was stabbed?" She made the sign for killing, a vicious twist.

I stared hard. "How did you know she was stabbed?"

"You mentioned it the night you were fired. Remember?"

I eyed her warily. "No. Actually I don't."

"Well, you did."

"Did I, then?"

"Yes, and you should stay out of it. Poking around in a murder is dumb and dangerous."

"Interesting choice of words."

"Well, it is."

"Who said I'm poking around in anything?"

High color infused her face, confirming what I already knew. She and Rafe had been talking about me again, sharing every tidbit either of them had managed to unearth. All I had to do was pour something in Rafe's ear to have it come out Caity's mouth. And didn't that make me spit fire?

"I don't need Rafe to tell me what you're up to, P.J. If there's a crazy risk to be taken, you will."

"What I do is none of your business."

"No? You ask for trouble and it's none of my business?"

"That's right. None of yours and none of Rafe's. I'm a grown-up, independent woman, Caity, not your pet. You two can go off and enjoy your cozy little cabal, but leave me the hell out of it."

"There's no cozy cabal. Just two people who happen to care about you."

"More like two pushy overbearing pains in the hind end who make me want to rip my hair and scream. If the time comes when I want looking-after by your little Benedict Arnold Society, you can rest assured I'll make the formal application."

Caity's publicist had finished her call. She slipped in through the rear door with her thumb raised and a fat grin plastered on her face. "We've done it! We've got the special with Oprah, the whole enchilada plus teasers and promos!"

They traded hugs and squealed like stuck hogs. A celebratory frenzy erupted in the car, a warm-up for the impending excursion to one of Caity's many favorite celebration spots: the River Café in Brooklyn. There I'd be doomed to suffer no end of congratulatory cocktails and triumphal food and far more self-referential cheer and banter than I was fit to bear. As the driver revved the limo's engine, I mumbled my excuses and slipped away.

■ **The offices of Aureus Press and its many sister com-**
panies occupied a soaring steel- and smoked-glass tower on
the Avenue of the Americas, which used to be known as Sixth
Avenue, just as I used to be known as passably sane. The
lobby featured checkerboard marble floors, huge palms in
mammoth silver planters, a rotating modern art display, and
the sort of intense security I had not thought to expect. Anyone seeking admission to the office banks had to pass through
metal detectors and submit to a search of packages and bags.
Following that, employees peeled off through yet another
bank of detectors which scanned their coded photo IDs.
Posted instructions directed visitors to stop at the information
desk at the center of the cavernous space and sign in.

I waited there at the broad, brushed-steel counter, while the
plump silver-haired woman in front of me pleaded her case to
the guard. "He's so talented, my grandson Leonard. Imagine,
the child's written a whole, entire three-hundred-page story,
full of spies, killings, the whole nine yards. And only this winter turned sixteen."

The guard was slim as a sipping straw with an ash-smear

mustache and droopy, downcast eyes. "That's nice, ma'am. But we can't take manuscripts here. You'll have to send it in."

She wagged a finger. "No, you don't. I know what happens when you send things in to one of these places. No one pays them any mind at all."

"They'll get around to it. Takes time."

"My foot. I used to write a bit myself when I was younger: stories, poems. Some of them pretty good it happens. Even finished most of a whole book once. And you know what I got back when I sent it in? One of those awful ready-made letters that don't even bother with your name. Call you 'Dear Contributor,' like you're a big fat nobody. Don't you think most of a book that took a person two whole years to write while she was looking after a husband, five kids, two dogs, and the house deserves better than that?"

Sad eyes smiled kindly. "Tell you what. You send it in with the name Leonard marked on the front in big bold letters, and I'll ask a friend of mine in the mail room to keep an eye out for it, see it gets sent to the right place."

She seized his hand. "Would you do that? What a sweetheart! Wait until I tell Leonard. He'll be thrilled."

"Most things that come in never see the light of day, ma'am. Probably not a good idea to get the boy's hopes up."

She pressed the manuscript to her ample bosom. "Guess you're right. I won't say a word. Be our little secret."

I stepped into the spot she vacated. "Aureus Press, please."

"To see who?"

"Albert Dunston's editor. Or his publicist. Either way."

"Your name?"

He checked his list. "Sorry. I don't see any Lafferty."

"I don't have an appointment. All I need is a minute of their time."

He folded his arms. "No can do, not without an appointment."

"Can you call up and let me speak to someone?"

"Not allowed to unless you're on the list. Sorry."

I pulled out my cell phone. "I'll try myself. What's their number?"

He told me, but the call would not ring through. I strode about trying to find service, but the lobby was a cellular black hole. Staring down at the signal indicator, I walked slowly toward the door. And that's how I happened to strike gold.

In this case, the find came in the form a sun-blaze yellow visitor's pass, discarded by someone who had missed the trash. The adhesive backing was pebbled with lint, but I scraped a bit and pressed until it stuck.

I peered across the lobby at Sad Eyes. At this hour the bulk of the building's traffic flow was outbound, and a few minutes elapsed before a couple approached the guard. While he was distracted with them, I hurried to the elevator banks and slipped into the first open car.

I'd hoped to find a company directory on board, but no such luck. Hastily, I pressed all the buttons. At each floor, I leaned out and searched for Dunston's publisher. I was starting to fear I'd have to sneak downstairs and find a building directory when the door opened on twelve to the welcome blaze of the Aureus name and starburst logo in oversize brass letters across the hall.

To the right loomed the entrance to the publishing operation. Reception was tucked behind a glass wall, allowing me a clear view of the bespectacled young man who served as the gatekeeper.

"P. J. Lafferty," I told him. "I'm here about Albert Dunston's *Dark Reckoning*."

"To see Maggie Corson?"

"Maggie Corson, exactly."

He called in on his phone.

"Maggie's not in," he reported.

"You're kidding."

He shrugged. "Want to leave a message?"

"I came all this way to see her. Can't imagine how she could forget. What about the other one who works with Dunston?" I frowned, pretending to troll for the name.

"Anthony Pericolosi?"

"Anthony. Right. Would you try him?"

He did; it worked. "He's on the phone. Be with you in a few minutes."

"Great."

On my way to the cluster of squat, gray chairs, I passed a bookshelf crammed with volumes by Aureus authors and stacks of glossy promotional materials. Ruffling through, I found a press kit for *Dark Reckoning*.

A moody black-and-white head shot rendered the author in crags and shadows. His somber face was distinguished by thick Chinese-hat eyebrows and eyes the pale gray of sanitized exhaust.

The brief bio that followed described Dunston as the British-born son of peripatetic parents. His father had been a career diplomat and his mother an archaeologist unable to resist the lure of far-flung digs. Early on, they had entrusted their children to the care of boarding schools, where Albert, the youngest of five sons and four daughters, had shone as a brilliant, if eccentric, student. He held an alphabet soup of advanced degrees and a consuming fascination with warped creeps like Blake Madigan. *Dark Reckoning* was his first book for the general public, though he'd written or contributed to hundreds of professional journals and texts. Copies of a few of his key scholarly articles were included in the kit, and as I read, my desire to talk to the man about Charlie Booth grew even greater. Over the years he had made an exhaustive study of what he termed *violent-possessive* personalities, and he was considered the world's leading expert on that brutal criminal type. He was often called upon to consult with police departments, victims' families, corporate and political entities worldwide, and he was credited with helping to crack any number of seemingly hopeless cases. A spate of glowing endorsements described him as dedicated, tireless, and insightful in this particular pursuit. Dunston was touted as the man who could deliver when all else failed.

The receptionist called my name. "Pericolosi can see you now. It's through that door. Down the hall, turn right, then right again. His office is the first on your left."

Inside, gravel-colored carpeting muffled my steps as I passed between windowless cubbyholes walled by chin-high charcoal dividers. Each held a gunmetal desk fitted with a computer console and a phone, an armless royal blue chair on wheels, and an array of adjustable shelves. People toiled amid the standard jumble of personalized coffee mugs, framed photos, greeting cards, and cloying knickknacks.

At the end of the hall I veered right. Here, the offices grew larger and brighter, with windows and genuine walls, many of them hung with bookshelves crammed with books and boxed manuscripts. Fresh-faced entry-level types occupied an interlocking grid of conjoined desks across the hall. One more right turn brought me face to face with a door marked *Pericolosi, A.*

Dunston's editor exuded boyish, disheveled charm. His sandy hair was a mass of unruly waves, his khakis crinkled, and the tail of his blue-striped shirt drooped free. He greeted me with a warm, disarming grin.

"Thanks for seeing me, Anthony. I really appreciate the time."

"Sure. You're here about *Dark Reckoning*?"

"I am."

"Quite a story. Couldn't get it out of my head for weeks."

"It does stay with you."

He folded his hands on the desk. Nice hands they were, lithe and strong. "So what's your interest in the book?"

"Actually, it's the author I'm interested in. I need to talk to him about a case."

"Sorry. Dunston's out of commission. Could be for a while."

"How long is a while?"

"Hard to say."

"Is he on vacation? On a case?"

"Look, I don't like to play cloak-and-dagger, but I can't tell you. Dunston's request."

"Is there any way you can get a message to him? It's very important."

"Important how?"

I summarized the situation. There had been a murder, a young woman slashed, but the authorities refused to pursue the obvious suspect in the case. The prime suspect bore uncanny, chilling similarities to Blake Madigan. Dunston's expert advice might well help to save the killer's little boy.

"All I need is to talk to him. Get his ideas on how to approach this."

His look went grim. "Before the book came out, Al Dunston and I had lunch with Madigan's surviving daughter Gail. She was so sweet and soft-spoken, and she seemed so incredibly normal. It was as if she'd put a wall between what her father did and herself. But after a while, Dunston got her talking, and she described some of what went on in that horror house she grew up in. One of Madigan's favorite tricks was holding his kids' feet to the fire—literally. Hard to believe creeps like that exist."

"That's true. And I'm afraid Charlie Booth is just as bad."

He spewed air. "His poor kid."

"That's the problem exactly: his poor kid."

"I'll pass it along, P.J. That's the best I can do."

"Please explain to Mr. Dunston that I wouldn't be bothering him if it wasn't critical, if not for that little boy."

"I will. I'll call and let you know, one way or the other."

"Thanks, Anthony. And please tell him this is one of those situations where time is of the essence. It's impossible to tell when that little boy's luck will run out."

CHAPTER

16

■ I raced down Second Avenue and caught the bus on the fly. Ten minutes later we were bumping across the rutted roadbed on the upper level of the Fifty-ninth Street Bridge, passing through a cottony fog that swallowed my view of the dark currents swirling far below. The veil began to lift as we approached Queensborough Plaza, and the wind chased off the last feathery wisps by the time the bus stopped to discharge its capacity load. Across the vast, busy intersection, friends and relatives of Rikers Island inmates parked their forbidden cell phones and other prohibited items at a corner candy store that did a land-office business babysitting anything that happened to be on the prison's extensive contraband list. That done, the visitors moved down the block and waited in a jittery mass for the Rikers Express.

I stood aside, silently rehearsing my pitch. I was confident that I could count on my ex-boss, Will Creighton, though, as it turned out, completely mistaken about what I could count on him for. From my first day on the job, Dr. Creighton had advised and encouraged me. He'd been a perfect mentor, the sort who recognized my unfortunate clown tendencies and did his level best to keep me from tripping over my own fat, floppy feet. Even lately, when the demands of his ever-expanding family and professional interests seemed to be catching up with him, leaving him weary and preoccupied, I was sure I could always count on him in a serious pinch.

The bus to Rikers finally pulled up, and I held back until the bulk of the mob had boarded. I handed the driver my transfer and settled on the vacant seat nearest the rear exit. As the doors shut with a pneumatic sigh, I fought the urge to flee. There was a real risk that I might run into one of Chief Daley's nasty squad or—large gulp here—Daley himself. I had no interest in finding out whether he would make good on his threat or what the ugly specifics of his making good might be.

The bus meandered in the gathering dusk through ever-shifting ethnic enclaves—Ecuadorian, Thai, Greek, Guatemalan, Korean, Japanese—stopping every few blocks to cram in more passengers. Regardless of their backgrounds, visitors to the prison complex were easy to identify. They all bore the same air of weariness and pained resolve. While no one was detained on the Rock for long, one stay tended to lead to another. The recidivism rate was so sky high; plenty thought the state might as well install revolving doors. There was also the matter of near Darwinian inevitability. Kids in certain families seemed destined to follow their mothers or fathers to a life of crime and punishment in much the same way that kids with professional parents so often took up medicine, business, academics, or the law.

A half hour later the bus reached the prison parking lot at the mainland terminus of the Island Bridge. I charged out and scampered down the stairs before the surging tide of oncoming passengers had the chance to sweep me back on board. Jungle rules applied here. It was eat or be eaten.

The bus soon continued onto the bridge, and I was left standing alone at the lip of the desolate lot. I backed away from the road, where I was less likely to be spotted by chance, and stared at the steady line of cars and trucks streaming off the bridge in my direction. If he was following his standard routine, Dr. Creighton would be on the next bus out. I spotted his dark green SUV crammed with baby seats in its customary place at the rear. Given his tenure and position, Creighton could have claimed a coveted reserved spot on the island within convenient walking distance to his office. But he clung to the egalitarian (and arguably psychotic) view that, to the greatest extent possible, he should experience the same maddening annoyances as everyone else.

My breath caught at the sight of an approaching bus, but it held speed and zipped by, laying a trail of oily fumes. The passengers, a group of visiting Japanese dignitaries, from the look of them, regarded me with unabashed curiosity. Several snapped my picture, as if I were another interesting oddity of the bloated American penal system.

Fifteen more minutes elapsed before the next bus came into view. This one stopped. Passengers streamed out and drifted toward their cars. I recognized a few prison employees among the visitors who had parked in the lot. But they all ignored me with a vengeance. Daley must have made good on his promise to spread the word of my unsightly demise.

Dr. Creighton was last to alight. When I waved, he shaded his brow with cupped fingers and squinted to wrest my identity from the glare of the streetlights that had just flared on.

He approached me warily. "P.J.?"

"Hi, Dr. Creighton. Great to see you!"

"I must say I'm a little surprised to see you. Everything all right?"

"Mostly."

"What brings you here?"

"I called you a couple of times."

"Yes, and you've been on my to-do list. Unfortunately, I've been tied up."

"Of course, I understand."

"From now on, if I'm slow to get back to you, just call and remind me please. Or better yet, send an e-mail pointing out that I'm being negligent and rude. I promise I'll get the message and the hint. You certainly didn't have to come all this way."

"This isn't about your not calling, Dr. Creighton. I came to ask a favor."

"What's that?"

"I need a piece of information from Jeannie Bagshaw's autopsy report. The Medical Examiner's office won't release the postmortem results to me, but as an official with the Corrections Department, you're entitled to it."

"Is that so?"

"Yes, and I'll be eternally grateful for your help, sir."

He peered around the lot, clearly not eager to be seen with me himself. He seemed relieved that everyone else had driven off. "Walk me to the car, would you, P.J.? I'd like to put these down."

A quartet of canvas totes hung from his hands. They were crammed with dark green files. "Of course. Sorry. Let me help you with those."

"That's fine. I can manage."

As we approached his SUV, he pressed a small red button on his key fob to pop the rear hatch. He deposited the files beside three enormous soft packs of Pampers and two folded double strollers.

Creighton's first wife of more than thirty years had died before I met him. Shortly after I started working at Rikers, he'd married a journalist named Molly Calloway, whom he'd met at a grief support group. Molly had been there researching a story for *New York Magazine* on the hottest new trends in death and dying: designer headstones, themed memorial parks, living funerals, grief groups that doubled as places to meet and greet, and the like. When she learned that Creighton headed up psychiatric services at Rikers, she took his card. Ambitious reporters always have their news nose trained to catch the scent of the next big story. A few weeks later Molly sold the idea of a feature on mental illness in prisons to the *New York Times Magazine*. Creighton liked to quip that it was craziness that brought him and Molly together and that lunacy was the Krazy Glue that bound them still. Their family situation was lunatic quality, to be sure. They had produced four little ones in as many years, a feat even more mind-bending when you consider that Molly was north of forty and Creighton had kids older than me.

He brushed his hands. "Why don't we stop somewhere? We can catch up and discuss this further."

"Sure, if you have the time."

"I'll make the time."

Soon he was weaving his way through local back roads. "Excuse me for just a second." He drew out his cell phone and invoked the voice dial for home. "Hi, honey. Just wanted to let you know I'll be late. I ran into P.J., and we're going to go somewhere and talk awhile. Right, exactly. Yes, sweetheart. Love you, too."

He swerved left and pulled into the broad lot behind a Greek seafood restaurant.

"I'm sorry to make you late going home, Dr. Creighton. I can't imagine how Molly manages all day with four little kids."

"It's like the little old lady who was able to lift a giant cow. The trick is to start with a tiny calf and just keep lifting." His pale eyes lit with amusement. "Of course, the two nannies help a bit as well."

"You have two nannies?"

"That's the bare minimum. One would never take all four kids on, and plenty demand a one-to-one ratio. Of course, there's also the cleaning woman, a laundry person, a dog walker, a couple of relief babysitters, and the cook."

"Makes sense to me. I couldn't imagine taking care of one baby, much less four. To manage a brood like yours, I'd believe I'd need general anesthesia, and probably martial law."

"Everything makes sense except the payroll, but so it goes. Cost of doing business, I suppose."

"Cost of staying sane."

"Same thing."

At this hour the large restaurant was empty except for a scatter of men tippling in front of a televised ball game at the bar. The owner, a hassock-hipped woman with dark lacquered curls and a voice like a tuba, greeted Creighton warmly by name. She installed us in a red vinyl booth at the rear of the back room and gave us menus.

"Just coffee," I said.

Creighton eyed the giant bill of fare. "Hungry? They have terrific grilled fish."

After a brief consultation with my stomach, I discovered that I was ravenous. "A little, but I don't want to hold you up any longer than necessary."

"It's necessary. I haven't had a thing to eat all day."

Creighton stirred the air with an index finger, and the owner countered with a crisp thumbs-up. "Striped bass okay?"

"Great. Whatever you suggest."

"OK, then we'll have some hummus first, and tzatziki. That's a cucumber and yogurt dip. And Greek wine. Sound all right?"

"Wonderful. Thanks."

He signaled the rest of the order. "So? How are things?"

"OK."

"Honestly?"

"Well, if you want the whole unvarnished truth: I'd have to say things pretty much suck."

He looked utterly approving in the way that therapists can seem to approve of almost anything to get you to spill the sewage roiling in your guts. *So you're sexually fixated on lawn fawns, are you, Mr. Smith? Do tell.*

"In what way?"

"So many, I barely know where to begin."

He sat back as if he had all the time in the world. Like approval, silence of whatever necessary duration is a devilishly effective way to coax out the emotional trash.

"I screwed up with a patient Nina Present referred, so that's probably the end of my short-lived career in private practice. And then there's Chief Daley and the drugs and the whole Booth business that just keeps pulling me in deeper and deeper. Which is why I need the autopsy report. It's going to take solid evidence."

Creighton raised his hand. "Whoa. One thing at a time, P.J. You screwed up with a patient, you said?"

I held my head. "I objected to the way she was treating her daughter, mistreating actually, and she went off the wall."

"Woman named Adler?"

"Yes. How did you know?"

"Nina mentioned it to me. Doesn't sound like you screwed up in the least. Nina said, and I quote, 'That dried prune has had it coming for years.'"

"Really? I thought she must be furious. I called to tell her what happened, but I haven't heard back."

"I'm afraid Nina shares my less-than-stellar record for returning phone calls. But rest assured, there's nothing for you to worry about on that score. If she wasn't completely in your pocket before, she's certainly there now."

"You can't imagine what a relief that is."

"Fine. One worry down. Now, what's this about Chief Daley? And did I hear you say something about drugs?"

I fiddled with a small rip in the red plastic covering on the booth. Even in the telling, the story had the power to make me squirm. I described the roadblock and the cop boarding the bus as we crossed the Rikers Island Bridge on the day I was fired. I recounted the humiliating search and the planted table sugar. And I repeated Daley's warning. "The chief is very angry with me. That was the message. If he decides to ruin my life, I'm over."

"Surely, you wouldn't take a thing like that seriously, P.J. The only thing shorter than Cal Daley's fuse is his memory. Ten minutes after you were out the door, I'll bet anything he'd forgotten all about you and moved on to fuming over somebody else."

"Then why would he send that cop after me? And why the threat?"

"Short fuse, as I said. And big frustration. Bringing down the crime rate at Rikers has been Daley's top priority since he came on the job. That's why he was hired, and that's what's going to make or break him as a chief. Jeannie Bagshaw's murder was one in a string of violent incidents at the prison in the past couple of months. Suddenly the statistics have gone from great to grim."

"Is that true? I hadn't heard."

"No one's rushing to broadcast the news. In fact, the powers that be will do everything they can to keep it hushed up as long as possible."

"What do you think is behind it?"

"My opinion? Daley's scare tactics worked for a while, but the magic has worn off. Research has shown again and again that you can only get so far with good old-fashioned authoritarian repression. After a while the inmates stop feeling intimidated. Sooner or later they start acting out, and more violence results. Cal Daley isn't about to ask me for advice, but if he did, I'd suggest he try some more inventive, effective strategies."

"Such as?"

"Faith-based programs; group-dynamics approaches; initiatives to isolate and rehab nonviolent prisoners. Things like that. They're working very well in the private prison system."

"Really? Last I heard there were huge problems in the contract jails. I was under the impression that whole movement was on a major downswing."

He scowled. "That's what the public prison administration and the prison workers unions want you to think. And the media goes along. Failure always makes a juicier story than success. It's unconscionable. Damned pack of lies!"

"You sound pretty passionate about it."

"I am. It's a flat-out sin. Private prisons are the right answer to the mess our public facilities have become, and that's where the money should go. You know as well as anyone what goes on in these places, P.J. And what doesn't. But all these people give a damn about is their own self-interest!"

Creighton's irate outburst succeeded in shutting my mouth. Normally he played in a far lower key, and I'd never seen him so heated about anything. Maybe four years of sleep deprivation and diaper overload were finally catching up with him.

I ate awhile in silence, feeling increasingly the fool. Creighton looked weary, older, more than a little strung-out, and I'd been too blinded by my own problems to notice. "I didn't mean to go on and on like that, Dr. Creighton. You've got more than enough on your mind without having to hear my whining. All I really came to talk to you about is getting Jeannie Bagshaw's autopsy report."

"We will, P.J. But let's take our time and discuss the rest before we deal with the issue of the postmortem." He pursed his lips in thought. "There was something else you mentioned. Something about a booth?"

"Charlie Booth was Jeannie Bagshaw's husband. A witness called and told me she saw him at Rikers behind the exercise yard at the women's prison on the day of the murder. The witness said she saw Booth using a hose to wash off Jeannie's blood."

"And she knew it was Jeannie's blood how?"

"She didn't know; she made the logical connection."

"Who was the witness?"

"That's not important."

"Maybe not, but I'd like to hear anyway."

"All right. I'll tell you, Dr. Creighton. But I'm asking that you reserve judgment until you hear me out."

"I'm listening."

"It was Millie Williamson. She recognized Booth from his picture in Jeannie's cell. I understand she's not a paragon of reliability, but in this case, I'm convinced she was telling the truth."

"This is *Big Millie* you're talking about?"

"Well, yes, but—"

"The same Big Millie who called the governor and the president of Turkey and the American Ballet Theatre to complain about little blue mugwumps crawling in through her ears without wiping their feet first and tracking muddy footprints on her brain?"

I tried not to wince. "Green mugwumps, yes, sir, but this is different. And it's not only Millie. Jeannie's aunt believes Booth killed her, too."

"Wait a minute. Am I to understand you've been talking to Jeannie Bagshaw's relatives?"

"Jeannie was murdered, Dr. Creighton. Charlie Booth is a sadistic abuser who has custody of their little boy. The aunt has gone to the police and to DCYS many times to report the terrible injuries Booth has inflicted on the child, but nothing comes of it. Crazy as it sounds, her complaints simply disappear."

"From which you conclude what?"

"That someone has to look into it. Someone has to prove that Booth murdered Jeannie and see that he's arrested before he has a chance to do the same thing to their son."

"And you believe that someone should be you?"

"No. I believe it should be anyone *but* me. Unfortunately, no one else is willing to take it on. I've gone to the cops, and they refused to listen. But if I get solid enough evidence, they'll have no choice."

"What about this aunt of Jeannie's? Why doesn't she pursue the case against Booth herself if she's so sure he killed her niece?"

"She wants to. She's willing to do everything she can. But she's terribly sick. Sounds like leukemia. Apparently, she's not long for this world."

"Is that everything?"

"Pretty much."

Creighton sat back and folded his arms. "You've been honest with me, P.J., so here's my honest response. You're right. It does sound crazy. Completely off-the-wall."

"I know, sir. But those are the facts."

"As I see it, the fact is you're acting on the strength of the word of one woman who's criminally insane and another who's dying of a serious cancer that might well have spread to her brain."

"It's not like that, Dr. Creighton."

"No? Have you any proof that what they're alleging is true? Have you checked any of it? Is there even a way to check it?"

"Maybe not. I don't know yet. But even if I can't, that doesn't mean Charlie Booth is innocent of Jeannie's murder. He's a monster, Dr. Creighton. I saw pictures of the abuse he inflicted on Jeannie and their son. They were hideous, unthinkable."

"You saw pictures of injuries."

"Terrible injuries, yes. The boy's aunt took photographs. Enough to turn your stomach, sir. Believe me."

"And that somehow proves who inflicted them?"

"No, but—"

He shot me the sort of pitying look you'd give a three-legged dog.

"Booth did it. I know he did."

"No, you believe he did, and that's a whole different ballgame. Belief doesn't give you the right to go after somebody. Belief doesn't hold up in court."

"Maybe not. But that doesn't give you a get-out-of-hell free card if you simply sit back and let the worst go on."

"The point is you don't know what's going on. It's all circumstance and supposition. Do you honestly think it makes sense that someone could inflict all that harm and the police decide to sit back and let it continue?"

"No, but that's what happened."

"That's what someone claims," he corrected. "That doesn't make it true."

"Then why do I feel so positive about this, Dr. Creighton? Tell me that."

"Only you know the true reason, P.J., but I can make a stab at it. When bad things happen, we crave closure. We want someone accused and punished so we can move on to more pleasant concerns and wipe the ugly incident off our hands. It's natural, and perhaps protective in a way, but that certainly doesn't give us the right to leap to unsubstantiated conclusions or to act on them."

"What about instincts? What about common sense?"

"Those things are fine, but they're no substitute for facts and evidence. We're all innocent until proven guilty, not presumed. Those are the crucial elements that keep our legal system afloat. I don't have to tell you that."

"Evidence is precisely what I'm after, Dr. Creighton. That's why I need Jeannie's autopsy report."

His exasperation escaped in a rush. "May I speak frankly?"

"Of course."

"You've been under a great deal of stress lately. Jeannie's murder, losing the job. Not to mention all the family problems you've carried around for so many years. It's perfectly understandable if that feels like too much to bear."

"You think I'm imagining things? Making things up?"

"What I think is that you're under a great deal of stress and you could benefit from a safety valve. You deserve to unburden yourself, P.J."

"*You deserve to unburden yourself* is code for *you need a rubber room*. I'm not crazy. Or maybe I am crazy, but that doesn't mean I'm wrong about Charlie Booth."

Our food arrived. Creighton slathered a chunk of pita bread with hummus. Eyeing my plate, I discovered that my appetite had fled.

"I don't think you're crazy," he said. "But I do believe you're not thinking clearly, P.J. This isn't like you. This isn't the thoughtful, intelligent young woman I thought I knew."

I cared intensely what Creighton thought, and my face burned with the shame of his disapproval. "So what do you suggest?"

"I suggest you to talk to someone and get this sorted out."

"I am. I'm talking to you."

"A neutral party, I mean, and I'm not that. How long since you've been in therapy?"

"Not since my training analysis." And what a memorably wrenching process that had been. Staring my parents' death in the eye, acknowledging the depths of my brother's craziness, not to mention my own, made big Millie's rude, brain-soiling mugwumps look like a day at the beach. Sure, I had learned a great deal about myself, so I suppose one could argue it was worth the agony (not to mention required for entry into the profession I so wanted to call my own), but I can't say I've ever had the least desire to go at it again.

Creighton sipped his wine. "So it's been almost ten years."

"About that."

"Extreme stress or no, that's far too long. I go for a refresher every year or so for a few sessions, at least. Think of it as routine maintenance, a tune-up, if you will."

"What about the extreme stress on my wallet?"

"That excuse won't fly, and you know it."

"The therapist I worked with is probably retired by now."

"No matter. I was going to recommend someone new in any event. Terrific woman. Some of her techniques are a bit unconventional, but there's no arguing with her results."

He found her vital statistics in his Palm Pilot and copied them on the back of his card. "I'll tell her to expect your call."

"I'll think about it, Dr. Creighton. But this isn't a good time. There's too much going on. I'll call her when things settle down."

"Now is the perfect time. As soon as you get home this evening, I want you to phone her and set it up."

"Is this really necessary?"

"Yes. And seeing you battle the idea only confirms that. You need to do this, P.J. Trust me."

I glanced at the card. The psychiatrist's name was Yolanda Groome. She practiced something I'd never run across before called psychokinetic integration, and her office was unthinkably far away in TriBeCa, the southwestern end of the island, which was technically part of Manhattan, but in my view might as well have been a suburb of Mars.

"You don't honestly expect me to *schlep* all the way to Hudson Street."

"You're a bright, insightful young woman, P.J., and as Nina said, a gifted therapist as well. I have tremendous admiration for you. Always have. From that very first day, when you came to my office for your interview, it was clear to me that you had what it took. So, you're right, I don't *expect* anything. I *know* you're going to do what's necessary to get yourself back on track."

I felt a tiny bud of a smile blooming, my first in days. "When you put it that way."

"Is that a promise?"

"I promise to give it serious thought."

"No sale."

"What about requesting Jeannie's autopsy report? Will you do that for me?"

"Once I hear from Dr. Groome that you've kept up your end of the bargain, that you've signed on and participated fully, we can talk about that further."

"No fair. You're asking me to do what you want and I get nothing in return."

"On the contrary. You get clearer thinking, better perspective, and improved peace of mind. That's what you offer your patients, P.J. And, as someone who cares about you, that's what I want for you."

"OK. I'll do it. But can't you please request Jeannie Bagshaw's autopsy report now? I'm terribly worried about her little boy."

"I'm not talking about a major delay. I'm sure Dr. Groome will make time for you when I explain what's going on. And I suspect it'll only take a few sessions with her to get things straightened out. You'll be far more use to that little boy, and everyone else, once you take care of yourself. The last thing you should be doing is getting involved in something so complex and uncertain when you're struggling to deal with so many other issues."

"Damn it, Dr. Creighton. Must you always make sense?"

"I don't always, believe me. But it is a great deal easier, as you well know, to be logical and objective about someone else's issues. That's another reason I go to see a therapist myself from time to time."

"All right. You've made your point. I'll call her as soon as I get home."

"Excellent." Creighton's approval warmed me through the rest of the meal, on the convoluted ride home, and as I strode down my dark, quiet street. Only when I stepped inside my tiny apartment and locked the door did I begin to fret about what I'd agreed to do.

CHAPTER

17

■ **Of course, because I was reluctant to see her, the** therapist Creighton recommended had a last-minute cancellation for early the following day. She instructed me to wear comfortable, loose-fitting clothing, preferably a leotard or sweats. And I thought, if they have wardrobe for her brand of psychotherapy, why not a stand-in for the balky likes of me?

I took the subway downtown, lurching amid the rush-hour crush of flesh and attitude. Surfacing at the stop nearest Dr. Groome's office, I was relieved to discover that I still had many long blocks to traverse. The closer I got to her address, the more leaden my steps became. My brain kept reeling off excellent reasons to run. There could be a terrorist attack right here and now, or an escaped convict or a tiger fleeing the non-existent local prison or zoo. If none of the above was likely, why had my internal danger indicator shot into the screaming red-alert zone? I recognized my symptoms as toddler-quality resistance. I was acting like a small child with a full, screaming bladder who would rather jiggle about in a classic pee-pee dance than confess the pressing need. What was I afraid of? No idea. But I understood that by going through with this, there was a serious risk I'd find out.

Dr. Groome's office perched amid a cluster of small businesses on the seventh floor in a pleasantly shabby commercial building in the city sector known as TriBeCa because of its location in a triangle below Canal Street. A creaky elevator redolent of mildew and cleaning fluid delivered me slowly to seven. There, I passed a door marked Gordon Wiesbaden, Bookbinder, another for Samuel Matthew Goldstein, Attorney At Law, the accountancy partnership of Tretter & Lavolsi, LLP, a sculpture studio cleverly named The Sculpture Studio, J. M. Larkin costume design, and an enigmatic operation labeled with nothing but its name: RemarkAbilities. Yolanda Groome's door, in similar fashion, read simply: Psychokinetic Integration. Her name was nowhere in evidence, nor was the alphabet soup of advanced degrees Creighton had reeled off in describing her. It would seem she was content to allow her presence to speak for itself.

And quite the eloquent presence it was. The therapist stood over six feet tall, and every inch, from the skunk-streaked onyx hair that was slicked back and knotted at the crown, to her slim bare feet with silver-polished nails, could best be described as majestic. She was also lithe and limber, gliding swanlike as she ushered me inside. The office was devoid of furniture, except for the slim ivory Parsons table pressed against the wall that held a telephone, a computer, and the kind of card file some therapists use to organize their patients' contact information.

When she reached the center of the rubbery black floor, she sank as if someone had stolen her bones. "Join me, P.J."

I tried, though her descent resembled the gentle downward drifting of an autumn leaf, while mine was more like the creaky collapse of a rickety folding table.

"You have trouble letting go, I see," she said, scoring a bull's-eye with unnerving ease.

"Maybe I just need oiling," I quipped.

"Then that's what you shall have." She rose like a vapor and drifted to the side of the room. There she opened the well-camouflaged door to a supply closet and retrieved an amber bottle from the upper shelf. "Shall I apply it for you, or would you prefer to do it yourself?"

"I was joking."

"Nevertheless, it might be useful. Try some. I think you'll find it pleasing."

I eyed the bottle. "Is this really necessary?"

"Why? Does it frighten you?"

"Of course not. That's ridiculous."

"Fine. Then let's proceed."

"This doesn't feel like therapy, it feels like a silly game."

The frown barely rumpled her alabaster skin. "I don't play games, and I don't want to make you feel any more uncomfortable than you already are."

"Then why are you?"

"As a therapist yourself, you know the answer to that. You've constructed a careful fence around the things you find too painful and difficult to face. By coming here and working with me, you recognize there's a strong possibility that your protective fence will be compromised."

I folded my arms hard across my chest. "What's wrong with a nice, sturdy fence, I ask you?"

"Two things. Nothing gets in and whatever is inside, good or bad, can't get out."

"I'm fine."

"No one is suggesting you aren't."

"I'm only here because Dr. Creighton insisted."

"I understand, but since you're paying for the hour, why not get your money's worth?" She held out the bottle. "May I?"

"I can do it." I twirled off the metal cap, unleashing rich essences of lilac and thyme, and another scent, sweet and soothing, that I couldn't identify. I allowed a stingy drop or two to drip on my fingertips. Then I replaced the cap and returned the bottle to her.

She opened it again and poured a generous measure of oil into her cupped palm. Wordlessly she invited me to imitate her as she drew the heady-scented essences toward her face. She inhaled so her ribs flared and her features slumped with blissful calm. Then she spread the oil from palm to fingertips, fingertips to wrists, pulse points to forearms, and so on, moving in slow rhythmic rounds.

Feeling ridiculous, I copied her movements, fingerpainting along my hand and arm. Dr. Groome caught my eye and mutely encouraged me to slow down. I did, matching her pace; circling smoothly; inhaling the rich heady aromas of the oil. From some inscrutable source, soft, restful music filled the room. So relaxing. My muscles uncoiled. My mind cleared of loud, jumbled thoughts, and I found myself adrift on the tuneful currents.

Dr. Groome's voice was a warm, embracing breeze. "Close your eyes and let your mind go."

I tried to stay grounded, but my brain had its own agenda. Reality receded, and a scene from my childhood wavered into view.

I saw a vast meadow glazed with brilliant wildflowers and the thicket of hard-packed dark evergreens beyond. Fierce sunshine lit the jewel-clear sky. Caity and I had fixed the picnic for this celebration of my mother's birthday, planning and fussing over it as if we'd somehow known it would be her last. In deference to the day's importance, we'd packed good silver, table linens, even fine glasses and china plates swaddled in newspaper, as if we were moving to France. The basket weighed a ton, and Jack and Daddy strained red-faced to carry it between them. Jack scowled at me and Caity, and teased his worst. *What did the little twerp twins pack anyway? Cement sandwiches? Concrete pudding? Barbecued bricks?*

"What do you see, P.J.?" the therapist prodded.

"Can't see anything," I said, more sharply than I intended. "My eyes are closed."

"What are you thinking about, then?" she asked with unstinting patience.

"Thinking about what's for lunch," I said, musing about how delightfully misleading the truth could be.

"Try to let go, P.J. See where your thoughts take you."

They propelled me back to that meadow in the part of that terrible day that was filled with such cruel, empty promise. My mother had been what then? Thirty-six? Could that be? Only four years older than Caity and I are now?

That day, at that time, I was still a believer in the magical powers of lemonade, sugar cookies, oven-fried chicken, and the clumsy coleslaw two eager girls had prepared. Surely, all that effort and excellent intent had the power to keep us laughing, fooling happily, and having a grand, memorable time. And that's how it went until my brother got it in his head to joke that it was a damned good thing God had seen fit to behave himself and give us the perfect weather Jack had ordered up.

Not just a good thing, he'd said, a *damned* good thing, as if a person could say *God* and *damned* in the same breath and not get my mother riled up. But Jack was so tickled by his own cleverness, he fixed on it completely. That was how my brother got sometimes, like a greed-crazed dog. He would sink his teeth into something, and you'd have to near squeeze the life out of him before he'd even consider letting go.

"What are you thinking, P.J.?" Yolanda Groome asked.

"About how dogs hold on to things like a Chinese puzzle. The harder you pull, the harder they persist."

"What meaning does that have for you?"

"Nothing in particular. Just a thought."

"I suspect you're a bit of a Chinese puzzle, too," she said.

I opened my eyes. "Sometimes a cigar is just a cigar, Dr. Groome."

She nodded. "If you're not ready to take me along, that's all right, P.J. Close your eyes again and go on your own."

"I'm not going anywhere. I'm right here."

"Go. See what you see."

What I saw with painful clarity was that look on my mother's face that told you surer than words that you'd crossed the line. Her mouth went tight as a miser's purse, and her green eyes darkened like the sky before a storm. Those slim hands of hers, white and smooth as milk despite all the work she did, clumped in bloodless fists. Anyone with a lick of sense recognized those signs as a clear warning you'd best stop whatever it was you happened to be doing to bring them on. My mother liked a good joke as well as the next person, better maybe. She could even take a raunchy story now and again in the right place and time with the right folk, but she had no sense of humor, whatsoever, when it came to God. The way Jack was carrying on, it wasn't a stretch to say he was being disrespectful, even downright blasphemous. He wasn't claiming he'd prayed for the warmth and sunshine like a good little Catholic boy. He was suggesting in all suicidal seriousness that he held the power to boss God around.

Somehow, Jack failed to see my mother's rage, though

from the way she was glaring at him, I half expected his head to burst into flame. She was mottled with the fury; splashed with fiery blotches of outright rage. And there was my brother in all his clueless, reckless glory, sticking his neck farther and farther into the noose.

Dr. Groome must have seen my grimace. "You look pained, P.J. What just went through your mind?"

Now I saw my father, neck cords bulging, all but dragging Jack into the woods. Jack stumbling and mewling in fear. Dry twigs and underbrush cracked beneath the weight of my brother's terror and my father's cold, silent rage.

The sharp distant thunder of their words filled the air. Dad's sledge of a voice pounded Jack's scared shrill, stretching his words into wisps of tremulous bravado. Terror roared in my ears, and I clutched Caity's arm so hard she yelped.

All this thrummed in my memory. And then, try as I might to keep it submerged, to stop the forward roll of time, I felt the moment rising, that impossible instant that shattered our glass-blown lives.

My eyes snapped open and I swallowed hard.

"What is it, P.J.?" Dr. Groome urged.

"Nothing. Something came to me, that's all."

"What?"

"One of those movie scenes where the audience knows that something terrible is about to happen, but the victim is unaware. I wonder if it's useful or useless to have advance notice when something bad is going to happen."

"What do you think?"

"Don't know. I suppose you'd only be better off knowing if you had some way to change the way things were going to go. But fate is fate. By definition you can't change it. So all you'd get is more time to feel hopeless and scared."

"Wouldn't you also have more time to prepare?"

"There's no way to prepare for some things."

Her brow peaked. "Such as?"

I peered at my watch. "Such as our time running out, which it has. So I'd better go, Dr. Groome. Good to meet you."

* * *

On the way to the subway, I called Dr. Creighton from my cell phone. "I saw your shrink friend, Dr. Creighton. Mission accomplished."

"I'm glad, P.J. It's going to do you a world of good."

"She's—interesting."

"Unorthodox but most effective, as I said. Nothing wrong with thinking outside the box."

The scent of her oil wafted from my hand. "So, I wanted to let you know I've satisfied my part of the bargain, and I'm really looking forward to seeing that autopsy report."

He chuckled. "Jumping the gun a bit, aren't you, P.J.?"

"I'm not jumping anything. The deal was that I go to Dr. Groome and then you get the autopsy report."

"No, the deal was that you go to Dr. Groome and sort things out, after which we *discuss* whether or not it makes sense for me to request that report."

"Come on, Dr. Creighton. This can't wait. The longer Charlie Booth is around, the greater the chance he'll seriously hurt his little boy. I'll go back if you want me to; I'll do the work. You have my word."

He sighed. "I know this may be hard for you to understand, P.J. But if I help you to go off half-cocked, you could be the one putting that child in jeopardy. You wouldn't be doing him any favors, and you might well be putting yourself at serious risk as well. Innocent or guilty, no one is going to welcome your snooping around. There could be legal repercussions, and worse. It would be irresponsible of me to encourage or enable that, and I'm not going to do it."

"Fine. If you won't help, I'll find another way."

There was a long, bristling silence on the line.

"Dr. Creighton?"

"I'll agree to a compromise, P.J., but that's it. If you go and see Dr. Groome for intensive work every day this week, I'll request that report, if only to convince you you're being misguided."

"Every day? That's too much."

"No, it's not. Not in the least. Given the scope of the issues you're dealing with, it's merely a beginning. But I'll consider it a show of good faith, on one condition."

"Traveling to the ends of the earth to meet with that voodoo lady every day isn't enough of a show of good faith for you?"

"My condition is that you put forth A-plus effort. If Dr. Groome tells me you've done that, I'll request the report."

"How can she judge the size of the effort I'm making?"

"I believe she can."

"What if she doesn't like me? What if she's a tough grader? What if she's in a bad mood?"

"She'll be fair. I'm confident of that. Complete your part of the bargain and I'll see to mine."

I had reached the subway. "You don't leave a person much wiggle room."

"Something tells me you've been wiggling for far too long, P.J. It's time to look yourself hard in the eye and put those issues you've been carrying around to rest."

"I hear you," I said, though what I meant was that, given no choice in the matter, I'd concede to his overbearing, outrageous, and seriously endearing demands. Creighton cared, and he understood the depths of the emotional swamp I'd been slogging through, both of which meant more than I could say.

"OK. You win."

"No, P.J. You do."

I hung up, descended into the station, and swiped my MetroCard at the turnstile. The uptown express met me at the platform. As the train picked up speed and plunged into darkness, I clung fast to the cold metal pole. What could be more dislocating than barreling full steam ahead, thrust by propulsive forces over which I had no control?

CHAPTER

18

■ In the absence of his beastly wife, Ted Demetrios struck me as taller, surer, brighter, and better looking than he'd appeared in her noxious shadow. He shook my hand firmly and locked with confidence onto my gaze.

"I'm glad you suggested seeing us separately," he said.

"It's helpful to get to know the parts of a couple as individuals."

He settled in the smaller green chair and splayed his arms on the rests. His tan corduroy blazer gaped to reveal the fanciful fish pattern on his crimson necktie over a trim, dark blue linen shirt.

"I heard a lot from Clarissa, Ted, but not much from you. How do you feel about your marriage?" I asked.

He showed his palms. "I don't think anyone would describe it as a marriage. It's more like a tour of combat duty that just goes on and on."

"Then may I ask why you don't seek a discharge?"

"Honorable or dishonorable?"

"That's a different question. Let's try to answer the basic one first."

"I don't get out because it's not an option."

"Why is that?"

He brought his hands together now, folded as in prayer. "Several reasons."

"Such as?"

"I work for Clarissa's father in the family business. When we got together, he made it clear what was expected of me, and if you think my wife is a piece of work, you should meet the old man."

I nodded, acknowledging the point with as much neutrality as I could. Therapy was about leading horses to water, not dragging them against their will. "Giving up financial security is certainly not a trivial issue."

"Financial security has nothing to do with it. That's not why I stay with Clarissa or why I'm still working for her father." He pulled out his wallet and passed me a snapshot of a young girl, a gawky child with a crooked grin and outsized teeth. Thick-lensed glasses gave her eyes the look of lusterless stones submerged in a murky bowl. The irises were off-kilter, their targets uncertain, and her expression seemed off as well, like an ill-fitting dress.

"She's why. That's our daughter, Robbie. Our only child."

I offered the best that came to mind. "Sweet."

"Yes, she is. Robbie was born with a rare metabolic disorder that has caused all kinds of problems over the years. Language delay, developmental delay, uncontrolled seizures."

"Sorry. That must be tough."

"Not easy. But when you have kids, you do whatever's necessary to take care of them."

"True." I thought of the countless hours my mother had spent at the kitchen table patiently working with my sister so that she might overcome her disability, learn to communicate despite the deafness, and eventually become so adept at everything she tried she wound up leaving me—the "able" one—in the dust.

Ted Demetrios smiled at his daughter's crooked image. "Robbie tries so hard. And she's been making good, steady progress, even starting to read a little, but nothing she's done has ever been anywhere near good enough for Clarissa or her folks. To them, she's defective, a factory second, and nothing less than top-of-the-line perfection will do for them."

"I'm sorry to hear that."

He sighed. "She was diagnosed when she was only a few months old. Clarissa and my in-laws have been lobbying to have her institutionalized ever since. I've had to battle them constantly to keep her home. Kids do better with their own families, no one questions that. But to Clarissa and her folks, it's all about image. Robbie's like a stain on the wall: unseemly."

"Many people have difficulty dealing with disabilities. It's possible that they see a disabled child as a reflection of their own inadequacy."

"Maybe so, but their inadequacy is not what concerns me. The only thing I'm worried about is my daughter. If Clarissa and I split up, Robbie will be shipped off to a residential program so fast it'd make your head spin. And I assure you, they wouldn't worry about the quality of the place. Their only interest would be getting her out of sight and mind."

"Couldn't you have Robbie come live with you?"

His lips pressed in a grim line. "You don't know those people. They run on revenge like some cars take diesel fuel. If I divorced Clarissa, they'd have me declared an unfit father. I wouldn't get to see my little girl, much less take care of her."

"They can't have you declared unfit because they want to."

"You'd be surprised. They've got the money and power to do what they please. They have politicians in their pocket, judges, you name it. In all the years I've known Clarissa, I've never seen those people hit a wall."

I eyed him steadily. "Talk to me, if you will, about the cross-dressing."

He laughed. "Don't tell me you believed that nonsense. If you're willing to listen, Clarissa will claim I'm a pedophile skinhead junkie and every other goddamn thing she can think of. It's all part of setting up a case against me so they'd be guaranteed full custody of Robbie in case I ever dared to consider filing for divorce."

"So there was no dressing up in her underwear?"

"Hardly. The day she was talking about, Clarissa pulled one of her little disappearing acts and I was with Robbie. My daughter loves to play dress-up, so I turned her loose with a boxful of clothes Clarissa had put aside to get rid of. Last year's things, no matter what they cost, are trash to my wife. She won't even allow them to be given to charity.

"Anyway, at some point Robbie took one of her mother's frilly nightgowns and draped it around my shoulders like a shawl. Then she put a hat of Clarissa's on my head, a silly straw thing with fake fruit on the brim that probably cost a zillion dollars. It was one of those idiot fad items she can't live without and then never even wears. That was the extent of my so-called cross-dressing."

"Why didn't you say so when she brought it up here?"

"Because I know what I'm up against. Clarissa's like a wild animal. When she comes after you, the only reasonable strategy is to play dead."

We talked more about Robbie and the steel cage that was Ted's life. There are some corners you can get painted into that seem to offer no viable escape. As a therapist, it was my job to help him examine the alternatives and decide which was the most tolerable. Sometimes, there was no neat, happy solution. Sometimes, life was about compromise, acceptance, and doing the best you could under the unfortunate circumstances. Sometimes, life meant merely getting by.

CHAPTER

19

■ **"This the hoppy rater? Hurry up yo' ass and get me** P.J. I got to talk to that girl now!"

"You are talking to me, Millie."

"Don't give me that. Think I'm rope-a-dope or something? Think I don't know the difference between a tapeworm, a whale sperm, and a do-si-do?"

"What is it, Millie? Why did you call?"

"Think you can roll me over, bowl me over, tease me, have my foal?"

"You're talking nonsense, Millie. I'm not going to listen if all you're doing is running at the mouth."

"White coral bells upon the silver squawk," she trilled. "Lilies of the Valley make the hard-on talk."

"I'm hanging up now, Millie."

"Whoa doggie. Wait a hog. Hey, P.J. That really you?"

"Yes, Millie."

"'Bout time. Where you been? Been trying to get through to you since the dawn of grime."

"What is it, Millie?"

"Seen that Jeannie girl's sumbitch husband again, that's what is. Seen him off like nobody's business, laying a duck."

"Doing what?"

"Duck work. You know. Taking all those shiny pieces of duck and firing them all up together and laying them in a big ole mother ducking line."

"You mean ducts?"

"That's what I said. And what's that sumbitch think he's doing going around laying ducks like nobody's business when he should be getting his own fool duck boned and fried?"

"Are you sure it was Booth, Millie? Are you absolutely, positively sure?"

"Watched that sumbitch till my eyes was all dry and googly. That's how sure I was. Watched him till he packed his duck tools and climbed up in his mother ducking truckling and drove his sumbitch self away."

"What kind of truck, Millie? Did you get a good look at it?"

"You betchum. It was the kind with people seats up front and one of them wide open behinds, the kind stuff belches out of onto the road."

My heart was knocking fiercely. "What color?"

"Dark. Black maybe, or maybe green."

"What about the make or license number, Millie. Did you happen to notice either of those?"

"Can't say as I did. Had my eye on Jeannie's sumbitch husband and his ducks. But that truck had a little man on it with a curly hat looking out one of those windows they got in boats. Maybe Mexican. Maybe from that other place in China: tie-one-on."

With a person like Big Millie, the line between sense and mugwumps was slim indeed. "Sure. A little Mexican or Taiwanese man with a curly hat looking through a porthole. Got it."

"So what you gone do bout it?"

"I'm going to study the situation carefully, Millie. I have to go now. My next client is at the door."

Clarissa Demetrios strode about with pursed lips and her pert nose wrinkled with distaste. "Am I to take it that you live here?"

"Why do you ask?"

"Do you actually find it acceptable, this place?" She shuddered in disgust.

"We're here to talk about you, Clarissa. Please sit."

She flipped the clasp on her Prada purse, plucked a cigarette from a slim, gold, monogrammed case, and waved it batonlike. "Is this all of it, one grim, little room?"

"I don't allow smoking."

Her brow dipped. "You don't *allow*? What gives you the right to allow or disallow anything?"

"You're welcome to follow my rules or find another therapist."

"That's cute, your little power trip. Reminds me of how dogs stop to piddle on all the trees. I suppose they think it accomplishes something. Makes them feel important somehow, affirmed in their silly, meaningless lives."

I sat unflinching. Poison fumes were harmless if you refused to suck them in. "When you're finished posturing, we can begin."

She perched on the arm of the couch. "What did you and Ted talk about yesterday? Man came home smiling like a fool."

"That's confidential."

She sniffed. "Confidential why?"

"Because it would be unethical for me to reveal anything a client tells me. That goes for you as well, Clarissa. Whatever you say to me stays strictly between us."

"That's absurd. Ted's my husband."

"Doesn't matter. The rules of confidentiality apply to everyone. Spouses are no exception."

A nasty smirk curled her lips. "What's the big intrigue? Did you have sex with him or something?"

"What I have with all my clients is confidentiality, Clarissa."

"I hear therapists do that with their clients—have sex— though it's hard to imagine doing so with someone as utterly repugnant as my husband. I haven't let that creep near me in years. You'd have to be extraordinarily dedicated, I'd think. Or dumb and blind."

"Confidentiality is essential in psychotherapy. It allows people to freely speak their mind."

"Is that what Ted did, speak his little mind? Did he whine to you that I'm a nasty, hideous bitch who makes his life a living hell? Because I won't dispute that. Not at all. I'll proudly admit that his misery is one of my few true pleasures."

"Why is that?"

"It simply is."

"Don't you think there could be better satisfactions in life than making someone else miserable?"

"You mean like having sex with your grotesque clients? Living in a dreary little dump? Frankly, no."

"Your life could be better, Clarissa. You don't have to be so bitter and angry."

"How encouraging." She went coy. "Did Ted tell you he was molested by his father as a little boy? The old man used to diddle him in the bathtub. Moved on to—shall we say—bigger things as Ted got older. I suppose that's why my husband has such a thing for little boys. Did he tell you about how he watches the ten-year-old who lives next door? I caught him staring at the child through binoculars while the poor kid was getting undressed. Ted was all red-faced and panting like a dog. Made me sick."

"Tell me about Robbie."

She flinched. "I have no interest in talking about that."

"Why? Do you find the subject too painful?"

"Too tedious. The girl should have been put away years ago. Everyone would be far better off."

"Would Robbie be better off?"

"What possible difference could it make to her? She doesn't know enough to swallow her own drool."

"All children benefit from love and caring."

She sniffed. "It's bad enough I have to deal with Ted. One freak in the family is quite enough."

"You don't have to stay with him, Clarissa. You choose to."

"That's what I admire most about you, Ms. Lafferty. You may not know anything, but that doesn't stop you from stating your idiotic opinions as fact."

"I'll be glad to recommend another therapist."

"Absolutely not. You're precisely what I want. Totally useless."

At times like that, I wished I'd become a veterinarian. When animals act like animals, fair enough. "Time's up for today, Clarissa. I'll have those recommendations for you tomorrow."

Her voice dropped to a hiss. "Don't even think of trying to pass me off to someone else. I'm sure you wouldn't want to have me file a complaint against you for—"

I didn't blink.

"I was going to say for sexual harassment, but that's far too mundane. Don't worry. I'll think of something perfect if need be."

CHAPTER

20

■ **The hospital sprawled like a sleeping giant behind a** line of waiting cabs and ambulettes. As the automatic doors gaped to admit me, I was struck by a wave of dizziness. My knees buckled, and I erupted in a chill sweat. I braced against the wall, pulling air, until the awful sensation passed.

With extravagant care, I crossed the lobby. I inscribed my name in the visitors' log and then joined the short queue at the patient information desk. Standing there, I realized what was wrong. The last time I had ventured into this kind of hospital was the night my parents died.

True, I'd gone to visit my brother Jack in any number of psychiatric and rehab facilities, but those were different. This was the sort of place where I'd learned that people could be wheeled from a wailing ambulance into a swirl of comforting chaos only to be ferried out again, mere hours later, under a sheet. This was the kind of place where young children sat weary and bewildered for a cruel eternity while strangers plied them with far too many sweets and allowed them to color with expensive fountain pens on forbidden things like personalized memo pads and patient information pamphlets. This was a place where a child might enter in a rational lifetime and exit, before a single night played out, to a world that made no sense at all. A place like this held the power to turn a living, breathing child into an insensate mass of leathery grief.

"Everett Waite, please," I told the kindly-looking, gray-haired gentlemen at patient information, repeating the code-name Dunston's editor at Aureus Press had instructed me to use.

The old man keyed in the necessary strokes. "That's 1410 West." He handed me a pale blue pass and pointed toward the elevator bank at the end of the hall. Mount Sinai Hospital was a rambling health-care complex on upper Fifth Avenue with a namesake medical school and more than a thousand beds.

Passing the nurses' station on the fourteenth floor, I spotted the name Everett Waite amid the cluster of file charts that dangled from a square metal frame. Down the hall, the same name occupied a slot outside the room. The other slot was empty.

I rapped on the doorframe. "Mr. Waite. It's P. J. Lafferty. Anthony Pericolosi said you'd agreed to meet with me."

"Yes. Come in."

Albert Dunston reclined on a hill of pillows, surrounded by machines. Around him, everything pulsed in discordant beats: the drip of solutions infiltrating his veins, the strident bleat of electronic monitors. Cloudy fluids slithered from the tubes that snaked beneath the covers.

He nodded toward the door. "No guard outside?"

"No."

"Excellent timing. He must have ducked out for a bathroom break or a smoke."

"Why do you need a guard?"

"I don't. Don't need one, don't want one, but I have one just the same. Sit, Ms. Lafferty. Please."

The only chair in the room held a powder-blue device with a mouthpiece connected to an accordion tube which was attached in turn to a cylinder filled with small colored balls.

"That's to keep up my breathing, which happens to be fine," he explained. "Feel free to throw it and the rest of this nonsense out the window and make yourself as comfortable as you can."

"How are you feeling, Mr. Dunston?"

He sniffed. "Cranky, that's how. Crabby, irritable, out of sorts, and put upon. It's bad enough being attacked without having to suffer a further assault by all these insufferable, overbearing do-gooders. I told them I'd be fine if they'd just patch me up and let me go about my business, but they refused to listen. I'm a virtual prisoner here, Ms. Lafferty. That's the fact."

"I'm sorry to hear it, sir."

"It's the bloody lawsuits. A person doesn't dare sneeze in this country without getting the damned lawyers to sign off in triplicate first."

"Is there anything I can get you? Anything I can do to help?"

A glint of mischief lit his pale gray eyes. "You're doing it. I do believe you're about to rescue me from what might have proven to be lethal boredom."

"My pleasure."

"No. Mine. And do let's take a moment to bless young Anthony. He recognized the importance of your request and chose to ignore the ridiculous edict against anyone contacting me until this little puncture wound heals. He's a good man, Pericolosi. Always liked him, and now I'll be forever in his debt."

"Me, too." I set the breathing apparatus on the nightstand and settled in the chair.

"First I'll satisfy your curiosity, Ms. Lafferty, and then you can satisfy mine," Dunston said, gingerly touching the bandaged span of his abdomen that still wept with bilious drainage. "This happened while I was interviewing a man up in Connecticut who was about to go on trial for a string of murders. They called him Doc Picasso. Perhaps you've heard of him."

"I have." The case had inspired plenty of gruesome headlines. Doc Picasso was the nickname imposed by the press on a man named Vernon Seeley Vaughan. Posing as a plastic surgeon named Dr. V. S. Villum, he had lured patients to his private clinic in a small hamlet near the Massachusetts border. Vaughan had placed ads in several major cities, hoping to attract out-of-towners seeking surgical bargains, especially those who showed particular concern with keeping such procedures secret. After patients signed up for his "state-of-the-art enhancements" and paid in the untraceable cash he demanded, Vaughan rearranged their faces and assorted other body parts, turning them into grotesque, and very dead, abstractions. Vaughan in his lunacy believed that human design was flawed, and that he was destined to improve on it. When things went horribly wrong, as they always did, he chalked it up to a difficult but necessary learning curve and buried his mistakes in a wooded area behind his house. The crimes went undiscovered for years and might have indefinitely. But after a rainy spring that left the ground soft and sodden, a golden retriever in the neighborhood dug up a young woman's shin bone, carried it home, and presented it to his owner as a gift.

"The fact is I got what I deserved," Dunston said. "This was my own fault, to be sure. I'd been corresponding with dear Mr. Vaughan for months. Getting to know him, so to speak. We were relating as well as one can relate to such a person. He had offered several telling bits of personal information, which, I'm ashamed to admit, put me off guard.

"He told me he'd been born with hypospadias, which means the opening of his penis was not in the proper place. Correcting that normally involves a simple procedure, but according to Vaughan, something went wrong and he was forced to endure a series of corrective operations that caused him considerable pain and embarrassment during a formative phase in his childhood. People like Vaughan rarely disclose such intimate details, so I'm afraid I was dangerously confident that he and I had clicked.

"His tactic when we met on the day this happened was also quite clever. Over the course of our conversation at the prison, which lasted about an hour, he slowly dropped his voice to induce me to step nearer to his cell. I took the bait, though I stopped at what I considered to be a safe distance. Unfortunately for me, Vaughan had fashioned a diabolical little device, a spring-loaded projectile with a metal end that resembled a fish hook. When I came within a few feet of him, he was able to catch the skin on my neck, and pull me off balance so I staggered toward his cell. As soon as I got close enough, he impaled me with a charming weapon he'd fash-

ioned from a ballpoint pen cartridge and razor blades. Most
ingenious, really. Made quite the spectacular hole. Too bad
his real talents for invention couldn't have been channeled in a
more positive way."

"Thank heavens you're all right."

"If you choose to play with the bad dogs, you learn to take
the bites, Ms. Lafferty. I am all right, as is evidenced by my
ability to tell the tale, and I'll be far better when they release
me from this appalling place. Now why don't we move on to
something of far greater interest? Do tell me everything you
know about your Mr. Booth."

Dunston listened intently as I recounted the story yet again.
He seemed captivated, even energized by the grim tale of in-
human brutality, and I could relate. My interest in the dark
side of the psyche went back as far as I could recall. While
other children were biting their nails on behalf of Little Red
Riding Hood, I was fixated on what forces might have conspired to turn the wolf so bad. Did evil run in his family? Had
something knocked him off course growing up? Could he be
suffering from a sickness? I imagined a sweet apple rot that
rendered his brain soft and brown.

Dunston propped on his elbow, flinching with pain. "Mind
if I ask you a few questions, Ms. Lafferty?"

"It's P.J., please. And of course, ask anything you like."

"Why do you believe that Big Millie person when you ac-
knowledge that she's a severe, intractable paranoid schizo-
phrenic?"

"It's like the old joke, sir. Just because you're paranoid,
doesn't mean they're not talking about you. I've known Big
Millie for years. She's off her trolley most of the time, but
every so often, she slips back on track. What she told me
about Charlie Booth sounded credible. Everything followed
logically, so as dumb as it may seem, I believed her. I believe
her still."

Dunston set his jaw. "It doesn't seem dumb at all, though
perhaps a bit naive. I understand the scope of your predica-
ment, and it's considerable. There's a child in jeopardy, and
you wish to keep that child out of harm's way, but to do so,
you have to go up against both his mother's possible killer and
the system that sometimes seems designed to let the worst

among us get away with the worst things they do. I say that's naive in the sense of tilting at windmills. Hardened cynics would throw up their hands and walk away."

"You make it sound hopeless."

"Not hopeless, no. But it's not simple either, not by any means. I've spent most of my life working to bring down men like Charlie Booth, and a good deal of that work has gone into figuring out how to coax the powers that be into acting in their own self-interest. This is never an easy feat. I can assure you."

"But you've been able to do it."

"At times."

"How? What can I do to build a solid case against Charlie Booth?"

He fell back against the pillows and drew a shuddering breath. "I wish I was in a position to help you more actively with this."

"Me, too. But you're not."

"No, and if the blasted doctors have their way, I won't be for some time. While I'm lying here, moldering like a compost heap, my obligations are piling up. When they finally do let me out, it'll take me months just to get back to square one."

"I understand, Mr. Dunston. But you can help by advising me. What should I do?"

With a quivering hand, he lifted the paper cup at his bedside and pulled greedily at the straw. "What you *don't* do is try to convince anyone of anything without hard proof. That takes a disciplined approach, logical and sequential. First you have to verify the charges, make certain that the crime in question actually happened as described and that the alleged perpetrator is in fact the likeliest, and hopefully the sole reasonable suspect."

I took this down on a notepad. "Verify. Got it. But how?"

"It's a fencing match, thrust and parry. You provide an answer to every question that might be posed. Was he in the right place at the right time? Did he have access to the victim? Did he have access to the weapon? Had he used that kind of weapon in the past? Had he committed a similar crime in a similar way? Is he capable of the acts you're trying to prove he did? Was there ample opportunity and motive?"

I wrote furiously, fearful of missing a word.

"Next, you amplify. By that I mean you have to collect enough supportive data to make an impeccable case. That involves bolstering every step of your argument with hard facts. How do you know he was in the right place at the right time? Who can attest to this? What's the proof? Is the word of your witness more credible than that of any counterargument Booth or his witnesses may present? Can you accumulate enough evidence and testimony so there's no way for even the cleverest defense to knock it down? This is where sheer patience comes in, the sort no one has in nearly sufficient quantity."

"I'm afraid that goes double for me."

"Perhaps it does. But remember what I said about the lawsuits. Everyone's running scared. Given the threat that they might be accused of arresting someone without cause, many in law enforcement would sooner risk the threat of allowing even the most heinous criminal to remain at large. That's why you amplify. Build them a structure so firm and unassailable that they can't knock it down. Give them hard facts, bulletproof, earthquake- and tornado-proof. Lawsuit-proof. You can't rush it. One crack, one flaw, and the entire thing can fall apart. There's a reason the oldest pyramids have lasted for 4,500 years, P.J. They were built to perfection, stone by stone by stone. No mistakes. No shortcuts."

I reached for the breathing device and fiddled with its stem. "I'm on my own here, Mr. Dunston. I don't have the benefit of thousands of strapping souls and engineering geniuses to help me move and place those stones."

"Then you'll have to figure out how to do it yourself. And that's not all. After you build the case, you'll need to deliver it. Step three is to notify the necessary people in a correct, unassailable way. Foul that up, play it wrong politically, and you may as well try to whistle through your ear. Everything is politics."

"My favorite."

"Mine as well. I believe the word comes from the Greek *poly,* meaning many, and *ticks,* referring to small annoying insects."

"I hear you. I'm a lousy politician, but I'll try."

That earned an approving nod. "The final piece is to testify, which you will likely be called upon to do as well. And that can be quite a challenge in itself. Men like Blake Madigan and your Mr. Booth are unabashed liars and manipulators who tend to keep company with like-minded souls. They'll say or do anything to have their way. Being a person with built-in boundaries, with decency, can put you at a considerable disadvantage. Try to keep that in mind when the time comes."

"I hope I get that far."

"You will, P.J. I'll help you. You'll come back. And we'll talk about your Mr. Booth. We'll discuss how you need to approach him, how you'll dope him out so you minimize his advantage and maximize yours. We'll devise the roadmap, and set you on your way."

CHAPTER

21

■ **My first task was to verify that Charlie Booth had** been at Rikers at the time of Jeannie's murder. Since no visitors were allowed on Tuesdays and Rafe had uncovered no recent arrests in Booth's record, the likeliest scenario was that he had been at the prison as part of a work crew. Big Millie's assertion about seeing him "lay ducks" bolstered that view, if, by any wild stroke of good fortune, it happened to be true.

When I called Lottie Dray, Dennis John picked up. Chirpy music played in the background, the upbeat strains of a parody counting song on some kiddie show: "*Goodness, gracious, eight balls of wire.*"

"Hello. I can't talk to you. Call back later."

"Wait, Dennis John. It's P.J. I need to speak to Aunt Lottie."

"She went to get the laundry, so I'm not allowed to talk to anybody until she comes back."

"I'm sure she meant strangers, sweetie. People you don't know."

"I'm not allowed to answer the door; I'm not allowed to answer the phone; I'm not allowed to go near the stove or feed any M&M's to my new goldfish. Not even one."

"When did you get a goldfish?"

"Tomorrow. Are we going to have our playdate?"

"Sure we will."

"Today?"

"I can't today, but soon."

"When's that?"

"Before long."

"When's that?"

"Soon."

"OK. Here's Aunt Lottie. Bye."

The receiver clashed with a hard surface, filling my ear with grating noise. There followed a long, breathy pause before Lottie came on the line.

"So glad to hear from you, P.J. Have you gotten any further with our—friend?" She wouldn't mention Booth's name in front of his son. Then, the man was the very definition of unmentionable.

"Not yet. I'm working on it."

"You'll figure it out. I know it. Hold on a second, will you? There now. Dennis John's gone off to play, so we can talk."

"Good. I'm trying to prove Booth had access to Jeannie on the day of the crime. Do you know who he works for?"

"Not sure really. He bounces around so, it's tough to keep track."

"Maybe Dennis John knows."

"I can ask."

I listened to the silence while she did so. Lottie sounded winded when she came back on the line. "Nope. He doesn't know, either. He remembers a place called Artco, and so do I but I'm pretty sure Charlie had a fight with the boss and left there some time back. Wish I could be more help."

"That's okay."

"I could ask next time he comes for the boy. Not likely he'd tell me, though. Charlie doesn't like people poking in his affairs."

"No, don't say anything. I'll think of another way."

"You sure? I'll do what needs be."

"I'm sure."

I ticked that idea and the call to Lottie Dray off my to-do list. The next item up was far more daunting. I headed out and walked briskly downtown under an ornery sky that itched to spit rain. The wind was foul-tempered as well, a leftover blast of winter, blowing harsh. I huddled deep in my ancient peacoat, wishing I'd had the sense to wear a scarf and gloves, not to mention carry an umbrella. As I drew closer to the elegant Eastside neighborhood known as Sutton Place, I also wished I'd had the foresight to dress a bit more grandly. Talking my way into the rarefied home of Taffy and Allston Grainger was bound to be difficult, at best. Scruffy jeans, a faded work shirt, battered loafers, and the Salvation Army–quality peacoat I'd bummed about in since college did not a fabulous first impression make.

But I was not turning back, especially now that the sky was delivering on its threat and the first fat raindrops plunked against the sidewalk. In moments the rain intensified. Pelting pins fell, tinting the pavement an oily gray. I slipped my arms out of the peacoat, tented it overhead, and broke into a clumsy run.

I'd found details about the Graingers' home, including photographs of the facade, among the endless references to their crammed social calendar online. Fortunately, Sutton Place only spanned a handful of blocks and held a limited number of the private homes New Yorkers refer to as brownstones, no matter what color they happen to be.

Theirs was red brick with gleaming black shutters, bright white trim, flower boxes brimming with forced early blooms, and shiny brass accents. At the door I took a moment to catch my breath and compose myself. I thought of my sister, who could coast through the most intimidating situations, and I resolved to imitate her regal posture and commanding stride. Caity also did this amazing thing with her head: a sharp, efficient toreador toss of the hair that made me want to bow. I would have tried that, too, but surely on me it would look like a tic. Identical though we were, my twin could deftly pull off things I couldn't do in my dreams. Fashionable hats that looked charming on her perched on my head like laying hens. The high-heeled pumps she strolled about in so gracefully made me wobble like a broken stool. Despite her lack of hearing and need for an interpreter, Caity was an eloquent, charismatic public speaker, while I'd as soon face a firing squad as a podium, a microphone, and a crowd.

I rang the Graingers' bell, triggering heraldic chimes that sounded the opening bars of Beethoven's Fifth. Moments later light flared behind the intricate stained-glass panels that flanked the double doors. The doors soon opened to reveal a slim, blond woman. She was dressed in a navy cardigan over a print silk blouse and matching skirt. A dainty pearl choker bound her neck. I took her for the social secretary, one of those unflappable sorts who make no end of perfect arrangements. But then, her eyes bugged at the sight of me and she clutched her chest.

"Caitlyn Goldstein! My word, can it really be you? My daughter's a huge fan. Beyond huge! She'll be thrilled to death."

I bit back a ruinous instinct for honesty, and smiled.

"Where are my manners?" she prattled on. "I'm Taffy Grainger, Ms. Goldstein. Come in, please. Let me take your coat."

I clung to it with a shy smile and pretended to shiver.

Entering the brownstone, I felt queasy, and not solely because my shabby peacoat now smelled like a soiled wet dog. Like many twins growing up, Caity and I had enjoyed trying to fool people into taking one of us for the other. We'd sought opportunities to play the game, not so easy in our case given the hearing/deaf thing and the fact that Caity was so obviously *foie gras* to my chopped liver. But still, we managed to pull it off several times, including the delectable occasion when I passed as Caity in junior high English and got her a C-minus on a written report in lieu of her typical A. Then in high school, when the clique of popular snooty girls took to treating my sister like a leper, I made the brilliant decision to go to the locker room when they were changing for cheerleading practice, pretend to be Caity, and hear what they might have to say behind her back. My diabolical plan was to catch them red-handed in the act of speaking ill of a deaf girl, which would no doubt leave them feeling so guilty that they'd embrace Caity, and by default, me. Except for being tragically misguided, the plan was foolproof. Unfortunately, the whole thing hinged on the premise that the subject of their scorn was my sister. What I overheard in that locker room instead was aimed squarely and solely at me. Turned out I was the one they'd been shunning. Their ringleader, a brilliant, pretty, and universally well-liked girl named Meaghan McCloat, observed that it was a terrible shame for a girl like my sister to be stuck with an annoying creep like me. I was the social liability, the leprous annoyance that kept them away. That was the last time I'd dared to take such a risk. Decades had passed, and still the memory stung.

The Grainger house was wall-to-wall posh, with no end of hand carving, polished stone, and delicate antiques. I'm the sort who measures such things in terms of hours required to tidy, polish, dust, and tend, and by my careful calculation, the answer here was far too many, and then some.

Oil portraits in extravagant gilt frames lined the walls. Most of the pictures appeared to be of dead, foul-tempered relatives. A few depicted regal family pets. The place of honor over the ornate living room mantel held a large painting of Taffy Grainger flanked by her two gorgeous blond, blue-eyed children and the gorgeous blond, blue-eyed man who completed the set.

"Would you care for some tea, Ms. Goldstein? Or perhaps a bit of sherry to warm you on this nasty day?"

She was behind me, and I had the presence of mind to pretend I hadn't heard. Turning, I did my level best to look quizzical.

Now her mouth worked in slow, exaggerated rounds, as if showing me her dental work might somehow help me to understand. "Would—you—care—for—some—tea? Or—a—glass—of—sherry, perhaps?"

I shook my head and brought my fingers together crisply: the sign for no.

Now it was her turn to fix me with a blank stare. I fished in my purse for the notepad. *Nothing thanks,* I wrote. *Sorry to stop by without calling first. But I had a question for you.*

She gave me an odd look, and I could tell what she was thinking. How on Earth would a deaf person call first? Well, they could, in fact, via a special teletype phone called a TTY or TTD, which if need be could be relayed through a call center, as Caity often did to communicate with the hearing, but I hadn't come to fill her educational gaps.

"Not at all," Taffy Grainger said. "A distinguished author like Caitlyn Goldstein is always more than welcome in our home." I followed her to a sitting room done in soft yellows and dainty blue floral prints.

"What was it you wished to ask me, Ms. Goldstein?" Taffy Grainger said this with grand deliberation, while I pretended to study her lips. In truth, I was fascinated by the crisp white military precision of her teeth.

I'm working on a new book, I wrote. *I set a scene in a brownstone very much like this one. The owners are hosting a charity event, and someone disrupts it. My editor told me she thought something like that happened to you, so I was eager to hear about it. Of course, I'd fictionalize it completely. It wouldn't be recognizable as having happened here.*

Mrs. Grainger read my note then shook her head. "She must have us confused with someone else."

I took up the pen again. *But you do have charity events here?*

"We do. Several each year, but I can't imagine anyone trying to disrupt one of them."

No one ever made a commotion outside during one of your events? Someone acting crazy?

Now her look registered alarm. "Most certainly not. How dreadful!"

The police never contacted you about anything like that? You never filed a complaint?

"Never. I hate to even consider how such a thing might undermine all our hard work."

The horror on her face was the genuine item. Charlie Booth had fabricated the story that landed Jeannie in the crazy ward, as Lottie had said. What I couldn't fathom was how he'd managed to sell it to the police.

My editor was obviously mistaken, Mrs. Grainger. Sorry to bother you.

"No bother at all. Quite the contrary. It's an honor to meet you."

You're gracious, thanks. I should be going now.

Taffy Grainger moved to show me out. As we crossed the foyer, a teenage girl burst in and stood dripping onto the marble floor. I recognized her from the family portrait, though just barely. These days she sported a brow ring and magenta streaks in her sodden dark-blond hair. She had that look of utter adolescent exhaustion that told you how incredibly hard she worked to drive her parents mad. She beamed raw, festering hatred at her mother. But the poison attitude dissolved the instant she caught sight of me. "Oh, my God! Is it really you? Am I dreaming? Is Caitlyn Goldstein really, truly standing in my house?"

Before I could answer, she gestured wildly. "No, wait. I can sign that for you. I've been learning since I read my first Eva Everheart book." Clumsily, she formed the words *Are you.* Then, with increasing fluidity, she finger-spelled my sister's first and last name.

I signed *yes*, cringing with the lie.

Tears glazed her opalescent eyes. "I *love* your books. I've read every one of them, again and again. Before Eva, I totally hated reading. Totally."

"That's true," Taffy Grainger said. "Until Olivia discovered your books, we could not motivate her academically. Nothing we tried worked. But now she reads all the time. And her schoolwork has improved so much. She's like a different child."

"My God, Mom. Would you stop?" the girl whined. "She's a famous writer. She doesn't want to hear how I'm doing in school."

"No. I do. I'm glad you're doing well," I signed in all sincerity. "Education is extremely, terribly, incomparably important."

"I remember that. Eva said it in *All About Eva.*"

So now I was quoting Caity's dumb books. My cheeks went hot. "I guess she did."

"I remember thinking it made so much sense," Olivia said. "It was like a lightbulb went on in my head."

"I'm glad," I gestured. "That's good."

The girl eyed me with reverence. "Eva's my hero. Her and you."

"I don't know what to say." And in truth, I did not. I'd never looked Caity's accomplishments in the eye like this, never imagined her having such a striking impact on a child. But here was hard, undeniable evidence that she had. My sister had given this girl the love of a book, the gift of a reason to learn. Because of my twin, this child's education and quite possibly her entire life had taken a better turn. Caity's work had made the girl more tolerant as well. Deaf people had risen so high in Olivia Grainger's esteem that she'd bothered to learn to sign. The sap of tears rose in my own eyes, a gush of awe and pride. She was something else, my sister, and damned if that didn't make me ache to poke Her Royal Highness in the eye.

CHAPTER

22

■ **I arrived to find Dr. Groome sitting cross-legged on** the floor. She beckoned me to join her, and I tried. But I could not begin to match the pretzel twist of her endless legs or the flagpole true vertical of her spine. Slowly she inhaled. I watched her inflate, rib by rib, and then somehow stretch taller.

"Imagine a string from the ceiling pulling you straight up, P.J. Imagine yourself rising light as air."

I did my level best, but the only dangling string I could picture was a noose, and the light-as-air image put me in mind of a fat, ugly blimp.

"What's wrong?" she asked.

"I don't feel light and long. I feel like a big old stinky wet English sheep dog."

"That's because your mind is full of noise. If you learn to block it out, you'll find how incredibly powerful your will can be."

I shrugged, and the meager starch I'd managed to force into my spine gave way. Slouching was my steady state, and my back felt most natural bowed like a shrimp. "I'm afraid my will is no match for my won't."

"Have you always been so down on yourself?"

I leaned back on my elbows, which felt better still. "Always? I don't think so. My mother used to say I was the happy-go-luckiest little child."

"When did that change?"

"Good question."

"And?"

"I don't know." Even as I spoke the words, I could taste the bitter metal of the lie. My life was scored by the sharpest dividing line, a raw, bleeding rip in the universe that could not be made to heal. The wound could be traced to the day of my mother's birthday picnic, when my father dragged Jack off to the dark of the woods. Everything until then made solid sense. Afterward, there was only chaos.

"Tell me about your parents," she said.

"They've been gone for years, both of them. Nothing much to tell."

"What did they die of?"

"Same as everyone: shortness of breath."

Her look held a pointed warning.

"All right. It was a car accident. They went out for a drive in the country, to talk, they told us. It was raining hard, though the day had been glorious hours before. But a storm came up suddenly, and they went off a slippery back road. The car flipped and burst into flame. Both of them were tossed free, not wearing their seatbelts for some odd reason. They were unconscious when the ambulance came for them, never came to. A blessing, everyone said."

"And what did you think of that?"

"That it was the biggest crock of lard I ever heard."

"Maybe they were trying to ease the blow, to give you comfort."

"Some blows can't be eased, Dr. Groome, certainly not by trying to paint a nicer name on the door to Hell."

"Clumsy attempts to help make you angry?"

"Hot, snapping furious is more like it. Nothing I hate more than a bunch of clucking well-wishers. How I wished they'd kept their empty sentiments and smelly casseroles and phony sympathies to themselves. I knew what they were thinking, every blasted one of them: better those dead souls and their poor cursed orphan kids than me or mine. Best not get too close in case the jinx is contagious."

"Is that what you imagined they were thinking?"

"That's what I knew they were thinking, that and worse. People who hold the luck see themselves as superior. Like the smile of fate is something they deserve, and I don't."

"Do you?"

"Sure. Or maybe not. Who knows? What's the definition of deserving anyway? And who decides?"

"All fascinating questions."

"The kind with no answers, you mean."

"True."

"They call me P.J., you know, Dr. Groome. Stands for Poor Julia. That's the name someone hung on me after my parents died, and it stuck. I suppose everyone thought it simply grand that I wear all the misfortune. That way none was left to fall on them."

"Why did you let it stick? Why do you?"

"Because it's true that my luck stinks. Has from the start. I was born with a broken leg. And it's gone from there to worse."

"Must have been a tough delivery."

"You'd have to ask my mother about that, which would take quite the long-distance call."

The straighter she sat, the more I slumped, so by now, I was too hunched over to suit even my taste. My capacity for sheer, stubborn, self-destructive spite was truly boundless.

"Is this your notion of cooperating in therapy?"

I could barely meet her accusatory gaze. "Sorry. Sometimes the smart remark's the first that springs to mind."

"You don't have to apologize. The question is whether you want to try to accomplish something here or simply run out the clock."

"That would depend on the accomplishment. Frankly, there are some things I find too hard to look in the eye."

She slouched as I did, until the tortured arch of her spine made mine ache. "Such as?"

"I find it too hard to talk about them, too."

"You and I both know there is no way to shut something out if it needs to be addressed, P.J. The poison will bubble up in some other way. You'll have headaches or ulcers or feel the need to drown the pain in drink. Eventually, you're going to have to face whatever it is head-on and deal with it."

I stared at the rubbery floor. They were tiny dimples everywhere, and I wondered if they might harbor a hidden code. Wouldn't it beat all if the secret of the universe was right here for the taking, inscribed on my therapist's floor? "I like the word *eventually*," I said. "It sounds so nice and far away."

"The sooner you face your demons, the sooner you can whittle them down to manageable size."

I traced a row of bumps, trying to read them like Braille. Unfortunately, I couldn't read Braille, so the exercise wasn't all that useful. "And I'll do this by going back to the womb and doing it all again?"

"Nothing like that." She walked to her supply closet and retrieved a brightly patterned box. "It's like trying to open this. If you examine the outside, there doesn't seem to be any way. Go ahead. See for yourself."

I took the box and scrutinized it from every angle. The lid was fixed in place; and the seams on the bottom firmly sealed. I kept turning the maddening cube over and over in my hands, searching for a way in. Finally I tossed it down in disgust. "It's impossible."

"No. It can be done."

"If you're trying to judge my frustration tolerance, you needn't bother. I haven't any. If you'd asked, I'd have saved you the trouble of the test."

"It only looks impossible." She pressed on one end of the box while pulling the opposite corner. The sides fell open to expose the perfect peach-colored rose anchored in a chemist's tube inside.

"Cute trick. But I'm not a magic box, and anyway, you won't find any prize hybrid roses inside this girl. Stinkweeds are closer to the fact."

"We'll see. Lie down, P.J. Let me help you relax."

"I am relaxed."

"Humor me."

"Do you consider humoring the therapist therapeutic?"

"No. But I do understand that a commitment by both parties to work honestly and hard is essential."

I settled to the floor, holding fast to an image of Dennis John. I pictured him as a gap-toothed six-year-old and, much further down the road, a swaggering, adorably impossible adolescent. I conjured him as slim, tall, and athletic, not to mention heartthrob handsome, along with the brains. He'd play basketball, I thought, and I flashed to a scene of him as a star center on his high school team, running in grand strides, wearing a white jersey that set off the blaze of ginger curls.

"Focus on your breathing, P.J. That's right, inhale deeply, exhale fully, and then repeat. Tense your toes, and release. Now tighten your calves. Hold as long and hard as you can, and then let go."

Knees . . . thighs . . .

I was carried by the inexorable tide of her voice, swept again to the day of the picnic. It was much later now. Dusk seeped like smoke through the spotless panes of our kitchen window. The air in the room began to jitter and swirl, and I thought I must be light-headed from the hunger. When my parents had left hours earlier, they'd said they'd be right back. Right back had to mean any minute, so I'd sat at the kitchen table in frozen anticipation. Caity perched across from me, and neither of us had the courage to risk draping our fear with words. Wishing could surely bring them home, and so I tuned the full might of my yearning to the task. I conjured the weighty crunch of their tires and the spit of displaced gravel on the drive. I imagined the phantom slam of the car doors, the bright, certain bursts that would declare our world was safe again, and right.

They had to be back in time to give us dinner. My mother always had something warm and soothing on the stove. Stew with vegetables or hearty soup or roast chicken with creamed spinach and mashed potatoes, suffusing the house with the lovely perfume of parental concern. True, Caity and I were capable of filling our own bellies if it came to that. We'd fixed enough food to feed the fleet for my mother's picnic, after all. But my parents had been home then, reminding us to put away the milk and clean the sink and take care not to burn down the house.

And so, I sat unmoving, staring until my eyes ached and the vacant rumbling in my belly built to a growl. We hadn't seen Jack since the battle with my dad, and his absence ached like theirs. In a way Jack being gone scared me more. He'd been acting increasingly strange in recent months, wobbling off-kilter like a tire that threatened to slip its wheel. Soupy darkness gathered, and my fear grew fangs and claws. A monstrous voice within me taunted *Something's wrong*.

"Is it about your parents' death, P.J.? Is that the pain you're feeling?"

"Blasted floor is hurting my butt, if you must know."

"Your brother, then?"

"I don't remember talking to you about my brother."

"Hmmm," she said. "Interesting."

My eyes snapped open. "I know the ploy. You say *interesting*, and I'm supposed to feel compelled to rush in and explain myself. But I don't."

"I hear you."

"And my brother has nothing to do with anything. Jack is Jack, a fact of life."

"Your brother doesn't mean anything to you?"

"Sure he does, he means plenty, and most of it bad, but I've learned to live with it. Jack is what he is."

"Oh? And what is he?"

"He's mad, or if you're given to political correctness: clinically insane. Jack's delusional, unpredictable, impossible, irresponsible, reckless, and maddening. But he's also my brother. I love him dearly, and I care about him deeply. I think of him constantly and miss him intensely, and it would suit me fine if he'd gently fall off the planet and I'd never have to deal with him again."

"You're estranged?"

"No such luck. Jack turns up every so often like a bad flu. You know it's coming, and you do everything in your power to ward it off. You take your vaccine and gobble your vitamins, but sooner or later it gets you, nonetheless."

"Where does he live?"

"No one has an answer for that, not even Jack. Wherever the bad wind blows him, there he is."

She went to the supply closet again and retrieved an object I could not see. "Sounds very much like my son."

The secret in her hand was a gold locket containing a tiny

snapshot of a young man. She passed it to me. "Martin destroys whatever he gets his hands on, especially Martin. This is the only picture of him I've been able to rescue, even partially."

The face in the picture was a harder, darker version of her own. Martin had the same dark hair, pale skin, and cool, piercing gaze, but the bearing that draped like regal raiment on his mother hung on him like an ill-fitting sack.

I tossed the locket back as if it burned. "Why would you tell me about your son?"

"Why wouldn't I?"

"Because it's out of bounds, not done, that's why. The therapist should appear as *tabula rasa*, a blank slate," I said, quoting a prime rule from Practice of Psychotherapy 101. "Revealing personal information is a barrier to effective transference."

"Stonewalling by the patient is a far greater barrier, wouldn't you say?"

"That's hardly a contest I feel qualified to judge, Dr. Groome."

The smile she shot me could liquefy steel. "I can see why Will Creighton is so fond of you, P.J. You're a true original."

"That doesn't sound like much of a recommendation."

Her smile held steady. "Quite the contrary."

"I'm trying."

"You certainly can be. But I think we're going to succeed despite that. I think you want answers even more than you want to run and hide."

I felt suddenly nine years old. "It's possible."

"Good."

"But I don't know if I can find those answers, Dr. Groome. Maybe that takes courage I don't have."

Her gaze glanced off her watch. "Let's pick it up right there tomorrow, P.J. I have an idea."

CHAPTER 23

■ **Back home, I found a giant heap of bad news on my** stoop. "What are you doing here?"

"Sitting. Waiting for you."

"Trespassing's more like it, Rafe."

"I signed up for the office softball team. Couldn't find my lucky mitt. Figured it had to be here."

"It's not exactly softball season."

"No, it's not, but we start practice next week in a cage."

"You in a cage. Imagine that." I caught a whiff of his no-fair cologne; the very one he used to slap on to lure me into one of those extra-friendly, up-all-night moods.

"So I was in the neighborhood and I thought I'd stop by and get the glove."

"Well, you thought wrong. If you want something that happens to be here, the procedure we agreed upon, you, me, and Mike the Mediator, is you call first and make the formal request. Then I decide when and if it's convenient for me to get whatever it is to you. And then you don't ask again, as is covered in paragraph 17-3a of the separation agreement, my favorite, which is the one about how we agree not to molest or annoy each other in any way, shape, or form. Plus, to make the fine point, you had plenty of opportunity to come by and pick up your things when we split."

"If you'll make an exception this once, I promise next time I'll call."

"Why, pray tell, should I do that?"

"Because I really need the glove."

I faced him squarely. "Want to know your problem? One of your problems?"

"What?"

"I'm not nearly as dumb as you think I am, that's what. So happens you don't need a glove to practice in a batting cage."

"That's not why I need it. I have to break it in."

This put me in mind of how he'd slept with his glove under the mattress for most of a month when he first got the blasted thing. He would set a ball in the pocket and bind the whole bulky bundle with rubber bands, and every night before bed he'd lovingly rub it—not me, mind you—with mink oil no less, and then slip it under the mattress where it lay ready to jab me whenever I chanced to move about in my sleep.

"That glove's been broken in plenty, Rafe. As have I."

"Come on, P.J. Let me get my glove, and I'll go."

"The answer is no for three reasons. One: This is my place and you have no business here. Two: I'm tired and not in the mood. And three: I have plans."

"What plans?"

"Not that it's any of your business, but I plan to go inside, whip up a grilled-cheese sandwich, put my feet up, and see if there's anything suitably idiotic to watch on the tube."

"I don't see how that has anything to do with my glove."

"And right you are. So good night, Rafe. Safe home."

"We had a fight, P.J., not a catastrophe. I can't for the life of me understand why you can't let it go."

"It wasn't a *fight*. What we had was a profound, complete, irreconcilable difference in our basic world views. I believe in family loyalty, and you believe in the company line."

"That's not true."

"It's completely true. And who'd have guessed the other woman would turn out to be a big, fat overblown copy of the New York State Penal Code?"

"What we disagreed about was the right thing to do for Jack."

"I know what's right for him, Rafe. He's my brother, not yours."

"You know?" His brow shot up. "Pray tell, exactly what is right for Jack?"

"I have no interest in discussing that with you. The point is you have no right showing up here, expecting me to take you in."

"I don't expect that at all. All I'm asking for is some common courtesy."

"Here it is, then. Would you please, thank you, you're welcome, don't mention it, kindly leave?"

"There's no reason to be so bullheaded when it would take exactly five seconds for me to get the glove and leave."

"There are lots of reasons."

"Name three."

"Damn you, Rafe! Would you quit trying to lawyer me into thinking with your head? It happens to be a nasty, miserable day, and I don't care to catch my death for the dubious privilege of standing out here arguing with you."

"You don't have to. We can argue inside."

"No, we can't."

"What if I told you I have more information about Charlie Booth?"

I glared at him hard as I could, but he refused to be vaporized. "Five minutes, Rafe. By the clock."

He trailed me into the house like an eager stray, and I knew how persistent strays could be if you were dumb enough to give them a lick of hope. I offered him nothing, not even a chair. "You needn't bother taking your coat off, Rafe. You'd just be putting it right on again in four minutes thirty-three seconds."

Naturally, he shed the camel coat, the brown calfskin gloves, the navy sports coat, and the Burberry cashmere muffler, and left them where they dropped.

"Ever hear of a thing called a closet? Brilliant new invention. Works amazingly well."

At that, he scooped up his things and dumped them on my closet floor. "Want me to open a bottle of wine?"

"Sure, Rafe. You do that soon as you get home."

"Not very hospitable, are you?"

"The thing is I don't happen to have any wine at the moment. The architect and design team are in the midst of redoing my cellar, so I've had to send my entire collection of Chateau Hoity Toits and Vintage High Malloys off to storage."

"Not a problem." Leave it to Rafe to pluck a bottle of Dom Pérignon from his briefcase. "I remembered it's your all-time special-occasion favorite," he said.

"No, Rafe. My all-time special-occasion favorite is having my place to myself."

He popped the cork expertly. "Celebrate early and often, I say. Can we use your glasses, or would you rather we drink from the bottle?"

I shrugged, which he took for a cue to help himself. He chose two mismatched goblets from my mongrel assortment and poured the champagne. "To you, P.J." he said.

I stood and watched him drink.

"What?"

"Wanted to be sure you weren't trying to poison or dope me, Rafe. It makes me mighty suspicious to see you acting so blasted thoughtful and sincere."

Now he plucked a wedge of perfectly ripe Camembert from the briefcase, a box of my favorite water crackers, and a package of those sinful cheddar cheese sticks that have the perfect little cayenne sting. "Plate?"

"In the cabinet where they've always been. Now are you ready to tell me what you have to say, or did you come packing the whole surf and turf?"

He spread cheese on a cracker and handed it to me. "Nope. This is it. *Salud!*"

The bubbly charged directly to my brain. "What about Charlie Booth, Rafe? What did you learn?"

"Bad guy," he muttered behind the hand that cloaked his food-stuffed mouth. "Very."

"I thought you said all you found on him was that one sealed juvenile case."

"True, but I asked around, put out the word."

"Asked who?" I sipped more champagne, enjoying the froth of mind.

Rafe raked his hair, dead giveaway that his nerves were doing a jig. "I floated his name by a couple of detectives assigned to the prosecutor's office, and they floated it on the street. Turns out Booth has quite the reputation. He's a tough guy's tough guy, if you know what I mean. The word is if you want to stay healthy, you don't go anywhere near him."

"Is that so?"

"Yes. He's serious trouble."

"Well, thanks for the news flash. I'll keep it in mind." I held out my glass. "And I'll have a touch more of that champagne before you put a cork in it and hit the road."

"You have to take this seriously, P.J. You can't just blow it off."

"No? You hand me anonymous warnings from nameless people who floated things by other nameless people you floated things by, and I'm supposed to hide under the bed? So happens I'm aware that Charlie Booth is not a nice guy. That was spelled out for me clear as day in Jeannie Bagshaw's blood."

He chewed on that and a cheese stick. "Where are you with all that anyway?"

"Floating it by people. And then they float it by other folk and so on. Doing lots of floating. Just like you."

Now he settled in an easy chair with his elbows propped on his knees and his hands folded. "Sit, P.J. At least hear me out."

I checked my watch as I sank in the facing seat. "You've got fifty-eight seconds to go, Rafe. Then your pumpkin turns into pumpkin rot."

"You're making a serious mistake, and I can't just stand by and watch you do it. You can't go after someone just because you want to see him caught. That's not how it's done."

He'd eaten up twenty seconds. "Are you done?"

"No. You have no idea how reckless it is to poke around like you're doing. It isn't the movies. A bumbling amateur doesn't turn into James Bond because she means well."

"Oh, my. And here I was counting on exactly that."

"I think you are, P.J. I think you believe you can wear your good intentions like body armor and not get hurt."

"Five seconds, Rafe."

"People talk. Even people who may be on your side.

Things slip, no matter how innocently, and next thing you know, this Booth guy comes after you."

"I understand the risks, Counselor. Believe it or not I'm smart enough to know that scorpions sting."

"Of course you are. The question is can you keep from getting stung by them?"

"Time's up."

"Come on. At least hear me out."

"Bye now." I collected his things from the closet.

"Goddamn it, P.J. Do you think you're invisible? You think you can go poking around in a murder case and nobody sees? You don't know what the hell you're doing. Not the first god-damned thing!"

He was on the stoop now, standing in the chill rain that had started anew.

"Oh, I see all right, Rafe. I see that you think I'm a puppet, that you have only to pull the strings and I'll dance to your tune. I see you and my sister, the bloody pair of you, sticking your damned noses where they don't belong like you always do and then complaining about the smell. Well, here's a bulletin, Rafe. I don't need your interference, and I'm not going to put up with it. I've had my fill of the pair of you poking around in my affairs, and it's going to stop right here."

"All we want to do is help, P.J. That's all either of us wants."

"Well, I don't want your help. What I want is for you to give it up, Rafe. Get off my case and tell Caity to do the same." I shut the door with a satisfying *thwack* and pressed my back to it. "So happens I'm perfectly capable of floating all I need to on my own."

CHAPTER

24

■ **My next appointment was due to arrive in ten minutes.**
I brewed a strong cup of tea, reviewed my notes, and struggled
to evict Rafe and Caity from my mind. If I could manage the
violent crazies at Rikers, I could certainly handle a simple
pair of overbearing control freaks like them.

I focused on Nina Present's latest referral instead. She had
described Mark and Emily Porter as a delightful young couple, and Emily had sounded perfectly normal when she called
to make the appointment. Still, given the charmers Nina had
sent my way to date, the sound of the doorbell raised a puff of
dread.

Waiting on my stoop, the Porters held hands. They traded
adoring glances and sat close together on the couch. Physi-
cally they were a fine match: both young, trim, and attractive
with dark, wide intelligent eyes.

I took my place opposite them. "What brings you here today?"

They began speaking at once. Then each hastily offered the
floor to the other. Finally they laughed and came to a rapid,
unspoken agreement.

Emily pulled a resolute breath. "We've been thinking of

starting a family. But first we wanted to talk the whole thing through with a professional and make sure we're ready."

Mark nodded. "It's a big decision."

"What are your concerns?"

"So many, it's hard to know where to start."

"Wherever," I said.

Emily eyed her husband anxiously. "Do we stay in the city or move to the suburbs? Does one of us stay home or do we hire a nanny? Can we really afford a child right now?"

"And what will it mean for our relationship?" Mark put in. "We're used to having time alone together, time to do pretty much what we want. A baby will change that."

"He means no sex," Emily explained.

"Well, that's what everyone says."

"So we'll be different."

"That's what everyone says, too."

"But we will be. You'll see."

He smiled and squeezed her hand. "I like the sound of that."

"I'm much more worried about the career thing," Emily said. "Things are going so well right now. I got a promotion last month, and Mark is on track to become a partner soon. Is this really the right time for either of us to pull back?"

The notes I'd taken were rife with question marks. Still, the unwritten one loomed largest by far. How did anyone ever leap to the terrifying, perilous conclusion that they were ready to raise a child? "Which issue would you like to discuss first?"

"Well, we both love the city, so I doubt we'd move," Mark said.

Emily nodded. "And we've pretty much decided that it makes the most sense for me to cut back and work part-time, at least for the first couple of years. My company has been pretty good about that in the past, though there are no guarantees."

He squeezed her hand again. "It's not in stone, honey. We can always decide to go the other way. I love kids. Could be fun to play Mr. Mom."

"I can't see that being necessary, though flexible is good," she said. "And of course a baby will change the way we live, but I think we're ready for that."

"I think so, too," he agreed. "Within reason."

"There will be sex, Mark. You'll see."

"You sound ready," I observed. Though they were both years younger than I was, they were much further along on the game board.

Mark eyed me with reverent hope, as if I held the wisdom of the ages instead of the middleweight screwup championship of the world. "I guess my main problem is fear, plain and simple. Am I really ready to take responsibility for a child?"

Emily pressed his hand. "That makes two of us. I keep thinking it wasn't that long ago that I was a kid myself. What if I turn out to be an incompetent mother? I can imagine forgetting I have a child and leaving the baby in a cart at the supermarket or driving away with the infant seat on the roof of the car."

"And I keep worrying I won't be able to tell when he's hungry or tired or sick. So we're both scared," Mark said. "And maybe for good reason, at least, on my side. Remember what I told you happened with my parakeet, Em?"

"If you leave the window open, the baby is not going to fly away," she teased gently. "And you know when a baby's hungry. I remember from my little brother and sister. They let you know exactly what they need. It's when you drive away with the kid on the roof of the car that things get serious."

Mark shook his head miserably. "But I couldn't even take decent care of a pet bird. After that, my parents wouldn't let me have any pets. First, they said I had to prove I could take care of one of those Japanese toys; the ones that react to how much attention you pay to them, to how well you meet their needs. I managed to kill mine in less than a week, which is quite a feat. This is not a terrific recommendation for parenthood."

"You were a child then yourself," I said. "Children aren't expected to have the means to take care of themselves, much less anyone else." I knew that from excruciating experience. After my parent's death, Jack, Caity, and I had been forced to band together like three spindly twigs left to brace up our whole, unwieldy world. My mother's cousin Fiona, a spinster lady from Ireland, had been dispatched to look after us, but she was an odd mousy soul who sat all day knitting ugly striped scarves and listening to Christian radio, and almost never spoke at all, except to pray. Aunt Fiona coming was like having an ungainly new appliance delivered to the house; one we were leery of and could never quite decipher how to use.

"But who says I have the means now?" Mark said. "Em knows how absentminded I can be. I'm afraid I'm still just the same scatterbrained little kid in a bigger package."

"The kind of love and concern you're both expressing is an excellent indicator," I said.

"But is that really enough? How are we supposed to know what's best for a child, what's right?"

"I believe it's as Emily said. Kids have an inborn talent for letting you know their basic needs. And you figure the rest out together as you go along." I said this with great conviction, as if I was flying by something sounder than the seat of my pants.

She smiled. "I like the sound of that."

"So do I," he agreed. "Maybe it's not completely crazy to think we can do this."

"No," I said, flashing on all the billions of souls there had been in the world, the overwhelming majority reared by parents who never gave their fitness—or lack of same—a passing thought. "I don't think it's crazy at all."

They traded the sort of adoring glance that made me understand how Moses must have felt gazing from an impossible distance at the land that was promised, though not to him.

"Thanks so much. This means more than you can imagine," Emily said. "If it's possible, we'd like to come back and see you from time to time, make sure we stay on track."

"Of course. Call whenever you like and we'll set it up. And great good luck to you."

Now, that was what the textbooks called a positive, productive exchange. The wistful grin hung on my face until the phone rang, and the operator informed me that Big Millie was calling yet again.

■ **"That's it, P.J. I'm telling you, that's the straw that** broke the whole Campbell's soup!"

"What, Millie?"

"You ever hear shit like that shit, or what?"

"Like what?"

"'Bout Jeannie's husband, that's what. Talking 'bout how that sumbitch Booth had hisself the unlitigated gall bladder to sneak onto the unit and right on up to my cell while I was at supper and leave me—guess what."

"What?"

"No, you gotta do the whole three guesses."

"Is this really necessary?"

"Three guesses is the way the game gets played. Now, go on and get guessing."

"All right. I'll guess he left a message, a cupcake, or a book."

"Wrong, wrong, and double wrong. Want a bonus guess? 'Cause I'm not trying to be no hard-fast stripe bass here. No one gonna 'cuse me of being hard-fast or tough-assed or no coal-hearted shit like that."

"No, thanks, Millie. I'm all guessed out."

"All right, then. Sumbitch left me a big, old, whiskery, blind-eyed, starting-to-stink dead rat."

"How do you know it was Booth?"

"'Cause I wasn't at supper neither, that's how. I was supposed to be; it was time and everything. But you know how once in a wild Tyree and me gets to playing poker down in the day room?"

"Yes, Millie. And you know gambling isn't allowed. Last time both of you wound up doing fifteen days in the Bing. Left you crawling the walls, remember?"

"Do I never. So we're real careful and we allows ourselves just the fewest, itty wittiest little hands of Texas Hold-em and next thing, I'm knowing it's got to be suppertime 'cause my stomach's carrying on something wild, grinding all up on itself and sounding like the little engine that could fart itself silly. So I go back to my place to get us some peanut butter crackers and corn nuts and beef jerky and cans of Sprite and all, and damned if I don't see that sumbitch Booth, sneaking off like a big old rat hisself."

"Did you talk to him?"

"Nope. But I 'spressed my feelings, like you always said I should. I was feeling real poorly inside, mad and angry and pissed off and starving hungry and all, so I went and let those nasty 'spression suckers out for air."

I cringed. "How badly did you hurt him, Millie?"

"Didn't hurt the man one eye odor. I just held him all gentle like a baby until he did like I tole him and swallowed down that rat."

"Whole?"

"You betchy. Cut up in pieces cost more."

"Good Lord."

"Don't you worry. Man's fine as wine, P.J. Chokey Dokey."

"Listen to me, Millie. Please. Chances are that was your imagination playing tricks. You mustn't hurt anyone, no matter who it is or what you think you see. When I said to express your feelings, I meant in words. Something happens, you report it. You talk about it with a therapist. Do you understand me?"

"Oh, I understand all right. You're one of those passy fits thinks it's wrong to kill a flea, fill a tree, or trill a G. Never thought you was that kind, P.J. Never imagined you as one of them tree-smacking paddy-whackers. But there you all lovey dovey no shovey are."

"You could get in serious trouble, Millie. You know that. You could wind up in the Bing for a year."

"What I know is that sumbitch Booth gone and killed himself an innocent rat was just twitching around, minding its ratty old business, and the Good Book says the man got to eat what he slews. A tooth for a Booth, Reverend Herbert always said. Ain't that so?"

"You're fixated on Charlie Booth, Millie. That's a setup for you to have delusions about him."

"I ain't having no such thing. And don't you dare go round laundering my sorry ass."

"You haven't been taking your meds, Millie. Have you?"

"Taking them where?"

"I'm serious."

"Nothing to be seery-assed 'bout, P.J. I line up for my meds every morning, first thing and again after supper."

"But do you take them? Do you swallow them down?"

There was a scuffle in the background, someone wanting to use the phone. I heard a crash followed by a pained, piercing shriek.

"Millie!"

"It's cool. That girl's gonna wait real patient-like, now I showed her what's what. You waiting real extra special patient, ain't you, bitch?"

"I want you to stop. Right now!"

"Already did. You should see how patient that girl got. She so patient, she can't hardly move."

"Listen to me, Millie. You're out of control. I need you to promise to take your meds and make an appointment to see one of the therapists."

"Right O'Roonio. I'll come on up and see you tomorrow soon as I get through with my part on *Days of Their Lives.* They paying me real fine to play Madame Puree, tell you that."

"It won't be me, Millie. I told you I'm not working there anymore."

"Why not? Someone mess with you? You tell me someone

messed with you, I'm gonna feed them way worse than a big, ole hole-in-one rat."

"It's not important. All that matters is for you to get the help you need. Mary Schoen and Chris Vacchio are both excellent. Why don't you arrange to see one of them? Ask Nancy at the desk. She'll set it up for you."

"You ain't listened to one word I said, have you, P.J.? I can't believe you'd take that rat-leaving sumbitch's part over mine."

"I'm not taking anyone's part. I'm asking you to take your meds and see a therapist, that's all. Things are going to look entirely different to you after that."

Big Millie covered the phone, and I caught the muffled clash of angry voices. A long minute passed before the line came clear again. "You trying to tell me you hungry for a rat sandwich, bitch? You just itching to taste my special rat tail mashed potatoes with a side of twitch, ain't you now?"

Millie was huffing hard. "Sorry, P.J. Now where was we?"

"We were talking about getting you back on meds and straightened out. Otherwise, it's going to be a very, very long time before you get released."

"I'm already straight as a gate. And I'm telling you just what-all happened, the real deal. Charlie Sumbitch Booth gave me a big old dead rat, and I gave it right back. It's like the Good Book says: Someone spites you, burn the other cheek."

"Hear me, Millie. You need to take your meds and see someone. We can talk in a few days and see how you're feeling then."

"Few days won't make no damned difference. I seen what I seen, and I can prove that sucker."

"How can you prove it?"

"You come here, bring your eyes, and you'll see."

"I can't do that."

"You can't come to jail? Day-um, P.J. You musta thrown some way foul ball!"

"I'm busy with a new job. That's all."

"Well, I'll show you how I'm gonna prove that sucker anyhow. In fact, I'm putting how right in an envy lope soon's we get off the phone. I'm wrapping how up and sticking a chicken licking stamp on that sucker and sending it your way."

■ **I awoke to the sound of the phone bleating, Lottie Dray** calling to report that Booth had paid an unexpected visit the night before.

"Said he wanted to see Dennis John, but it was past ten and the boy was long asleep. Charlie was drunk, even worse than usual. Staggering and slurring so I could barely tell what he was trying to say. I asked him to leave. Stood in the doorway to block him. But he pushed his way in like I didn't exist."

"Are you okay?"

"Got a little bumped is all. Trouble is I couldn't keep him out."

Cold fear gripped me. "Is Dennis John all right?"

She blew a breath. "Charlie went right to the bedroom and took the boy up out of bed. Held him so tight; Dennis John woke up in a panic. He started struggling in Booth's arms, trying to get loose. But the more he fought, the harder Charlie squeezed. It was like he wanted to suffocate the boy, like he wanted to crush his little bones. I kept begging him to stop, screaming 'Please, Charlie. Leave him alone!' But it was like he didn't even hear me. Man was so crazy mad, the pulse at his temple looked ripe to burst. So I prayed, P.J. God help me,

I prayed Booth would have a stroke right then and there and drop dead."

The scene came too vividly to mind: The little boy trapped and terrified; Lottie using what meager strength remained to try and help him. "Is he all right, Lottie? Please tell me, is Dennis John all right?"

"Yes," she breathed in a sharp, shallow rasp. "I went to the kitchen and got Charlie a beer. Lucky thing I had one in the fridge. I held it out to him. You must be thirsty, Charlie, I said. And thank God that turned the man's mind. He dumped Dennis John on the couch, downed the beer like he was dying of thirst, tossed the can, and left. Took off like he'd forgotten why he came in the first place, like it was all a bad dream."

"Thank goodness."

"Way I see it, Dennis John's got someone looking after him, and that someone was guiding my hand," she said. "At least, this time."

"All that matters is you're both okay."

"We are, P.J. Only—"

"What?"

"The thing is, Dennis John was so upset afterward, I had a terrible time getting him back to sleep. So finally I said he should make a wish, and whatever it was I'd do my very best to see it come true."

"What did he wish for?"

"That's the thing of it, P.J. He wished you'd come and play."

My daily trek to Dr. Groome's office normally took about forty-five minutes, door-to-door. But nothing was normal about today. My route to the subway was blocked by a mammoth water-main break. A squalling tangle of emergency vehicles blocked the streets, and the horde of gawking onlookers made it nearly impossible to move. Once I managed to skirt the mess and reach the station, the train took forever to come. I stared down the rails at the dingy tunnel, waiting for a ray of hopeful light. When at last it came, the car I entered was clean and had several vacant seats. That should have been more than enough to arouse my suspicions, but no. I sat back, folded the paper into a neat, manageable rectangle, and prepared to enjoy the daily bounty of wretched news.

The train pulled out and rocked in lurching percussion against the rails. Drums of spark-spitting steel set the clattering backbeat for all the lurid tales of intrigue, pestilence, greed, malfeasance, natural and economic disaster, betrayal, and that all-time popular favorite: violent death. A banner headline declared that the country's murder rate had edged up again after more than a decade of steady decline. I mused about a connection between this global trend and the recent increase of stabbings and slashings among Rikers inmates I'd learned about from Dr. Creighton. The article's first few paragraphs detailed the who, where, what, and how of the rise in homicides. For speculation about the why, I would have to turn to the jump on page A27. As I did so, folding with care to keep the rotten news from slopping over onto the old man on my right or the girl on my left, the train went dark and screeched to a wrenching stop.

Subway cars stall all the time, and most often it's a brief, annoying tease. Seasoned riders learn to ignore these common lapses. Soon enough the engines roar to life again, the lights blaze on, and you're rolling. But this time the dark silence held until it was pierced by a slim, reedy shrill.

At first I took the sound for a recorder or some other amateurishly played horn, a no-talent Samaritan trying to entertain us during the outage. But it soon gained force and built to a piercing scream. Next came wild, desperate thrashing on my left. My paper was wrenched and propelled across the car in a wild crackling burst. I was shoved hard and then pummeled with a flurry of knob-edged thwacks. Head—hip. A breath-stealing jab to the ribs. A kick connected with my shin, shooting a fiery bolt of pain.

I raised my hands in defense. "Stop!"

The scream dimmed to a spare, breathy plaint. "Please help me. Please. I'm so scared!"

"Shhh. It's okay."

"Turn the lights on. Please."

"Easy," I urged. "Take a breath."

"Let me out of here!"

"It's okay," I soothed. "You're okay. Nothing's going to hurt you."

The words rode a sugary sigh. "It's too dark," she moaned. "I can't stand it."

"You can. It's all right. Just breathe."

"Make it stop now!"

"Soon. Try to calm down."

"But I can't do this. Don't you see?" I could sense the seismic groundswell as her terror built again. "You have to make it stop!"

"Look. They've come to help."

A pair of transit cops had muscled in at the end of the car, brandishing torch lamps. "Everyone all right here?"

By the wavering flash beams, I studied the girl. She looked about sixteen; a spindly waif with spiked hair bleached to the yellow-white of mayonnaise and ears rimmed by a thicket of cheap silver rings. Her face looked drawn and oily as if she hadn't been properly fed or washed for a very long time, and her bony chest worked like a piston beneath a worn denim jacket. Dipping stiffly, she scooped up her things: a bulging, camouflage-colored backpack, a thick green woolen poncho, and a bald baby doll with one vacant eye socket and a fractured skull.

The cops trailed through the car. "You all right, ma'am? You, sir?"

The girl clutched my arm. "I'm sorry. Don't say anything. Please."

As the first of the cops approached us, the engine quaked and came alive. Overhead, the lights blinked on, and the train lurched forward, clacking sharply along the rails.

"You ladies all right?"

"Yes," I said. "Fine."

"Someone pulled the alarm," the cop said. "You?"

"No. Wasn't me."

"Sure you're okay?" he asked the girl.

"Positive."

At the next stop she scurried out, and I trailed close behind. "Wait!"

Angrily she stopped and wheeled to face me. "I said I'm sorry. Now back off!"

"Are you doing anything? Taking care of it?"

"Of what?"

"Fear of the dark is a phobia. A very common one. And not hard to cure. There are specialists, clinics."

She smirked. "Yeah, sure. Specialists."

By the bold light of the station, I noticed the black electrical tape that bound the soles of her sneakers. Her clothes were soiled and tattered. The backpack bulged with what I took to be her worldly possessions. Shrugging into it, she started off again at a determined clip.

I followed awkwardly, slowed by soreness in the places she'd thwacked. "Wait! Did you run away? Are you alone?"

The girl kept walking. "What's it to you?"

"I'm just asking."

"You a cop or something? A narc?"

"Nothing like that. You just look like you could use a little help."

Stopping again, she faced me with a cold, jut-jawed glare. "What are you, then, a perv? A chicken hawk?"

"Of course not."

"I didn't ask for your goddamned help, lady. Don't want it, don't need it. Buzz off!"

"I can put you in touch with a clinic. You wouldn't have to pay."

"I said, leave me alone!" She held the doll by a foot and whipped it at me. The plastic fingers grazed my arm and tore the sleeve of my peacoat. A passing stranger, a ferret-faced guy with a buzz cut and pointed jaw, caught her arm and held it so she couldn't swing again.

"That's enough," he ordered the girl.

"Get your hands off me!" she shrieked.

"Leave her alone," I said. "It's okay."

"Go. I'll take care of this."

Before I could protest, he marched her toward the exit and turned her loose. He had the look of someone who took such things in stride. An off-duty cop, I thought. Or a plainclothes detective.

The girl shot me the bird, and then charged toward the nearest stairway. My self-appointed rescuer took off in the opposite direction without a backward glance. I was left standing there with my mouth agape, eyeing the ruined sleeve of my jacket and rubbing the soreness on my arm. I wondered how many good intentions it took in total to pave the road to Hell. And I mused about how many of those pavers were my own.

CHAPTER 27

■ **I was fifteen minutes late for my appointment with Dr. Groome.** Overnight, she'd transformed her office. A pair of shoji screens defined a cozy square at the center of the room. Within the rice-paper cocoon, an Oriental carpet in soothing earth tones was capped by a plump, bronze-studded brown leather couch. Dr. Groome perched on a high-backed leather chair beside the couch. She wore a flowing skirt over her standard leotard.

"What's all this?"

"It's for you, P.J. Something different. Please lie down."

"You're joking."

"No. I'm not."

"It's been a tough morning, Dr. Groome. The last thing I need right now are more of your games."

"It's no game," she said. "Yesterday, when we talked, I remembered something I learned from the wisest teacher I ever had. His name was Martin Ruhlmann. Ever hear of him?"

"Founder of the Ruhlmann Institute?"

"Yes. Remarkable man. And so approachable. Students were always welcome to come to him with questions, even at home. As long as his porch light was on, you could wander in, talk awhile, and clear up whatever was on your mind."

"Nice."

"Indeed. One night I was studying for finals in the graduate library. I was memorizing comparative details about the major schools of thought in the field, poring over a giant stack of books and notes, and it occurred to me that I had one big fat central question Ruhlmann might be able to answer. So I went to his house, and sure enough the porch light was on. He invited me into his study, and I explained what was bothering me. There were all these different, often opposing philosophies, and each of them was backed up by complex logic, convincing studies, and typically a pretty impressive body of work. But which was the best approach for patients, I wanted to know. How on earth did clinicians make the choice?"

"That's the $64,000 question."

"True. I expected him to give me a long, rambling, equivocal response. But in fact, Ruhlmann surprised me. He had the answer right at his fingertips. And as usual, he was completely correct."

"What was it?"

She smiled. "He said the best approach for any given patient was the one that worked. Simple as that."

"That's pretty obvious."

"The most brilliant observations always are."

"So suddenly you've decided to play Freudian analyst?"

"Not at all. I've decided to try something specific that Freud and many others have used: trance induction."

I backed away until I bumped the screen and it wavered behind me. "Hypnosis? I don't think so."

"Why not?"

"It's creepy, that's why not. It's like having you crack my skull open and go mucking around in my brain."

"It's perfectly safe, P.J."

"In the right hands for the right reasons. And on the right subject, which happens to not be me."

"You can rest assured I've trained extensively. And I've seen excellent results with clients even more resistant than you."

That brought a scowl. "More resistant, is it? And here I thought I was the undisputed champ."

"It'll be painless. I promise."

"I don't like the idea, Dr. Groome. Bunch of hocus-pocus, if you ask me."

"It's simply another means to access the subconscious. A different door in, if you will. You can't be made to do or reveal anything unless you wish to, as I'm sure you well know."

"No? Then what do you call sensible folk making chicken noises? Holding their arm up like a statue's for hours?"

"Those are parlor tricks, entertainment, and not therapeutic hypnosis at all. I don't have to tell you that."

"Doesn't matter. I don't like the sound of it. Not one bit."

"Then you can elect not to use it in your practice."

"I can also elect not to participate here."

She doffed her half glasses and pinched the bridge of her nose. "Let's be clear, P.J. I'm asking you to cooperate."

We traded weighty frowns. "Actually, what you're doing is telling me I have no choice."

"If you prefer to put it that way, fine. I'm telling you this is how I wish to proceed. And I'd like to get to it without further delay."

My hand grazed the seat of the couch. The leather had a cool, reptilian feel that somehow evoked an image of Charlie Booth, veins bulging over knobs of sinew as he all but squeezed the life out of Dennis John.

"What do I have to do?"

"Settle back, close your eyes, and focus on the sound of my voice."

Instead, I clung fast to the lifeline she'd tossed me earlier. I could not be made to do or say anything against my will. That included going under some bloody spell.

"You hear nothing but my words," she said in a soothing lilt. "Listen."

Her warm honeyed voice had the proven power to sweep me away, and so I clung to the kind of thoughts that were guaranteed to keep me grounded. I fixed on the dark things, the fevered worries that jolted me awake in the dark of night. I thought of Booth, Aunt Lottie, and Dennis John. I thought of my lack of a job and the gaping void that left in my future. I thought of being alone, playing the odd unmatched sock in a world full of neatly rolled pairs. I considered the possibility that I might stay that way for good. I imagined coming to the end alone, having no one to help ease me out the door. As if that barge of standard worries wasn't enough, this coming Friday was my brother Jack's birthday, his thirty-fifth, and that was always a prime occasion for him to show up.

Poor Jack, I thought, and, as my nickname so aptly noted, Poor Julia. Somehow, Caity was able to deal with our brother at a sensible emotional remove. My way was to dive into his murky waters headfirst, even though I could see the horrors waiting, even though I was all too familiar with the pain of the sharp, looming rocks.

My thoughts swerved to my mother and the small, white pills she used to shake from an amber bottle when she thought no one would see. Somehow, I'd known to hide in the dim hallway until she replaced the vial behind the flour tin where she kept her mother's wedding ring, her father's gold watch fob, and the bit of cash she liked to call her mad money. Once when I was alone, I'd climbed on the counter and taken the bottle down and tried to divine her secret, but the label had been removed. And so I had dared to experiment and swallowed one of those pills myself. The effects had hit me instantly: acute remorse, crushing guilt, and fear so fierce it tore away my breath. Caity had found me crumpled on the kitchen floor, not my mother, thank the Lord, and nursed me in her way. She'd helped me to our room, brought me tea and biscuits, and then sweetly laid out all the things I'd have to do to keep her from spilling my beans.

Suddenly a dark green pickup bumped into view. It sped across the dusty road, raising a fog of grit. Charlie Booth hunched high in the cab, nearly lost in a swirl of blue smoke. And there was Blake Madigan slumped in the blood-slicked cargo bed, surrounded by trash bags plumped with the bodies of dead infant boys. As they careened through the quiet lanes of Ste. Cat's cemetery, past my parents' pristine graves, Madigan tossed the bags out, one by one. One struck my mother's headstone with a hollow *thud*. Another landed with a dull *thwack* at the foot of the grassy mound that marked my father. Madigan counted backward as he threw. "Ten . . . nine . . ."

"Three . . . two . . . one." There was a bone snap followed

by Dr. Groome's voice. "You're wide awake now, P.J. Alert and refreshed. Open your eyes."

I found her sitting beside me, looking far too pleased. "I'd say that was an excellent start, P.J."

"Come now, Dr. Groome. Don't tell me you're so easily fooled. I wasn't under, you know. Not really."

"Is that so?"

"It is. I was just lying here, it so happens, thinking about the most mundane things."

"Such as?"

"So routine, they're barely worth the mention. A friend's birthday coming up. An illness I had as a child. Dealing with the trash."

"You certainly had me fooled."

"Did I now?" I dearly hoped she'd take the flush of the lie for a glow of self-congratulation.

"That's fine, P.J. Tomorrow we'll try again. I'll pretend to hypnotize you, and you can pretend as hard as you like that it doesn't work."

CHAPTER

28

■ **As I entered the grim lobby, I was surprised to find** Lottie waiting on the couch. Dennis John, sporting a precious look of mock fury, was reveling in one of those orgies of mindless violence boys of all ages so enjoy. From his bunker behind a stained, shackled chair, he fired off round after blistering round, pausing after each lethal strike to imitate a small, flame-haired, freckle-faced explosion.

"Wham! Kerpow! Gotcha!"

His aunt sat clutching her purse like a lifeline.

"Lottie? What's wrong?"

"Oh, it's nothing," she said, with a pointed nod toward the child. "Feeling a little under the weather is all. Could be a cold coming on."

"Anything I can do?"

"There is, actually. Doc said he'd fit me in, so I hate to ask, but could you maybe look after Dennis John for a bit?"

"Of course. We can take you to the doctor and wait for you there."

"Best not. This doctor has a special office for grown-ups only. Lots of hands-off things, so no children allowed." She winked. The evasion would be our little secret.

"Anyway, that nice Emma Wolcott, the lady from Children's Services I told you about, is going to drive me. Should be here any time."

A black Ford soon pulled up outside and Ms. Wolcott emerged. She sported a silver suit and gray pumps and projected an air of sturdy calm. I walked Lottie out to the car and gave her my cell number.

I returned to the building as Dennis John reared back to lob an invisible grenade. He cringed through the imagined explosion that followed, and then peered up at me.

"So what do you want to do?"

"Why don't you choose?"

He scrabbled to his feet, whipped out his arm rifle, and blasted an unseen enemy with a long, jolting, automatic round. "That's it. Everybody's dead!"

"How comforting."

His face scrunched with concentration. "Wanna play—?"

"What?"

"I know. We can play Captain Hook. You be the pirate ship and I'll be the brave guy who rescues the treasure—okay?"

"The pirate ship, sure."

"You have to be really, really quiet and really, really scary," he directed. "And you need to have a great big trunk full of buried treasure and a scary pirate flag with bones on it and a parrot that talks."

"Quiet, scary, treasure trunk, flag, and talking bird. Got it."

"And you have to say yo ho ho."

"How can I say anything if I have to be really, really quiet?"

He shrugged. This clearly fell in the category of my problem.

"Okay, then. I think I'll be the kind of pirate ship that takes a little boy onboard and carries him off in search of an ice-cream cone."

His eyes narrowed. "You sure pirates eat ice cream?"

"Sensible pirates would."

"Parrots, too?"

"I'll have to look that up."

He tugged my sleeve. "You forgot to say yo ho ho."

"Sorry. Yo ho ho, and I'll have to look that up."

I would also have to listen intently and be prepared to answer all manner of impossible questions. Everything we passed on our walk aroused the child's ravenous curiosity. Wasn't a church God's house, and if it was, why did God need so many houses? How come they called it Tuesday? What were pigeons saying when they cooed? And why didn't that man have a potty at home, so he wouldn't have to tinkle in the street?

"I don't know."

"But doesn't tinkling on the street like that make his pee-pee cold?"

"Another bit I'll have to research, Dennis John."

His face fell. "Why did God send his chariot for my mommy?"

"I don't know, sweetheart."

"Aunt Lottie says God knows best."

"As does your aunt Lottie. Now it's my turn to ask a question. Are you a chocolate man or vanilla?"

"Yes," he said with an emphatic nod.

"Which?"

"Chocolate man and vanilla man."

"Both? Sure you have the room?"

He lifted his shirt to show off his ice-cream storage tank. A hollowed hammock over the bone sling it was, but he believed.

"I see."

When it came to ice cream, the child was most decisive indeed. The cone would have two scoops; it would wear a maraschino cherry hat and a heavy coat of chocolate sprinkles. Dennis John watched with unblinking solemnity as the chubby, acne-pocked boy behind the counter filled his request.

To be sociable, I ordered the same, and we perched on tall stools at the narrow counter that faced the main road. There, Dennis John continued his inquisition between sweeping licks. "How come that lady walks funny? Why is she having a baby? Can cats sing? Why can't cats sing? Does the train always have to be so loud?"

"How come you ask so many questions?"

"Are questions bad?"

"Definitely not. Questions are an excellent way to learn."

"How come?"

"Because then you get answers to the things you don't understand."

"Do lions ask questions?"

"Perhaps in their way."

"Do frogs?"

"I suppose, if they're sufficiently curious."

"What questions would a cow ask?"

"I don't know, but you know what an owl asks?"

"What?"

"Who?"

He giggled at the dopey joke, and I felt unduly pleased.

"Whose Mommy are you?"

"Nobody's."

"How come?"

"Because I don't have any kids."

"Why don't you?"

"Because. Your ice cream's dripping, sir. Best get to it."

For a while he licked in blessed silence, but that was soon broken by a chirped summons from my phone. "Must be your aunt Lottie."

It was Emma Wolcott in fact. She told me Lottie was in talking with the doctor, and she'd call again to let me know when they were headed home.

I held a smile for Dennis John's benefit. "Everything OK?" I asked her.

"As OK as it can be," she said.

By the time I flipped the phone shut, Dennis John was tugging my sleeve to recapture my lapsed attention.

"Sorry, sweetie. I'm off now."

His eyes brimmed with tears. "Look."

His ice cream lay spreading on the floor, a murky, sprinkle-dotted ooze. "It was an accident. I didn't mean it. Don't be mad."

"I'm not, sweetheart. Not at all."

His eyes sparked with terror. "Don't hurt me, please!"

"Of course I won't. Never. I'll get you another cone. No harm done at all."

As I stood to do that, my gaze strayed across the street,

where a dark green Toyota Tacoma pickup was angling toward the curb. Once in the space it idled, belching plumes of exhaust. Then the door flew open, and Booth stepped out.

Hot fear infused me. "Let's go, Dennis John."

"But my ice cream."

"Not now. Hurry!"

"But you said we could get a new one. You promised."

"We'll get one later. Right now we have important pirate business to do. You understand?"

"No."

"We have to get away fast, before the bad guys come and steal the treasure."

"The bad guys are coming?"

"That's right."

He gripped my hand. "Hurry, P.J. Run!"

I held fast and raced outside. The light had yet to change. Broad lanes of whipping traffic separated us from Booth. But any second that would change.

I clung to the shadows cast by storefront awnings and the cover of milling passersby. I kept peering over my shoulder. The green light flared, and Booth started across the street. He flicked off the spent butt of his cigarette and lit another, cupping the flame as it dipped and quivered in the wind.

Dennis John hung back, dragging his feet. "I'm tired of playing pirates. I want another ice cream like you said."

"We'll get one in a little while, sweetheart. But first we have to find a good place for brave rescuers and pirate ships to hide."

"Do we have to?"

"We do. For just a little while."

"I know. Here." He broke loose and dashed toward a slim door tucked between the tidy produce displays at a greengrocer and the neighboring tailor shop.

Glancing back again, I saw no sign of Booth. But that only increased my apprehension. My skin crawled with the sense of him angling closer, honing in.

"Wait," I urged. "The bad guys are too close. We should get farther away."

Heedless, he ran inside. Trailing as fast as I could, I entered a long, dim hall.

"Dennis John?"

My voice echoed eerily. The child was nowhere in sight. I jiggled the knob on the first door I came to, but it was locked. Poised on tiptoe, I peered through the high, murky transom.

Nothing.

I hurried to the next door, pounded uselessly and battled the unyielding lock. The bristling silence slipped beneath my skin.

People disappeared, especially kids. How many times had I heard such hair-raising stories on the news? The victims were there one minute, gone the next. Sometimes their bones turned up later in a shallow grave or washed up bleached and laundered by the tides. Sometimes, perhaps years later, someone confessed. But sometimes the mystery remained.

"Hey? Where are you?"

Still nothing. My thoughts raced in frenzied circles. There was Booth closing in, somehow catching my scent, while the Earth gaped to swallow Dennis John.

"Please, sweetie, please! Don't do this. Say something. Come out from where you're hiding."

There was a thump followed by an odd sighing sound and low, rhythmic tapping like an impatient foot. I trailed the sounds to a room at the end of the hall. Peering inside through the small glass panel in the door, I saw a large, gaily-decorated space. Dennis John was in the company of six other little ones. They were supervised by a young man in red gym shorts and a white T-shirt with a whistle around his neck. He had the broad, slightly demented grin of someone who had passed a dangerous excess of time chanting ditties to little kids. A bright banner tacked to the wall read: *Cubby's Music Club*.

Three of the children played with a candy-striped parachute. They lofted the bright, silken fabric and ducked beneath, chortling in delight as it drifted down to envelop them. Dennis John and two others marched about to the beat of a lively CD, wielding old-fashioned rhythm instruments. Yet another little boy hung by his knees from a low-slung parallel bar like a gap-toothed bat.

I crossed the room and crouched beside Dennis John. "You mustn't take off like that, sweetheart. You scared me."

"But you wanted to hide, so I came in here to music club."

He clashed his cymbals to punctuate the point. "Cubby's club-bers can drop in any time."

"We have to go," I said.

"But I don't want to."

"Now, Dennis John." I kept glancing nervously at the door. "You'll come back another time."

"I want to stay! It's my turn after Billy on the bar!"

I tried to pry the cymbals from his grasp.

"No!" he screeched. "Get off me."

The teacher came up beside us, still grinning. "What's up, Denny boy? Who's your friend?"

The child now lashed out angrily with the cymbals. Cubby caught his hands and gently disarmed him. "Easy, Chief. People are not for hitting, remember?"

"But I don't want to go yet, Cubby. She can't make me."

"Who's your friend," the teacher asked again.

"She's P.J., a big pajama head. And I'm not going."

Cubby turned to me, still holding the smile. "You know Denny how?"

"I'm a friend of his aunt Lottie's. She had a doctor's appointment, so she asked me to watch Dennis John." My eyes swerved to the door again. "And we really have to go."

"She's a friend of your aunt Lottie? Aunt Lottie left her in charge of you? That true, Slugger?"

"Yes, but I want to play more instruments. I want to hang from the bar."

"We have to go, Dennis John. It's time."

"NO!"

Cubby beckoned me aside and whispered, "Give me two minutes. I'll get the other little clubbers to sing the goodbye song to Denny, and he'll be good to go."

"Is there a back way out?"

"Through the fire door."

"Is there some place on that street I can get him an ice cream?"

"Market on the corner."

"You're a lifesaver, Cubby," I told him. "That's the fact."

CHAPTER

29

■ **A hulking guard hunched on a folding chair with his** back to Albert Dunston's door. He had a sloped simian brow, a neck wider than his head, and overblown muscles that strained the seams of his khaki uniform. From inside the room, I caught the drone of a news radio broadcast over the dissonant bleat of monitors and drips.

I showed my pass.

"Sorry. No visitors."

"Mr. Dunston is expecting me."

"Nobody here by that name," he said sharply.

"Mr. Waite, I mean. He's expecting me. You can ask him."

"No visitors. No exceptions."

That brought the roar of Dunston's wrath. "She's my guest. You are to let her in this instant!"

The guard went sheepish. He leaned toward the door and spoke in a low, soothing hush. "Sorry, Mr. Waite. You know the drill, sir. No can do."

"Don't give me that. I invited her here and you're to admit her without further delay."

"I don't make the rules, sir."

"Then run along and get whoever does."

"Can't do that, sir. Sorry."

"You're going to be." There was a loud grunt followed by a harsh metallic crash.

The guard's square jaw twitched. "You OK in there, Mr. Waite?"

No answer.

"Mr. Waite?"

The silence held. The guard bolted out of his chair and burst into the room. Dunston sat at the side of the bed, pale legs dangling below the flimsy skirt of his hospital gown. He had hurled his entire dinner tray across the room: a graphic ode to rage rendered in meatloaf, mashed potatoes, and grass-colored Jell-O flecked with fruit.

The effort had left him limp. His grin flickered like a dying bulb. "I'd say that's a pretty good arm for an old wreck, wouldn't you?"

I shot him a big thumbs-up. "You definitely burned it in there, sir."

"Most fun I've had in days. Come in, P.J. Sit. We have lots to discuss."

"No, you don't." The guard gripped my elbow, whirled me around, and steered me into the hall. "You heard me. No visitors."

He shut the door firmly behind him; righted the chair he had toppled in his haste, and resumed his post. "You know the way out, lady. Use it."

"Let her in, you big galoot!" Dunston shouted. "I'm warning you."

"Better take it easy, sir. Docs want you to rest. Don't want to hurt yourself."

"Is that so? Watch me."

Suddenly both the radio and his monitors went still. Their absence echoed like the thrumming aftermath of a blast. The expectant silence held for a beat, and then the alarms began to shrill in strident cacophony. An urgent voice boomed over the paging system. "Code blue! Fourteen-ten,Walter. Code blue!"

A young man, lab coat tails flying over sea-blue scrubs, raced toward Dunston's room. Two other doctors soon followed. Yet another pair burst from the elevator, wheeling a crash cart that limped and simpered on a wonky wheel.

Nurses appeared, as did a somber gray-haired man in a fine silver suit who had Big Cheese written all over him. His stride was weighted with grim resolve, his craggy face tight with irritation.

The lot of them formed a human barricade around Dunston's bed, so I couldn't see what was going on. But soon enough, his irate voice broke through. "I will not be told whom I can and cannot see. You read me, Dr. Parkman? Have I made that clear?"

The man in the suit backed off a step, affording me a meager peek. He tamped the air. "Be reasonable, Mr. Dunston. We're only trying to keep you safe and secure."

"You let that young lady in or I'll take my leave and visit with her elsewhere. Your choice."

I witnessed the silent negotiation that ensued: hard dipped brows; cocked heads; the skyward twirl of exasperated eyes.

Parkman gestured for the others to leave. The nurses peeled away first, and then two of the doctors walked out pushing the crippled crash cart. A young woman in a white coat reconnected Dunston's monitors, checked his vital signs, and then awaited a confirmatory nod from Parkman before she trailed the others into the hall.

Parkman scowled. "I can't have you causing such commotions, Mr. Dunston. This must stop immediately."

"I agree, Dr. Parkman. I've been a naughty, naughty boy, and I think you should demand that I leave."

"I'm not suggesting that at all, I'm asking you to be reasonable. This is a hospital. Many of our patients are seriously ill."

"Really? What with Rambo out there and all these gulag-quality restrictions, I naturally assumed it was a jail."

"We're only doing what we've been instructed to do by the police. Apparently, there are others you've interviewed and written about who might choose to harm you. The authorities are concerned about the potential for further assaults and very anxious to do whatever is required to prevent them."

"Is that so?"

"Yes, Mr. Dunston. And so are we. As a patient, you're entrusted to our care. And we take that trust very, very seriously."

"So all this hullabaloo is about preventing further assaults?"

"Exactly."

Dunston presented me with a dramatic sweep of his hand. "And does she strike you as someone who might assault me, Doctor? In your expert, professional opinion, is she one of those *others* I've interviewed and written about that the police are so very concerned about and anxious to keep away?"

"Well, no. Of course not."

"Of course not," Dunston repeated with a resolute dip of his chin. "In fact, this charming young woman happens to be my daughter. The only attempted assault she's ever made is on my wallet, and I can assure you I'm more than capable of rising to my own defense in that regard."

"Your daughter?"

"Daddy's little girl. Yes. Apple of my eye. We call her P.J."

Frowning, Parkman checked the patient notes that hung in a file at the foot of the bed. "According to this, you don't have any children, Mr. Dunston."

Dunston sighed. "Don't you think I'm aware of whether I have offspring or not, Dr. Parkman?"

"I would imagine."

"You're missing the point. This has nothing to do with whether I have five heirs or none."

"What does it have to do with?"

"With trying to make things easier for you."

"Sorry. I don't understand."

"Why don't we say this is the daughter that happens to have been omitted from my chart by mistake, the one you learned about, and, of course, concluded was a reasonable exception to the no-visitors rule? Close family always merits an exemption, as do attorneys, so if you like, feel free to explain that my daughter happens to be my legal counsel as well. You're also welcome to describe her as my spiritual and psychological counselor and/or my personal physician, shaman, guru, trainer, couturier, whatever suits your needs. So naturally, she's welcome to visit as often as she likes."

Parkman stiffened. "You're asking me to lie to the police."

"Nothing of the sort. The *little fabrication*—I'd prefer to call it—is strictly mine; my invention, if you will. I hold the copyright, and I'm assigning that copyright, without restriction, to you. Either you avail yourself of that or you're welcome to speak the whole, unvarnished truth when you explain to the police how you left me with no reasonable alternative but to leave this repressive environment."

Parkman lost the stare-down. "All right, Mr. Dunston. I'll instruct the guards to admit her, but only on the condition that she's the sole exception and that your *little fabrication* remains strictly between us."

Dunston shook on it.

"And no more tantrums." Parkman glared pointedly at the spattered food on the wall.

"That was not a tantrum, Doctor. It was a restaurant review."

The administrator puffed his lips. "All right. I'll have menus sent up from local restaurants. You're not on any dietary restrictions, so you can have what you want. I'll arrange it, as long as you behave."

Dunston waited until Parkman was well away. "Now, where were we, P.J.?"

"Ready to discuss Charlie Booth."

"Ah, yes, your Mr. Booth." He melted back against the pillows.

"Maybe you need some rest, Mr. Dunston. I can come back later."

"Not at all. I'm perfectly fine."

"Are you sure?"

"Yes. And don't you dare start clucking over me like the rest of them."

"Right, sir. No clucking. You have my word."

"Good. Our first task is to take a good, hard look at your Mr. Booth, to put him in reasonable perspective. Find an appropriate slot for him."

"I don't think he has a slot."

"Certainly he does. He's a man, an ordinary mortal."

"All due respect, Mr. Dunston, I don't think anyone would describe Charlie Booth as ordinary."

"That's correct, and it's a major part of the problem in cases like this. There's a tendency to overestimate such people, and that enhances their power immeasurably. In fact, Charlie Booth, Blake Madigan, Jack the Ripper, the lot of them, are simply defective human animals."

"Who happen to be very effective at inspiring fear and trembling."

"That's the media squeezing mileage out of lurid events and the public lapping it up. The reality would make poor box office."

"The reality?"

"The sorry truth, yes. Such people are unfit to live in society, to be productive, to have real relationships or to lead anything that even approaches a normal life. They're quite pathetic really."

"I've thought of plenty of my patients that way, but not Booth. It would be mighty hard to dredge up a drop of sympathy for the likes of him."

"Of course it would. But sympathy is not the issue here. What I do, what you're trying to do, is fundamentally about gamesmanship. To succeed, you must first recognize that while your Mr. Booth is unfettered by rules, while he feels free to trample boundaries of decency to get what he wants, you have a considerable advantage as well. You can catalogue and predict his behaviors in ways that he could never begin to reciprocate or expect."

"I can?"

"Yes. People like Mr. Booth always have distinct behavioral features we can identify, analyze, and ultimately utilize against them." He enumerated on his fingers. "They have personal quirks, defining patterns, preferences, and aversions. Above all, they can be relied upon to act as they have in the past. History is destiny, so to speak. See where they've been, and you know where they're headed. Learn what they've done, and you've read the crystal ball."

"Sounds like everybody else."

"Bingo. Normal people have the capacity to recognize that; those like your Mr. Booth do not. They have no instinctive understanding of human nature; no grasp whatsoever of how people function, including themselves. Plus they're incredibly arrogant, either by delusion or design. Ironically, this renders them powerless to avoid the simple mistakes that ultimately lead to their demise."

"But until then, they damage and destroy." My gaze strayed to the bandaged swell of Dunston's abdomen. "Especially the people who try to catch them in those mistakes."

"True. There's a considerable danger in pursuing people

like Booth. And yes, I'm living proof of that." Dunston held me in his unflinching sights. "But you have a choice. You can bow out, P.J. You can walk away any time you like, and not a reasonable soul in the world would judge you ill for that. Mr. Booth is neither your responsibility nor your job."

"But what happens to Dennis John if I drop it?"

He wove his hands behind his neck. "Ah yes, there is the matter of the little boy."

"He should have better than me behind him, you know. That child deserves to have the best there is taking his part against that brutal son of a bitch they call his father."

Restlessness drove me to the window. On the street far below, an ambulance limped toward the emergency entrance, howling its outrage at the tangle of traffic that slowed its way. I thought of the poor soul inside, dangling over the abyss by the slimmest strand of time. And I thought of Dennis John, dangling, too.

"All right then, Mr. Dunston. Let's get on with it."

"You're sure?"

"I am."

"Fine. We'll proceed."

He rose slowly to his feet. Leaning hard on the IV pole, tubes and monitors trailing, he began to pace.

"Are you sure you should be out of bed?"

"Could that be clucking I hear?"

"Sorry."

The thin gown gaped behind him. As he walked, I caught a glimpse of his pale, slack behind and the huge, livid bruise that held him in gruesome embrace.

I cleared my throat. "Excuse me, Mr. Dunston, but you're catching a bit of a tailwind there. Perhaps you'd like me to get your robe."

He craned his neck, peered down, and shrugged. "If you'd be so kind."

I retrieved the thin blue cotton robe from a hook at the side of the room and draped it across his shoulders.

He kept up the slow, labored circuit, though the effort left him pale and pinched with pain. "Before we go any further, P.J., I want you to tell me what happened."

"What do you mean?"

"With Mr. Booth. Something transpired between you. And it has changed you. I can see that."

"It was nothing."

"Indulge me, please."

Reluctantly I did, though I downplayed my bristling terror on spotting Booth across the road. I confessed that I'd fled from him with Dennis John, chased by the horrifying certainty that somehow Booth had the power to sniff us out. "So that's the whole of it. We slipped out the back of the building, stopped to buy ice cream, and then made our way to meet Lottie at her place when she got back from the doctor's. In fact, nothing happened at all."

"On the contrary, something very important happened. You handed Booth the power, played mouse to his cat. And that will not serve you well, not at all."

"He had no way of knowing how I felt. Chances are he didn't even know we were there."

"It's what you know that concerns me, P.J. What you know, and how you react."

"That's all I did: reacted. It was a shock, seeing him there, and my instinct was to get the hell away."

"I understand. But you must learn to put such instincts aside, to override them. You could have reasoned the situation through and assessed it differently. You might have chalked the episode up to simple coincidence. Booth lives and works near where this occurred?"

"Somewhere nearby, yes. I don't know exactly where he does, either. The boy's aunt says he moves around so much it's near impossible to keep track."

"Nevertheless, you spotted him in what is known to be his home territory, which suggests there was nothing in the least odd about his being there. Chances are he simply stopped to buy something, to visit someone, to keep an appointment. Chances are it had nothing whatsoever to do with you."

"All perfectly logical, Mr. Dunston, which obviously I'm not."

"Navigating alien territory without a road map would leave anyone scared and confused. Let's provide you with that map, shall we?"

"That would be wonderful."

"It can seem a bit complicated. You may want to take notes."

"I would, definitely." I found a pen and a few rumpled scraps of paper in my purse.

He shambled to the nightstand, extracted a thick yellow legal pad from the drawer, and handed it to me. "I want you to bring me up to speed on everything you've learned so far, and we'll work from there to fill in the blanks. Take it step-by-step. You'll need to tackle this systematically."

"I'm all for that."

"Good. Rule one: People like Booth don't simply happen. They're born, formed, or both."

"Does it really matter why he is or where he came from? Isn't the real question what he is?"

"No, the real question is what he's going to do. And the only way to find that out is to go back; as far back as it takes, and see what the man has done."

■ **The list was overwhelming. According to Dunston, I** had to learn about Booth's background, including any anomalies in his childhood and his history of violent behavior. Aside from inflicting sadistic harm, what interested him? Did he have any known fears? Did he suffer from any persistent physical or emotional weaknesses, aside from the lack of a soul?

Still, none of that would count for anything unless I could prove that Booth was at Rikers and that he'd had access to Jeannie Bagshaw on the day she was killed. Everything hinged on that.

In the front room at Artco Sheet Metal, a chunky woman with daisy-blond hair sat at the desk. She huddled close to her computer monitor, squinting at the screen, engrossed in a game of spider solitaire.

"Sorry to interrupt you," I said in all sincerity, having been hooked on the blasted game myself for months until I went cold turkey about a year ago and deleted it. Obviously, I hadn't expunged it from my own hard drive. As I scanned the board for moves, my fingers twitched.

"You've got a play there with the seven on the eight of spades," I told her.

"Hey, thanks." She did as I suggested, and completed the king-to-ace run. The cards flipped onto the discard pile with the addictive trill that the game's devilish designers had built in to fuel the craving. I recognized this as the compelling might of intermittent reinforcement. Give a mouse a pellet every time it presses a lever, and sooner or later the mouse gets full and disinterested. Give it never, and before long the mouse gets wise and stages a job action. Dispense those pellets at random, and the mouse will keep pressing that lever until its little paws give out, at which point, that mouse will likely take up spider solitaire.

Somehow the woman wrested her brown eyes from the screen and settled them on me. "Help you?"

"I'd like to speak to whoever's in charge of personnel about someone who once worked here. I only need a minute of his time."

"Okay."

She printed the name of the man I was to see in bold block letters on a sheet of copy paper. Then she handed me a pair of foam earplugs and plastic goggles so scratched, the world went plaid. "Should be in there."

The moment I pulled open the ponderous fire door to Artco's workshop, I was besieged by brain-stapling noise: stammering nail guns, the blistering *whoosh* of torches, the biting scream of ripsaws, and the harsh strike of hammers on steel. Long benches crisscrossed the dust-laden floor. At each, men loomed like giant insects behind dark goggles, plastic face shields, and silver apron carapaces that covered them from neck to knees. Spark showers burst at intervals. And everywhere were sheets of annealed metal, scrap metal, metal filings, and mammoth coils of solder. Everything was carpeted by a dense layer of glimmering debris. Metal bits shimmered in the air, and with every breath I caught its bitter taste.

I passed from station to station, showing each giant bug the name, but all heads swerved in the negative. Out of options, I returned to the welcome quiet of the reception area. Despite the plugs, my ears rang with the deafening din.

"He's not in there."

"I know," she said, staring at a new game of spider solitaire, which I recognized immediately as a sure loser. "Thought he was, but then I saw him head out back."

A door at the rear led to a dingy storeroom. There, amid drums of solvents and shelves laden with tools, supplies, and parts, I encountered a gangly mustachioed man. He sported a chessboard flannel shirt and tight jeans crammed into sharp-toed boots. A thick brown belt with an ornate silver buckle underscored his medicine-ball gut. A scatter of metal dust rode the brim of his bad-guy black ten-gallon hat and a ratty mess of dirt-brown hair spilled out from below to his shoulders.

"Mr. Jones?"

"Who's asking?"

"My name is P. J. Lafferty."

"So?"

"I was hoping you might be able to help me. I need information about a man who used to work here. The lady at the desk told me you're in charge of personnel."

"The here and now ones I am. They don't work here anymore, they're not my headache."

"I understand, but I have to find out where this man went to work after he left here, Mr. Jones. It's very important."

He slapped his chest, hips, thighs. "Oops. Must have left my crystal ball at home."

Somehow I held my tongue. "I'd be most grateful if you'd check your records. He might have left some forwarding information. Or maybe someone called looking for a reference and you have a record of that."

He cracked the seal on a box of mechanical pencils, scooped up a fistful, and then did the same with a box of Post-its.

"Could you please look?"

"I could, yeah. But I can't think why I'd want to."

I fished through my wallet for a promising incentive, but all I found was the same measly rumpled five-dollar bill that had been rattling around alone in there for days. My first client checks had yet to clear, so it was the empty wallet shuffle for me. Nevertheless, I offered him the bill, leaving myself with the grand sum of fifty-seven cents, praying there was a subway ride remaining on my MetroCard. The walk home from Nowhere, Queens, was mighty long. "That's all I have on me, Mr. Jones. I could send a check."

He snickered. "Sure. You do that. Make it out to snowball's chance in Hell."

He loped out of the storeroom, and I trailed close behind. "Maybe you don't even have to look it up. Maybe you know where Charlie Booth went to work after he left here."

At that, he stopped cold. "This is about Booth?"

"Yes."

"That no-good, rotten piece of crap? That's who you're after?"

"It is."

He shoved his thumbs in his waistband. "You his friend or something? Old girlfriend maybe?"

"If he had friends like me, he'd have no need of enemies, Mr. Jones."

He chewed on that and the wad of gum that plumped his scruffy cheek. "Booth screwed me over big time. Cost me my biggest account."

"Charming fellow," I said.

"That wasn't the worst of it. Scumbag robbed me blind. Stole money, materials, tools. Didn't even care who knew it. Man who cleans up was here one night after hours and saw Booth walk off with a five-thousand-dollar saw. Called the cops to report it. Turned out to be about as useful as peeing up a rope. Got nothing for my trouble but double talk and bullshit excuses. Gave up and ate the loss eventually, but it didn't go down easy. Tell you that."

"Booth gets away with things. I've heard it before."

"Yeah? Why you think that is?"

"Wish I had the answer."

"Dumb luck, I figure. But sooner or later his luck'll run out. I want a front row center seat when it does."

"That would be quite the ticket line," I said.

"So what is it you want with him?"

I hesitated, reluctant to show all my cards. But his hatred of Booth struck me as genuine, and I had to take a risk to win his help.

"His wife was murdered. Stabbed to death. I'm trying to prove Booth held the blade."

"You think you can pin a murder rap on him? That true?"

"I hope, with the right help."

"Follow me."

He led me back through the shop and out a rear door to a corridor lined with offices. His was the last and, from what I was able to see, the largest. A broad window behind his desk offered a panoramic view of the rusted car carcasses and other trash that littered the adjacent auto body shop. Tepid light leaked in through the murky panes, brightening the fronds of a large, plastic palm. Antique rifles and handguns shared the wall and shelf space with a striking array of Elvis paraphernalia. My personal favorite was a smiling, wind-up Hawaiian Elvis doll in a grass skirt and flowered lei, strumming a ukulele.

Jones perched on a pony-skin stool and started rifling through a drawer in the file cabinet. His record-keeping system was impossible to divine, and likely nonexistent. I saw no identifying tabs, no names or numbers, nothing in the way of an obvious code. Nevertheless, he walked his long, twiglike fingers across the packed records and extracted several files.

My optimism dissolved as he went through each in turn, muttered angrily, and tossed it aside. "Nope. Not that either. Damn!"

"Is there anything I can do to help?"

He shot me a melting scowl. "Yeah. You can sit down and shut up!"

Jones kept plucking files from the packed drawers and discarding them in a heap, growing visibly angrier as he did. His face went florid and he kept swearing, not quite under his breath. "Damned whore Eleanor. Dumb slut is nothing but a tit-stand on heels."

Finally he retrieved a thick folder crammed with rumpled sheets. "Yeah, doggie! This could be it."

His lips moved as he read, like Dennis John's, and it struck me that all his costumed swagger might be intended to camouflage a case of illiteracy.

"I'd be glad to take some of those and help you go through them, Mr. Jones. Would be faster that way."

"Thought I told you to shut up."

"Yes, sir. You did. But I hate to see you doing all that work on my account."

His fury warped in a hard, knowing grin. "That so? Well, aren't you just too thoughtful for words?"

"All I want to do is help, to make things easier for you if I can."

"That so?"

"Yes."

He pulled out the drawer and flipped it, dumping the contents on his desk. The files spilled over, papers flying, and I had the distinct sense that this was not the first time he'd used this exact means to express his displeasure. That would certainly account for the utter disorder he continued at intervals to blame on the aforementioned "incompetent slut Eleanor."

I huddled cringing in my chair as his temper gathered steam. Then Jones surprised me. He leaned back on his stool and calmly wiped his hands of the situation.

"You want to help, be my guest. I got plenty of better ways to spend my time. Look all you like. When you're through, put everything back. Every last bit of it, you hear?"

"Yes. I will, Mr. Jones. Thanks."

"You find something that puts the screws to Booth, more power to you. World would smell much better without him in it. Tell you that."

CHAPTER 31

■ **"So you get what I sent you, P.J.? Did you see?"**

I rubbed my gritty eyes. My bedside clock read 3:52 a.m. "You can't call me like this, Millie. It's the middle of the night."

"Get the lead out you bed, Momma. Squirrely bird's the one what catch the sperm."

"You're supposed to be in your bunk, Millie. They catch you making a call in the middle of the night, it's right to the Bing."

"Bing-a-ling, baby. Bing a ding dong ding."

"I'm serious. You know the rules."

"Got my own truly rulies, girlie goo. Anyone try to play bing bong with me, I fry they pond golden. Drain them good."

"What is it, Millie? What do you want?"

"Want to know did you get the thing. Want to know do you see I was telling the whole truth and nothing but the Booth."

"I didn't get anything."

"Bet you did, too. I sent that sucker special hurry up with a stickem lick and a half. Wrote 'mergency all over that sucker and air mail and all that shit. Got to be there by now."

"Nothing came, Millie. Maybe you wrote the wrong address."

"Wrote it right. Zip code and everything. Just like I saw."

"Where did you see my address? I'd like to know where you got that and my phone number."

"Don't you be getting all coy malloy with me, lady. As a reporter, I got to keep my sauces comfy dental. But I know you be livin at Number 38 Alderman Place, first floor. New York, New York, one double ought two one. That's you, right?"

It was, and it didn't please me that she knew my address, much less had it committed to memory. Millie's stays on the Rock were frequent, but all too brief. The last thing I needed was to have her showing up on my doorstep.

"Maybe it got lost, then. Or maybe you only imagined you sent it."

"'Magined my ass. Don't you be messing with me. I ain't no woo woo doesn't know which way's a puppy."

"I'm not messing with you, Millie. I'm telling you I didn't get it. That's how it is."

"No way, pomade. I'll tell you how it is. Now those sumbitches from the mother ship be messing with the mail. First it's the streetlights, then the mangoes, and now it's the whole entire United States pose office. Stoop to nuts, they be taking over. This shit's got to stop, P.J. And lickety quick!"

I yawned broadly. "Listen to me, Millie. I want you to pull your thoughts together, to concentrate."

"Okey dokum."

"Are you concentrating?"

She grunted. "Sure am."

"I want you to go back to bed and sleep until it's light out. Then I want you to go see the nurse, take your pills, and make an appointment with a therapist. You got all that?"

"Yuh uh."

"Repeat it, then. What did I ask you to do?"

She started clapping, grooving, singing in her gospel voice that was a cross between Mahalia Jackson and a factory whistle: "I got the whole whirl in my Hanes. I got the little bitty baby in my Hanes . . ."

"Stop, Millie. You're not concentrating."

"Am so. I concentrate any harder, I'm gone mess your pants."

"Go back to bed now."

"Who gone watch the sat delight if I go back to bed? Who gone stop 'em when they come knocking on the ferris wall? Tell me that."

"I'll take care of everything, Millie. You get some sleep."

"Promise you'll watch them good, especially the smallish ones?"

"Definitely."

"Watch them real hard now. Otherwise them smallish sumbitches slip right through."

CHAPTER

32

■ **The Club, so rarefied and exclusive it required no fur-**
ther name, had soaring ceilings where winged cherubs flew,
antique urns nestled in softly lit niches, and the kind of outrageously fine carpets my mother used to make us take our
shoes off in the presence of and then walk around nonetheless. I felt too edgy to sit on one of the regal crimson velvet
sofas and chairs perched in cozy groups at intervals around in
the lobby. Instead, as I waited for Nina Present, I stood shift-
ing my weight like a skittish bird. *Fidgeting*, my mother
would have accused with that look that told me she'd sooner
see me whip a baby seal. I felt utterly out of place in the presence of all the poised, impossibly fashionable people who
passed me on their way in or out. Did one say hello, or was
that not done? Was a nod passable, a smile? And if the latter
was acceptable, how energetic a smile did one chance? An
offhanded lip curl? A vague dimpling of the cheek? A hint of
teeth?

I'd been jittery about this meeting since Nina called early
this morning to ask me to lunch. She'd apologized for the
short notice, though in fact, that had been a mercy. More time
in advance would have given me more time to fret about what

she might want to discuss. I'd toyed with several possibilities, none of them good.

In fear of being late, I'd arrived half an hour early. Nina, naturally, appeared a genteel twelve minutes after the appointed time. I spotted her drifting down the majestic stairway in the company of an older woman with a honeyed tan, soft green eyes, and blizzard-white bobbed hair, who bore a nagging resemblance to Nina. They approached me in lockstep, but then the older one kissed the air beside Nina's cheek and walked off. From this, I concluded that while the average person might think it polite to trade introductions and greetings, the truly well-bred understood that it was far more appropriate to treat people we didn't know like broom handles.

Nina gripped my hand in both of hers. "P.J. Wonderful to see you. I hope you haven't been waiting long."

"Not at all."

"So glad you could come. I've been eager to get together and hear how things are going."

"They're going," I said. "Thanks again for the referrals. It's meant more than I can say."

"My pleasure. I made a reservation in the grill room. I hope that's all right."

"Great. I love grill rooms," I blithered.

I followed her to the elevator, a brass Art Deco jewel box manned by an old man in a maroon brass-buttoned uniform and a hat that resembled an overturned flowerpot. We soared with knee-crushing speed to the twelfth floor, where we were deposited in a small, gracious anteroom that connected in turn to a paneled room featuring a fireplace, a lavish buffet, and a wall of sparkling windows. The panorama was a glorious view of New York's famed Central Park, now resplendent with blooming trees, bright flowers, and a carpet of lush emerald grass. The view made me want to slurp my breath, and I battled against the ruinous urge.

Elegant people in pairs and quartets occupied the tables surrounding the buffet. Like Nina, they were all done up in designer suits and impeccable accessories, while I sported the selfsame black skirt, jade sweater set, and irritating pumps Caity had insisted on buying for me years ago when I was interviewing, fresh from school, for jobs. My sole pair of hose had a runner on the thigh the size of a rope ladder, which I'd patched with clear nail polish, and a safety pin held the waist-band of my skirt, which had somehow shrunk while hanging in my closet and now refused to close.

We ordered iced tea and then ventured to the buffet, where I kept a keen eye on Nina and took care to fill my plate as she did hers. I claimed one lonely shrimp, a splinter of beef, and a speck of poached salmon barely flecked with dill sauce. Salad filled the gaping void on her gold-rimmed china plate, and so it did on mine. Naked greens and crispies. No dressing, of course. No bread. My stomach churned in angry protest as I set this piteous display of virtue at my place. At the dessert station the crème brûlée beckoned, not to mention the most fabulous-looking blueberry cheesecake and an apple crumble with fresh whipped cream that any sensible person would have bartered without hesitation for a chunk of her soul. Nina would no doubt sooner swallow a hornet's nest than yield to such temptations. That, I brilliantly concluded, was why she was built precisely like Aphrodite, and I bore the far stronger resemblance to Aphrodite's horse.

She nibbled on a lettuce leaf. "Are you enjoying the prac-tice, P.J.?"

"At times. It's different, to be sure."

"But you'd like to be back working in the forensic area."

"I would." I tried to harpoon a cherry tomato with my salad fork, but only succeeded in chasing it about the plate. "Very much so."

She folded her hands. "If I tell you something, can I count on you not to repeat it to anyone else?"

"Of course."

Leaning closer, she dropped her voice. "There's an excit-ing new program in the works, a full-service center for people with persistent psychiatric problems, with a special program for those recently released from hospitals and jails. It's still in the development phase. And they haven't started hiring yet. But the force behind the project happens to be a dear old friend."

"They'll have use for counselors like me, you think?"

"Yes. I'd say you fit the bill exactly. But it's early, as I said. So you'll have to sit tight for a bit."

I made a final stab at the tomato, but it slipped the fork and landed on the floor. When I moved to retrieve it, Nina set a light hand on my arm. She gave me one of those ultra-kindly looks that shrink you by a foot. "The waiter will get it."

"Of course," I blithered again. "They always do."

"What I'd like to do is arrange for you to meet Brett Carnival. That's the friend who had the idea for the center and is working to raise the funds. Brett is a sweetheart, and I'm sure you'll hit it off. Then, soon as the time comes, he can bring you in for a formal interview and start the ball rolling right away."

Having such a place for my brother Jack had long been my fantasy. What a blessing it would be to have a haven filled with people who knew Jack, dedicated souls who could spot the storms brewing and avert them. And what an incredible opportunity it would be to work there.

"When will that be, do you suppose?"

"Hard to say. You know how it is. These things always cost twice as much and take twice as long as anyone predicts. And then there are the regulators, licenses to get, wheels to grease. On and on."

"So it could be quite a while."

"It could be. Things like this typically are. People are so resistant to change."

"Human nature," I said as I coaxed the stubborn tail off my shrimp. "The devil you know and all that. There's a powerful comfort in sameness."

"True, but it is too bad. So many important changes get delayed or go by the boards out of meaningless resistance."

She sipped her tea, and I watched in amazement as her brilliant red lipstick failed to leap off her lips and transfer itself, as mine always did, to the rim of the glass. She was a walking magic show, Nina was. And here she was, breaking bread—or to be technical, celery—with the likes of me.

"Take the contract jails, for example," she said. "We should have so many more up-and-running by now. They're such an improvement over the public system. It's a sin that it's taking so long."

"Dr. Creighton mentioned that the other day. He said it's because the unions are against it, and the powers that be."

"Will's as passionate about the issue as I am. It's maddening to think we wind up running in place because some special interests have the more powerful voice."

A bit of something crisp had lodged itself between my teeth, fitting retribution for the prank I played in suggesting that Caity had gone through her signing in similar condition. I drilled for it with my tongue, but the blasted thing refused to budge. Giving up, I hid behind my hand. "Results don't lie. If the contract jails are really working, people will have to come around."

"Eventually, true. But in the meantime, how many inmates get sacrificed on the altar of the status quo and those who stand to profit from it?"

I thought of my brother Jack. "One is too many."

She clinked my glass. "I agree with you wholeheartedly, P.J. Even one is too many. We have to do everything we can to turn things around as quickly as possible."

I clinked back. "To turning things around."

"Yes," she said. "Amen."

■ **"We need to talk." Caity dumped the grocery bags on** my counter and started signing with the flapping fury of fighting cocks.

"I have nothing to say to you." I plucked out the magazine she'd brought, scrunched in my chair, and settled in for a nice, long sulk.

It's no simple feat to give the silent treatment to a deaf person, and at the risk of seeming immodest, I do this quite well. Caity's lack of hearing deprived me of virtually all the other time-honored means siblings used to vent their rage. Shouting at her was useless, as was sniping or teasing or calling her nasty names. She had only to turn her back, and I ceased to exist. And could I simply retaliate with the cruelty she so richly deserved? Sadly, no. As soon as we grew old and aware enough to detest each other properly, my parents had imposed a strict prohibition against physical violence that inhibited me still. Under no circumstances was I to hit, shove, trip, kick, bite, yank out fistfuls of Caity's hair, gouge her eyeballs, push her out of any windows, or so much as attempt to wrench any of her appendages from their rightful locations, not even a measly finger. It took me years to figure out that my best remaining strategy was simple *quid pro quo*. I could ignore my twin with the same maddening ferocity that she ignored me. I could disregard her into a veritable frenzy of blazing frustration. At least, I could pretend to ignore her. And how immensely satisfying that has proved to be!

She came up behind me and attempted to wrest my attention from this week's issue of *People* magazine, which she had brought with the fixings for a dinner of spaghetti with mixed seafood, a beet and assorted other nonsense salad, and company I did not wish to have. But no matter. Being unwelcome was of no consequence to Caity. Nor was she put off in the least by my raging indignation about her chummy little conspiracy with my ex. What kind of sister takes the part of her twin's former husband, I ask you?

The answer: one that sucks!

Caity was boiling, too: beets, shellfish, and a stewpot brimming with salted water for the spaghetti. In typical fashion she had all the burners fired up far too high, so the pots hissed and jittered beneath their lids. Well, she could cook herself silly for all I cared; she could reduce herself by half and still be half again too much for me.

Turning the page, I discovered that a startling number of major celebrities I'd never heard of had been indicted, fired, engaged, divorced, married, sued, honored, surgically altered, debilitated, recovered, and/or deceased since last week's edition. That was followed by a rundown on the countless books, music, films, tapes, video games, and TV shows I would have to consume before the next issue unless I wished to risk being hopelessly out of touch. Next, I came to the section of the magazine that focused on the deeds of "ordinary" folk: a man who'd invented a means to flush the toilet by thought alone, a three-year-old girl whose abstract oils commanded six-figure prices, a couple with nineteen children and three on the way.

Caity kept stomping over to gesticulate between me and the magazine. I caught the signs for *mule-headed*, which doubled for *stubborn* and *ass*, the one for *impossible* and the alternating taps of middle finger to palms intended to invoke a crucifixion, which meant *Jesus Christ*. But still I refused to react.

She added her snout voice to the demand for my attention. "It's not going to work, P.J. I'm staying right here until we talk things out."

I read on. A man from New Zealand, cute though obviously a card or two shy of a full deck, had crossed that enormous sprawl of a country in a ceaseless series of cartwheels, forward rolls, and back flips, and planned to do the same around the world. Barkley, a smug-looking Yorkshire terrier, had somehow managed to heal a feud between two families on the upper Michigan Peninsula that had simmered for five generations.

"You're being ridiculous," Caity railed, signing and speaking both. "When are you going to start acting your age?"

Glancing up, I smiled sweetly. "So happens I have that penciled in for a week from next Thursday, right after lunch."

I turned another page, and there it was: a picture of Caity and Eva Everheart, locked in an adoring hug thanks to the magic of deceptive photography. The story spewed the usual claptrap about how the fictional Eva had appeared to my sister fully formed and how Caity was merely the channel through which her deaf superheroine communicated with her millions of devoted fans. "I'm simply a vehicle for Eva," Caity had told the interviewer with the sort of burning sincerity that only unbridled ambition coupled with a total lack of scruples can inspire.

"A vehicle is it?" I mused aloud. "Being a *vehicle* doesn't stop her from cashing the checks or sucking up the attention, does it now? Being a *vehicle* doesn't keep her from wearing her fame like a blasted tiara and expecting the world to bow." Disgusted, I tossed the magazine aside.

"You could say something, P.J.," Caity whined. "You could be big enough to say 'Nice going, Sis. Good for you.'"

At that, I stood and faced her. "No. I could not. I'm not nearly that big, it so happens. So you're famous. So you're a big-deal, hotshot star. That doesn't give you the right to go behind my back and gossip about me with Rafe, of all people. I'm not your plaything, Caity. I'm not here for your amusement, and I'm not yours to manipulate and control. Not yours and certainly not Rafe's. Despite how the pair of you sees me, I happen to be a serious, independent adult."

She cracked a fistful of spaghetti and dumped it in the water that had come to a grand, spitting boil. Steam wafted beneath her chin, giving her the look of a cauldron-stirring witch. "Serious and independent, is it?" Her voice was gaining angry heft and clarity, sinking to a chillingly normal tone. "Hah!"

If she insisted on talking, I would sign. "Despite how you see me, so happens I am."

"I don't think so. Not close. Serious, independent adults don't go around impersonating their sister. They don't show up at Taffy Grainger's brownstone, of all places, pretending to be that sister. And if they happen to be idiotic enough to try such a stunt, they certainly don't drop their stupid glove on the way out so Taffy Grainger has to call that sister about the lost glove and arrange to get it back to her!"

My cheeks caught fire.

"What were you thinking, P.J.? That's what I'd like to know."

She refused to take my tongue-tied shame for an answer.

"What were you thinking?"

"I suppose, technically, I wasn't thinking at all."

"Technically, indeed," she huffed. "So happens there are consequences to what you do. You get it into your reckless head to go snooping around at the Graingers' and the next thing I know, I get roped into speaking at one of her stupid charity functions on behalf of orphan tadpoles or endangered persimmons or some such idiocy."

"You could have turned her down."

"No," she signed sharply. "You set it up so I had no choice. You made it look as if she had done me a favor, which meant I owed her one. That's how serious, reasonable adults deal with one another. So I did what I had to do to keep from embarrassing you any more than you had already embarrassed yourself."

"You're right about the Grainger thing. It was dumb, and I'm sorry."

"The fact is you could be much worse than sorry." Signing again, she struck the tips of her cocked fingers to drive home the point. "Make a mistake like that with other people, with say—murdering lunatics—and they can pay you back with way worse than a charity appearance. They could pay you back so you'd never turn up anywhere again."

"I said I'm sorry. You don't have to beat it to death."

"Yes, I do, damn it. It or you." She started shucking oysters, gouging flesh and sinew with chilling glee.

"It just happened, Caity. She mistook me for you and I went with it. I didn't plan it that way."

She tossed the knife so it landed point down, impaling an innocent unpaid phone bill against the countertop. "T-A-F-F-Y G-R-A-I-N-G-E-R," she finger-spelled furiously. "What's next, P.J.? You go to Buckingham Palace and try to pass yourself off as me to the Queen?"

"I thought *you* were the Queen."

"No you are: queen of the reckless jerks!"

We locked angry eyes, and I knew the game. Last one to stop beaming poison death rays won.

This turned out to be me. Caity's arms flared in lovely surrender. "That's it. I give up. You want to be a stubborn idiot, I guess there's no way I can stop you."

"I'm trying to do the right thing, Caity. That's all."

"That's not all."

"Yes, it is."

"What is it with you? Why are you so obsessed with that little boy?"

"I'm not obsessed with him. I just think the poor kid deserves a break. Bad enough his mother gets killed. Bad enough her blood is on his father's hands. But now his great aunt, the only one he has left to look after him, is dying. Somebody has to care for the boy, Caity. Someone has to see to it that nothing even worse happens to him. It's only right."

She plucked a tissue from the flowered box on my coffee table and handed it to me. That's how I came to learn I was leaking tears.

"That's good, P.J. Get it out. Have a good cry."

"I'm not crying, damn it. Must have gotten something in my eye."

"Sure. That was my second guess."

The tears flowed harder, coursing down my cheeks. "Well, it's sad, damn it. Horribly sad and unfair. Children aren't supposed to be left with no one to hug them or love them or sing them to sleep. Left with no one to pack their lunch boxes or admire their school projects or kiss away the hurts. Kids are supposed to have loving grown-ups to protect them from the cold, cruel world."

Her eyes brimmed with sympathy. "You're right."

"I know I am."

"I'm agreeing with you."

"Well, stop, damn it! Don't give me a hard time."

"I have to. Someone does. Feeling for that little boy is one thing. What you do about it is quite another," she signed with a hitchhiker's twirl of the thumb. "Be his pal if you like. Buy him toys; take him to the movies. Those things make sense."

"Those things don't keep Dennis John safe. They don't stop his father from terrorizing the kid, from hurting him, maybe even . . ." I couldn't put words to the darkest possibility. Words might have the power to make it so.

She scowled. "Maybe even going after the fool who's dumb enough to go after him. Consider that. And while you do, you may also want to ask yourself why you have such a death wish. Could be useful for you to know." She tapped her forehead, the sign for knowing and wisdom and all the other virtues she was convinced I lacked.

"I do not have a death wish."

"Yes you do. That's why you choose to work with crazy dangerous people and live in crazy dangerous places like this. And that's why when, heaven forbid, you're happy like you were with Rafe, you find some way to ruin it."

"I ruined it? Fat lot of rubbish, that is. Rafe's the one who drove a stake through our marriage, not me."

"Rafe loves you still, you blooming dolt. Despite the way you treat him, despite everything, he's crazy about you. The man would do anything to have you back. Don't you see?"

"Sure. I see perfectly. He joins forces with you to try to run my life. Now there's an irresistible act of undying love."

"You're not going to listen, are you? No matter what I say, you're going to keep up this lunacy until something terrible happens."

"Something terrible is far more likely to happen if I drop it."

"You don't know that."

"No. But I don't want to find out the hard way that I'm right."

"If you think someone is about to get hit by a runaway train, you don't jump in front of the locomotive, P.J. That makes no sense."

"I'm not jumping in front of anything. I'm looking for a way to stop it."

Dripping disgust, Caity sniffed. "Fine. Go stop your train. Tie yourself to the tracks for all I care. You want to grow up to be roadkill. Fine with me. Your choice."

"My choice? That would be a refreshing change."

"You've got it. Complete independence. Freedom to be as stubborn and reckless as you like. Knock yourself out."

"Are you telling me you and Rafe are going to back off?"

"You bet."

"Promise?"

"Cross my heart and hope to fall off the *Times* best-seller list. I'm done with it. It's finished. Let's eat."

Caity hefted the unwieldy pasta pot, ferried it to the sink, and dumped the boiling contents in a rush. Angrily she portioned out two plates, and we claimed opposing seats at the table. We shared a face, but as she ate, hers went light with the blessed absence of caring for me, while mine bore the increasingly weighty burden of knowing that I'd won. I'd gotten exactly what I wanted, in spades. Caity and Rafe were off my case. And for good or ill, I'd have to live with that.

CHAPTER

34

■ **If ever the good Lord invented a gift for the snoopy** curious, Google was its name. I went online and with a few keystrokes learned that the Sheet Metal Workers' Union represented thousands of people in industries ranging from fine tin work to heating, roofing, and air-conditioning to laying rail and shipbuilding, and on and on. During my search of the chaotic files at Artco, Charlie Booth's former employer, I'd discovered little of use beyond the fact that the company was strictly a union shop. Logic suggested that if Booth had paid the dues and held the required union card, he had likely landed at another company that operated under the oversight of the New York Local, number 28.

I tracked their offices to the fifth floor of a small building on Greenwich Street in the West Village. The door was locked. As the sign directed, I pressed the button beneath the adjacent speaker.

A deep, menacing voice soon bellowed through the grate. "Help you?"

"Yes. I hope so. It's about one of your members."

He buzzed me into a cramped space plastered with flyers, announcements, and a copy of the union's mission statement, which boiled down to getting members the wages they deserved along with their due of pride, security, and respect. I mused that if Chief Daley had a mission statement, it would boil down to getting heads on stakes.

The stocky bulldog of a man who had authorized my entrance perched behind a broad gunmetal desk. He had the mashed nose, plumped ears, and lumpy brow of a seasoned fighter who'd taken far too many crushing blows.

"Something about a member, you said?"

"Yes. He used to be at Artco Sheet Metal in Queens. I'm trying to find out where he works now."

"See your member ID?"

"I'm not in the union."

"Member information is for members only."

I played my trump card, the one I didn't exactly have. "Denton Jones from Artco suggested I check here. He's eager to get a line on this person, too."

"You know Cowboy Jones?"

"I do."

He chuckled. "How's he doing anyway? Been an age."

"Like always. You know."

"Do I ever. Some kind of character, that one."

"He is."

"So who's the guy you're trying to track down, you and Cowboy?"

"Someone who used to work for Jones. His name's Charlie Booth."

He paused for a beat and plucked a pen from the holder on his desk. "Booth, you said? With or without an E?"

"Without. And it could be under Charles."

"And you are?"

He printed my name below Booth's on a message slip.

"What is it you want with this guy?"

"It's about a job. Rush thing I'm hoping he can help me with."

"And Cowboy? Why's he looking for Booth?"

I displayed my empty hands. Coming up with lies on my own behalf was hard enough.

"Wait here."

He lumbered into an adjacent office and shut the door. I

presumed he must be enlisting someone's help in the search or maybe checking filed records. My eye drifted to the papers on his desk: a dues reminder, a lobbying letter destined for a state senator, notices about the annual convention to be held in Las Vegas next June.

Suddenly a light flared on his phone console, and I caught the deep drone of his voice as he talked on the line. I edged closer to the door until I was able to catch scraps of what he was saying. He invoked Booth's name and mine and then went silent. When he spoke again, it was in a near whisper. "OK. I will. But make it quick."

I froze.

What if he was talking to Booth? What if he'd called to report that a bloody fool named P. J. Lafferty had come around asking about him? I could all but hear Booth's vicious wheels turning. *Keep the bitch right where she is. I'll take care of her.*

The receiver clunked as he hung up. I heard the deep thud of his approaching steps.

Heart stuttering, I lunged for the door. I raced out and down the hall toward the exit.

"Hey, Lafferty," he howled as I slipped into the staircase. "Where'd you go? Hey!"

I charged down the stairs, hurtling at the perilous edge of control, nearing freefall. When I reached the bottom landing, I fairly melted with relief.

Mercifully the lobby was deserted. But then, as I passed the elevators, a light flared, a bell pinged, and the door slid open. I stiffened with horror, braced for the clutch of hands and his crushing grip.

The car was empty.

I ran full out. Turning off Greenwich, I tracked the maze of small Village blocks that jutted off at odd, unpredictable angles.

Most of a mile away, I finally thought it was safe to stop. Pressed in a doorway, I waited for my galloping pulse to slow. My lungs seared and sweat plastered my shirt to my back.

I tried to think like Albert Dunston, to put the incident in perspective and avoid leaping to the worst-case scenario. The phone call might have had nothing at all to do with Charlie Booth. Maybe the bulldog had called his boss or whatever union official was in charge of fielding impertinent requests from nosy strangers. Maybe Booth had stolen from other shops, as Cowboy Jones said he had from Artco, and Bruiser had thought that the police, or whoever else was investigating, might want to talk to me.

But then again, maybe he had phoned Booth in fact. Right now, Jeannie's killer might be bloody furious at missing a chance at me. Right now he could be planning some other devilish way to pay me back.

CHAPTER

35

■ **"Sorry I'm late again, Dr. Groome. My earlier appoint-**ment took longer than I expected."

"Sit, P.J. Just sit for a moment and breathe."

"I am breathing."

"You're breathing like a plant, not an animate life form."

"I'm doing the best I can."

"Then I'll teach you how to do better. Watch."

Psychokinetic integration, a system of her own invention, was based on the theory that you could achieve emotional mastery through physical control, and vice versa. Decades of study and observation had led Dr. Groome to the unshakable conviction that bolstering one built the other and favoring one or ignoring either caused dangerous imbalances. Proper breathing was crucial.

I tried to match the slow, steady rise and fall of her chest.

"What is it, P.J.? You're trembling."

"Nothing. I'm fine."

"What has you so frightened?"

I shrugged that off. "My imagination, same as always. Truth is I've never managed to outgrow the ghosts in the closet or those evil goblins that hide out under the bed."

"So what was it this time, the ghosts, the goblins, or something else?"

I stared at the palm of my right hand, noticing for the first time how my life line came to an abrupt dead end. The crease beneath it, the one for love if I had the order straight, started firmly enough but then jogged off in sharp little pips so it resembled a mass of brambles. Or perhaps it was the other way around and my love life plunged early off the cliff while the rest of my life was destined to veer from thorn to thorn to thorn.

"Here's a riddle for you, P.J.," she said. "Suppose you're walking in the jungle, and as you approach a clearing, you hear a great, deep, angry roar. What do you do?"

I shrugged. "That's easy. Run my bloody head off."

"And then?"

"Keep running my bloody head off."

"And when you believe you've gotten safely away? What then?"

"Run farther for good measure and then a bit more."

"And when you're satisfied?"

I smiled. "That's when I collapse."

She doffed her glasses and slipped the end of an earpiece in her mouth. "And then what?"

I gave that a bit of serious thought. "Soon as I found the strength, I imagine I'd head home and pour myself a drink, maybe a couple."

Her eyes pressed shut.

"I gather that's not the answer you were hoping for."

"I was hoping that you might use the opportunity to ask yourself why you'd happened into that dangerous place and how you might avoid winding up in such a situation again. The best result of adversity is learning, don't you think?"

I thought of the lion, licking its chops as it savored my last juicy bits. "No. I'd say the best result is coming out of it in one piece."

"Do you ever ask yourself why it is you're always poking around the clearings where lions might be?"

"Now you sound like my sister. Caity thinks I have a death wish, which I can assure you, I do not."

"I agree. You don't."

"No? I was sure you'd be lining up to buy a front-row seat on that bandwagon."

She nodded. "I might if your sister suggested that you don't believe you deserve to live happily and well."

"How is that different from a death wish?"

"It's very different. You don't want to die. But I believe you do suffer from overwhelming guilt, and since you think you deserve to be punished, you seek ways to bring that punishment on."

My left palm proved no more encouraging. The life line drooped from the outset and petered out prematurely like the one on the right. The heart line looked stiff and uneasy and ended at a featureless fork in the road, so there could always be the path not taken, a cause for regret.

"My background is Irish Catholic with a touch of the wandering Jew, Dr. Groome. Guilt comes with the territory."

"Perhaps, but there's guilt and there's guilt."

"Are you talking degrees?"

"No, types. I'm sure you're familiar with survivor's guilt."

"Me? Not at all. My sister's the survivor. Talk to her."

Even her smirk was elegant. "Lie down, P.J. Close your eyes. Focus on the sound of my voice."

I tried not to, anything but. I nipped the flesh inside my cheek and dug my nails hard into my palms. But even as I worked to remain connected, my mind was slipping out the back door.

The phone sounds, bleating shrilly as in pain. There's a light for Caity to see when a call comes in, and a flash matches each jarring ring. Neither of us moves to answer. We know there's nothing we care to hear on the other end.

The ringing continues, jeering now. Caity shifts uneasily in her chair, tucking her legs beneath her as if she's spotted something horrid on the floor. She strokes her nose as she used to when she was small and sucked her thumb. My blood runs cold at the sight of iron Caity needing such primal comfort.

The phone rings again and again, an insistent plaint that creeps beneath my skin. I count six rings, ten, a dozen. And then finally, mercifully, it stops.

My sister stands. Trancelike, she drifts to the refrigerator. She drinks milk from the carton. Then she scoops peanut but-

ter from the jar with her finger and eats it the forbidden way: plain. The rule about that was unequivocal. Plain peanut butter was out of the question. You had to eat it with apple slices, crackers, or bread and wash it back with ample quantities of juice or milk. How many times had my mother warned that plain peanut butter could plug your throat and choke you? She'd drilled it in so the thought alone was enough to make me cough and clutch my neck. And of course, you didn't drink anything directly from the carton. Not if you were our mother's child.

I scream so hard it feels like cat claws raking in my throat. No, don't, Caity! You can't do that! Stop!

She's turned away, staring into the fridge, but somehow, she can hear me. And suddenly she can speak every bit as clear and normally as me.

It doesn't matter anymore, she tells me coldly. Why pretend?

She'll kill you, Caity. You'll see. Mom will come home and murder you dead.

My sister's laugh is dry and mean.

I scream again, and the scene shifts. I'm in the bathroom where Jack is lying in the tub. His face rides low in the water like a frog in a murky pond. His eyes look glazed with shock. A wispy blush stains the bathwater.

Once, I read that a human body holds six quarts of blood, which, on its journey through a person's veins, arteries, and capillaries, traverses a staggering twelve thousand miles each day. Imagine making two round trips from New York to California without stopping. Imagine doing it without as much as a movie or a snack.

Jack is slack, wet, unwieldy; he weighs a ton. I poise behind him, loop my arms across his chest, and pull hard as I can, but he doesn't budge. I tug so fiercely, I lose traction on the slick tile and crash on my rear. The fight goes out of me, and I dissolve in an agony of tears.

Right then Caity shows up, unfazed and confident as you please. She takes cool, fast, unflinching command. She opens the drain so the bloody water sinks. Soon, it slurps its last and gurgles out. She drapes a towel over Jack so he's decent, though he's clearly not. Then she dials 911 and hands me the *phone. She signs exactly what I'm to say. Tell them we live at 210 Grove, she orders. Say it's serious bleeding.* Internal bleeding, *she adds mysteriously. There are no slashes on Jack's wrists. No cut marks I can see. Cold terror grips me. Could a person's internal organs simply choose to bleed? And if it's internal, how did the blood seep into the water?*

That's when I spot the curl of a C *and the bold capital* B *carved on my brother's back. I move with extravagant care, sidestepping the dying goldfish that litter the floor and the splinters of glass from their shattered bowl. Jack starts to tease.* "Look at P.J., dancing like a stuck fool while Father Patrick Q. Muldoon is laying coins on her mother's eyes."

"No, Jack. Hush. Don't say that."

"One quarter, two."

"It's not true. You can't say that. Ask Father Muldoon."

"And now on her daddy's: three quarters, four.

Snap.

"You're awake now, P.J. Open your eyes. Sit up."

"No more of that, Dr. Groome. It was awful. I feel bloody horrible and strange."

"Of course. The answers you dredged up are very disturbing."

"What answers?"

"About Jack, P.J. About what happened with Father Muldoon."

"Father Muldoon?"

"You called his name. It's got to stop, you said."

I blink at her, trying to bring things clear. "Muldoon was the parish priest when I was a kid. He retired ages ago and moved away. I don't see what he has to do with the price of broken eggs."

That won me a warm, approving smile. "That's exactly what you have to figure out, P.J. You have the pieces; now all you have to do is figure out how they all fit."

CHAPTER

36

■ **Lottie's good days were growing scarcer, but this** promised to be one. We met on Fifth Avenue near the Plaza Hotel and crossed the busy street to Central Park.

Dennis John was fizzing with excitement, chattering non-stop. "Can we really go to the zoo? Can we really go to the playground? Can we really buy a pretzel from the guy?"

"Yes, yes, and yes," I told him. "That's the deal." The real deal was that checks from my clients had finally cleared, so I could afford the modest treat.

"Can you push me really, really, really high on the swing?"

"Depends. How high is three reallys?"

He pointed skyward, squinting at the sun. "All the way to the clouds!"

"There aren't any clouds. Sky's clear."

"To the moon, then? Can you push me all the way to there?"

"This is daytime, sweetie. The moon's asleep."

"Can you push me all the way to the moon's bedroom, then?"

"Sounds like a pretty tall order."

He turned to Lottie. "But she'll do her best, right?"

"Definitely, honey. I'm sure P.J. will get you as close to the moon's bedroom as she can."

He skipped happily between us as we ran the gauntlet of portrait artists, street vendors, rollerbladers, human statues, and the assorted other people and pets bent on enjoying the glorious day, even if it killed them.

The child preened. "You know what I can do? I can go down the slide headfirst."

"And you know what I can do if you do that? Have a heart attack."

He rolled his eyes. "Don't worry, Aunt Lottie. She's just fooling."

Our first stop was the children's petting zoo. I bought a dollar's worth of animal food from a vending machine to dole out to Dennis John so he'd be happily diverted while I picked Lottie's brain.

"What can you tell me about Charlie Booth's childhood?"

"Not much, I'm afraid. Didn't meet him until after he and Jeannie married and moved north."

"Jeannie didn't talk about his family? Say what he was like as a kid? Where he went to school? Things like that?"

"Jeannie didn't like to talk about the past. Suppose there wasn't much worth remembering."

"She and Booth lived near each other as kids?"

"Near enough. Jeannie's parents had their place in a town called Beaufort and Charlie's family was from the next town. Place called Bluffton."

Dennis John had fed the last of his pellets to a baby goat that now trailed him adoringly.

"Can I have another quarter, P.J.? Baa-Baa's starved."

"His name is Baa-Baa?"

"Yup."

"Baa-Baa Streisand?"

"Just Baa-Baa."

I fished around, found a quarter at the bottom of my purse, and made the buy. "Give him just a couple, okay? You don't want him to get a tummyache."

"Just a couple, Baa-Baa," he told the goat. "You heard her. You'll get sick."

They drifted off, deep in negotiations.

"Who would know about Booth's childhood?" I asked Lottie.

She frowned. "His parents, of course, but I think Jeannie mentioned they passed on. Must be someone else down where he used to live, but I honestly can't say who. Never did hear much about Charlie's family, but I figured his folks washed their hands of him soon as they could. Wouldn't blame them, that's for sure. You love the children God sends, but it was something else entirely that sent him."

"Bluffton you said? That's where he was from?"

"Right. Named for the bluffs that run along the May River. I went down to the area many years ago to help out awhile when Jeannie's great-grandma Annabelle took sick. Wasn't much to those towns back then. Handful of locals lived there year-round. Rest were families from Savannah and the like who built summer homes near the river. I heard you wouldn't recognize the place now. Full of golf courses and condos. Land they could barely give away is worth a mint."

A pair of sheep now trailed Dennis John along with the goat, and he came back to gather more feed.

"That's the last quarter," I said. "Tell them you're not an all-you-can-eat buffet."

"I'm trying, P.J. They won't listen." He walked off working to feign annoyance as a haughty little llama joined the parade.

"Is anyone left down there on Jeannie's side?"

"Last I heard, her mother was, but she didn't turn up for the funeral, so who knows? Not likely she'd have much to tell you in any case. That one was never right, if you know what I mean."

"Doesn't sound very promising."

"Wait. There is someone." She pressed her temples. "Jeannie talked about a neighbor lady, woman who helped Jeannie out when she could. Wasn't easy with those crazy parents of hers. They didn't take kindly to the idea of anyone getting too close to their business. If they caught Jeannie so much as talking to the neighbor, they'd beat her raw. So she only dared to see this lady once in a great while when both her parents were out and things looked to be safe. I can't tell you how much that girl appreciated the kindness; given how little human treatment she ever got at home."

"And you think that woman might have known about Charlie Booth?"

"Way Jeannie told it, this woman got real upset when her folks arranged for her and Charlie to get married. Said he was bad business, always had been. So yeah, sounds like she had a line on him."

"That could be a big help, Lottie. What's the neighbor's name?"

"That's what I'm searching this thick head of mine to find. I sure heard it enough. Jeannie used to remember that neighbor lady in her prayers."

"It'll come to you. Don't worry."

Dennis John came back, this time with a baby mule in tow. "This is Dunk, the donkey. He wanted to meet you."

"Is that so? A pleasure, sir. I'm P. J. Lafferty and this is Dennis John's aunt Lottie Dray."

"Dunk says he's hungry, too."

I checked my watch. "We'll feed him next time, sweetheart. We have to be at the big zoo in ten minutes if we want to watch the trainers feed the porpoises."

He leaned close so the mule wouldn't hear. "I have to go to the bathroom first. OK?"

"I'll take you," Lottie said.

The strain of the outing was starting to show. "No, I will. You sit and rest."

I took him to the boys' room and hovered outside. A suspiciously long time passed.

"Dennis John?" I called through the door. "Are you all right?"

"Fine."

We were fast closing in on porpoise time. "Hurry it up then, OK?"

"P.J.? How come the porpoises get to have lunch and donkeys don't?"

"Everyone gets to have lunch at the zoo, only not all at the same time. It's the porpoises' turn now, so let's get a move on and go watch."

"Do porpoises like people watching them eat lunch?"

"We can ask them when we get there."

He emerged looking sheepish, with dripping hands and large damp blotches on his shirt.

"What happened?"

He shrugged. "I took a drink."

"Do they have one of those hand dryers in there?"

"I think so."

"Good. Go turn it on and dry off."

"But won't we miss the porpoises' lunch?"

"Not if you hurry."

Two minutes later he emerged. I took his hand and spoke over the din of the blower that was still churning hot air inside.

"Come, let's get Aunt Lottie and hustle over to the porpoise pool."

At that instant the noise of the hand dryer stilled, and the air split with a loud, wrenching scream.

CHAPTER

37

■ **A dense crowd had gathered. I spotted them as we** rounded the giant tree that separated the restrooms from the rest of the zoo. The adult faces registered horror and disgust; the children looked dazed and terrified. The air was thick with nervous talk and tearful wailing. A child screeched, "No, Mommy. No!"

Instinctively I gathered Dennis John close, pressing his face to me so he'd be shielded from whatever ugliness had stained this beautiful day.

"What's the matter, P.J.? What's wrong?"

"I don't know, sweetie."

His voice pinched with fear. "Where's Aunt Lottie?"

"I'm sure she's waiting right on the bench where we left her."

I hoisted him onto my hip, and he clutched me hard. He buried his face in my neck, and my ears filled with the sharp, shallow whimper of his fright. "I don't like it."

"I understand, sweetie. Commotion can be scary."

"I feel sick."

His cries were creeping under my skin. Truth be told, I

wasn't feeling all that terrific myself. "Shh, sweetheart. Try to stay calm. Everything is going to be all right."

"But where's Aunt Lottie?"

The bench where we'd left her sitting was beyond the huddled crowd. I carried the boy toward the mass of people and slowly worked my way through.

"What happened? What's going on?" I asked again and again.

A woman hitched her shoulders. "An accident, I think. Someone hurt."

"I heard it was one of the animals," said a woman standing behind a double stroller. "Can't really see."

"Oh, my God!" a woman cried. "Oh, Lord!"

Her shrieks were soon swallowed by the howl of approaching emergency vehicles. I kept pushing forward, eager to get to Lottie. Almost through now. Dennis John clung to me fiercely.

Cops and medics rushed the scene. "Move out, folks. All of you. Back off!"

By now I'd reached the forward fringe. What I saw there sent my stomach lurching.

"What, P.J.? What is it? What's wrong?"

I held his head. "Shh, sweetheart. It's OK."

"Where's Aunt Lottie? I want to see her."

"I'm looking. Maybe she went to the bathroom, too."

I tore my eyes from the bloody horror on the ground and scanned the benches. Lottie was no longer sitting where we'd left her, and I couldn't spot her in the tense, milling crowd.

As I drifted in search of her, a cop blocked my way. "You see who did that, miss?"

"No, I didn't. It happened while we were at the restroom."

He spewed breathy disgust. "Place is packed. Has to be someone who saw that go down."

"That makes sense, Officer. But I didn't."

"Where's Aunt Lottie, P.J.? We have to find her," Dennis John pleaded.

"We will, sweetie. Maybe she took a little walk."

I glanced back, as drawn to the grotesque scene as I was repulsed.

"But she's OK? Nothing bad happened to her?"

"No. This is not about Aunt Lottie. One of the animals got sick. That's all."

That was hardly all, but it was as close to the gruesome truth as I dared to step. The cheeky little goat that had been following Dennis John so eagerly, nagging in his charming way for food, now lay staring blankly at the sky. A spreading crimson pool stained the ground beneath him.

The boy issued a big squeaky yawn. "Honest? You promise God didn't send his chariot for her?"

I stroked his hair and rubbed soothing circles on his back. "She's fine, Dennis John. I'm sure she is. You'll see."

"Which animal got sick?"

"You needn't worry yourself about that. The zoo doctors will take care of him."

"Does he have a sore throat?"

"I don't know." I swallowed hard. The boy had come uncannily close to the fact. A gaping slash traversed the base of the baby goat's neck, the kind of wound hardened homicide cops referred to as a second smile.

By now, more officers from the Central Park Precinct had arrived at the scene. They fanned out to join the first responders, questioning everyone.

"Does the animal have a headache? I had a bad headache once."

"I don't think so, sweetie. I don't think he's hurting at all."

"How come he's sick, then?"

"Because animals get sick like people do."

"How come?"

"It's just natural. That's how come."

He yawned again. "I'm tired."

"Take a rest, then, big guy. You can nap right here on me."

His breathing went smooth. Mine quickened with every passing second. Where was Lottie? What if the monster who had slaughtered that little goat had moved on to her next? What if the monster was Booth?

I could almost hear Albert Dunston's patient chiding. *You're getting ahead of yourself, P.J. Jumping to conclusions. Giving your Mr. Booth more power than he deserves.*

Dennis John seemed to grow heavier with each step. I spotted a vacant seat on a bench, and sat for a moment to regroup.

A rescue van pulled up, and a trio of uniformed medics hurried to the spot where little Baa-Baa lay. One of them crouched, pressed a stethoscope to the animal's chest, and shook his head. Another medic draped a blanket over the dead kid. There was the squawk of two-way radios, strident questions, more outraged cries.

The frenzy subsided as still more officers arrived and demanded that everyone clear the area. Uniformed personnel urged us toward the exits. People started filing out. Soon the place was nearly deserted.

I hung back, still hoping to spot Aunt Lottie, until a young female guard approached. "Have to ask you to leave, miss."

"Sure. Just give me a minute."

"Afraid you'll have to go now. They'll be glad to issue a refund at the gate."

My legs threatened to buckle as I stood, but I drew the kind of deep, slow, invigorating breath I'd learned from Dr. Groome; and I mustered sufficient strength to follow the last stragglers toward the ticket counter. At the exit I shifted Dennis John to my other hip and supported him in the sling of my interlocked hands.

Through the gate I headed left toward Fifty-ninth Street, where we'd entered the Park. It felt as if an eternity had passed. I kept searching for Lottie, scanning frantically. Still, I almost missed her where she sat, slumped on a crowded bench with her head lolling on her chest.

"Aunt Lottie. There you are. Thank heavens. Are you okay?"

She straightened slowly. "Fine, P.J. Better now."

The old man seated beside her rose and strode away. Gratefully I sank in his place, settled Dennis John in my lap, and smoothed his hair. "Did you see that bloody horror at the zoo?"

Lottie shivered. Her face was ashen. "It was him, P.J. A warning."

"Booth?"

She nodded tightly. "Soon as you left to take Dennis John to the bathroom, Charlie came up behind me. Told me don't turn around. My head must've moved. A reflex. And next thing, I feel something sharp pressing hard against my back.

Felt like a knife. I told you not to move, he said. Called me an awful name."

"Are you hurt? Should I call an ambulance?"

"No. He meant to scare me. That's all. Kept threatening, asking where was Dennis John. I said the boy was off with a friend, hoping Booth would get bored like he does and leave. But he stayed there right behind me, and he laughed that ugly way he does. A friend, he said. Is that what you call her?"

My heart was stuttering like a jackhammer. "He was talking about me?"

"Who knows? Could've been hot air. But Charlie was plenty mad. Said I had some nerve letting the boy out of my sight. Said maybe he should get me thrown in jail for neglect."

"He was trying to scare you."

"Only thing that scared me was thinking you'd come back and he'd take after you and the boy. So I did like he said. Close your eyes, he told me. Keep them closed until you count to a hundred, real slow. When you open them again, I want you to take in what you see. Take it in real good. That's just a preview. Next time it's you and your friend."

"That's exactly what he said?"

"Word for word. I can still hear him. Figured the best I could do was go along. So I closed my eyes and started counting. Next thing, I hear a little girl scream. Mommy look, she kept yelling. Look!"

I set my hand on hers and noticed the papery dry fragility of her skin. "Then what happened?"

She shivered. "I looked. Knew it didn't matter anymore. Never takes that man but a minute to do his worst."

"Why did you come here, Aunt Lottie?"

"Charlie said to. Said I should count to a hundred and then leave the zoo and walk. Must've looked a fright, scared for you and Dennis John like I was. But no one noticed with all that was going on."

"It was chaos."

"Would be. Hard to imagine a thing like that happening with all those people around, all those innocent little kids. You don't expect it, that's the thing. Who'd think anyone had the nerve?"

"I'm so glad you're all right."

Now she squeezed my hand. "I'm the one who's glad, P.J. Gladder than I can say. I was just sitting here, thinking how I plain couldn't stand it if anything happened to you or that precious boy. Killed me to have to walk away. What I wanted to do was stay put; make sure he didn't do anything bad to either of you. But I know Charlie. If I dared disobey him, he'd do something awful for spite. So I left like he said, and I walked."

Dennis John stirred in my arms and muttered, "Aunt Lottie?"

"Right here, lovey. Look at you all tuckered out."

"Something happened at the zoo, Aunt Lottie. One of the animals got sick."

She brushed a stray curl from his forehead. "That's OK, sweetheart. He'll be fine in no time. Mark my words."

A crooked little smile fluttered briefly, and then the child's eyes drifted shut again.

Lottie watched until she was sure he'd fallen back to sleep. "I kept walking until I found this empty seat. Don't think I could've managed another step, I was that exhausted. I sat here, hoping the weakness would pass. Kept thinking there was nothing I could do but pray Booth would leave before you got back, that he wouldn't do either of you any harm. Problem was, my mind wasn't all that clear after what went on. When I tried to think up a prayer, all that came to me was Jeannie on her knees, saying her God blesses like a little child before she went to bed. By then she had Dennis John, though she was barely grown herself. But with all she'd been through, she still held on to what little comfort she could get."

"Poor Jeannie," I said, thinking that even my childhood qualified as a bed of roses compared to hers.

Lottie's head dipped sadly. "It all came back to me so clear, sitting with Jeannie while she said those blessings. Girl needed mothering something awful, so I tried to give her as much as I could. After we got Dennis John settled in his crib, I'd help Jeannie get ready to turn in. I know it's babyish, she'd tell me like she had the need to apologize. And I'd say, no it isn't, sweetheart. Not at all. Anything that makes you feel better is fine. Only thing that calls for an apology is hurting someone else."

"It was dear of you to look after her like that."

"Wasn't anything. Jeannie may have been my sister's child, but to me, she was like my own. So I'd wait until she was all ready to turn in, and I'd sit beside her on the bed the way she liked." Her eyes drifted shut.

"Sounds like a nice memory."

"Sitting here, it all came back to me clear. I could hear that sweet little voice of Jeannie's, see her pretty little face. God bless Dennis John, she'd say. And God bless Aunt Lottie. God bless Grandma and Grandpa and Lacy and all the good people in the world. God bless all the bad ones, too, and help them be good."

"Sweet," I said.

She turned to me and smiled. "Better than sweet, P.J. Because then I remembered the rest of it, I remembered how she always blessed that nice neighbor lady last of all. And I remembered that nice lady's name."

■ **Dennis John slept through the cab ride and stayed** asleep when I ferried him to my place. My queen-sized bed fairly swallowed his mite-sized form. He snuggled under the plump quilt I tossed over him, flame curls flattened on the pillow, and the tension on his face dissolved.

I brewed chamomile tea for Lottie, sweetened it with honey, and, after she drank some, urged her to rest on the couch. She protested, but soon enough, she settled back and drifted off as well. Treading lightly to avoid disturbing her, I found Officer Martinez's card near the phone and dialed her number.

She did not sound pleased to hear from me nor the least intrigued when I told her I had information about a case. "What is it this time, Lafferty? Did one of your patients find an image of the Virgin Mary in a baked potato?"

"Actually, I was in the park today, at the children's zoo, when a baby goat was killed. I know what happened, but apparently you're not interested. So that's it, then. Over and out."

"Wait!"

I held the phone away and let her stew, enjoying the pleading that rapidly built to a frustrated shrill.

"Lafferty? Are you there? Lafferty!"

I kept still, gazing fondly at the phone, and it occurred to me that Mr. Bell's invention had never been adequately appreciated for its potential as a torture device.

"Come on. I know you're there, Lafferty. I can hear you breathing. Damn it. Now, pick up!"

In slow motion I lifted the handset to my ear. "Hello? Is someone there?"

"It's me, Martinez. Don't play games."

"Oh, my. You're still holding on, Officer Martinez? I thought our little conversation was finished."

"Is it really necessary for you to be so difficult?"

"I'm the one who's difficult, is it? And here I thought it was you suggesting you couldn't be bothered to hear information about a case."

"Are you home?"

"Of course I am. Where else would I be sitting by the phone, waiting to receive calls from mental patients about Blessed Virgin baked potatoes?"

"I'll be right over."

And so she was, in less than ten minutes by the clock. She showed up alone this time, looking grim. I pressed a finger to my lips. "The boy I told you about is sleeping inside, and that's his aunt on the couch. Whole ugly episode knocked them out."

"I see that. Now would you like to tell me what happened at the zoo?"

"I would. Come in."

"I caught the call about it on the two-way. Heard more on the radio news coming over. Whoever did it is not going to win any popularity contests."

"The three of us were at the zoo when it happened. So was the boy's father, Charlie Booth."

Now she started taking notes, scrawling eagerly. "And you saw this Booth guy attack the goat?"

"No. Not exactly."

The smirk was edging back. "What exactly?"

"I took Dennis John to the bathroom. His aunt was waiting for us near where it happened, and Booth approached her."

Lottie was snoring gently, mouth agape.

"Then I'll have to speak to the lady," Martinez said. "What's her last name?"

"It's Dray. But can't it wait? Be a pity to wake her. She's sick, and all that really wiped her out. Whole thing was pretty hard to take for anyone, sick or not." Saying the words, I went queasy again myself.

"I'm sure it was, but if she's a witness, I've got to hear what she knows. Sooner the better." She bent down and nudged Lottie gently. "Sorry, ma'am, but I need you to wake up now. There. That's the way."

Lottie's eyes snapped open, and I could read her blazing fear. "P.J.?"

"It's OK," I said. "This is Officer Martinez. I called her about what happened today at the zoo."

Grunting with the effort, she sat up. "You shouldn't have."

"I had to. The police should know."

"There's no point. I told you, when it comes to Booth, cops just turn a deaf ear."

"I don't know what's happened in the past, Ms. Dray. But believe me, I'm going to listen to you very carefully," Martinez said.

Lottie's face hardened. "Wasted my breath lots of times. Cops who started out all nice and interested like you."

Martinez perched on the smaller green armchair. "I hear that you don't trust this, ma'am, that you don't trust the police. And that's fair enough. People have to earn your trust; and it doesn't come cheap. Plus, I can't promise I can do what you'd like. Cases go the way they go, which frankly isn't always how they should."

Lottie sniffed. "Don't have to tell me that."

"What I can promise is I'll take in everything you tell me. I'll evaluate it the best I can, and if it adds up, I'll do my level best to see it gets the attention it deserves."

The old woman locked eyes with Martinez, and her expression slowly lost its wary edge. "Suppose it can't hurt to try."

"So you were at the zoo?" Martinez prompted.

"In the children's part. Waiting for P.J. and Dennis John to get back from the bathroom. I was sitting on a bench, warming my bones and feeling good for a change. Warm and relaxed, like I didn't have a care. Then, all of a sudden I feel something behind me. Sense it really, like a storm coming. Next thing, I hear that awful voice of his. And it's like a bad wind kicked up and blew out the sun, like the day went dark. 'Don't turn around,' he tells me. 'Shut your eyes keep them closed. Bitch,' he calls me, and worse. I don't like saying such things, Officer, but that's how Charlie talks."

"How can you be sure it was Charlie Booth?"

Lottie blinked. "I know his voice, that's how. I know how he sounds and the awful things he says. It was him. No question."

"Lots of people have similar voices, ma'am. Similar voices and patterns of speech. Lots of people use bad words and make threats."

"I know Charlie's voice," Lottie repeated firmly. "Like my own."

Martinez nodded slowly. "Did you get a look at him?"

"Didn't dare. You cross Charlie, no telling what he'll do. Dennis John was right nearby. Coming back any time. P.J., too. All I wanted was for Charlie to get done with whatever he had in his mind, and leave."

"You did fine," Martinez said. "What happened next?"

Lottie's eyes went murky. "I sat there for a time, and then I decided to look for P.J. and the boy, to warn them Charlie was around. Tell them to stay away."

"He told you to count to a hundred, remember?" I prodded. "You opened your eyes when you heard the little girl scream."

She studied my face. "Sure. That's right. I heard a scream."

"And then, you left the zoo, like Booth told you to do," I said. "You wandered around until you found a vacant seat on one of the benches, and you were there when I came along a little while later, remember?"

"Please, Ms. Lafferty," Martinez said. "We call that leading the witness, and it won't stand up here much less in court. All the lady can tell me is what she remembers herself. Only what she heard and saw and knows for a fact on her own. According to the law, nothing else counts."

"But it's true what P.J. said," Lottie insisted. "I got confused for a minute, tired and all, but I remember now, clear as day. Charlie said I should sit with my eyes shut and count to a hundred, real slow, and then he said for me to leave the zoo and walk."

"But you never saw him? Is that right, ma'am?"

Lottie's head swerved in annoyance. "I told you no, he said not to, and I knew better than to cross him. But I recognized his voice. It was Charlie Booth behind me, sure as I'm sitting here."

"I understand," Martinez said softly.

"Sorry?"

Now the officer spoke with greater force. "How's your hearing, Ms. Dray?"

"Fine."

"May I ask when's the last time you had it checked?"

Lottie flushed. "Nothing wrong with my ears. My sister always said I could hear a fly land on the neighbor's porch."

"I don't doubt that," Martinez said. "But you have to understand, these are the kinds of questions a defense lawyer would ask you on the witness stand."

"And I'd tell him what I told you: I hear fine. Better than fine. Always did."

"All due respect, ma'am. People lose hearing as they get older. Happens to everyone. It's perfectly natural, and certainly no shame. But a jury would have to take it into account. That, and the fact you never got a look at Booth. You're not an expert on voice recognition, so fingering someone on voice alone would be a mighty tough sell. All that amounts to a great big mountain of reasonable doubt. A case based on that kind of evidence would never even get to court, and if it did for some weird reason, it would never fly. Judge would toss it right out. Grant a dismissal. Booth would walk. And then he'd be free to thank the people who tried to testify against him however he saw fit."

Lottie's look hardened. "I know what I heard. But it's always like this with the cops, so why should you be any different? Booth has the lot of you in his pocket. Don't know how, but he does."

Martinez pressed her palms in prayer position. "I'm not in anyone's pocket. I happen to be on your side, whether it seems that way or not. Problem is the law boils down to rules, piles and piles of them. To make the system work, imperfectly though it does, we have to live with those rules. Like it or not."

Lottie's hands balled in furious fists. "I don't like it. Not one bit. How far does this have to go before that man gets what's coming to him? How many more does he get to hurt and walk away?"

"I hear you, ma'am. It's not easy waiting until justice sorts these things out."

"Maybe it's you has the hearing problem, Officer," Lottie said. "This isn't about your precious law. It's about real flesh-and-blood people, about an innocent little boy and his sweet young momma who lies rotting in her grave. Don't you talk to me about a bunch of rules!" The old woman was quaking with rage.

"Take it easy, Aunt Lottie," I urged. "We'll find another way."

"Have to. Got no choice."

Martinez stood. "I'm sorry there's nothing more I can do right now. But if anything else comes up, any time, I want you to let me know."

"Sure, Officer. I'll call you the very minute I find that sacred baked potato," I said. "Seems that's the sort of thing you consider interesting and important. When it comes to vicious psychopaths and their murdered wives or abused children, you turn your back."

Her face dripped with disgust. "I don't believe you fail to get it, Lafferty. I think you just enjoy spinning my wheels."

"No, Officer. So happens you're wrong. The fact is I don't get it, and I never will. I agree with Aunt Lottie. I'll never understand how that little boy is supposed to be sacrificed on the altar of your blasted rules. And trust me; I don't enjoy any part of it."

She made for the door. "What I said before still goes, Lafferty. Get me something solid, and I'll be all over it. You have my number."

"That I do. And you don't have to worry about hearing from me again. Next time I have something to report, I'll try to find someone who gives a damn."

"I told you, call me."

"Not likely."

She beckoned for me to follow her out on the stoop. There she stood in bold relief, backlit by the glow of the sinking sun. "Listen to me, Lafferty. I'm only going to say this once. If you claim I said it, I'll deny it. If it's my word against yours, mine wins by an uncontested landslide. You understand?"

"I'm listening."

"Listen carefully. I'm the best you've got, maybe all you've got. You read me?"

"No, I don't. Exactly what is that supposed to mean?"

"There are the written rules I talked about. And then there are the unwritten ones. They're the ones that make the world go round, or flat, as the case may be."

"Such as?"

"Who's the real boss, for one thing? Who runs the show? Whose word is really the last? Which informal directives do you follow if you're smart, especially if you're smart and ambitious? You don't cross certain people, Lafferty. Not if you want to get ahead in this job. There are very few of us dumb or honest enough to cross that line."

"And you're saying you're one of the rare ones that will?"

"Could be."

"What is it, Martinez? Dumb or honest?"

She sniffed. "Seeing I put up with you, it must be some of both."

"You already gave me the speech about how all you really care about is keeping your nose clean and serving out your time, sending the young ones to dental school. All that grand, noble rot that's just a lame excuse for copping out."

"You missed the punch line, Lafferty. I care about all that. You bet I do. But I care even more about what's right. That's why I went into this frustrating, low-paying, dangerous line of work in the first place. That's why I'm in it still."

"So you're trying to tell me you're a good, honest scout. One of the brave and few who's prepared to risk everything to do what's right."

She glared at me. "So happens I've gone out on that shaky limb more times than I care to think about. And if it's necessary, I mean really necessary, as in some well-meaning idiot has managed to get on the wrong side of exactly the wrong person at a crucial time, yes, I'm willing to crawl out after them and risk the consequences again."

"You mean Chief Daley?"

"I'm not going to spell it out for you, Lafferty. You'll have to draw your own conclusions. But do it in invisible ink."

"You'd go out on a limb for me?"

Now she laughed. "Not hardly. If it was only you, I'd sooner cut the damned limb off. I don't think I've ever met anyone more exasperating, ungrateful, or pigheaded. And those are your good points. You're so out there at the head of the pack of people who've driven me nuts, I'd be hard-pressed to name a runner-up."

"You're being sincere," I accused.

"I am. I'm telling you how it is because I do care about what happens to little boys and their mothers. I'm telling you that if you're dumb and headstrong enough to keep this up, which sadly I believe you are, and if by some crazy accident you happen to stumble onto something worthwhile, you should bring it to me, though to be one hundred percent honest, I won't be the least bit disappointed if all of this, including you, goes away."

"You're a good person, Officer Martinez."

"My cross to bear."

She started away. "You dropped something, Lafferty. There, behind the bush."

"Thanks."

As she retreated down the block toward her squad car, I knelt and stretched around the privet hedge to reach a soot-gray envelope in a plastic bag. One of those standard form apologies from the U.S. Postal Service, expressing their regrets for mangling my mail, was taped to the front.

The envelope's flap was torn, and a large chunk had been ripped from its side. I recognized the writing and, of course, the return address. When I slipped the letter from its plastic cocoon, the paper was sodden. Who knew how long it had been lying there, probably dropped by the postman when he tried to stuff the typical surfeit of junk in my small metal box?

I took the envelope inside and dried it in the microwave, sixty seconds at a time, testing between hits for doneness.

Lottie had fallen asleep again, but she was awakened by the sound of the microwave. "What's that?"

"I'm cooking the mail. Sorry to disturb you."

At the table I unsealed the envelope and extracted the contents. What I found left me reeling.

True to her word, Big Millie had sent the promised evidence. I turned it over and over again, ran my fingers over the smooth surface, and held it up to the light, marveling that it was exactly as advertised: proof that she had tangled with Charlie Booth. As a bonus, this confirmed where he worked. While I'd been out risking my neck, bumbling in the dark, that huge raving psycho had simply reached out and grabbed the perfect thing.

CHAPTER

39

■ **Creighton phoned with the kind of good news that** turned out to be anything but. "I requested the postmortem you wanted, P.J. Came in earlier today."

"That's wonderful, sir. I can't thank you enough."

"No thanks required. A deal's a deal, as you like to say. I spoke with Dr. Groome, and she told me you've been putting in the effort and making excellent progress."

"I'm glad she recognizes that."

"She does. She's very pleased. I trust you're going to keep up with it."

"I will, Dr. Creighton. She's good, in a weird sort of way, and I'll keep seeing her. But not every day."

"I don't expect that, P.J. But since you've achieved the right momentum, it's important to stick with it."

"Believe it or not, I agree with you. It does feel as if we're closing in on something important."

"That's good to hear. What sort of modified schedule do you have in mind?"

"We've talked about dropping back to twice a week for now. See how it goes."

"Sounds reasonable."

"Glad you approve, sir. When can I see the report?"

"Right now, if you like. I'm in the neighborhood. On Seventy-ninth. There's a small place on the southeast corner. We can meet there in ten minutes, if you're available."

"I'll be there."

Lottie had left with Dennis John shortly after five p.m. As soon as they were out the door, I'd yielded to the strain, exhaustion, and a mammoth craving to be swaddled in cozy pajamas, furry slippers, and my lumpy afghan. I had a pizza delivery planned as soon as I could muster the mental acuity to decide between sausage and pepperoni. This loomed as an even more monumental undertaking than choosing between the red plaid nightshirt and my Old Faithful blue flannels.

But now all that went by the board. Creighton's news raised me from the dead. I dashed into the shower, took the human equivalent of a drive-through carwash, and tossed on what I considered to be presentable clothes: black slacks, a striped blouse with no obvious stains on the front, socks, and loafers. I brushed on a trace of mascara, blush, and lip gloss, ran a comb through my damp hair, and hurried out.

Dr. Creighton sat alone at the broad mahogany bar, staring at the TV where a perky blond reporter was filing her story live from Central Park. Soon she was eclipsed by a taped feed and the anchorman's voiceover. A chill ran through me as I watched the scene at the petting zoo again. There was the throng of horrified onlookers, a close-up of the blanket over the small, inert bulge that mere moments before had been cheeky little Baa-Baa Streisand.

He ticked his tongue. "Murdering baby goats. Jesus."

I mounted the stool beside him. "I was there; it was awful, sir. Truly."

He stirred his martini, raising a bright, oily swirl. "You were there? I must say, P.J., I'd never have taken you for a denizen of the children's zoo."

"I was there with a friend and her little boy. Certainly wasn't what you expect when you take a little one off to enjoy a beautiful day in the park."

"My kids love that petting zoo, but you have to wonder if there's any place in the world that's safe."

"You don't have to wonder, Dr. Creighton. There isn't."

"Sadly, I think you're right. What amazes me is they have no idea who did it. Imagine someone being brazen enough to slit an animal's throat right there in public in the light of day and no one sees."

"He is that, Dr. Creighton. Brazen as it gets."

"He?"

"Charlie Booth. The very same Charlie Booth who stabbed his wife during that fire drill at Rikers."

He frowned. "My understanding is that no one came forward about the case. If you know that for a fact, why haven't you reported it?"

"I tried to, but I don't have sufficient proof. I had taken the boy to the bathroom when it happened, and the lady with me who had a run-in with Booth only heard his voice. He made sure of that."

"Too bad."

"Yes. But maybe he's not as clever as he thinks."

"Meaning?"

"I'll explain. But please, can I see that postmortem first? If I have to wait another second, I'll explode."

"Care for a drink? Sounds like you could use it."

"I could, now that you mention it. What you're having would be grand."

He ordered, and while the bartender poured the ingredients in a shaker, Creighton ruffled through his briefcase for the autopsy report.

"Have you read it, Dr. Creighton?"

"Haven't had the time. It came in moments before I left the office."

"I'm dying to know if Jeannie was slashed in the shape of a *C* or a *B*, which is signature Booth. He likes to mark what's his. That's typical of the violent possessive personality."

I leafed through the report. Like all postmortems, this one was filled with no end of numbing details. There was the standard identifying data: the victim's age, marital status, last known address and phone number, height, weight, general condition, obvious health issues (aside from the central fact that her health was not an issue anymore). Following that was a blow-by-blow description of the autopsy. The coroner detailed how he'd accessed, visualized, removed, examined, and evaluated every organ. I held a chilling image of Jeannie Bagshaw's remains on the harsh metal examining table, a gaping intersection carved from her abdomen to her chest, her skull cut away. The cap of thick red curls tossed aside.

"Where did you hear that term?" Creighton asked.

"Which?"

"Violent possessive personality? It's vaguely familiar."

"A British forensic scientist identified that particular criminal type. His name's Albert Dunston. Have you heard of him?"

He frowned. "I don't think so. But there are so many."

"Quite an amazing man. Brilliant really." I kept scanning the report as I talked, desperately searching.

Creighton drained his drink and surprised me by summoning another. He'd never been much of a tippler, or so I'd thought. "Sounds as if you know this man Dunston personally," he said.

"I do. One of those weird coincidences. I happened on a book of his, *Dark Reckoning,* while I was at one of Caity's signings. The subject was a monstrous horror named Blake Madigan who kept his wife and daughters prisoners in a secluded house. He tortured them, did unthinkable things. Eventually he killed his wife and older daughter. Dunston interviewed the surviving daughter for the book. He's been studying that brutal personality type for decades."

I read on, learning far more about Jeannie's heart, liver, and spleen, not to mention her stomach contents (tuna salad, white bread, grapes, apple juice, and a single ginger snap) than I cared to know. The M.E. described her organs of reproduction and excretion in excruciating detail as well. Apparently, she'd had other pregnancies in addition to Dennis John. There was evidence of at least one botched abortion, very likely a do-it-yourself home version, or one perpetrated by Charlie Booth.

The cause of death was exsanguination. Jeannie had bled to death secondary to a deep puncture wound that had struck a critical artery. Still, I hadn't come to the part about the nature of that wound. The shape of it. How it looked.

I heard the clink of Creighton's stirrer in his fresh drink. "How did you happen to meet Dunston?" His voice had a hard judgmental edge, but I refused to let his disapproval distract me. I answered without looking up. "I told you, I ran across his book. I couldn't get over the similarity between his subject and Charlie Booth. They were both violent possessive personalities. Both about the same age, with young, vulnerable wives and small children."

"I understand. But how was it that you and the author happened to meet?"

"I contacted his publisher. Told them I wanted to speak to Dunston about a case. And he agreed."

"So I take it he's here in New York?"

I marked my place and glanced up. "He is. At Mount Sinai. He was stabbed by a subject and badly hurt."

"Is he expected to survive?"

"Yes. At least, I hope so."

"To good outcomes," Creighton said grimly. "The end is what counts after all."

I wanted to quip that the means could be significant as well, but a harsh note in his tone kept me mute. Something had changed in my former boss. He seemed distant and far less approachable than I'd thought. Or perhaps I'd never known him as well as I'd wanted to believe.

I lifted my glass to meet Creighton's. Only after I took a sip did I remember that martinis are too strong for me by far. A sip left me sputtering and coughing. My hand quaked, slopping gin, vermouth, and anchovy-stuffed olives across Jeannie's autopsy report.

Creighton took a pile of cocktail napkins from the stack in front of him and blotted the worst of the mess. My knees were damp, my dignity—such as it was—in tatters. Dr. Creighton had been spattered as well. Damp spots freckled his silver trousers, and an olive rested atop his spit-shined right shoe.

"I'm so sorry, Dr. Creighton. What a clumsy oaf."

"Don't worry about it. I'll get you another."

"Make it a glass of wine this time, would you, sir? White to be safe."

I returned to studying the report. Scars from countless old external and internal injuries were graphically described. Jeannie's slender young body was a mass of fibrous tissue, contractures, and adhesions. There were ugly patches where she'd been cut or burned. Her spleen had been ruptured, and more than two dozen old fractures had left their mark on her bones.

I was nearing the end, and still I found no description of the lethal wound. The medical examiner had recorded its depth at 10 cm, almost 4 inches, and stated that a 4 cm tear had been discovered in Jeannie's descending aorta. But what had appeared on the surface?

The final page contained the coroner's certification, the requisite statement that he had completed the examination personally and that the findings as reported were, in his professional opinion, accurate and complete. Puzzled, I flipped through the rest of the pages again. Nothing.

"I don't get it. Where's the description of the lethal injury?"

"It has to be there." Creighton took the report from me and flipped to the section he sought. "Here it is. On page three, paragraph four, it says 'Cause of death: exsanguination. Manner of death: deep puncture wound to the descending aorta. Probable weapon: long sharp instrument such as an ice pick or awl.'"

"Yes, but it doesn't say how that wound looked on the outside."

"That's implied. It says a deep puncture wound, probably made by an ice pick or similar instrument." He turned to the bartender. "Can I trouble you for another olive?"

He delivered three in a shot glass. Creighton plucked one out and impaled it horizontally with his martini stirrer. When he removed the stirrer, a small, neat round hole remained. "On the surface, a deep puncture wound looks like that."

"That can't be."

"Why not?"

I stared at my hand, wondering if there was such a thing as a brain line and what, if anything, could be done in the tragic case of someone like me who'd been born without one.

"Because I was counting on finding out that Charlie Booth had carved his initials on Jeannie," I said dully. "That's what he does. He burns or slashes in the shape of a *C* or *CB*."

"That's Booth's modus operandi?"

"Yes. All violent possessives have their little quirks, and Booth's is to mark what's his. He's not particular, uses whatever's handy: lit cigarettes, razor blades, broken glass. But he always makes his mark."

"Which means?"

I sipped my wine or, to be completely accurate, tossed it back as if I was trying to douse a fire.

"Could mean nothing. Maybe he made an exception, this once. Maybe he didn't have time to do the engraving. A fire drill only lasts so long. I'd bet Booth was about to do his standard marking after he killed Jeannie, but then he heard someone coming, and he ran."

He sniffed. "Anything's possible." The rest went without saying. If anything was possible, it was possible that I was dead wrong.

"Booth killed Jeannie Bagshaw," I said. "He killed her, and I'm going to prove it."

Creighton's face expressed his contempt. "It would seem the postmortem you were so desperate to get your hands on is not going to prove a thing."

I scowled at the autopsy report. "That was just one idea. I've got plenty of others."

Now he blew an exasperated breath. "Listen to me, P.J. I understand what you're going through. Some things grab hold of us, and it's incredibly hard to let go. But those are the very things we must give up before they consume us completely."

"That's not what's going on here, Dr. Creighton. There's a big difference between wanting to resolve an unthinkable injustice and being obsessed."

"Keep working with Dr. Groome. I suspect you'll discover soon enough that all this murder business is a smokescreen."

"That's not true."

"You'll discover what's true when you're prepared to accept it. In the meantime, I understand that nothing I say is going to dissuade you from playing this thing out."

"True."

He raised his glass and drank to my stubborn futility. "You said Booth wasn't as clever as he thinks. What was that about?"

I shrugged. "Probably nothing, Dr. Creighton. Another one of my harebrained ideas. You know how it is when you get behind a smokescreen. It's plain impossible to bring anything clear."

CHAPTER

40

■ **"Why you be calling me middle of the night like this,**
P.J.? What right you got mucking up my pillow squawk? Tell
me that."

"I didn't call you, Millie. You called me. Anyway, it's not
the middle of the night; it's ten in the morning."

"What you say?"

"I said it's ten in the morning. Three minutes after ten,
exactly."

"That's it! That's the heartworm! You be talking zackly
shit like that, fraid I got to ask you for your brother's maiden
name."

"Stop, Millie. This is ridiculous."

"I'll give you dickless, girl. You do like I say."

"Men don't have maiden names."

"Tell me right now or I'm banging up this phone."

"All right. It's Goldstein."

"Dayum. You got some kind of bread on your shoulders,
you know?"

"Actually, I'm glad to hear from you, Millie. I was just
about to call you. I got what you sent, and it's a big help.
Thanks."

She snorted. "Lookee cookie. All I had to do was call up those red-eyed lickety gibbets and tell them what's who and next thing, they stop messing with the rain or shine."

"That's not how it happened, Millie. Your letter got damaged, and then the postman dropped it when he came to deliver it. Someone spotted it behind the hedge outside my building. It could've been sitting there for days."

"Pose man my ass. But all smells like men's hell, ain't that so? Now you can go on and lock up that Jeannie girl's sumbitch husband. Wreck a wedding get you twenty-some to life."

"I'm working on it, Millie. Have you seen Booth again?"

"Yes indeedy tweedy. Saw him first thing today. Me and Tyree was out in the yard, getting her ready for the booty contest and don't that sumbitch come up by the fence all looking upside his frying little strobe eyes like Tyree's booty got something in the world to do with him."

"Was he in the same uniform?"

"Nope. Had on a new one, wasn't all ripped to shit. Time I got through with his old one, that thing's weasel was so plopped."

"Millie. I'm going to ask you this once and I need you to think it through and answer very carefully. Are you absolutely positive that was Jeannie's husband you saw? Are you completely sure you tore the uniform on the same man you saw in Jeannie's cell?"

"Never saw no man in Jeannie's cell, P.J. Lest you count that one time Jeannie was feeling poorly and Ole King Coca-Cola came by to bring her tray."

"I'm talking about the man in the picture in Jeannie's cell. Her husband. Are you sure that was the same person you saw washing off blood with a hose after the murder, the same one who left you a dead rat? The same one you saw near the fence today?"

"You doubtin' my ferocity, P.J. Is that what I see goin down?"

"I'm double checking, that's all. I'm planning to take what you sent me to the cops. I'm going to ask them to check it out based on the strength of what you've told me. So I have to be able to rely on you completely."

"Lawdy Ann. And they say I'm the one got the prostitution complex."

"So it's true, then? I can count on it?"

"Course you can. Here's the actual factual. I did like you said. I been taking my pills all nice and regular, you know those big ole white ones smoothes you out real creamy and them little pretty bitty ones make you feel so squeachy keen? I been seeing the shrinky dink all regular, too. Bearing my parts. I'll tell you square as air, sometimes my mind gets goin' so it's hard for my brain to keep up. But right now, I'm flat in the groove.

"You're sure?"

"Sure as I ever been. Sure as tootin. Doo dah day."

■ **I had expected Albert Dunston to be delighted. And he**
was, though not with me. The tray before him held a bright
linen cloth, fine tableware, and a sumptuous-looking dinner
Dr. Parkman had arranged to have delivered by Primola, one
of the city's most popular Italian restaurants. Heady aromas
wafted from the soup. A gleaming slick of olive oil and bal-
samic vinegar capped an antipasto of cheeses, meats, and
grilled vegetables. For the main course, there was veal with
wild mushrooms in a rich red wine sauce, and pasta with
black truffles. Dunston munched happily on a breadstick.
"Care for anything, P.J.? It's delicious."

"Thanks anyway, sir. Honestly, all I want is to hear what
you think."

"There's only one thing to think: it's risky."

"Risky how?" Again, I showed him the photo I'd taken of
the fabric scrap Big Millie had sent. There it was: real, undeniable hard evidence.

"As you well know, things are not always as they appear."

"That's exactly as it appears: a torn piece from a workman's uniform with the name sewn over the pocket."

"That's what it would seem to be."

"No. That's what it is."

He took the picture from me and squinted slightly as he examined it from a variety of angles. "Are you willing to entertain a different possibility?"

"Like what?"

"Suppose you're walking on the beach and you find a bottle that's washed ashore. Inside, you find a note, written in a weak, shaky hand. The message is a desperate cry for help. Obviously, the person who wrote it is at the end of his rope, barely holding on. You read the note again and again and you decide you have to find the poor fellow, the one whose sailboat capsized in a freak storm. Somehow he managed to survive, and he washed up some time later, near dead of exposure and dehydration, on a deserted island."

I gave in and tried a breadstick, which was a homemade and incredibly good. "What a nightmare."

"Naturally, that's how you react. You're overwhelmed with concern for this unfortunate young man. And it seems fated that since you're the one who discovered his note, you're the one who must figure out a way to rescue him."

"That would be quite the tall order."

"True, but compelling, as you might imagine."

"I can, but I don't see what this has to do with that evidence."

He smiled. "You will. You become more and more obsessed with finding that poor lost soul. You can barely think of anything else. You decide to quit your job and work on it full-time. People try to reason with you, but you're beyond that. Eventually your friends and family grow disgusted and drift away."

I felt a surge of indignation. It was my life, my choice. What right did anyone have to judge? "So it goes."

Dunston's head dipped. "You remain true to your mission. And then one day the most amazing thing happens. You're out on your boat, the one you've sacrificed everything to buy, and suddenly, there it is!"

"The island!"

"Yes. The exact island described in the note. You recognize it at once. Every detail matches the mental picture you've held for months; including the crude sign your victim said he'd posted on a piece of driftwood near the shore."

"There you are!"

"Ah, yes." Dunston tried his soup, and his eyes drooped with pleasure. "The triumphal moment at long last. Barely able to contain yourself, you land your boat and race ashore. You race over the rise, where the lost sailor said he'd built his lean-to. And do you know what you find?" His blooming smirk punctured the fantasy.

"Sure I do. A great, ugly pool of quicksand."

"Close. What you find in fact is an exclusive, five-star resort where many years back, a couple of bored teenage sons of wealthy visitors decided to stuff that note you found in a bottle for kicks."

"This is different," I railed. "Way different. Look." I tore the photo from his grasp. "There's his name. There's the company he works for. This is not some goofy teenage prank, and I'm no addled Don Quixote. In this case, one and one happens to make two."

Dunston remained unmoved. "Possibly."

"Possibly my foot. Big Millie ripped that fabric from Booth's uniform, plain and simple. This is hard evidence, something real and solid you can hold in your hand." I brandished the picture like a victory flag. "This is your precious verification."

He handed me another breadstick and a chunk of Parmesan cheese. "I'm not suggesting that you're mistaken or irrational. In fact you may be completely correct, there's a good chance of that."

"Hallelujah! You're admitting I could be right."

He raised a moderating hand. "Of course you could. But you could also be wrong. Remember what I said about building an unassailable case, one that can't be torn down. That fabric scrap could be an important piece of evidence, as you suggest. But it doesn't stand as a certainty on its own."

"Why not?"

"Several reasons. The person who gave it to you is insane. You have no chain of evidence. You can't prove that it came from a uniform on your Mr. Booth. You can't even prove that it came from a uniform. Before you run with it, I'm urging you to seek the necessary corroboration."

"And I'd be glad to. But how am I supposed to do that? Cure Big Millie? Find the instant replay of her encounter with Booth that doesn't exist?" I flopped on the chair, frustrated nearly, but not quite, beyond words. "It's ridiculous."

Dunston's smile dripped with maddening forbearance. "You've answered your own question. Obviously, you can't prove it beyond a reasonable doubt, which is the standard you'd have to meet. So the best answer is to pursue a different and hopefully more fruitful line of investigation, something that can lead to unassailable proof. I know how difficult it can be to admit you've come to a dead end and cut your losses, but given the facts, that's the only reasonable way to proceed."

"I disagree. This isn't some random note in a bottle that washed ashore. It's real, tangible evidence, and it makes no sense to throw it away."

"Have you considered what you might be throwing away instead?"

"Such as?"

"Such as the confidence of your contact in the Police Department. Can you honestly afford to risk losing that?"

Angrily I bit the head off another breadstick. This one tasted grainy and dry.

"Can you?"

I chewed glumly.

"You've already given that fabric scrap to Officer Martinez, haven't you? That's why you're showing me the picture and not the real thing."

I hitched my shoulders. Why waste precious words?

"Then it would seem this conversation is moot," Dunston said. "No point discussing it further."

"Martinez was all over it," I said. "She thanked me for bringing it to her and promised to get on it right away."

His left brow hiked ever-so-slightly. "Care to try the veal, P.J.? It's wonderful."

"She's going to question Booth's boss about ruined or missing uniforms. Find out if Booth was on a crew at Rikers on the day Jeannie was killed. If he was, we have proof of access. And we certainly have motive. Booth got Jeannie locked up in the first place because he wanted her out of the way. So now he decided he wanted her out of the way permanently."

His expression shifted into neutral as he chewed.

"After that, all we'd have to do is interview his coworkers, prove Booth went missing at the time Jeannie was killed, and there's your unassailable case."

"One way or another we shall see." He lifted the remote from his bedside table and flicked on the TV. "Let's have a look at the news, then, why don't we? It's always good to know what's going on."

■ In psychotherapy, the resolution of a knotty, resistant problem can come in the most unexpected way. In the case of Clarissa Demetrios, the means to defuse her sadistic anger toward her husband turned out to be garden-variety displacement. In the space of a few short sessions, her flaming rage at Ted had been simply and effortlessly redirected toward me.

She was pacing, dripping contempt, slashing the air with a long, bloodred fingernail. "You know? I've been doing a great deal of thinking, P.J."

"Is that so?"

"About you."

"I see."

"Highly unpleasant thoughts. Disturbing. And it strikes me that this should not be the result of expensive, time-consuming counseling sessions. I'd think at the very least, the client should derive a measure of contentment."

"Actually, the goal is personal understanding, Clarissa. A realistic appraisal of one's circumstances and improved capacity to cope with them. I suppose you could call that contentment, but I think there's more to it."

She scowled. "I don't give a damn what you think. The fact is you're so far beneath me it's absurd."

"I understand that you feel that way. And it follows that it makes no sense for us to make further attempts to work together. Let's call this our final session."

She sat, crossed her legs decorously, and lit a cigarette. "What a pathetic little person you are."

Ted hunched on the couch beside her, staring at the floor.

"Put the cigarette out, Clarissa, or follow it outside," I said.

She took another drag, sucking her cheeks to the bone. Mentholated plumes spilled through her nostrils. "I do as I please, you silly twit, not as you tell me."

"You can do as you please elsewhere."

She snickered and took another greedy pull on the cigarette. "Precisely what do you plan to do about it?"

"Me? Nothing."

"I didn't think so."

I gestured at Ted, and he trailed me quickly through the bedroom door. As we crossed the threshold, a signal flared on the smoke detector in the living room. Harsh clanging followed, and water burst from the sprinkler above Clarissa's head. Shock rooted her in place as the cold shower doused everything from her fancy hairdo to her ostrich purse, pricey green suede suit, and billion-dollar shoes. The cigarette she was holding sizzled and then melted to a sodden droop in her hand. The dense spray doused her face as well, melting her careful makeup into muddy mascara trails, rivulets of flesh-toned base, puddles of lavender shadow, and livid tendrils of peach blush.

"The nerve!" she sputtered when she found her voice. "You'll pay for this!"

The white cashmere coat she'd thrown on the chair was soaked as well. Blind with rage, Clarissa tossed it on. "You'll hear from my attorney. And from the licensing board. I wish I could be there when they strip you of your credentials. Wouldn't that be fun?"

I surveyed the damage to my apartment. Some hard time with the hair dryer should take care of restoring things to their former substandard state. That was a big advantage of having little of value; there was precious little to lose.

She dropped the soaked cigarette and ground it into the floorboards with the toe of her saturated pump. "I'd say that constitutes an assault," she said, brightening. "An assault, at the very least. Somehow I don't think the police will be amused by the notion of a therapist attacking a patient in the middle of a session. Imagine the scandal: a psychologist who completely loses control of her behavior and hurls a huge pot of scalding water at someone attempting to unburden herself. A client entrusted to that therapist's care, no less. Outrageous!"

Head cocked at a coy angle, she eyed the pasta pot Caity had used days ago, the one that still rested on the burner where I'd left it to dry after I washed it. "What do you think, Ted darling? Would the judge be sufficiently impressed by second-degree burns, or shall I have Dr. Serafin make it third-degree? Perhaps a mixture of second and third would be better. Over thirty, or perhaps forty percent of my body. Thankfully, nothing on the face. Details like that are so very convincing, don't you think?"

"Stop, Clarissa," Ted rasped.

She cupped her ear. "What was that? Did I hear you say you'd prefer I tell them you were the one who hurled the hot water at me? Is that what you said, Ted my sweet?"

His jaw twitched. "I said stop. You got what you deserved. She asked you not to smoke, but you chose to anyway. So you set off the sprinkler. It's your fault. Don't take it out on her."

"My, my. Aren't we getting cheeky? That's what incompetent counseling can do, I fear. Make a person lose all sense of what he can pull off." The wet suede squeaked when she folded her arms. "You'd best get a grip, darling. It would be a dreadful pity if I had to have you committed for a sudden nervous collapse. Imagine how your precious daughter would miss you. And I'd simply have to send her off to one of those residential programs you're so opposed to. Given the situation, your psychotic break and all, what choice would I have?"

Ted went pale. "You wouldn't."

"Actually, I would."

"Actually, Clarissa, Ted's right. You wouldn't and you won't."

"Watch me."

"First, *you* watch me." I crossed the room, sidestepping the puddles, and stopped beside the cabinet that held my TV and the recorder I used to tape all my sessions. I pressed the Eject button and extracted the tape from this hour. "You can go on and tell whatever you like to whomever you like, Clarissa. This will expose you for precisely what you are. By the way, lodging false charges is a serious criminal offense. Punishable by imprisonment."

Her eyes flashed and then skittered madly. "This is outrageous. The nerve of you to make a recording without my permission. My attorney will see about this."

"You tell your attorney I'll be happy to provide a copy of the permission you signed at the beginning of our first session, the one that states you agree to have the sessions taped." I checked my watch. "Now, would you look at that? We're fresh out of time."

Ted bore a look of stony resolve that told me he'd be all right. Weakness was catnip to Clarissa. As soon as you learned to bark back, she went in search of less challenging prey.

After the door closed behind them, I reveled in a moment of soggy triumph. Everything seemed to be coming together at last. Of course, that's the exact thought I had before harsh, insistent rapping at the door signaled the opposite: that in fact, everything I had built to this point was poised to come apart.

CHAPTER 43

■ **Officer Martinez stood on my stoop, sporting a look** that chilled me to the bone.

"Come in," I said. "You have news?"

She didn't budge. "I wouldn't call it news."

"What then?"

"Have you ever stumbled on one of those amazing coincidences, Lafferty? The kind of coincidence that makes you believe that there must be some cosmic puppeteer lounging around on a big puffy cloud, pulling our strings and laughing his fool head off? A puppeteer with a really sick sense of humor?"

"Would you like to come in and tell me what you're talking about, Officer?"

"Actually, no. What I'd like is for you to come with me. No wait, let me be completely accurate. You are *going* to come with me. We're going to walk down the block to my squad car, and I'm going to drive you to the precinct house. Then I'm going to take you up to my office where I have some nice visual aids to help you to understand what I'm going to tell you."

"I don't need visual aids. Tell me now."

"We're going to do this my way, Lafferty. Every bit of it. Do you read me?"

I did, and my insides went tight with fear. "Sure, fine."

"Get your coat."

She settled me in the back of the squad car and shut the bulletproof panel between us. The 19th Precinct was only a five-minute ride, but it seemed far longer before we arrived at the vintage fifties brick building whose doors and windows were framed by garish blue trim.

Martinez parked on the street and led me inside. The cops we passed eyed me with open disdain. I felt like a kid on the way to the woodshed who knows for a certainty that he's about to be paddled raw but has no idea what he's done to earn the privilege.

Her office was a cramped, cluttered square. Files and reports perched everywhere. She closed the door and motioned for me to sit on the stiff metal folding chair beside her desk. From the large bottom drawer she produced the fabric scrap I'd given her, a stack of photographs that she laid facedown on the blotter, and several documents, which she also turned over so I couldn't see what they were.

"So here's the story, Lafferty. I went to Star-Tech Heating and Air, as you suggested. I took this so-called evidence you gave me, and I showed it to the boss, a man named Petrovich. Nice guy, very serious and sincere. Probably in his early sixties by now, and he's been with the company since he graduated from high school."

"Could you please just tell me what happened?"

She wagged her finger. "Lafferty, Lafferty. What you need is to learn a little patience. Make that a lot of patience. Now, why don't you sit and listen, and practice being patient, while I tell this in my own good time."

"But—"

"Oops. See what I mean? I'd say impatience is one of your biggest problems, maybe *the* biggest. So I'm going to do you a big favor and help you find the cure. Now, you sit back and zip it."

She stared at me, her face set in a dare.

"Good," she said. "You get half a smiley face. Now, where

was I?" She hummed. "Right. Mr. Petrovich takes a great deal of pride in the company, views it as his in a way. Can you understand loyalty like that?"

"Sure."

She ticked her tongue. "No talking, remember? You're to keep still, even if I ask you a direct question. You got that?"

I kept still.

"Petrovich cares intensely about the quality of the work Star-Tech does and about preserving the company's reputation, the reputation he's worked so hard for so many years to build. That makes sense to you?"

I pretended I was posing for a still life. I imagined I was a perfect, ripe, speechless apple—a Granny Smith.

She rewarded that with a grudging nod. "In fact, it was that impeccable reputation that helped Star-Tech to win the public bidding for a fat contract to replace some of the many miles of outmoded ductwork on Rikers. The job was huge, and highly competitive."

"That's exactly what Big Millie told me. She saw Charlie Booth laying ducts."

She shook her head. "See there? You're being impatient again. And talking, which is just what I asked you not to do."

"Sorry."

She pressed a finger to her lips. "If you mouth off one more time, if you even speak a word, I'm afraid I'll have no choice but to lock you up in one of our hospitality suites downstairs."

I opened my mouth to protest the absurdity of that, but quickly shut it again. I could see that she meant what she'd said. Every precinct had a couple of holding cells, and a person could be detained in one for a day or two for almost any reason, which in my case would be felonious failure to imitate a piece of fruit.

"Turned out the Rikers job was going very well," Martinez said. "So well, Star-Tech was on track to snag the bonus built into the contract for bringing the job in ahead of schedule. So imagine how upset that nice Mr. Petrovich was when his best welder up and disappeared. Petrovich called the guy again and again, left message after message, but he heard nothing. For the life of him, he couldn't figure out what was going on. This was his top man, someone who had always been hardworking and reliable. All of a sudden—poof, he doesn't come in one day and that's that.

"At first, Petrovich figured the guy must have gotten sick, maybe came down with a bad flu or something and felt too lousy to talk on the phone. Or maybe he had laryngitis and couldn't talk, even if he wanted to. The guy was divorced and lived alone, so there was no one to call for him. Petrovich even considered that maybe this guy had met someone and lost his mind for a couple of days. Poor man was lonely, after all. Or maybe he'd gone out to a bar and one thing led to another and he'd gone on a bender. This guy wasn't like that normally, but things happened.

"Still, when he hadn't heard anything by the third day, Petrovich started to get really worried. Maybe the guy had had a heart attack, or a terrible accident. Maybe he'd slipped in the tub or gotten a piece of food caught in his throat. Who knew? So Petrovich sent one of his other men around to check on this guy. The man he sent was gone for about an hour. When he got back to the office, he told Petrovich he was able to see the missing guy walking around behind the shades; so obviously he wasn't dead or hurt or even terribly sick. But the guy wouldn't answer the door. Wouldn't respond at all."

She went mute again, playing me. I seized the opportunity to gnaw a hangnail on my thumb.

"You see, Lafferty? Now you're being patient. I knew you had it in you if you tried."

I tried really, really hard.

"So finally Petrovich went to the man's house himself. He stood outside and kept knocking every few minutes, wouldn't take no for an answer. And after about a half hour, the guy finally gave in and opened the door. Petrovich was shocked by his appearance. The guy looked like he'd been through a meat grinder. His lip was split, he had a pair of world-class shiners and there was a giant, ugly bruise on his neck. He could barely speak, had only a whisper of a voice. A couple of his front teeth had been knocked out, and his tongue was so swollen, Petrovich couldn't imagine how he could breathe.

"At first the guy wouldn't tell Petrovich how he'd gotten so messed up. But gradually, the story came out, though as you can imagine, with a tongue like that and a bruised voice box, he wasn't talking all that clearly.

"Seems he was at Rikers, minding his own business, laying a section of heating pipe, when one of the inmates came up from behind and attacked. Beat the crap out of him with a length of ducting. Caught him by surprise, so he was badly hurt before he even had any chance to react. The beating went on and on until he lost consciousness."

With that, she flipped over the stack of pictures. They documented the man's monstrous injuries as they'd looked three days after the fact. It occurred to me that since Booth came into my life, all the photographs I'd seen depicted sheer horror.

"Take a good look at that man, Lafferty. Does he look in any way familiar to you?"

He had dark hair, a square jaw, a thin mustache, and a broad, flattened nose. Bruises aside, there was no way anyone could have mistaken him for Charlie Booth.

I shook my head.

Martinez shook hers as well, a comment on the pity of it all. "Thankfully, by the time he came to, his attacker was gone. Despite the awful shape he was in, he managed to stagger to his truck and drive home. And there he stayed. He didn't want anyone to see him all busted up like that. For some reason, it made him feel ashamed. And of course, there was no way in hell he was ever going back to Rikers to work. After an experience like that, it's all he can do to get through the day."

I waited for the punch line, as did she. "Come on, Lafferty. Aren't you burning with curiosity? Aren't you going to ask me what the great big astonishing coincidence was?"

The most I dared to risk was a shrug.

"You don't have to ask. I'm going to tell you anyway. You ready? The battered guy's name was Charlie. Imagine that. There's actually another Charlie in the world, and he happens to be a sheet-metal worker, just like Charlie Booth. How amazing is that, I ask you? Two Charlies who both work in the same kind of job. And in the same city no less. What will they think of next?"

Swallowing hard, I raised my hand. With a dip of her jaw,

Martinez granted me permission to speak. "Does Charlie Booth work for Star-Tech, too?"

"Turns out he doesn't. Mr. Petrovich never heard of a Charlie Booth. But Matilda Williamson attacked this poor guy nevertheless. Amazing, don't you think?"

I cringed. "It was Big Millie who beat this other Charlie up? You're sure?"

"I have to admit I'm not. The lady who attacked him didn't even have the decency to introduce herself. Pretty rude, if you ask me. But this Charlie fellow—the *other* Charlie as you put it—described his assailant as a very, very large black woman who was rambling about aliens taking over the U.S. mail while she beat the crap out of him. So my strong guess is yes. It was Big Millie, as you call her. And I'm sure that'll be confirmed beyond a shadow of a doubt now that Mr. Petrovich has convinced the *other* Charlie to pursue his legal remedies."

She turned over the top document in the stack, which was a complaint naming Matilda Williamson as the defendant in the matter of an assault with a deadly weapon, reckless endangerment, and a host of other charges including attempted homicide against one Charles Franklin Randolph Delavan Jr. Next up was a notice of a civil suit filed against the Department of Corrections, the City and State of New York, Matilda Williamson, the corrections commissioner, and—Lord help me—the prison's chief administrator: Calvin Daley.

"He's suing Daley?"

"Indeed he is, along with all those other deserving souls. Once Mr. Delavan became aware of the fact that he wouldn't have been harmed in that way had Ms. Williamson been under proper supervision and restraint, he overcame his shame and depression and got pretty pissed off about the whole business. He got even angrier after Petrovich insisted that he have a thorough checkup. One of his eyes was damaged permanently. Man can't go back to working as a welder with only one good eye. Poor guy is thirty-eight years old. Has an ex-wife to support, and two young children. All that could add up to a big, fat, juicy jury award and a very large embarrassment for a lot of government officials who don't take embarrassment well at all."

"He's suing Daley?" The impossible thought kept looping in my mind. Daley would murder me. He would murder me slowly and brutally, and after I was lying blue-cold without a hint of a pulse or brain wave, he would muster his fury and murder me again.

"And there's more!" Martinez said. The next document in the stack was a statement signed by Big Millie herself. I recognized the outsized, erratic writing. "Read this, Ms. Lafferty. An officer took it down during an interview with Ms. Williamson earlier today. I do believe you're going to find it— how shall I put this—most interesting."

In typical fashion, Big Millie's train of thought kept skipping the rails. Few sentences made anything close to actual sense, and the paragraphs failed to follow at all. That is, until the final assertion, the one right before Millie's signature, which was hideously lucid and clear. *I hereby affirm and attest that my former therapist, Julia (aka P.J.) Lafferty, did order me to "take care of Charlie and make sure he doesn't hurt anybody else." I acted on Ms. Lafferty's orders in putting Charlie out of commission. The man posed a danger to himself and others. And so I did what P.J. told me and took care of him. So help me God.*

"That's ridiculous. I never ordered her to hurt anybody."

Martinez sat back. "Don't tell me, Lafferty. In fact I'd prefer it if you never told me anything ever again. I stuck my neck out for you and almost got my fool head chopped off for my trouble. So as of now, I'm making it official. I'm wiping my hands of the whole nasty business, including you. I take back everything I said about coming to me. Whatever happens, don't."

"But Millie swore to me. She described Booth in perfect detail."

"I'm going to remind you one last time that Matilda Williamson is the poster girl for paranoid schizophrenia, and homicidal to boot. In plain English, the woman is nuts, Lafferty. And since you happen to be a professional in the field, I'm sure you know exactly what that means. You should know, at least. And I damn well should have known better than to be taken in by your bunk."

"I only told you what I believed to be true, Officer Martinez. I'm so sorry that it turned out to be wrong. The last thing I wanted was to make trouble for anyone."

She stood and opened her office door. "Save it for someone who gives a damn, Lafferty. I'm sure you'll have plenty of chances to make all the excuses you can think of for the judge."

CHAPTER
44

■ **I was up all night, tossing and pacing, agonizing over** my monumental screwup, trying to figure out how I could have been so dumb. Why hadn't I seen things as Dunston did? Why hadn't I recognized that it was risky, verging on criminally idiotic, to act on the strength of Big Millie's word? I went over it, every misguided step, again and again.

As the first light of dawn crept through my window, I arrived at the only sane conclusion. The trouble with going back is that you can't. The damage was done—period. That included Chief Daley and my impending dismemberment. All I could do was try to pick up the pieces and move on. The crucial facts remained unchanged. Dennis John was still in jeopardy, and Charlie Booth was still roaming free with Jeannie Bagshaw's blood on his hands.

Trying to shed an impossible excess of nervous energy, I walked uptown. The moment visiting hours at the hospital commenced I was on the elevator, headed to the fourteenth floor. By now the clerk who sat at the information desk knew me well enough to wave me through without the need of a pass.

I was desperate for Dunston's advice, though I was sure it would come with a large, indigestible helping of disdain.

His door was shut. No sign of the guard. I knocked gently, recognizing that he could still be asleep.

Silence.

I rapped again, harder this time. "Mr. Dunston? It's P.J. Sorry to come by so early, but it's serious. I have to speak to you right away."

Still nothing.

I turned the knob and peered inside. The blinds were drawn, the space steeped in gloom. After the glaring light of the corridor, it took a moment for my eyes to adjust. When they finally did, I saw that Dunston's bed was empty. The sheets had been stripped away, and a pile of freshly folded linen lay at the foot of the bed.

The nurses' station was deserted as well. Everyone was gathered in the lounge across the hall, exchanging patient information during the change of shift from the midnight-to-eight crew to the day staff that worked from eight a.m. to four. I tried without success to catch someone's eye. And then, fizzing with the impatience Martinez had failed to cure, I strode back to the central desk to wait.

Five minutes later people started filing out of the lounge. Some of the nurses headed for the elevators and home. Others wandered down the hall and into various patient rooms. One, a rangy woman with cropped auburn hair that I recognized from a previous visit, approached me. "Can I help you?"

"I'm here to see Albert Dunston. Is he down in X ray or something?"

"Dunston?"

"Everett Waite, I mean."

She frowned. "You a relative?"

"I have permission to visit him. You can check with Dr. Parkman."

She did just that. She picked up the phone on her desk and keyed in Parkman's extension. "This is Cindy Sherwin on Fourteen West. Would you tell Dr. Parkman that a Ms.—?" Her brow shot up.

"Lafferty," I told her.

"A Ms. Lafferty is here to see Mr. Waite. She says Dr. Parkman gave her permission to visit. Is he around?"

Hanging up, she waved me off. "Dr. Parkman's in a meeting. Shouldn't take long. Why don't you wait in the lounge?"

"OK. Sure." The lounge had a view of the elevators, so I'd be able to spot Dunston as soon as he returned from whatever he was off having done.

One nurse remained in the lounge. She was knitting furiously, needles trailing a ragged white beard, as she watched a morning talk show.

"You see that one?" she said. "The blonde?"

"Mm-hmm."

"Must've put on ten pounds. Maybe fifteen, plus what the camera adds. And there she is, stuffed in those pants so it's a wonder the girl can breathe."

"Mm-hmm."

"And him. What can he possibly be thinking with that hair? Looks like a squirrel got run over and wound up on his head."

"Indeed."

"To look at some people, you'd think they don't own a mirror."

I glanced at her. All this had come from a woman with a pelican pouch beneath her chin, a hairy mole on her right temple, and hair so wispy, you could read the bumps on her pink, scaly scalp. "Maybe they don't."

She scowled, and stopped talking, though not for long. "Look. There's that actor, what's his name?"

I shrugged. "Jeff something."

She snapped her fingers. "That's right. Jeff. I hate him."

At that, the rangy nurse came for me. "Ms. Lafferty? Dr. Parkman is waiting down the hall."

"He didn't have to come here. I just wanted him to confirm that I'm allowed to see Mr. Waite."

She walked off. I followed her past Dunston's room into a small examining suite at the end of the hall. Parkman was there, talking on his cell phone. As soon as we entered, he hung up.

The nurse turned back and shut the door behind her.

"Have a seat, Ms. Lafferty," Parkman said.

I caught the off-note in his expression. "What's wrong?"

He filled his chest. "I'm sorry to have to be the bearer of bad news, but Mr. Dunston passed away during the night. The guard discovered his body when he went in to check on him."

"Passed away?"

"Yes, I'm sad to say."

"But it can't be. I saw him yesterday. He was fine."

"It's difficult to absorb, I know. Mr. Dunston was a strong, determined man, but his injuries were very grave. He'd lost great deal of blood, and that, along with the trauma, can place a dangerous strain on the heart. Or sometimes a clot forms that can break loose and lodge in a crucial blood vessel to the heart or brain. A sudden infection may have developed and multiplied rapidly. Unfortunately, in a case like his, things don't always go as we hope."

"Dead?" I said again, trying to make sense of the word. "Dunston's dead?" In a rush, I went woozy and cold.

"Are you all right, Ms. Lafferty?"

"It can't be. This is all a big mistake."

"Lie down," he said. He walked me to the examining table and settled me flat on my back.

My breath came in short, shallow stabs. When I tried to pull more air, I was struck by the spicy shock of smelling salts. "Stop!" I sputtered, coughing. "Get away!"

He pressed his fingers to my wrist. "You can sit now, but take it slowly."

I shook my head to try and clear it. "You're wrong. It has to be a mistake."

"It's no mistake. We'll understand better what happened after the autopsy."

"If he's dead, someone killed him."

"That's impossible, Ms. Lafferty. There was a guard posted right outside his door."

"I don't care. He must have stepped away for a minute, taken a break. Otherwise it makes no sense. Didn't anyone hear the monitors?"

"It would seem not. The guard discovered him, as I said."

"That's impossible. How could the monitor alarms fail to go off? There must have been five of them."

"The police are looking into it. Maybe it was a glitch in the power to the room."

"Are you telling me if there's something wrong with the power, a patient can simply die and no one knows?"

"Well, no, of course not. There's battery backup."

"Exactly. So where was Mr. Dunston's battery backup?"

"I can't say. I wasn't there. But it's possible that Mr. Dunston simply disconnected his monitors as he did before. And if he wanted to end his life, it makes sense that he would have waited until his guard stepped away."

"Albert Dunston was not suicidal. No way."

He scowled. "I'm not a detective, Ms. Lafferty, and neither are you, so there's no point in our speculating about what may or may not have occurred to cause Mr. Dunston's death. But I'm sure all the questions will be answered once the police investigation is complete."

"So they think it's foul play."

"I'm not going to speculate about what they think."

"Police don't investigate unless there's a reason to."

"Perhaps that's so, and perhaps it isn't. At this point, all anyone knows as a certainty is that a patient died. There's nothing to be gained by making wild assumptions or leaping to unsubstantiated conclusions."

I shivered as the terrifying facts of my situation sank in. With Dunston gone I was flying solo, not to mention out of work. Getting rid of Clarissa Demetrios meant I no longer had her to push me around, but it also meant I no longer had a way to pay the bills. I'd pushed Caity and Rafe away as well. And I'd fixed it so Martinez would no longer help me. Aunt Lottie's heart was in the right place, but she needed every scrap of her diminishing strength to get by. So there I was: nowhere. And if, as I strongly suspected, Dunston's death proved to be a homicide, who knew how high the body count might go?

CHAPTER

45

Parkman gave me two minutes more and then es-corted me to the elevators.

"Will you let me know when you find out what happened to Mr. Dunston?"

"Why don't you try to put all this unpleasantness out of your mind, Ms. Lafferty."

"Please, Dr. Parkman. It's important. I have to know."

"All right. Give me your number. Should I hear anything of note, I'll contact you."

Outside, I wandered in a daze. Drifting was the best I could think to do. I let the traffic signals guide me. Don't walk. Go. And what was the meaning of blinked caution? Stand there, scoot across, run in place? How comforting it felt to be free of the impossible burden of actual decision-making. I even felt a twinge of envy for a leaf that blew past me, floating unfettered on the brisk morning breeze. A leaf didn't even suffer the need to interpret uncertain traffic signals. That was the sort of boundless freedom I craved.

At some point I happened into a neighborhood bodega, where I bought a cup of sweet, light coffee and a buttered roll. The dark, earthy, buttery, sugary smell of the place along with the grinding hunger in my belly conspired to drag me inside, so even there I wasn't taking the risk of creating friction with the will of fate. Wasn't it true that if I did nothing, I couldn't do anything wrong?

In that spirit I kept roaming, heading vaguely toward home. But when I reached my block, I turned away and continued on. I couldn't imagine what I would do in the apartment once I got there. Given Albert Dunston's unthinkable absence from the universe, anything as mundane as making my bed or reading the paper seemed obscene.

The sun glared with ever-increasing ferocity, and the clothes I'd thrown on early this morning, in what now seemed another lifetime, now hung too heavy and warm. Some twins are designed in mirror image. One can be left-handed, while the other is an unambiguous rightie. Or a mole on one twin's right cheek may be replicated on the opposite side of the other twin's face. With Caity and me, the diametrically opposite traits were coolness and warmth. I perspired twice as much as the norm, which meant she didn't have to spill a drop of moisture for the pair of us to break even. So there she'd be, Princess Caity, cool as a clam no matter how much pressure she was under, bright and perky despite the most crushing, oppressive heat; while the slightest hint of adversity or even the threat of a balmy day reduced me at once to a puddle of unsightly goo: hair a dripping string mop, shirt glued to my back, great dark splotches spreading beneath my arms, mouth capped by a bubbly sweat moustache like Tricky Dick Nixon's.

This was my condition when I found myself, hours later, in Midtown. In fact, my aimless meandering delivered me right in front of the Club. And wouldn't you know, at that very moment a sleek black limo pulled up to the curb and disgorged Nina Present along with a ruggedly handsome man. He had thick dark hair with a tease of silver at the temples and the commanding stride of someone who knows just where he's going, and why.

"P.J. Talk about perfect timing," Nina gushed. "That's what I call getting off on the right foot. Meet my friend Brett Carnival. He's the one who's putting together that fabulous program we discussed. Brett, this is P. J. Lafferty, the wonderful, young psychologist I've been bending your ear about."

He shook my hand. "Delighted."

"Sure. Me, too."

I was grateful when Nina took firm command. "I've made a reservation for us to have lunch in one of the executive suites upstairs, so we'll be private. I hope that's all right with both of you."

"Perfect," Carnival said.

"Perfect," I echoed, though in fact it was anything but. I was a grubby, disheveled, muddle-headed mess. Dunston's death had wiped my mind clean. Only now did I remember that Nina had arranged this meeting so I could hear about the psychiatric center Carnival planned to open downtown and sell him on my virtues as a potential employee. "I hope you'll both excuse me. I had a bit of a tough morning. I'm sure I look like a stretch of bad road."

Nina flapped a hand. "Not at all. You look wonderful as always, P.J. Sorry about the tough morning, though."

I shrugged. "It's an honor to meet you, Mr. Carnival. I'm very eager to hear more about your project."

He had the most infectious, engaging smile. "That, you will in spades. Once I get started on the subject, it's pretty hard to shut me up."

"Sounds as if you're suffering from a severe case of passionate enthusiasm," I said. "Could be contagious, but I'm willing to take the risk."

His grin grew even more magnetic. I recognized it as one of those powerful force fields that could suck a person in. "You're a brave woman, Ms. Lafferty. Lead the way, Nina."

In the suite I excused myself and went to the bathroom, where I cleaned up, collected the remains of my senses, and pinched a bit of color into my cheeks.

When I emerged, a somber man in a tuxedo was waiting to take our lunch order. Carnival requested a steak sandwich, fries, and a beer, and when I hesitated, suggested that I have the same. Nina smiled in approval, and then for herself requested a Perrier and a naked Cobb salad, minus the ham and cheese.

If the success of the proposed psychiatric center rested on brilliant salesmanship, Carnival had it made. In a few broad strokes he painted a vivid, compelling image of the place. I could imagine my brother Jack as one of many lost souls who would come to view the center a haven. There, he could find help in a crisis, a smooth, reassuring constant in the lurching roller coaster of his life.

As he'd threatened, Brett Carnival went on and on. "We're going to try out all the modalities: art therapy, music, sports, pet therapy, journaling, community outreach, alternative and complementary strategies. Acupuncture looks promising for some of these people, especially in terms of reducing compulsive behavior and disarming phobias. It's amazing how many possibilities there are when you approach this with an open mind. Of course, a lot of our clients will need medication, not to mention good, solid, regular counseling, which is where you come in. But I believe what these people need above all is stability, a reliable, well-constructed home base. That means we have to build in social relationships, learning opportunities, vocational training, a meaningful reward system, productive work. All these things tend to be missing in the lives of the very people who need them most. We just wait for them to skin their knees and then slap on a Band-Aid, and when that doesn't work, we claim we had no choice but to put them away."

"That's so true. I have a brother who's been in and out of jails and psychiatric hospitals for years, and all he gets is worse. Stability is what he needs. The kind you're proposing. It would be an honor to be involved in a program like that, Mr. Carnival. A dream, really."

He trained his killer grin on me and then on Nina. "With any luck, that dream will become a reality very soon."

"Do you have a time frame?" I asked, too brittle by far to play coy.

"I do, and as it turns out that time frame accelerated considerably just last night."

Nina cocked her head. "Do tell."

Carnival sat back. He wore a suit and tie, but it was easy to picture him in tennis whites or boat shoes and a captain's hat, tanned and shirtless. "Zachary Chafetz was in town for a meeting. Remember him?"

"The one from Yale who made a killing in Hong Kong real estate?"

"That and other things. Turns out his foundation has been looking for a project like this. We were supposed to get together for a quick drink before he went off to a dinner. After we talked awhile, he called to make his excuses, and we wound up discussing the center and reviewing plans until almost three in the morning. Before he left to catch his early-morning flight, he asked what it would take to get the project up-and-running. I told him we were still looking for six million more to build the center and get our staff and programs underway, but Zach disagreed. He said it was going to take at least twice that, and believe it or not, that's the check he wrote."

By now Nina's eyes had bugged so they resembled the hefty Greek olives in her salad. "He didn't have to get approval from his board? He didn't ask to review the business plan or consult with his lawyer? He just wrote a check?"

Carnival laughed. "When I say it's his foundation, I mean it's *his* foundation. Twelve million is a spit in the ocean for Chafetz, and he assured me that if the project goes well, there'll be plenty more. His concept is even grander than mine. He thinks we should offer recreation facilities, a gym, a weight room, even a Jacuzzi and sauna. Getting these people in good physical shape should be part of the deal. And he wants us to have a clinic on property as well, where we can do checkups, blood tests, and such. He was completely correct to say that these are not the kind of people we can easily refer out for routine services. Once they're with us, we should be able to get their teeth cleaned, their eyes checked, the whole shebang. And he wants residential rooms on premises for clients who need more intense supervision for a while, not to mention respite care so families and caretakers can get a break."

"It sounds amazing. I'd give anything for my brother to be involved in a facility like that."

"He can. We plan to meet the need where we find it, and

with people like Zach in our corner, we won't have any trouble meeting that goal. Where's your brother now?"

The question brought a squeeze of guilty fear. "I'm not sure. Normally, he turns up for his birthday, but this time he didn't."

"I'm sure you'll hear from him soon, P.J.," Nina said.

"I hope so."

"I can put out feelers, if you like," Carnival said. "In doing the preparatory work for the center, I've made a lot of contacts in the field."

"That's dear of you to offer, Mr. Carnival. Let me check on my own first. See if I can track him down."

"Sure. Glad to help any time. Now tell me about yourself, P.J. I want to hear all about your training and professional experience. I'd like you to describe how you envision your professional future, and I want to hear what sort of role you'd like to play at the center, if you come to work with us."

■ **"Your life certainly isn't boring,"** Dr. Groome said.

"Boring would be good for a change. I'd seriously welcome some nice, dull, numbing routine."

"Would you?"

I tried to imagine myself floating on a lake of blissful calm, reveling in the ceaseless sameness. But even in the fantasy a vicious swell kicked up and swamped my boat. "I would, but routine is not the way my life tends to go."

She had restored her office to its former state. The Freudian leather couch was gone, as were the shoji screens and the Oriental carpet. We sat again in the largely empty room, facing each other cross-legged on the rubbery black floor.

"You say that as if things simply happen to you, P.J., as if you're a passive member of the audience, sitting back and observing your life rather than playing the starring role."

"You say that as if we have a total control over what happens to us. Do you actually believe a person has the power to write the script for her existence and then direct the part and act it any way she sees fit?"

"No. I think our lives progress according to some combination of outside force and personal determination. But I strongly believe that the balance is tipped in favor of personal choice."

"So if lightning happens to strike me and burn me to ash, it means I wasn't determined enough to turn the bolt around?"

"Interesting example. In that case, what I might suggest instead is that you made an unfortunate decision to stand out unprotected in a storm. That's where personal determination would make the difference."

"So it's back to me having a death wish."

"If that's how you see it."

"Is it necessary for you to be so blasted logical all the time?"

"I'm afraid it goes with the territory. Don't you strive to be logical with your clients?"

I slumped on my elbows, wondering how this all but empty room could feel so full. The slightest move sent me colliding headfirst with yet another painful truth. "I get the message, Dr. Groome. You're telling me to quit whining and get on with it."

"You're welcome to whine all you like if that strikes you as useful. No particular harm in it that I can see. But yes, you might find it more productive to accept the facts of your current situation, no matter how unpleasant, and devote your energies to exploring what steps you can take going forward to improve it."

"You mean shoot myself?"

"Do you think that would be an improvement?"

Now I sprawled flat on the spongy, dotted floor. Acoustic tile lined the ceiling, and I took odd comfort in the notion that if all else failed, I could just lie here like this and tally up the holes. "No, but I don't see what else I could do to improve things. They are what they are."

"They are what you make of them."

"What's that supposed to mean?"

"Well, for example, you keep saying you feel helpless because you can no longer rely on Mr. Dunston's advice. But that's not really true. You still have the benefit of the advice he gave you before he died. You can continue to follow his suggestions if you choose to. In fact, you said he was extremely clear about how he thought you should proceed."

"He was. Verify, amplify, notify, testify. Go back, as far as it takes, and get to know the subject. If you want to know what's going to happen, learn how the subject behaved in the past. History is destiny."

"There you are."

"How come it feels like nowhere?"

"Good question. And you're the only one who can answer it."

"Let me ask you a philosophical question, Dr. Groome. If I counted the holes in one of those ceiling tiles and then multiplied by the total number of tiles, would you be confident that I'd accurately determined how many holes there were?"

"Why would you want to know how many holes there were?"

"That's a psychiatrist's answer; I want the philosopher's take."

"Then you'll have to ask a philosopher."

"That's begging the question, Dr. Groome."

"No. It's begging off on a question I don't know how to answer."

A sigh escaped me. "That never stops me."

"Here's a question for you, P.J.: How many psychiatric patients does it take to change a lightbulb?"

I mulled that over as I started counting holes. Three rows from the top the black dots started swirling. "I give up. How many?"

"Only one. But she really, really has to want to change."

"Do you really believe it's that simple? All I have to do is what Albert Dunston suggested and everything will fall neatly into place?"

"That's not what I said. What I suggested is that if you're still intent on trying to make a case against Charlie Booth for Jeannie Bagshaw's murder, and if you believe Mr. Dunston's methodology had merit, you can continue to follow that methodology despite the fact that he's no longer around to advise you."

"But you don't think I should. You agree with Rafe and Caity and Officer Martinez and Creighton and everyone else in creation. You think I should just forget about Jeannie's murder and the harm that might come to her little boy. You think I have no right taking on anyone else's problems when my own life is such a god-awful disaster."

"Time's up for today, P.J. We'll have to look at that question next time. But there are two things I'd like you to take away from today's session. One: Keep in mind that it doesn't matter what I think. What counts is what you think, not anyone else. As your therapist, my job is to help you identify what you really want, what you believe deep down, and perhaps help you figure out how to go about getting it."

I sat up. "But that's the devil of it. In this situation, what I really believe and what I want happen to be on opposite sides of the page. I can't have the nice, sane, sensible life while I'm busy tossing around the hot potato so it doesn't wind up burning the wrong hands."

"You'll figure it out, P.J."

"I'm trying to. Thanks, Dr. Groome."

She set a hand on my arm when I stood to leave. "That's the first thing I want you to take away. The other is the number of holes in the ceiling. It happens that all the tiles are identical. There are one hundred and sixty-eight holes per tile, fourteen tiles across from door to window, and eighteen from wall to wall. That's 42,336 holes in total."

"Why do you want me to know that?"

"Because now you never have to give it another thought, which means you're free to focus on more important things. I want you to have all your mental energies available to figure out what you want to do about those things. And then I want you to go out and do them and be done."

■ **Dunston's death had shaken me to the bone, but any**
doubts I had about proceeding with the case dissolved at the
sound of Dennis John's voice.

"Aunt Lottie's sick, P.J. They took her to the hospital last
night, and I had to stay with smelly old Mrs. Groves and her
yucky cat Mr. Prim who poops in the living room."

"I'm sorry, sweetie. He doesn't sound very prim at all."

I heard a woman's chiding voice in the background. "Now,
sweetie. That's not nice."

"Who's that with you now, Dennis John?"

"Miss Wolcott brought me to her house after school.
She's real nice. But it's only—what's that word again, Miss
Wolcott?"

"Temporary. It's only temporary. Let me speak to P.J. now,
honey."

She came on the line. "He's been trying to call you for
hours. Hope it's not a bad time."

"Not at all. Sorry I wasn't here. How bad are things with
Lottie?"

"Very." Somehow she kept her tone light and breezy. "So I
explained to Dennis John that his aunt Lottie needs to rest for

a while. Department rules say I can only keep him with me temporarily. But I promised to find him a great place where he can stay while his aunt Lottie rests. I know lots of terrific people, and I'm sure one of them will be delighted to have a wonderful little boy like him. Lots of my best families even have kids of their own or other kids staying with them who are right around Dennis John's age, so he'd have built-in playmates."

Now it was Dennis John commenting in the background. "But I want to stay with P.J."

"I explained to him that you have to work and all, P.J. I told Dennis John it's likely that staying with you is not in the cards. But he keeps insisting, so I thought it would be best if we got that off the table."

"I hate to say no to him, I really do, but things are pretty crazy right now."

"Of course, I understand."

"And what about his father?" The word alone made my spine crawl with prickles of fear.

"No way to get in touch," she said cryptically, "so I'm pleased to say that's not an issue, at least for now."

But that could change any time. If I took Dennis John in, Booth was likely to turn up sooner or later. Violent possessive personalities did not take kindly to people who interfered with their "possessions." Booth had only put up with Aunt Lottie because she kept Dennis John at his behest. I would be a very different story.

"I live in a tiny place, Miss Wolcott. And far from the finest. It's really not the best environment for a child."

"Sure. Don't worry. I'll work it out."

"I think that would be for the best." My firm conviction held for about two seconds, until I heard the boy's tearful pleas.

"Please can't I stay with P.J.? She's my friend. I promise I'll be good."

"It's OK, sweetie," Miss Wolcott told him. "He'll be all right," she said to me.

"Maybe I can work things out. I have an idea. Let me see if it'll fly and I'll get back to you."

"Sure. I promised Dennis John I'd take him out for pizza,

and then we're going to see if Aunt Lottie is up to a quick visit. You can call on my cell any time."

"You'll hear from me soon."

My sister and I were not on the best of terms, but the blood between me and Eva Everhart ran clear. On the way to Caity's posh co-op, I stopped at a market and picked up the fixings for Eva's favorite meal, the one she always had in celebration after bringing the bad guys down. The menu was baked ziti with meatballs and gobs of extra cheese, crusty French bread with butter and strawberry jam, and a large helping of plain steamed broccoli, which as Caity had calculated, had induced nutritionists and pediatricians to embrace and endorse her books. It was a testament to my sister's extraordinary influence and marketing savvy that after Eva extolled the virtues of broccoli in the second book in the series, sales of the vegetable had made significant gains for the first time since George Bush Sr. wrecked the industry by declaring that he hated broccoli, and as president, wasn't required to partake. I picked up a bottle of decent wine as well, or at least what passed for decent on my budget, and a small bunch of flowers on sale that were still more or less alive.

At Caity's glittery high rise the doorman worked the revolving door so I wouldn't have to, and then the man at the concierge desk scurried over and extended his white-gloved hands to relieve me of my bags. "How are you doing, Ms. Goldstein? Any new books?"

"I'm not Ms. Goldstein; I'm her sister."

"Wow. There sure is a family resemblance."

"Only on the surface."

Long ago Caity had left permission for me to enter without being announced. And I was pleased to discover that she'd neglected to revoke the privilege. I wanted the element of surprise, though as it turned out the biggest surprise was mine.

I let myself into her apartment, a sprawling eight-room glory on the forty-sixth floor with tooth-dropping East River views. I deposited my packages on the broad granite counter in her giant kitchen and then poked around until I found Caity in her study, where everything, except her, was built-in.

She was not alone.

My neck went hot. "Sorry to burst in on you two. I thought to make dinner and have a chat, but I can see this is not a good time."

"It's a fine time," she signed sharply. "Anything you want to chat about with me, you can say in front of Rafe, P.J. He's family."

"Ex-family," I said.

"Never mind. I'll go," Rafe said. "Maybe someday P.J. will stop thinking of me as public enemy number one."

Caity blocked his way. "No, Rafe. There's no call for you to leave on her account. As far as I'm concerned, if she's going to behave that way, she can climb right back on the high horse she rode in on and go." Her facing palms dipped. And then she stood, dripping smugness.

"Fine. I'm out of here." I was through the door and waiting for the elevator, before I remembered the reason I had come.

I let myself in again and marched back to the study. "So happens I came to see Eva, not you," I said.

Caity smirked. "Eva, is it?"

"Yes. I want one of those audiences she grants to people who have need of her superpowers."

Rafe burst out laughing, but not Caity. When it came to the fictional deaf wonder that had made her a rich, famous star, my sister was dead serious. "An audience with Eva Everhart is a big deal. She only grants one or two a book. What makes you think for a minute that you deserve such a privilege?"

"It's not for me. It's for a child, an extremely deserving one."

"Then the child has to make the request."

"It's a special circumstance, so I have to do it for him."

"What kind of special circumstance?"

"I'll explain that to Eva."

"You will if I allow you to speak to her, which I'm not inclined to do. Why should Eva even consider granting you a favor after the way you've been behaving?"

Rafe was still chuckling. "Now I've heard everything. Two intelligent women arguing about whether or not one of them will get to plead her case to a made-up character."

"Eva is much more than a made-up character, Rafe," Caity

signed. "That's like saying Cinderella is nothing but an invention, or Peter Pan."

Rafe raked his hair. "They're not?"

"Hardly. They're institutions, cultural icons on the order of Santa Claus and the Easter Bunny. Their power to inspire, to instruct, to transform, is awe-inspiring. It's like audiences of all ages clapping their hearts out to show they believe in Tinkerbell. Are you the one who's going to go to the microphone and declare they shouldn't bother, Rafe? Are you going to tell those people their hope and caring is all for nothing because Tinkerbell is made up?"

Rafe's hands flew up. "OK. Don't shoot. I have the highest regard for Tinkerbell. I do."

With a sharp glance Rafe's way, my sister claimed the victory. "Now back to this audience business, P.J. Why should Eva even consider doing a favor for you?"

"It's not for me. I told you. But obviously, she doesn't have to do anyone a favor. Like any good little cultural icon, she's free to do whatever she pleases."

She tipped her finger forward from her lips, the sign for true.

"And you know what? Even though I'm nobody's idea of an icon, I'm free to do as I please as well. It's all neat and tidy when you think about it. Eva can turn down your twin sister's request for an audience on behalf of a child in need, and I can turn around and hand the story to the press." With a sweeping gesture, I described the banner headline: "'Hard-hearted Eva turns a deaf ear to boy's cries for help.' Has a certain ring to it."

Rafe cringed. "I'm afraid she's got you there, Caity."

I smiled sweetly, for a bitch. "I'm going to go fix dinner now. You can hang around and join us, Rafe, if you don't mind being unwelcome."

"Not really."

"So be it, then. I'll get to it. We'll have a nice meal and a chat, and then Eva and I will have that little audience for dessert."

CHAPTER 48

■ **I'd imagined several ways Caity might react to Dennis** John, but going soft in the head for the boy was not among them. Under ordinary circumstances, my sister had no use for children, except for the lucrative fictional ones she'd invented and her young book-buying fans. I'd long relished the delightful irony that Caity's success required her to spend so much time around the very same grime-handed, drip-nosed, ill-mannered little tykes she so deplored. Countless times I'd watched her at fan events, struggling not to cringe. But with this little boy, she seemed genuinely enchanted.

"Why didn't you tell me Dennis John was such a charmer, P.J.?" she gushed, adding voice to her signing so the child could understand. "And so smart! It's hard to believe he's only five."

"Oh, my, she caught us. You'd best give it up and confess, Dennis John. Go on and admit that you're actually a thirty-five-year-old midget with a jelly-bean accounting firm and a doctorate in French toast."

Dennis John glanced up from his workbook, where he was practicing writing his *E*s. "She's being silly," he explained.

"I figured as much," Caity said. "You don't look a day over twenty-eight."

He giggled. "Your sister's nice, P.J." Then he leveled his pencil toward Rafe. "Him, too."

"Of course they are. Do you take me for the type of person who'd have some wretched pains in the rear for a twin and an ex-husband?"

"That's what you said on the bus, remember?"

I chuckled. "You're right, Caity. He's a definite charmer, that one."

"How come he's your ex-husband?" Dennis John asked, eager to keep playing bumper cars with his tongue.

"Because we got divorced," I told him.

"Then how come you still love each other?"

"We do not," I told him. "We hate each other exactly the way divorced people are supposed to."

"Nope. You love each other. Don't you love P.J., Rafe?"

"That's it, young man," I said. "Time for bed."

I supervised his tooth-brushing and heard his prayers, which centered on God not sending a golden chariot for Aunt Lottie. Then I got him settled in the guest room for the night.

"I don't want God to send a chariot for you either, P.J.," he said.

"I'm with you on that, sweetheart."

"So don't get sick. OK?"

I pulled the covers to his chin, leaving a puckish face framed by the curly flaming halo. "I have no plans to get sick, sir. Not a one."

"This is nicer than your place. It's giant."

"I'm glad you like it."

"Can I stay here with you until Aunt Lottie finishes resting?"

"I hope so. Keep your fingers crossed."

When I got back to the living room, Caity was fit to burst with excitement. "Sit, P.J. You have to hear this. It's so great!"

I sat. "What?"

"I'm so excited!" Her hands fluttered madly across her chest.

"I can see that. About what?"

She squealed. "You ready?"

"I don't know. You think my heart can take it?"

"Just listen. I've had the most amazing idea. It's a brand-new series starring a little boy, an orphan with magical red hair that enables him to battle the forces of evil."

My head bobbed. "Sort of Samson meets Little Orphan Annie."

"I love it! He won't be deaf like Eva, that would be too similar, but I can give him a deaf sidekick. I'm thinking about a brilliant dog, a chocolate lab that can read lips, maybe minds, too. Can you picture what a smash hit that would be!"

I smiled evenly. "Sounds like you're going to have another big success on your hands."

"Definitely," Rafe said. "I especially like the dog."

I hadn't seen Caity so excited since the unbearable week when Eva was prominently mentioned as a competitor in a feature on Harry Potter in *Time* magazine.

"It's not that I don't adore Eva," she signed in grand effusive sweeps. "And of course, I'd keep up that series as well. The fans would go berserk if I even hinted that I was going to retire Eva. But I've been looking for something different to do in addition, wracking my brain for just this kind of idea. It'll keep me fresh, and of course, there'll be no end of new readers. Isn't it the best?"

"Right up there," I said. "And you know what I can picture just as clearly as you having a second hit series?"

Her face tensed with suspicion. Rafe covered his mouth to mask the smirk. He knew me too well, damn him, but then again, not well enough.

"I can picture Dennis John's bank account growing nice and fat with his fifty percent of the action."

Caity sprung from her chair. "Are you crazy? Why should that little brat get half? It's my idea, my work, my name, and my reputation."

"You know? You've got a point," I said.

"You bet I do. Giving half to some scrawny little twerp. Fat chance."

"You're right. What would Dennis John do with that kind of money? All he needs is enough to make sure he'll be taken care of growing up, that he'll get a top-quality education and be able to start his adult life without a mountain of debt. Let's say you take that fifty percent including all subsidiary rights, of course: foreign sales, product tie-ins, movie rights, and such, and put it in a foundation to benefit Dennis John and other kids in similar situations. Of course, he'll be first on the list, but we can form a board of directors to decide which other children will benefit."

"I have a better idea. Let's say the hero of my new series is a little boy with blue hair, or maybe green. Let's say the idea had nothing in the universe to do with Dennis John, and that's the end of any ridiculous claim you think he might have on it."

"Now we're back to the same impasse we came to about that audience I requested with Eva. You're welcome to do as you please, and so am I."

She signed in a flailing fury. "What that's supposed to mean?"

"It means you're free to write your little fiction, and I'm free to tell the true story to the press."

Caity turned to Rafe and made a mute plea for his help.

Rafe assumed a look of lawyerly dispassion. "Maybe the best idea is to drop the whole thing."

At that, my sister moaned in despair. "No. I won't. I can't. If I don't have something to take my mind off Eva Everhart, I may have to strangle her in my next installment."

"I don't want to be unreasonable," I said. "Let's say we make it forty percent to the foundation."

"Thirty percent," she shot back. "But only on the first book in the series, and the donation is featured in the marketing campaign. That's as far as I'm willing to go."

"Twenty-five percent of all books and subsidiary rights. That's in all media, including those not yet conceived or developed, in perpetuity."

"One book, P.J. Don't be a jerk."

I shook my head. "All books, all sub rights, all the time."

"If you're going to insist on a cut of all the books, I refuse to go a single point over ten percent. That's it, P.J. End of story."

I conceded with grace and declined to mention that I would have been happy with half that. As my sister liked to say: More is more. We shook on it. "There are a couple of other tiny conditions," I said. "One: Dennis John and I get to camp with you until his social worker can find him a good placement or until his aunt gets out of the hospital, if she gets out."

"How lucky can I be? I get to share my apartment with not one, but two immature brats."

"You and Dennis John could stay with me, P.J.," Rafe said. "I have room."

"Thanks anyway. Caity's delighted to have us. She just doesn't know it yet."

"All right. You can stay here for a little while. But that's all. No other conditions," my sister signed.

"There's just one little thing." I pinched the air to demonstrate how minuscule it was. "I have to go out of town tomorrow, so I need you to pick up Dennis John after school and hang out with him until I get back. It could be late, and there's some chance I'll have to spend the night."

"No way, no how. You can rob me in broad daylight, but you are not going to force me to babysit. I have my limits!" She stormed out of the room, and her bedroom door slammed with a jarring concussion.

"I'll pick him up," Rafe said. "Just tell me where and what time. I can move my appointments around and hang with him until you get back. Rent a video, play Nintendo, whatever the little guy wants. We'll have fun."

"You'd honestly do that, Rafe?"

He shrugged. "I get along fine with little boys. We understand each other."

I had an equal urge to ruffle Rafe's hair—and tear it out. He had no right doing something so endearing. "Thanks. I appreciate it."

"No problem. Where are you off to?"

"I have to take care of some personal business. Hope to tie up some loose ends."

"Can you tell me what it's about?"

"Not yet, Rafe. But I promise I will if things work out the way I hope they will."

■ **The trip was meant to kill two birds with one stone,** and I dearly hoped neither would be me.

Things did not get off to an encouraging start. The flight was packed. Halfway through the boarding process, a nasty altercation broke out between two stocky men dressed for golf who'd somehow been assigned the same seat. Neither was willing to yield, not even when an accommodating passenger offered to relinquish her seat and wait for the next flight out. Security guards were summoned, and both men were muscled off the plane. That made us nearly fifty minutes late for take-off, but the unpleasantness did not end there. Behind me sat a whining toddler, a squalling infant, and their incompetent young parents, whose response to the cacophony was to ignore the little monsters and play hearts. I was wedged in a middle seat between an enormous woman, whose excess flesh spilled bloblike onto me, and a man who smelled like an overheated barn. I was starved, so predictably the flight attendant ran out of little peanut packets before she reached my row. As if all that wasn't maddening enough, someone had completed the crossword puzzle in my in-flight magazine and then torn out the last page which promised to reveal number one in a breathless countdown of the hottest new Hollywood hunks.

At the Charleston airport, we were held on the tarmac for fifteen minutes, awaiting an available gate. Then we waited another twenty minutes for a crew to deliver the forgotten jetway. When it finally rolled in place, my fellow passengers felt free at last to jostle, shove, claw, and elbow their way off the plane. That was followed by an interminable line at the rental car counter. When my turn came at last, the clerk couldn't find my reservation. Fortunately, I knew the trick, which was to make a loud, embarrassing scene, and then demand to see a supervisor, at which point a car miraculously became available.

I tried to remain philosophical. This was all proceeding according to the immutable laws of contemporary travel. The first law guaranteed that meticulous planning to get an early start, multiplied by the square root of the standard screwups, added to three times the sum of the headache blooming behind my eyes, put me on the road at the height of rush hour. What should have been a twenty-minute trip stretched to more than an hour. By the time I pulled into the lot at the Blessed Sacrament Retirement Home, it was past noon. His room, number 21, was empty, and the man I passed pushing a mop in the hall had no idea where he might be. I wandered around until I discovered a large sunny space where the residents and staff were congregated for lunch.

No one looked familiar, so I asked an aide to point him out. My heart thumped fiercely as I approached his table. I found it impossible to connect the frail wizened soul I found there with the stern, outsize man who had filled me with the quaking fear of God. His dark looks and fearsome warnings had convinced me I was doomed to spend eternity spinning on a spit like a chicken over the hottest raging hellfire the Devil's assistants could build. But time had shrunk and shriveled him. And now he seemed to be dwarfed by most everything: the slat-backed chair, the long communal table, even his lunch plate, heaped as it was with oversize helpings of pot roast, mashed potatoes, buttered bread, and sorry-looking peas with limp pearl onions. There was an outsize glass of milk as well, and for dessert, a large bowl of tapioca covered by a wrinkled skin. His dark shirt was stained and peppered with dandruff.

His face was coated with fine gray stubble, and he gave off the cloying smell of decay.

I swallowed a bilious swell as I sat opposite him. My throat burned and my voice thinned to a croak. "Father Muldoon?"

He blinked slowly.

"I'm P.J. One of the Goldstein girls, remember?"

"Tell them I don't like vanilla pudding, will you, young lady? I keep asking for chocolate, but they forget."

"You were our parish priest, Father. My mother, Nora, went to mass every morning, and my family never missed a Sunday until my folks were killed in a car crash. Remember that?"

"Don't care for vanilla. It's too sweet."

"You officiated at my parents' funeral, Father, our first Communions, all that. But no matter how many times my mother asked you not to, you insisted on calling my sister deaf and dumb."

His face widened. "That's right! We had a deaf, dumb child. A little girl."

"So you do remember. But here's the thing, Father, you were dead wrong. Caity wasn't dumb, not by a long shot. So happens she's a huge success: a famous author of children's book and rich as Croesus. My sister could line the church's collection plates with gold and diamonds every day of the week if she had a mind to, but that's not going to happen given the way her very own priest treated her, calling her deaf and dumb like you did, acting like all God's children were created equal, only the rest were a million times more equal than her."

"And grant you peace, Amen."

"Remember my brother Jack, Father? The two of you didn't get on well at all. He was forever cutting up, getting into trouble, and you were forever trying to punish him into settling down and doing things your way. I believe Jack held the world indoor record for Hail Marys and Our Fathers, not to mention smacks with a belt across the bum."

He blotted his mouth, and then he stood. "You be sure to tell them about the pudding, now. It's chocolate I like. Tell them write it down."

I trailed close behind. "Wait, Father Muldoon. I have to talk to you. Do you remember what happened with Jack before my parents were killed in that wreck?"

He muttered incoherently and hobbled toward the door.

"My father and Jack had an ugly fight that day. My father was furious, near out of his head. He wasn't thinking clearly, so upset I'm sure he wasn't minding the way he drove. That's why they went off that winding road, isn't it, Father Muldoon?"

"I don't understand."

"I think you do. And I need you to tell me. My parents had that wreck because of something that passed between you and my brother. Isn't that so? What happened between you and Jack was the reason he and Daddy had that fight."

He lunged ahead too quickly. The effort set him off-balance and he staggered. A burly man rushed toward us and caught the old priest before he went down. He gripped Muldoon from behind and walked him like a marionette. "There now, Father. That's the way. I'll take you to your room. Get you settled." He shot me a belligerent look. "Who are you?"

"An old friend of the father's. I was one of his parishioners as a little girl."

"You upset him."

"He doesn't like vanilla pudding, that's the thing."

"Is that right, Father? Was it the vanilla pudding got you in such a state?"

"Vanilla's too sweet."

"Can't argue with you there, Father. I prefer chocolate myself," the aide said.

I trailed along as he walked Muldoon to his room and planted him in the bed. "That better now, Father? You comfortable?"

"Tell them no more vanilla. Tell them write it down."

"Will do. You rest now, Father. Maybe get a little shut-eye."

"I'll be leaving in a minute," I said.

He frowned. "Man's had a stroke. Not good for him to get all worked up like that."

"I hear you. I'll see he stays calm."

Muldoon's roommate lay in the bed near the window with his eyes shut and his bony chest pulsing with syncopated breaths. He was frighteningly thin, his yellowed skin draped like a sheet across the skeleton he was soon to become.

"Tell me, Father Muldoon. Tell me what happened between you and my brother? What made my father so raging mad?"

He fixed his rheumy eyes on me, and I caught a trace of the old mortal threat. "Go away! Let me be."

"I will as soon as you tell me, Father. I've waited long enough. Too long. I have to know."

"Get out of here, I'm telling you. Go now!"

"Tell her, Patrick." The skeletal priest's voice was incredibly deep and strong. "You tell the girl, or I will."

"No." Muldoon crossed himself. "No!"

"All right then, she'll hear it from me. Bring over a chair, young lady," the old priest said. "It'll take a while to tell the story right."

CHAPTER

50

■ **The drive to Bluffton passed in a blur. Trees. Phone** poles. The windy rush of cars whizzing over the roadbed. I shot past billboards, their messages garbled by speed. I passed an endless string of churches, condos, strip malls, golf clubs, swamps. Nothing sank in, nothing could. Only one thought had the power to pierce the dense cotton batting that swaddled my brain.

I knew what had sent Jack over the edge. It was the telling, the unburdening, and then the hideous, painful lie. None of it was my brother's fault, but he'd shouldered the monstrous blame for my parents' death. That was the reason for the drugs, the running, all the futile attempts to escape himself.

Finally I knew. But what did the knowing solve?

Mrs. Reiner eased my bristling shock. I warmed to her at once, a sturdy soul with a warm, ready smile. Approaching the house on her narrow street, I spotted her staring through the broad bay window. She bustled out to greet me as soon as I turned into her graveled drive. She wore a flowered chintz housedress and a ruffled cobbler apron, the kind my mother always wore around the house. They put me in mind of bright wet floors tinged with ammonia and the joy of crisp, cool, freshly ironed sheets. I reveled in the memory, and for a moment the long-buried secrets eased their grip.

"How was your trip, P.J.? Where's your valise?"

"I'm not staying, Mrs. Reiner. I plan to catch the last flight from Charleston tonight."

"Doesn't leave us much time. Come on in, and make yourself at home. And please, call me Hayden. Formal never was my way."

I trailed her up the flower-lined stone walk toward a trim white Dutch colonial. As she trudged up the porch steps, my eyes drifted next door, to the shabby, built-out double-wide with striped awnings, where Jeannie Bagshaw had somehow managed to grow up. "Do Jeannie's parents still live there?"

"They left a few years back. Took off like thieves in the night. Must've quit paying their loan, because the very next day a man from the bank came by to foreclose. Rotten straight through, those two were. Makes you wonder what God could've been thinking, sending a sweet child like Jeannie to a pair of nasty, no-good characters like them. I wasn't sorry to see them gone. I'll tell you that."

The screen door squealed when she led me inside. The house was cool, gently lit, and suffused with sweet, rich baking smells. Bright nosegays in hand-painted vases perched on the tables. Clusters of flowers hung from the ceiling to dry.

"The one I miss is Jeannie," she said. "Not a day goes by I don't think of that sweet, kind-hearted girl. Can't tell you how it pained me see her go off with that awful Charlie Booth. Always hoped she'd get rid of him somehow. Maybe move back down this way. It would've been my pleasure to help her look after her little boy."

"I'm sure Jeannie would have liked that."

Her eyes pooled with tears. "So hard to believe she's gone."

"You made a big difference in her life, Mrs. Reiner. Jeannie was very grateful for your kindness."

"Yours, too. She wrote to me about you. Said you had a real good heart. Not like some others who worked in that miserable jail. Jeannie said you helped her, that you wanted for her to get strong."

"Of course I did. That's what I was there for."

"Not everyone does what's right, but you did. Now you sit and I'll fix you something to eat."

"Please, don't bother, Mrs. Reiner. What I really want is to hear what you know about Charlie Booth."

"Person can hear better on a full stomach," she said. "You like ham and cheese? Fresh turkey? Tuna salad? Or I can whip up a nice omelette?"

"Anything would be fine. Let me help you."

"Not a word of it. Put your feet up and relax. I'll be back in no time flat."

As soon as she left the room, my thoughts swerved back to the priests' retirement home. The shrunken old man in the bed beside Father Muldoon was Father Thomas. He had worked in the diocesan headquarters that included our parish. And so he'd been in on the investigation, and he knew all about what had happened between Muldoon and Jack. Father Thomas recounted it for me like a Bible story, a tale filled with horror and lethal lies and the even more murderous truth.

"There. All set." Mrs. Reiner was back, ferrying a hand-painted white tray heaped with sandwiches, a pitcher of iced tea, and sweets. "Help yourself, my dear."

She wasn't satisfied until my plate was brimming full. "Don't be shy. Traveling makes a person hungry. Never forget how ravenous my Walter used to be when he came home after being on the road for a week or two to call on his accounts. Man couldn't get enough to eat, rest his soul. Took down everything I put on his plate. Did my heart good to watch him."

She took a plate and dug into the sweets. "Already had my lunch. But here I go again."

I ate a sandwich and then savored the most incredible homemade brownie. It was creamy and chewy and sinful and meltingly light. "Everything's too delicious."

"Have all you like."

"I have. I couldn't eat another bite."

"You sure? You're not being polite?"

"Me? Never."

"All right, then. What can I tell you about Charlie?"

"Anything. Everything. When did you meet him? What was he like? Did you know him as a kid?"

Her mouth hardened with distaste. "I knew about him.

Most everyone did. Soon as he came along, things around town started to go downhill. Used to be a peaceful, friendly little place. Then there's Charlie, and all of a sudden, pets are turning up with their heads chopped off. People set out the trash for pickup, and the cans blow up. The mail goes missing, sometimes for weeks, and then they find it in a vacant lot somewhere, minus the checks."

"Booth got away with all that?"

"And more. His uncle Edmund Booth was the sheriff. Most he'd ever do was give that boy a talking-to like it was all a big joke. So the older Charlie got, the more misery he caused. He couldn't have been more than twelve when he took to stealing cars, having himself these little joyrides. He'd ride around a while, tearing up the streets, scaring everyone silly. Then when he got bored, he'd just drive the car through a chicken coop or someone's barn or garage. Charlie got a big kick out of wrecking things."

"I don't understand why people put up with the sheriff ignoring him. Why didn't they have him fired?"

"That's not how things worked around here. Booth was the sheriff, in charge of how the law went, period. You went along to get along, if you know what I mean."

"Nobody ever tried to change things?"

"One time. It was late May, back in '85. That spring the heat came on strong and early. Everything was parched and dusty and tempers were getting short. This one Saturday night, Charlie stole Maury Eastman's Buick. He drove it all over town, kicking up a fuss. And maybe four in the morning, he drove right through Gray Pitcher's barn. First thing the next day, Gray stormed right into the sheriff's office and demanded justice. Sheriff Booth told him to calm down, but Gray said no, he didn't want to calm down. He told the sheriff if he didn't take care of Charlie, he'd see to it himself the boy got the punishment he deserved. Sheriff brushed him off, and sure enough, Gray got in his car and he drove up one street and down the other until he tracked Charlie down. He roughed Charlie up a bit to scare him, and he warned the boy that if he so much as came near his property again, he'd get a backside full of buckshot for his trouble."

"Good for him."

"Wasn't as it turned out. Middle of the night a few days later, the Pitcher house went up in flames. Fire Department took its sweet time answering the call. The volunteers were friends of the sheriff and Charlie's dad. By the time they did show up, the house had near burned to the ground. The old lady, Gray's mother, got her lungs so full of smoke they couldn't save her. His wife Adelaide raised the cutest little Jack Russell terrier pups. Fire killed a litter of nine. Family up and moved out of town after that."

"Charlie set the fire?"

She shrugged. "We all knew he did, but what of it? Everyone was afraid if they raised a fuss, they'd be next. So Charlie got to keep doing whatever came to his sick little mind."

"Good Lord."

"After a while he got tired of the joyrides and moved on to terrorizing other kids. He'd pick the smaller ones, the weak ones. And he'd bully them like you wouldn't believe. Made it so they were too scared to go to school, too scared to leave their house even. Most of the families gave up sooner or later and moved out like the Pitchers did. Seeing how Charlie got away with everything, they didn't see a choice."

"Wasn't he arrested once? A friend of mine said there was a sealed record for a juvenile offense Booth committed back in nineteen eighty-five."

"True. Guess I try to forget that. It was before Jeannie. Charlie took a fancy to a new girl in town named Pam Greely. She was a pretty thing, way too smart to have anything to do with a no-good like Charlie. But he kept coming around anyway. Waited for her after school. Showed up at her house. Wouldn't take no for an answer.

"Finally the girl complained to her father. He told Charlie he'd better stop pestering his daughter. Said she had no use for him and never would."

"So what happened?"

Her eyes glazed with pained memory. "Never forget how Bill Greely cried. Never saw a grown man broken as he was by the grief."

"Booth killed Pam?"

She drew a pained breath. "Guess he figured if he couldn't

have her, he'd see to it no one else could. Charlie was maybe sixteen at the time and had dropped out years ago. But that day he walked into the high school cool as you please. He searched everywhere until he found Pam in the girl's room, washing the paint off her hands after art class. Charlie stabbed her with a long, sharp kitchen knife, the kind you use to carve a roast. Blade went clear through her heart."

"My God!"

"That's not all. Charlie wanted to get rid of the evidence, so he doused the hall with gasoline from a can he'd brought along and set the school on fire. Then he left and barricaded the door. A bunch of kids got serious burns, and that nice English teacher, Mr. Sternhagen, dropped dead of a heart attack."

"So the sheriff finally took action?"

"No, he didn't, not even then. I think Charlie would've gotten away with it altogether, like he did everything else, but the school had just installed a new security system, the kind they use in stores to nab shoplifters. Charlie was caught right there on the tape, spreading the gasoline."

"That was a lucky break."

"Not as lucky as you'd hope. Sheriff saw to it Charlie was tried as a juvenile. Boy was never even charged with stabbing Pam Greeley. They called it reckless endangerment, pack of nonsense like that. All he did was six months in one of those fancy boarding schools for troubled teenagers. Before you know it, he's out again. And he must've made some real interesting contacts in that place, because all of a sudden he's got plenty of cash, fancy jewelry, flashy clothes, even a souped-up sports car. Soon enough, he's going off to this place and that. And everywhere he goes, people die."

"Are you saying Booth became a hired killer?"

"Only know what I heard, P.J. Rumors. People said it was that way, that Booth knew people on both sides of the law. They said there were those who signed him up to do the killings and those who watched his back so he never got caught. May have been empty talk, but you know what they say about smoke and fire."

I thought of Albert Dunston's warnings about the need to separate fact from fearsome myth. Knowing what Charlie had done gave me a hint of what he might do in the future, and that could be useful. It wouldn't help the cause if the knowledge left me weak in the knees.

"Other than terror and torment, did Booth have any interests? Was there anything he particularly liked or enjoyed?"

She frowned. "Not some thing but there was always someone. Some poor boy he'd decide to take apart, piece by piece. Some poor girl he took to and wouldn't let go."

"I heard Jeannie's parents arranged for her and Charlie to get together, that he didn't even know her."

"That's true. With Jeannie it was different, strictly business. Way I heard it, Charlie and Jeannie's dad got to playing pool one night, and Charlie was winning big. When Kent Bagshaw ran out of money, he put Jeannie up to cover the debt and stay in the game."

"That's so hard to imagine."

"Kent was a horror, his wife, too. But Charlie was the worst. He *is* the worst."

"Booth is nothing but a man, a highly flawed human being," I said, quoting Dunston for her comfort and mine.

She nodded. "I like how you think, P.J. Right thing is to cut Charlie down to size."

"Someone very wise taught me that. He said monsters like Booth are actually at a disadvantage. They act predictably, but they can't grasp the fact that they do. Those predictable behaviors can be used against them."

"Wouldn't it beat all if someone could find a way to hang that man with his own rope?"

"The trick is to find the right rope. Was there any particular pattern to his crimes?"

"You know? Happens there was. I only picked up on it because my father was a fisherman, so in my house we always tracked the moons and tides. Still do, in fact. Daddy taught me if you know what the moon is up to you can predict how the seas are going to behave, when there's likely to be a sudden squall or freak storm."

"Is that true?" I asked.

"I'm sure a believer. Years ago I used to teach school over on Hilton Head. When the full moon came, there'd be freak storms and sudden squalls right there in my classroom. You know, that's why they call madness lunacy, because it's thought the pull of the moon drives folks insane."

"Interesting. But what does that have to do with Charlie Booth?"

"Whenever Charlie went on one of his rampages, I got to noticing it was a full moon. Moon came up full the night he burned Gray Pitcher's house down. It was full the night Charlie stabbed that poor girl and burned down the school. The day of the next full moon after Pam was killed, while he was out on bail before the trial, he had the nerve to turn up at the cemetery. Stood right at that poor girl's grave and went on and on about how she'd gotten what was coming to her. Said he was glad, that he'd loved every minute of it, and that he'd do it again if he had the chance. Charlie didn't notice that Bertie Argenbright was right behind him, planting flowers by her sister's grave. Woman heard every word Charlie said. Testified at his trial."

"You think the full moon drives Booth crazy?"

"Could be. Or it could be he fancies the idea of it. Legend has it evil blooms with the moon. Brings out the witches and werewolves. So maybe he figures that's the right time for him to howl, too."

My pulse was thumping madly. "Would you happen to remember when the last full moon was?"

She straightened. "I do, in fact. It was back on the Tuesday Jeannie died. Didn't occur to me until you asked about Booth's pattern."

"And the next one is coming up when?"

"This Sunday," she said. "Is that any help?"

"It could be."

"Hope that's true. Sure would be a blessing if Charlie Booth finally got what he deserves."

"I'll keep you posted." I checked my watch. "It's been wonderful. And so have you. But I'd better get moving if I want to catch that plane."

"Go on then. Take a sandwich. Take a couple, why don't you? Always good to be prepared, I say. You never know."

CHAPTER

51

■ **Rafe had no right looking so blasted happy to see me.**
Surely that was prohibited in the separation agreement. And
wasn't there a clause that barred him from looking so damned
cute? His hair was tousled, and he answered the door barefoot
in my favorite khaki cargo shorts and a lovely old work shirt
he'd buttoned incorrectly in his haste.

"How did it go, Rafe? Did you manage all right?"

"We had a great time. Dennis John said he was tired at
eight-thirty, so I put him to bed and he nodded right off.
Great kid."

"That's it? You didn't read him a story?"

"Sure I did. I read to him, sang, the whole nine yards."

"And I'm sure everything you fed him was perfectly nutri-
tious and organic, and wait—let me guess—you taught the
boy algebra and Latin as well."

His smile brightened. "Geometry and Japanese. Hope
that's okay."

"You must be exhausted, then. So I'll say thanks and take
him off your hands."

"No need. He's fast asleep. I can bring him back to Caity's
in the morning."

"Thanks anyway. You've done more than enough."

"It's my pleasure. Anyway, it'd be a pity to wake him up."

"I don't plan to. I can carry him down to a taxi and take him to Caity's. He won't even know."

Rafe hitched his shoulders. "All right. If you insist."

"I do."

"You sure? I promised to take him out for a pancake breakfast. Be a shame to disappoint him."

"Well, look at that. Perry Mason plays Mary Poppins. Who'd have thought?"

"I love kids. You know that. Always have." His look of sentimental longing made me ache to bust his jaw. "So can he stay?"

"OK, Rafe. But from now on, check with me before you make any promises."

"That's a deal. How was your trip?"

"Tough." The worst of the day came flooding back: the old priest in Father Muldoon's room; Muldoon lying in the next bed with his eyes closed, wailing his excuses to God.

"What?" Rafe urged.

I bit my lip, battled tears.

He wrapped me in a hug. Rafe was a great hugger, one of the best. "Tell me, P.J. Get it out."

Try though I did to hold them back, the words poured out. "Our parish priest kept coming after Jack, touching him, and after a time Jack told my mother. Of course she didn't believe him. In those days, nobody even imagined such a thing could happen. So my mother thought Jack had gone bad, maybe even possessed. For a long time she agonized about what to do. She couldn't eat, couldn't sleep. My father figured she was sick, and he insisted she see our family doctor. He found nothing physical wrong with her. Gave her pills to calm her nerves."

Rafe stroked my hair. "That's good, sweetheart. Get it off your chest."

I blew my nose, and then returned to the comfort of his hug. "The pills didn't work. My mother got more and more upset. At some point she decided the only possible answer was to confess. So that's what she did, she confessed to Muldoon."

He held me tighter, sensing what was next.

"Muldoon assured my mother she'd done the right thing. He acted all calm and forgiving, said he'd talk to Jack, counsel him. But in fact, Muldoon threatened Jack with hellfire and damnation. He punished and humiliated my brother until Jack didn't know what was what anymore. Jack started to doubt the whole thing had even happened. Eventually he decided to take the accusation back. We were on a picnic to celebrate her birthday when Jack told my mother he'd made the whole thing up. She told my father, and that was the beginning of the end. There was fury, fighting, terrible ugly words. Jack took off, and so did my parents. They went for a drive to talk, they said. But they never came back. The weather had been glorious, but soon after they left for their drive, a terrible storm came up. And that was that. I'm sure Jack held himself responsible for my parents' death, and that was the living death of him."

Rafe swayed gently, rocking me like a babe. "That's so awful, P.J. I'm so sorry."

I backed away and mopped my face with my sleeve. Oddly, I felt calmer, lighter than I had in years. "I'm okay, Rafe. Better now. But how am I going to tell Caity?"

"Like you told me. Caity can handle it, P.J. No question about that."

"I guess you're right."

He raked his hair. "I've been thinking a lot about that patient of yours who was murdered at the jail. It was wrong of me to blow it off the way I did, to say you were reckless to want the case solved. I'm sure I'd feel the same way if it happened to a client of mine. I'm sorry. And I want to help."

I locked eyes with him. "Is that the truth, Rafe?"

"Yes."

"The God's honest truth?"

"It is, P.J. What can I do?"

"If you really mean it, I know just the thing."

CHAPTER

52

■ **Rafe was every inch a lawyer; so of course, his help** came at a price. I had to agree to a long list of onerous conditions. I had to swear not to go anywhere near the designated trap, not during the time in question, not beforehand, and not for at least a week afterward. I couldn't go there myself and I couldn't ask anyone to go for me, though I couldn't imagine who that would be. I had to agree not to try to learn the identity of Rafe's contact, the person who would set things up and retrieve the equipment after the deed was done. Until it was done, I was not to call Rafe or attempt to contact him in any way. Not him, not anyone in his office, or any of his friends or relatives, no matter how distant or far removed. In fact, I wasn't to discuss this with anyone now or ever. The sole exception, if required, would be my formal testimony. Otherwise, I was to go about my business, pretend nothing was happening, and wait to hear.

Fortunately, I had Dennis John to help pass the time. I took him for yet another pancake breakfast at a diner in Caity's neighborhood, and as soon as we were finished, he asked about church.

"You want to go?"

"It's Sunday," he said as if that shut the lid on the subject.

A giant heap of Sundays had passed since any church last saw me. For some unknown reason, I thought it best to head for the big house: St. Patrick's Cathedral. We lit candles for Lottie and took our place among the congregants. When the time came, I went to confession. I owned up to all the sins I remembered, which was quite the list. "I'm sure there are others, Father. They'll come to me."

"The door is always open."

"Good to know."

After that, Dennis John and I strolled up Fifth Avenue and went for a walk in the park. Wordlessly we avoided the children's zoo. Instead, we headed west. We reached the little boathouse on the pond, and I rented a miniature sailboat that worked by remote control. Dennis John was awkward with the controls at first, eyes scrunched with concentration, tongue boring hard in his cheek. He puffed with pride as he slowly got the hang of it. "I'm the boss of the boat, right, P.J.?"

"Indeed you are. I think I'll call you Captain Dennis John from now on."

"You have to say aye, aye, Captain."

"Aye, aye it is."

"Do you have a boat?"

"I don't."

"Think you'll ever get one?"

"Not likely."

"That's all right. You can ride on mine."

I saluted. "Permission to hug the captain, sir?"

He submitted with his free arm and the attention he considered it safe to risk. "Aunt Lottie's real sick, isn't she?"

"Yes, sweetie. She is."

"Does it hurt?"

"I don't think so. She's pretty much sleeping all the time." She was in a coma, had been for days. And there was little hope she'd ever emerge.

"Why is she sleeping all the time?"

"Because of the sickness, sweetheart. It makes her very, very tired."

"Does that mean she needs to rest in peace?"

"Where did you hear that?"

"At Mommy's funeral."

"Likely so."

"It's up to God, right?"

"Sometimes it's hard to say why things happen. Sometimes we simply have to accept that they do."

He took that in with an incredibly grown-up look of acceptance and resolve. And suddenly, strangely, things fell into place for me as well. I couldn't change the facts, but I could control how I dealt with them. And that realization made all the difference in the world.

■ **Caity headed out early for a day crammed with oppor-**
tunities for fans to fawn and gush over her, and from time to
time kowtow. She offered to have her driver drop off Dennis
John at school, which freed me to agonize in peace. I paced
her enormous apartment, clutching a cordless phone, certain
Rafe would call any time.

But he did not. Not a peep from him all morning. Noon
crept by. One o'clock. Two.

By two-thirty I was ready to kill myself and him, though
not necessarily in that order. It was nearly three when the
phone finally rang.

"Tell me, for god's sakes. What happened? Did he show up?"

"He did. At about four."

"That's fabulous, Rafe. Where's the tape?"

A long silence played on the line.

"Something's wrong."

He sighed. "It was my mistake, P.J. Something I didn't account for. I'm so sorry."

"What are you saying?"

"Booth showed up at Jeannie's grave exactly like you said
he would."

"I knew it. It was the day of the next full moon after he killed her. He's done it before."

He blew another breath. "So you were right, and he did it again. He stood there talking for a good ten minutes, and then he left. My guy was watching through a high-powered scope. He saw the whole thing."

"So what went wrong? Booth realized he was being watched?"

"No. Nothing like that. My guy's a pro and extremely careful. He even waited until after the place officially closed to be sure there was no chance Booth might come back. And then he retrieved the camera."

"I don't understand. It sounds as if everything went off without a hitch."

"Almost. The camera's microphone was voice-activated. That was the only way we could think of to have the tape available all day. The problem is, the cemetery's near the airport, and planes kept flying over Jeannie's grave. The noise activated the audio part of the tape, and it ran out before Booth got there. You can tell he was talking, but there's no way to hear what he said."

"But you have the video?"

"I know what you're thinking, P.J. But it's hopeless. Booth was standing at an angle. You can see his mouth moving, but you don't get anywhere close to a full view. Caity's great at reading lips, but nobody's that good. I'm so sorry. I should've thought of it. My fault. What can I do to make it up to you?"

"Come here, Rafe. Bring the tape."

"What for? I told you, you can only see part of Booth's mouth."

"It may be enough. I happen to know someone who reads lips well enough to leave my sister in the dirt."

"Really? Who's that?"

"Eva Everheart."

Rafe chuckled. "I hate to break it to you, P.J. But Eva isn't real."

I welcomed the blooming smile. "That's where you're wrong, my friend. So happens she is real. And as soon as I can arrange it, you're going to meet her in the flesh."

■ **By six o'clock, when my sister breezed in, I'd watched** the tape at least a dozen times. Rafe had dropped it off on his way to pick Dennis John up at school and then take him to Cubby's Music Club. I ran it over and over again, studying Booth's ugly sneer as he stood at Jeannie's grave. I sneered myself as I fantasized about how that creep's swaggering bravado would crack when the judge announced how many decades he'd been sentenced to serve in a maximum-security lockup. I imagined him cooling his heels at Rikers until they found a place for him upstate. No doubt Big Millie would be glad to take a "sweetie pox" like Booth under her big, fat, incredibly powerful wing and crush his bones.

Caity glanced at the tape. "What movie are you watching? Looks old."

I flipped the set off by remote. "Sorry. I'm not allowed to talk about it."

With that, Rafe showed up with Dennis John. "You can make an exception for Caity, P.J. How else are you going to get Eva Everhart to read his lips?"

My sister signed in a flapping fury. "Eva? Have you both lost it? What's going on?"

I sent Rafe off to play with Dennis John. And then I assumed my best look of mock innocence. "Rafe helped me get Booth on tape at Jeannie's grave. I'm sure he said more than enough to hang himself for her murder, but the audio portion was voice-activated, and it ran out before Booth got there."

"How did you know Booth would show up there?"

"It's a long story. Complicated."

"What does it have to do with Eva?"

"With the character you claim credit for, nothing at all. I'm talking about the real Eva Everhart, the one you described to me as the most amazing lip-reader you've ever seen. I bet she could look at the tape and tell us what Booth said."

"Nonsense. There's no one like that. If anyone is capable of reading his lips, it's me. Let me see the tape."

I ran it again, and Caity perched at the edge of the ottoman to study Booth's mouth. She couldn't make out what he said, but I could read my sister like a neon sign. Caity was wild with frustration and getting more agitated all the time. "Why didn't they take multiple views? Why didn't they set the damned camera up to sweep the area? Why is the lighting so lousy?"

After the shot played of Booth leaving Jeannie's grave, I turned off the set. "So you can't do it."

"No one could. It's not possible," she signed with a harsh downward thrust of her fists.

"From what you said, the real-life Eva could. You told me about the time you watched her in a softball playoff. You said this girl was able to pick up what the pitcher and the first baseman were saying while she was running backward to catch a pop fly. You said it was unbelievable, that you'd bet she could read someone's lips while they were passing on a speeding train."

"Obviously I was exaggerating."

"That's a crock. You only exaggerate about yourself. Where can I find that girl now?"

"I have no idea. It's been years."

"Not that many." I picked up the phone. "Where does she live?"

"I told you, I don't know. I can't remember."

"I'm getting mighty tired of the game, Caity, but you leave

me no choice. Either you tell me her name and where the family lives so I can call the girl, or I'll tell it to the *New York Times*."

"Go on," she signed in a rage. "Do it."

"Fine, I will." I took up the phone.

"Knock yourself out. I'm not afraid of your threats."

"Directory assistance? I need the main number for the *New York Times*."

She turned on her heel and stormed out. But as soon as she reached the hall, she did another pirouette, strode back, and wrenched the receiver from my hand. "Her name is Ava Hanneman, and her family lives in Rye. She has a TTD, so I'll call her myself. But here's how it is. If she agrees to read Charlie Booth's lips, she'll probably have to testify in front of the grand jury, and if it comes to that, again at the trial. The defense will try to make mincemeat of her. They'll bring in a parade of certified experts who'll swear it's impossible to read what Booth was saying on that tape. Before they even begin to take her word, they're going to put her through the wringer, P.J. They'll attack Ava personally, try to discredit and humiliate her."

I frowned. "Then why bother to ask? Why would she agree to do it? Why would her parents allow it?"

"Because it's true, Ava did turn out to be the most amazing lip-reader imaginable. And who do you think taught the girl in the first place?"

"You?"

"Bingo. I started working with her when she was not quite two years old. I used a multimodal approach, and now she can lip-read, speak, and sign. Ava and her parents are so grateful, they'd do anything I asked. And for the record, I'm not asking because of you and your stupid saber-rattling."

"Why, then?"

"Because I'm sick to death of your obsession with Charlie Booth. And because if he's really guilty of murdering his wife, he shouldn't get away with it."

I signed contritely. "Thank you, Caity. Thank you from the bottom of my black, obnoxious heart."

"You are most certainly not welcome." She frowned at her watch. "Now, I have a dinner date, so I'm going to make the call, and then I'm leaving. But just so we're clear, Ava and her parents know all about her being my inspiration for Eva Everhart, and so does anyone else who cares to look."

She strode to the bookshelves and plucked out a copy of *Forever Eva*, the second book in the series after the surprise hit popularity of the first one. And there it was at the tail end of the lengthy list of acknowledgments: *And very special thanks to my amazing student Ava Hanneman, whose remarkable talents made me realize that an amazing girl like Eva could be real.*

CHAPTER 55

■ **My mother used to say that even the worst night ends** eventually. And so it seemed that at long last, this nightmare might be done.

Ted Demetrios had left me a message saying that Clarissa had filed for divorce. In exchange for his relinquishing all financial claims, she'd agreed not to contest his bid for full custody of their daughter Robbie. Emma Wolcott had called to say that she was close to securing the placement she'd hoped to get for Dennis John. Caity had delivered the tape to Ava Hanneman's home, and, as I'd hoped, the girl was able to make out what Booth had said at Jeannie's grave, albeit haltingly. For the past two hours my sister had been working with the amazing Ava to make a transcript, and she predicted they'd have it done in another half hour or so. As if all that wasn't enough to leave me swooning with delight, Nina Present called with amazing news as well.

"They've hired someone terrific to serve as executive director of the psychiatric center, P.J. He's leaving town tomorrow, and Brett wants you to meet him before he goes. Is there any chance you can make it for breakfast at the Club?"

"Sure. I'd love to. What time?"

"It'll have to be at seven so he can catch his plane. Brett's in meetings all day, so I offered to call you and set it up. I mentioned it to Will Creighton, and he's delighted, by the way. He said he'll be glad to give you a reference."

"That's wonderful, Nina. Very exciting. Only—"

"What?"

"No big thing. It's just that I've been staying at my sister's for the past few days, and I haven't anything decent here to wear."

"Could you borrow something from Caity?"

"Sure but I'd feel like a fish on a bicycle. No problem, though, I can run home soon as we hang up and grab what I need."

"Sorry to put you out like that."

"Are you kidding? This is the opposite of putting me out. I'm thrilled."

"Fine, then. I'll let you go so you can pick up your things. And as soon as the meeting is over tomorrow morning, I want you to call and give me a report."

■ **Only later, too late, did it strike me that several** things had felt wrong. I had to fiddle with my key, twisting it both ways and then back again before I could get it to work. In lieu of the standard glut, only one crumpled take-out menu littered my stoop, and when I pressed the door open, not a single ad or menu fell to the ground. When I looked back much later, when I was able to think clearly again, there was even something different about the darkness when I stepped inside. It seemed more solid somehow, more stifling, oppressive, and complete.

Thankfully, I knew how to locate the switch by feel. It was mounted beyond the small brass butterfly-shaped hook where I kept my key ring and the wood-framed mirror I'd picked up at a street fair. Eager for light, I slid my hand along the wall.

I felt the hook poking forth between extravagant brass wings. Continuing on, my fingers soon brushed the cool mirrored glass. I groped beyond, searching for the toggle that controlled the light.

But that was not what I touched.

Instead, my pinky grazed a rough, pliant bump. The bump jittered, almost imperceptibly. And I froze.

An instant later I was caught in a mad, grunting rush. Steel hands trapped my arms and wrenched back hard. Spikes of agonizing pain shot through my shoulders.

"Stop!"

The voice was a vicious taunt. "You're the one needs to stop, Poor Julia. You should know better than to stick your nose where it don't belong."

My mind bristled with disbelief. "Booth?"

Now his ropy forearm clamped my neck. I caught the stench of beer and tobacco. "What's the problem, bitch? You deaf like your sister? Didn't you hear me say to mind your own damn business?"

"I will. I swear it. Just let me go."

"Hey. That's good; I like it. Beg some more."

I kept still.

He squeezed my throat harder. I gagged and then coughed convulsively, struggling to breathe.

"If I tell you to beg, bitch, you beg!"

My mind ran in desperate circles, searching for a way out.

Booth ticked his tongue. "In my book you don't listen, you die."

The blade sliced my clothes with horrifying ease and split my flesh. I felt a harsh electric sting, a sticky rush.

"Please don't!" I groaned.

"Stop, Booth!" a man commanded. "Not yet."

At first I couldn't place the voice. It couldn't be.

"Come on, Creighton. You heard her," Booth said. "Bitch is aching to die. Begging for it."

"Dr. Creighton? What are you doing here? What's going on?"

"Hush, P.J.! Later, Booth. If you want the money, you'll do exactly as we agreed."

"Don't be such a tight-ass. Jesus, I hate freaking shrinks." The blade bit harder and a cry escaped me.

"What are you doing?" Creighton demanded. He flicked the switch, flooding the room with dislocating light. Eyeing the bloody cuts, he scowled. "I told you to wait!"

"What if I don't feel like waiting?"

"You'll do as I say."

Booth's sneer hardened. "Or what, old man? You gonna hit me with your cane?"

"Screw this up, and the party's over," Creighton said with chilling calm. "No more nice, big, easy-money jobs."

"I can promise you one thing, Grandpa, you wouldn't be around to see it."

"And here's the promise I can make to you. Should anything happen to me, anything at all, you'll be tracked down and finished like a dog."

My mind was buzzing with disbelief. "What are you saying, Dr. Creighton? What do you have to do with him? This is insane."

"It's entirely sane, I assure you. Sane and necessary, though I don't expect you to understand."

"Understand you dealing with him? It's completely crazy."

"I'm not interested in your opinion, P.J. Time to go. Take her to the car, Booth. Now!"

Booth snickered. "Get a load of you, all red in the face. Better watch you don't give yourself a heart attack, you old creep."

"I said take her outside. Now do it!"

"OK, easy, Pops. I'm doing it. We're gone."

Booth clamped my mouth with his calloused palm and forced me out on the stoop. In awkward lockstep we walked down my dim, quiet street. Creighton's minivan was parked around the corner. Another thing I'd failed to notice earlier, another clue that might have saved my neck.

I stalled as we approached the car, praying someone would spot us and sense something wrong. "Please, I don't feel well. I'm going to be sick."

"Sicker than you can imagine. Get in the car, bitch. Move!" Booth shoved me roughly into the backseat and then climbed over, wedging me between him and the door. One of the baby seats was still anchored in place. The others had been tossed aside to make room for this.

Creighton slid onto the driver's seat and headed south. "The child locks are on, P.J.," he said evenly. "So you needn't bother trying to get out."

"Don't do this, Dr. Creighton. You won't get away with it. You'll wind up in jail."

"There are worse things."

"Think of your family, then. Think of Molly and the kids."

"They're precisely why you're here."

"What are you talking about? That makes no sense."

"Shut up!" Booth roared. "Stop asking so many damned questions."

"That's all right, Booth. It won't make any difference if she knows."

Booth snickered. "Won't when I get through with her."

Creighton started driving south. "Go ahead, P.J. Ask whatever you like."

"Where are you taking me?"

"That, you'll see soon enough."

"What's going on, then? What are you doing? Christ, Dr. Creighton. I don't even know where to start."

"That's because you're still a child in many ways, P.J. You've never had any serious responsibility, never really had to care for anyone but yourself."

I caught a glimpse of his face in the rearview mirror. His expression was a cold, insensate blank.

"How does hurting me accomplish anything?"

"It's not about you, P.J. You just happen to be in the way. I warned you, time and again. I gave you every opportunity to stop delving into Jeannie Bagshaw's murder, but you simply refused to listen. Honestly, it pains me to have to end your life, but you've made it so I have no choice."

"Doesn't pain me, Grandpa," Booth said. "Can't wait." He ran his knife across my forearm, forging a long, bloody trail.

I kept thinking of Dunston, remembering what he'd told me, struggling to push away the terror that was building inside me like a trapped head of steam.

"You *can* wait, Charles," Creighton said. "And you'd better."

"What the hell's the difference? I can do her here, and then we can dump her wherever you say." He drew the blade across my cheek. "Think I'll slice you real thin, bitch. Do you nice and slow, the way girls like it. How's that sound?"

Creighton angled off the road. He put on the parking brake,

stormed out, and opened the rear door. "That's it. I'll sit with her from here on. You drive."

Booth menaced Creighton with the blade. "Don't feel like driving."

Creighton drew a .45 from his coat pocket and aimed the piece squarely at Booth's heart. "I think you do want to drive, Charles. Unless, that is, you're positively dying to avoid it."

Booth shrugged and went to take the wheel. As Creighton squeezed onto the rear seat beside me, I caught the tight set of his jaw. He exuded the dark, musky stench of a cornered animal.

Booth was speeding, weaving wildly back and forth between the lanes. "Stop it, you idiot! You'll attract the police."

"Think I give a crap? I got cops in my family going back generations. Cops look after their own, Grandpa. That's how it is."

"This is New York, Booth, not some one-horse, redneck, southern backwater. A traffic cop pulls you over, he's not talking it over with your uncle Bubba before he hauls you in."

"No sweat. Once he does, I make a call and I'm home free."

"I'm not going to argue with you. Don't forget what I told you. Screw this up, and you're history. Cop friends or no."

"Ooh. Now you've gone and done it, Creighton. Got me all shaky. Damn!"

He lurched the wheel. The car swerved, spun out, and nearly sideswiped a van in the left-hand lane. Brakes screeched, and I braced for a crash. But Booth turned away before we hit. Chuckling, he lit a smoke. Then he tuned the radio to a heavy-metal station and turned the volume up full.

I leaned toward Creighton and spoke in a rasp. "You don't have to go through with this," I urged. "It's still not too late to turn back."

He sniffed. "There's no turning back. I started down a path that leads in only one direction. I met dear Charlie back when he was just a pup in reform school. I was working there at the time, and it was obvious that he was a standout, even among those rotten kids. I passed his name along to some people who wanted to groom just such a kid, for a price. That was the first step. And how I agonized about it. I don't do that anymore. I simply do what I have to do. It turns out one sells one's soul in many installments, and the payments get easier and easier in time."

The radio was blasting so I could feel the thumping bass in my skull. "What does that mean, Dr. Creighton? And what does it have to do with me?"

"Nothing. I told you. But anything that gets in the way has to be removed, and right now that happens to be you." He stared at me mildly, as if things were normal, as if the Earth hadn't gone plunging wildly out of phase.

Now he smiled. "Molly is a wonderful woman, the love of my life, but she's always been impossible to please. She insisted on having four children, and then naturally, when they came along, she was overwhelmed and needed more and more help. We had to buy a much bigger apartment, and then a larger one still. Each one had to be grander and fancier than the last, and at the right address. Then there were the clothes and jewelry Molly felt she needed in order to fit in with the fancy neighbors. The children needed the trappings as well: the finest clothing, the most expensive toys, the best lessons, on and on. We had to have two cars, new every year. The most elaborate vacations. Memberships in all the right clubs. I won't bore you with the endless details. Suffice it to say the list goes on and on."

Suddenly he leaned forward and shoved his gun barrel into the small of Booth's neck. "Put out the cigarette, and turn off that goddamned racket. It's getting on my nerves!"

"Sure, Pops. Whatever you say." Booth stubbed out the butt on Creighton's leather seat. Then he switched off the radio, pulled off the knob, and tossed it out the window. "There you go. Anything else?"

"That's quite enough."

"Please, Dr. Creighton. I understand you're under pressure, that it's hard. But I don't see how you get from that to this."

"It progressed rather naturally. I was falling deeper and deeper in debt. With what they pay me at Rikers and whatever extra money I've been able to pick up here and there, there was no way I'd ever be able to dig out. The children would need private schools, summer camps, tutors, fancy parties, and all the rest. It could only get worse and worse.

"Then, a couple of years ago, Nina Present told me she'd invested in a company that was planning to build a network of private prisons. The minimum buy-in for investors was over my head, but it sounded like an incredible opportunity. So I scraped together everything I could. Took a second mortgage, the works.

"I knew I was laying everything on the line, but it seemed like a sure thing. And for the first few months, everything went as we'd hoped. Better. Violence was rampant in the prisons and getting worse. Prisoners' rights groups were on the warpath, demanding change. Politicians lined up to support our company's plan. We had to turn potential backers away."

"But then the roof fell in," Booth taunted. "I like that part, Grandpa. Go on and tell her how it all turned to shit."

Creighton shut his eyes. "Chief Kantrovic developed health problems and decided to step down. They brought Daley in to replace him, and that was the beginning of the end. As soon as Daley came on board, violent crime in the prisons dropped dramatically. The press ate it up. All of a sudden everyone started backing expansion of the public jails. As if that wasn't enough, a columnist for the *Times* wrote a scathing editorial about how private prisons weren't working."

Finally the whole ugly picture came clear. "So your investment was headed down the tubes."

He drew a shaky breath. "Based on all the positive projections, the board had authorized major commitments to buy land. They'd hired expensive consultants and had specialists draw up plans." He nodded toward the trunk, where I saw the same bags filled with dark folders he'd had when I met him in the prison parking lot.

"Those are the plans, the employee résumés, the proposed programs, the budgets. Everything I staked my family's future on. One day we're on top of the world, sky's the limit. Molly and I are talking about where to build our vacation home, thinking maybe we should have a place in the Hamptons and another in the islands, someplace warm. We're discussing chauffeurs, maybe even a private plane. Then Daley comes along, and all the company could do was hemorrhage cash.

They would have gone under in a matter of months. Taken me, Molly, and the kids with them."

"So you hired Booth to boost the murder rate, to make the public prisons look bad."

"Fortunately, I knew him. And so I brought him in. I had no choice."

"Of course you did, Dr. Creighton. You made the wrong one."

Creighton eyed me with contempt. "Be as noble and righteous as you like, P.J. For you, it's now or never, as they say."

We were in Queens, headed in a familiar direction.

Creighton caught my hideous glimmer of awakening. "That's quick, P.J. Very clever. Since I needed to dispose of you anyway, I thought: Why not have dear Mr. Booth do it where every corpse helps the cause?"

CHAPTER

57

■ **Creighton stopped the car on the mainland side of the** Island Bridge. He slid out, strode around, and changed places with Booth once again.

"Move it, P.J. Get down on the floor."

Booth crouched beside me and Creighton covered us both with a camp blanket.

"Not a sound, bitch," Booth rasped. "You try to pull anything, and I'll do the kid next. First, I'll let him know it's because of you. I'll make sure he's real clear on that, and then I'll slit his little throat so he bleeds out slow. I know how to carve out his voice box so he can't scream or cry. Not a real pleasant way to go. "

My stomach heaved. "I won't do anything. Don't hurt Dennis John, please."

"Up to you."

I felt the thrumming vibration as we crossed the bridge deck. The river churned far below and planes thundered overhead. It was stifling beneath the blanket, dark and close. Every breath brought a taste of Booth's acrid stench.

Beyond the bridge the pavement smoothed. Soon the car

slowed and then came to a stop at the guard station. Creighton slid his electric window down.

"Hey, Ben. How's it going?"

"Same old same old. They got you working mighty late, Doc."

Creighton blew a phony sigh. "The joys of paperwork. If I don't dig in and get my records done, the auditors will hang me."

"Better get to it then. Have fun."

"Fun, sure."

Creighton drove for a while, turning again and again. The prison complex was a large, confusing sprawl, and I lost my bearings. Where were they taking me? How long did I have? Was there any way in hell I could escape?

There were countless deserted spots on the island, especially at night. I reasoned they would take me someplace like that, where no one would hear if Booth's torture caused me to cry out.

Finally we stopped. Creighton's door slammed, and he came around to let us out.

Booth pulled off the blanket. "Last stop, bitch. End of the road."

I was startled to see we had parked beside the Rose M. Singer Center, "Rosie," the woman's jail where I had worked.

Booth jabbed his blade between my ribs. The pain shot through me, and I gasped.

He cupped his ear so the lightning bolt earring glinted in the beam of a sweeping flood. "I hear you right, bitch? You telling me you want that kid to die?"

"No," I said. "I'm sorry. I'll keep still."

As we passed behind the building, I cast a longing eye toward the day-room window. Big Millie could be there right now, forcing the others to watch whatever she wanted to see on television or monopolizing the phone so she could rant to anyone who'd listen about her latest delusion.

If only she happened to look out and spot us. I was one of the precious few people in the universe she trusted. If she thought I was in danger, she'd raise the kind of fuss that could not be ignored.

My heart leapt as a broad, looming shadow shifted along the day-room wall. But short of the window it paused, and then turned back.

Creighton seemed to read my mind. "Too bad about Big Millie."

I went cold. "What?"

"As I heard it, they took her down to the DA's office to question her about some workman she allegedly assaulted. They had her in a holding cell, and someone stabbed her. Happened just like that." He snapped his fingers.

"You killed her, too?"

Creighton sighed. "Sadly, no. I'm afraid that was not Mr. Booth's best work."

"Damn bitch had too much blubber on her. You'd need a goddamned Ninja sword to run that heifer through."

"Spare me the excuses, Booth," Creighton said. "On the bright side, she did lose a great deal of blood, and she's still on the critical list. So with any luck, Ms. Williamson will soon be counted as yet another victim of our dreadful public jails."

We were beyond the range of the day-room windows now, headed toward the yard. The yellow trailer Chief Daley used as an office was parked beyond. Daley liked to move around, go where he was needed, or better yet, where his was the last face anyone wanted to see.

Creighton smiled. "That, P.J., is what I like to think of as true poetic justice. Imagine our beloved Chief Daley's reaction when he turns up tomorrow morning and finds a dead body seated at his desk with a neatly printed page in front of her that says: *Death Runs Rikers*. The press will have a field day. I predict Daley's head will be the first to roll. Should be a hoot."

Booth slapped Creighton's back. "I got to say I like it, Grandpa. It's good."

"It will be if you do your job."

Creighton produced the key to the trailer and unlocked the door. "After you, my dear."

My gorge rose and my legs went soft. "I can't."

"Get in there, bitch. I waited long enough."

"I feel sick. I mean it."

"You're about to feel a whole lot worse." Booth scooped

me up and carried me to the inky darkness inside. The room still stank of the stray cats who'd taken up residence during the years the trailer had gone unused. Daley had evicted those strays when he decided to use this for his office, but so far all the disinfectants and scented candles had failed to eliminate their smell.

Booth lit a smoke, and in the wavering match light I could see the vicious pleasure on his face.

"Get to it, Charles. I want this over with."

"Don't rush me, Pops. Told you I prefer to take these things slow. Had to rush like all get-out to do my Jeannie. Same with that Dunston creep and the fat bitch. Too many people around, so I couldn't take my time. Wasn't near as much fun."

"You killed Dunston?"

"Sure did."

"But why? He had nothing to do with the prisons. What could you possibly hope to gain by hurting him?"

"In fact, P.J., you can consider Dunston's death your fault. As I said, I did everything I could think of to dissuade you from continuing to investigate Jeannie Bagshaw's death. I thought surely you'd give the whole thing up when your dear friend Mr. Dunston met such a shocking, unfortunate end."

"Why would I think that had anything to do with Jeannie Bagshaw? They couldn't tell why he died. They told me it might've been the loss of blood from his injury, that it could've put a strain on his heart."

"Strain on his heart my ass," Booth spat. "I cut that old man's throat so deep, his head near came off. Hospital made up that crap about blood loss to keep the story quiet long as they could. Guess they figured having patients turn up dead wouldn't be good for business. Bunch of lying creeps."

"You're the creep, Booth. Both of you are nothing but sick, pathetic, worthless pieces of crap!"

"Whoa! Look at you with your panties all in a twist. Too bad you got to go out all mad like that, bitch, but I say your party's over now!"

The glint of his blade split the darkness. He shoved me to the floor, reared back, and poised the knife to plunge.

"No!" I screamed. I caught his wrist and pushed the blade

away. But he drove it toward me with enormous force. My muscles quivered with the impossible strain. The blade edged toward me, closer and closer, until the sharp tip grazed my throat.

I brought my knee up and rammed his groin. Howling like a stuck beast, Booth recoiled. Desperately I twisted away.

I lunged for the trailer door, but before I reached it, Creighton cried out. "Stop! Make the wrong move and I'll blow you away. Now turn around slowly."

His .45 was leveled at my chest. I heard the click as he flicked off the safety.

My hands flew up. "No, please, Dr. Creighton. Don't!"

His face went tight. The room exploded with blinding light, a deafening blast. I was lifted off my feet and thrown flat. There was another flash. An earsplitting explosion.

And then the void.

CHAPTER 58

■ **"Look. She's coming around."**

"Don't crowd her. Give her air."

A fierce beam was trained directly at my eye. Squinting, I made out the hazy form of a somber cop. My mouth was bone dry, my mind a cotton haze. "Am I dead?"

He flicked the light off. "No, ma'am. You're very much alive. And mighty lucky."

"What about Booth and Dr. Creighton? Are they gone?"

I tracked his gaze to an idling ambulance. The EMTs were maneuvering a pair of sheet-draped bodies inside. "They're gone, all right."

The horror of those final moments before the blast came back to me. "But how?"

"You have the chief to thank for that," he said. "In fact, here he comes now."

"How're you doing, Lafferty?"

I sat too quickly and the sky spun in a dislocating swirl.

"Better take it slow. You've got some nasty cuts there."

"I wasn't shot?"

"Close, but no cigar."

"How could that be? I saw the blast. I felt it."

Daley rolled his eyes. "The shots came from my gun. And the hit you felt was Booth's body. He landed on you when I blew him away."

"You just happened to come along right then?"

Now he shook his head. "I didn't get to the top of my game by leaving things to chance. I was in the trailer, hiding out in the bathroom. My team had an eye on everything that happened from the minute you went to your place."

"But how did you know?"

"I've been watching your dear friend Will Creighton for quite some time. Man was living way above his means, and that's a big red flag. When a person's drowning, he'll grab whatever he thinks will keep him afloat."

"So you followed him?"

"Didn't have to. I made it my business to get to know his wife. Didn't take much before she decided to throw hubby to the wolves to keep them away from her door."

"Molly confessed?"

He snickered. "Not hardly. She played Little Miss Innocent to the end. Claimed she found out what was going on by accident."

"But that doesn't make any sense. Their investment in that company building private prisons was her bankroll, too. If she blew the whistle on Will, the whole thing was bound to fall apart."

"That's what you'd think, isn't it? But Molly saw it a whole different way. As soon as she gave Will up, she started going on and on about how she's going to write a book about the whole business, tell the story from the wounded wife's point of view. Woman's convinced she's going to have a best-seller on her hands, a movie deal. Make more money than she'd know what to do with."

"That's insane."

"Maybe, but not so it meets the legal definition. I met with the DA today. He's preparing a warrant for her arrest. Something tells me she's going to have plenty of time to work on that book of hers in a nice quiet cell."

"Four kids, Jesus."

His lips pressed in a hard, grim line. "Bad things happen, Lafferty. Somehow, kids get by."

I thought of my brother Jack. "Not always."

"There's another ambulance coming. They'll get you checked out and stitched up."

"I don't need to go to the hospital. I'm fine."

"You're no position to argue. So don't try." He started away.

"Wait, Chief Daley. I have a question."

"What?"

"If you were in on this from the beginning, how could you let them torment me that way? You let it go on while Booth cut me again and again. Do you honestly hate me that much?"

"Don't flatter yourself. Creighton's wife told me the plan, so I knew nothing serious was going to happen until they got you here. We had the trailer bugged, so I decided to wait until the two of them finished spilling their guts. The Dunston murder was a nice bonus. The attack on Millie Williamson, too. Always good to get those open cases shut."

"I could've been killed."

"What's your point?"

"Booth could have slit my throat a thousand times before you came out of the bathroom and blew those two away."

He shrugged. "But he didn't, did he? Because there you are, still mouthing off."

"And you think that makes everything all right?"

"You know what your problem is, Lafferty?"

"What?"

He tossed up his hands. "Beats the hell out of me. But if you ever figure out how to get that giant chip off your shoulder, give me a call. I'm sick of hearing how great you were, sick of everyone nagging me to take you back. We haven't filled the slot yet, so if you want to talk about it, let me know."

Despite everything, all the horror, I felt the blooming grin. "Sure, Chief. If that ever happens, you'll hear from me first thing." My mother had taught me never to burn my bridges, so I left the rest unsaid. Instead, as that pompous, arrogant, cruel, undermining, world-class jerk swaggered off, I whispered the words to myself. "But don't hold your breath, Chief. Or better yet, do. I'd sooner roast in the real Hell than do it here working for you."

CHAPTER

59

■ **For the tenth time in as many minutes, I pulled the** curtain aside and drifted out of the stifling little cubicle.

"No one's come for me yet?"

The nurse's patience was fraying; I could see the ragged edge. "Please go back inside, Ms. Lafferty. Soon as they come, I'll let you know."

"This is ridiculous. I'm perfectly capable of finding my way home myself."

"Sorry. I can't let you go on your own. It's against the rules."

"I'll sign something. I'll take an oath. Just please, let me out of this blasted place."

She showed her teeth. "I'd love to. Believe me. And I will, as soon as I can."

The cubicle was tiny, barely big enough to hold the side table and the oversized chair. Try doing any decent pacing in a space like that. My hatred for hospitals grew with every second that passed. I detested every inch of the place, every sanitized millimeter. I loathed the needles they'd given to numb the pain so they could truss me up like a Thanksgiving bird. As if that wasn't enough, they'd shot me again and again with antibiotics and a tetanus shot. And now they refused to let me go no matter how hard I worked to irritate the hell out of them.

What was the damned holdup anyway? I'd left messages on Caity's cell phone and on her special teletype phone at home. I'd called the relay center that translated her voice calls to text and told them it was an emergency. And where the hell was Rafe? He was supposed to be at Caity's, minding Dennis John, but I couldn't raise him on any of his numbers.

Again, I ventured out of the cubicle. And there he was at last.

"About time," I huffed. "Let's get out of here."

"My God, P.J. What happened? You look terrible."

"It's a long story, Rafe. For now let's just say the other guys look much worse."

My jacket was in tatters, and it hurt too much to put it on. Rafe took off his coat and draped it across my shoulders. "Ouch!" I shrieked. "Easy."

"Sorry."

"Where were you? I kept trying to reach you."

His eyes took a curious turn. "Dennis John and I were busy talking to Miss Wolcott. I had my phone turned off."

At that, I saw the boy, trailing close behind Rafe. His lip quaked and his eyes leaked crystal tears.

"God's chariot came for Aunt Lottie, P.J. So she had to go."

I held out my arms to him, but he hung back shyly. "You got hurt."

"That's true. But the doctor said I'll be fine as long as I take two hugs at least three times a day."

"You mean it?"

"That I do."

He melted against me, and he wept, and the tears pooled in my eyes, too. "I know, sweetie. I know."

I also knew what he didn't, that his father had died today, too. And rotten monster though Booth had been, his death was yet another loss to add to the painful heap. Soon, before he heard it on the news, I would have to tell Dennis John about that, and in the case of Charlie Booth, the story would have to be different. There would be no golden chariot sent by God, no thoughts of Booth lounging around on a bright, puffy cloud in the celestial firmament. From Caity, I'd learned that much about creating a plot. The ending had to follow what went before.

After a while Rafe gently eased the boy away. "Let's take P.J. home, big guy. I think we could all use some sleep."

Rafe helped me settle Dennis John in Caity's guest room. We sat with him until he drifted off.

"Your turn now." He helped me to my feet.

Standing, I shook loose of his grip. "I'm fine, Rafe. You needn't treat me like a broken doll."

I didn't stumble, not really. It was more that my feet disagreed. Rafe caught me before I hit the floor, walked me to Caity's study, and pulled out the convertible bed. Gratefully I slipped off my shoes and slid under the covers. I was running several quarts low on oomph, and a dense painkiller fog was rolling in.

Rafe perched on the bed beside me and stroked my hair. "I heard what happened, P.J. I got a call from one of our detectives. Thank God you're OK."

My tongue was gaining weight, growing fuzz. "A run-in with a knife-wielding psychopath, a bit of gunfire. A rude awakening or two. Two dead. Aunt Lottie gone. No big deal, Rafe. One of those days."

And it wasn't over.

As I was drifting off, in came Caity. At the sight of us, she brightened and went smug. "Well, hallelujah," she signed. "It's about time."

"Is that so? You've been waiting a long while for me to get cut to ribbons, have you?"

"What are you talking about? What is she talking about, Rafe? And what has she taken? She looks stoned."

I struggled to stay awake while Rafe filled my sister in. Her face registered disbelief followed quickly by horror, shock, and last but not least, my all-time favorite: rage.

She came at me, spitting mad. "Goddamn you, P.J. You could have been killed!"

"Next time I'll try harder."

Rafe signed for a time-out. "Stop. Both of you. It's been a terrible night, and everyone's upset. But that doesn't mean you should say things you'll regret."

"*She's* had a terrible night?" I railed as best I could. "Of course. What am I thinking? Poor girl probably had the agony of choosing between lobster and filet mignon."

Caity planted her hands on her hips and used the voice. "I never got to dinner, as it happens. The first emergency call I got was about Jack."

"Oh, Lord, Caity. No!"

"Relax. It's nothing terrible. He was arrested downtown, that's all. Simple assault. Public lewdness. Disturbing the peace."

I melted with relief. With Jack, you learned to be grateful for anything less than total disaster. "Where is he now?"

"Cooling his heels. I tried to post bail, but given Jack's record, the judge decided to have him admitted to Bellevue for psychiatric evaluation. He's all right. Or what passes for all right with him."

I was battling sleep, but sleep was pulling way ahead. My tongue felt so thick and heavy, I could barely lift it. "I found out what he and Dad had that fight about on the day they died, Caity. It was Muldoon."

"Bonnie Doon?" Caity said. "Sure it was. Go to sleep, P.J. We'll talk in the morning. You're not making any sense at all."

CHAPTER

60

■ **Could that really have been a mere nine months ago?**
Looking back now, it seems like a different lifetime. Sometimes, as I wait in my office between clients, I simply sit back and marvel at how things have changed.

The psychiatric center opened a few months after that dreadful night, and I was on board when it did, in charge of counseling services. My brother Jack has been with us from the beginning as well, and though I no longer see Dr. Groome for formal sessions, she comes in from time to time to discuss her son Martin, who is part of the program as well.

We've had a packed house from the outset. Many of our clients, like Jack and Martin, are referred by the courts. We quickly developed a reputation as a far better place for people with serious psychological problems to go than jail.

And so why was I in the least surprised when my next new referral came barging in. "You better haul ass, P.J.! And quick! They's a boogie woogly-eyed thing out there got himself some serious macular-weehawken rays."

"Good to see you, Millie. I heard you'd been released."

Huffing hard, she slumped in a chair. A leg gave way and

sent her sprawling. "You see that? You take down the slicing number?"

"That's OK, Millie. I'll get a stronger one. Meantime, you can sit on the couch."

Her eyes narrowed. "Is it true what I heard? You went and had yourself a kid?"

"Jeannie's son is staying with me. He asked to, and so far, it's been going fine."

That was the short story. The much longer one left me thankful and hopeful and more than a little bit scared. Dennis John had been miserable with the people Emma Wolcott found to take him in, try though they had to help him adjust. It wasn't a week later that she had come to ask if I'd consider keeping the boy with me. Caity had been skeptical to say the least, but Rafe said the magic words. I wouldn't be alone in this. He'd be more than glad to help. So of course, Caity—never to be outdone—said she'd be glad to help, too. And given my sister, she assured that her help would be bigger and better and generally more helpful than Rafe's. As I saw it, in the average case, it might take a village, but given how far from average this case was, the three of us would have to do.

"So look at you, P.J. You got yourself a bitty itty son of a who-knows what. Tell you this much. That boy act even one time like his sumbitch daddy, he do one eensy spider stucco sumbitch thing, you better put him on a rocket to Whoseback-istan and light the fuse."

"Have you been taking your medicine, Millie?"

"You bet. Twice a day and three times a doughnut. Don't you go trying to change the subject. We are not through scussing you."

"That's not what you're here for."

"Buzz my licorice I'm not. You got a father for that boy, P.J.? Boy don't grow up right without a man."

I smiled. Lately, I'd been smiling a lot, and musing about an impossible question: How did a person suddenly go soft in the head for someone she'd been fuming at for years?

The answer: If it feels so blasted wonderful, who cares?

"Maybe soon, Millie. Let's say things may be moving in that direction."

She shot me a sharp, warning look. "Best not be some rotten sumbitch like my Reverend Herbert."

"No. That he's definitely not."

One thing had not changed at all. Rafe's timing was impeccable. He knocked and stuck his head in. "Hey. Sorry to bother you, Julia. Ellen said she thought you were between appointments. I'll come back."

Millie bolted up and grabbed his arm. "You the one? You P.J.'s scallion-tree pie?"

Bless his heart, Rafe barely blinked. He offered Big Millie his hand. "Good to meet you. I'm Rafe Lafferty. And you're?"

"Lafferty? What you be doing taking P.J.'s name? Sounds like some kind of theft of nervous fits to me."

"Lafferty is Rafe's name, Millie. We used to be married, but we got divorced."

"Right," Rafe said. "And then when Dennis John came to stay with Julia, there wasn't enough space in her place, so they moved in with me."

"Why you keep calling P.J. Julia anyhow? She your smoothie pox, you better learn her Vidal Sassoons."

"Julia's my name, Millie. I've decided to use it instead of P.J. from now on."

Millie's head swerved from Rafe to me, and then back again. She shook her head in disbelief. "I got to tell you, now you gone and got my head all muffed out glue-wise. You two best sit right there on the strato-barkis, pull your beds together, and tell the whole thing slow."

National bestselling author
Judith Kelman

writes
"A POWERHOUSE OF A THRILLER."
—Harlan Coben

New York Times
bestselling author

LEE CHILD

DIE TRYING
0-515-12502-4

Ex-military policeman Jack Reacher returns in a gutsy
novel of heart-stopping action...

When a mysterious woman is kidnapped by a politically
motivated fringe group and taken to their compound,
Jack Reacher must help her escape with her life—from
the inside out.

"Tough, elegant and thoughtful."
——Robert B. Parker

"Opens with a bang."-——*Chicago Tribune*

"Engrossing."-——*Rocky Mountain News*

Available wherever books are sold or at
penguin.com